WOLF'S HONOUR

WHEN THE DOMAINS of the Space Wolves come under devastating attack from all sides by the Thousand Sons Chaos Marines, Ragnar and his battle-brothers launch a lightning strike counter attack on the Thousand Sons' base deep in the warp. The Space Wolves must triumph for Ragnar to have any chance of retrieving the Spear of Russ from his nemesis, the Chaos Space Marine Madox. For it is only through returning the Spear that he will be redeemed in the eyes of his battle-brothers and his Chapter.

Wolf's Honour is the conclusion to the thrilling Ragnar Blackmane tale, following on from the action-packed *Sons of Fenris*.

A WARHAMMER 40,000 NOVEL

WOLF'S HONOUR

By Lee Lightner

Special thanks to Mike Lee.

A BLACK LIBRARY PUBLICATION

First published in Great Britain in 2008 by
BL Publishing,
Games Workshop Ltd.
Willow Road
Nottingham
NG7 2WS
UK.

10 9 8 7 6 5 4 3 2

Cover illustration by Geoff Taylor.

A CIP record for this book is available from the British Library.

ISBN 13: 978 1 84416 389 2
ISBN 10: 1 84416 389 X

Distributed in the US by Simon & Schuster
1230 Avenue of the Americas, New York, NY 10020, US.

See the Black Library on the Internet at
www.blacklibrary.com

Find out more about Games Workshop
and the world of Warhammer 40,000 at
www.games-workshop.com

IT IS THE 41st millennium. For more than a hundred centuries the Emperor has sat immobile on the Golden Throne of Earth. He is the master of mankind by the will of the gods, and master of a million worlds by the might of his inexhaustible armies. He is a rotting carcass writhing invisibly with power from the Dark Age of Technology. He is the Carrion Lord of the Imperium for whom a thousand souls are sacrificed every day, so that he may never truly die.

YET EVEN IN his deathless state, the Emperor continues his eternal vigilance. Mighty battlefleets cross the daemon-infested miasma of the warp, the only route between distant stars, their way lit by the Astronomican, the psychic manifestation of the Emperor's will. Vast armies give battle in His name on uncounted worlds. Greatest amongst his soldiers are the Adeptus Astartes, the Space Marines, bio-engineered super-warriors. Their comrades in arms are legion: the Imperial Guard and countless planetary defence forces, the ever-vigilant Inquisition and the tech-priests of the Adeptus Mechanicus to name only a few. But for all their multitudes, they are barely enough to hold off the ever-present threat from aliens, heretics, mutants – and worse.

TO BE A man in such times is to be one amongst untold billions. It is to live in the cruellest and most bloody regime imaginable. These are the tales of those times. Forget the power of technology and science, for so much has been forgotten, never to be re-learned. Forget the promise of progress and understanding, for in the grim dark future there is only war. There is no peace amongst the stars, only an eternity of carnage and slaughter, and the laughter of thirsting gods.

PROLOGUE
Heart of the Wolf

THE FOUR THUNDERHAWKS swept in at full power with
the sun of Hydra Hydalis at their backs, plunging like
a sheaf of iron tipped spears at the dark leviathan
drifting before them. If someone – or some*thing* – on
the space hulk was watching for signs of attack, Ragnar Blackmane wanted to mask their approach until
the last possible moment, concealing their emissions
amid the raging solar winds given off by the system's
three suns.

It hung in the void like the pitted shard of a broken
world. Ridges of stone, plains of ice and towers of
trapped metal stretched for more than ten kilometres,
dwarfing all but the largest of Imperial battleships.
And not the biggest of its kind by any stretch, Ragnar
thought grimly, studying its ominous bulk through
the viewports of the lead Thunderhawk's command
deck.

Space hulks were the flotsam and jetsam of the warp, or so the theory went, drifting in and out of the immaterium as though carried on an invisible tide. Many were nothing more than hunks of lifeless rock, perhaps torn from worlds by the teeth of warp storms in ages past. Others, however, were studded with the hulls of entombed starships, some of them tens of thousands of years old and not all of them human in design. Such discoveries were legendary; often they contained treasure troves of lost technology and xenos lore.

Sometimes they also carried horrors hidden deep within their decks: foul alien raiders, hordes of twisted mutants, or worse.

When the space hulk first arrived at the edge of the system almost eight standard months ago the handful of decrepit ships that comprised the Hydalis system defence squadron drew close enough to perform a series of long-range auguries. Not long afterwards, the alarm had gone out via astropath, and three months later Fenris sent its answer.

Now all that stood between the oncoming hulk and the forty-five billion Imperial citizens of Hydra Cordalis was Ragnar Blackmane and his small company of Wolves.

The harsh light of Hydalis's primary gave the notional prow of the hulk a bleached out, blue-grey cast. Tendrils of steam wreathed the rocky surface as pockets of trapped ice boiled away beneath the suns' harsh glare. Here and there, the light flared painfully bright along a spar of metal or a shard of jagged hull plating. Abyssal shadows pooled in the depths of ancient impact craters. They seemed to shift with the changing position of the Thunderhawk, like the multiple eyes of some vast predator. The thought left a cold feeling in the Wolf Lord's gut. Ragnar was first and foremost a son of Fenris, and his people had a healthy dread for the horrors of the deep.

Baring his fangs in a silent snarl, Ragnar surveyed the red-lit interior of the command deck. It was a cramped space at the best of times, the pilot and co-pilot side-by-side at the forward end of the compartment. A master tech-priest and the senior augur operator situated directly behind them. The two bondsmen were fitted in bulky, armoured flight suits that made them look slope-shouldered and apelike, but Ragnar's power armoured bulk loomed head and shoulders above them all. With the Wolf Lord standing at the back of the compartment the atmosphere was nearly claustrophobic, but the crew did their level best to go about their work as though Ragnar wasn't there.

The Wolf Lord turned his gaze to the augur operator at his right. 'Any change?' he asked.

'None, lord,' the crewman replied, never taking his eyes from the wavering lines on the augur screens before him. The operator reached up with a gloved hand and made a minute adjustment to a set of brass fronted dials. 'No engine heat or augur signals. It's drifting at a constant rate, heading for the centre of the system.'

'Any power emissions at all?' Ragnar inquired.

The crewman shook his head. 'None so far,' he said. 'We'll know more as we get closer.'

Ragnar nodded thoughtfully, and then addressed the pilot. 'Where is the hull that the defence ships spotted on their augurs?'

The pilot glanced over his shoulder at the Wolf Lord; like Ragnar, the Space Wolf wasn't wearing a helmet. Bright blue eyes glittered beneath a pair of shaggy red eyebrows, and a web of fine scars indented the pale skin of his right cheek. 'We'll find it on the dorsal side of the hulk, lord,' the pilot said in a rumbling voice, 'roughly amidships, so they said. We'll be there in another few minutes.' Then he turned back and keyed the vox-bead behind his ear. 'Jotun flight: approach pattern Epsilon,' the pilot growled, 'and Snorri, keep your fat arse tucked into formation this time. If you get shot down again you're walking back to Fenris!'

Ragnar couldn't hear Snorri's reply, but the flight leader let out a booming laugh and pushed the throttles forward. The three other Thunderhawks in the flight shook out into a rough arrowhead formation, and their thrusters flared blue-white as they began the final phase of their approach.

The Wolf Lord shifted his weight and reached for a nearby stanchion as the assault craft pulled into a climb that carried them over the hulk's bulbous prow at a distance of less than a hundred metres. Jumbled plains of rock and twisted metal flashed by underneath the Thunderhawk's nose. Ragnar caught fleeting glimpses of broken hulls jutting from the surface: here the curved bow of an Imperial merchant ship, there the saw-toothed profile of an ork raider. Once he thought he caught the dull sheen of yellowed bone encased in a steaming sheet of ice.

Then he saw it, like a dark cathedral rising from a broken field of stone. 'There, off to starboard,' Ragnar said, pointing just to the right of their current course.

'That's it!'

'Where?' the pilot said, peering into the darkness. Then he straightened in his seat. 'Ah, yes. I see it now.'

The ancient warship rose from the centre of the hulk as though it had taken shape around her. Plains of broken stone stretched away on all sides, rising almost to the level of her dorsal turret deck. Her buttressed command bridge stood straight and tall, still remarkably intact after more than four thousand years. The prow of the Imperial battleship was almost completely buried, but Ragnar saw that instead of the customary eagle's head at its crown there rose the figure of an armoured warrior, sword and shield held ready.

The tech priest shifted in his seat and pulled a thick, leather-covered tome from a satchel tucked underneath his console. The priest flipped through the yellowed pages, comparing the winged statue on the warship with the images pictured in the book. Suddenly he sat upright. 'Here it is,' he said, his voice tinged with awe. 'She's the *Dominus Bellum*. One of Vandire's ships, according to the text. Disappeared right after the battle of Ophelia VII.'

Ragnar studied the derelict carefully. The condition of the ancient battleship was crucial to his plans. As soon as he'd received the report from the Hydalis defence squadron he knew that his lone strike cruiser, the *Stormwolf*, had no chance of destroying the hulk on its own. If the *Dominus Bellum's* reactors were still intact, however, it was possible they could destroy the drifting hulk from within.

'Any power readings?' the Wolf Lord asked.

The augur operator studied his screens and shook his head. 'No lord. It's... wait!' He began tuning a set of dials, and the lines on one of the screens suddenly spiked. 'I'm picking up energy spikes along the dorsal hull and z-band augur signals!'

'Morkai's teeth!' the pilot cursed, grabbing for his mic. 'Jotun flight! Evasive action!'

Just as he spoke, Ragnar saw pinpricks of fire flash and stutter along the length of the battleship's upper deck, and suddenly the Thunderhawk was engulfed in nets of tracer fire and blasts of explosive shells. Hammer blows rang against the Thunderhawk's armoured hull, and the Wolf Lord was thrown forward as the assault ship dived even closer to the hulk's treacherous hull. The other Thunderhawks of Jotun flight followed suit, smoke streaming from minor hits along their fuselages and wings.

Ragnar tightened his grip on the stanchion as the Thunderhawk plunged through the chaotic storm of fire. The battleship's defensive turrets blazed away at the oncoming assault ships, filling the void with a wall of energy bolts, shells and streams of high-velocity slugs. Shrapnel from near misses raked at the Thunderhawk's flanks, and a blow like a Titan's fist smote the craft on the starboard side. Lurid red icons flashed urgently on the tech-priest's console, and the young crewman began flipping switches hurriedly as he whispered a prayer of salvation to the Omnissiah.

The Wolf Lord growled under his breath. The plan had been to try and find an intact hangar deck to land on, but that was out of the question now. Ragnar realised that any hope of a rapid and orderly sweep of the derelict had just been thrown out of the airlock. He reached forward with his free hand and gripped the pilot's shoulder. 'Full assault profile!' he yelled. 'Get us on board any way you can.'

Nodding his head, the pilot keyed his vox-bead to relay orders to the flight. Another blow shook the assault ship, and Ragnar's keen nose caught the smell of burning circuitry. Quick as he could, the Wolf Lord turned and stepped through the rear hatchway, heading down the ladder beyond to the assault bay where his Wolf Guard and the company's priests waited.

Ragnar dropped down to the metal clad deck with a clang. The cavernous assault bay, large enough for thirty fully-armed Space Marines, was crowded with ten warriors in massive Tactical Dreadnought armour. Though slow and ponderous, the ancient suits of Terminator armour were ideal for the close confines of a space hulk's passageways, and Ragnar had brought every one of the ancient suits he could muster. Power fists flexed and armoured heads swivelled to regard the Wolf Lord, and a chorus of rough howls greeted Ragnar from the Wolf Guard's vox-units. Jurgen, the company's Iron Priest, waited at the far end of the bay, flanked by four powerful thrall servitors. Jurgen was locked into his assault cradle like the other Wolves, his helmeted head bowed as he read a litany of protection from a small, metal clad book in his gauntleted hands.

Next to Ragnar, an adamantine helmet worked in the shape of a massive wolf skull turned slightly to regard him. Pale golden lenses the colour of lupine eyes studied him from the depths of the helm's black oculars. The vox-unit on the Wolf Priest's Terminator suit crackled. 'I take it the hulk is hostile,' he said laconically.

Ragnar chuckled, stepping to his assault cradle and reaching for his waiting helmet. Normally he hated wearing the thing, preferring to feel the thunder of battle and the hot touch of blood on his skin. That sort of thing required air, however, and there was no way to know if they'd find any inside the battleship's hull. 'Frankly, it never occurred to me that it might be otherwise,' he replied. 'I didn't expect this hot a reception, though.'

He pulled the helmet on and locked it into the adamantine gorget. There was a moment of darkness, and then, immediately, the helm's optical systems flickered into life. Icons and readouts shone in dull colours at the corners of his vision, showing the status of his suit and those of his pack. With a murmured command, he tapped into the Thunderhawk's command channel and received status icons from the rest of the company as he locked himself into the assault cradle. The Wolf Lord noted grimly that three icons in Hogun's Blood Claw pack were flashing amber. *Jotun Four's been hit hard*, Ragnar thought grimly. *Three men out of action and we haven't even reached the target yet. An ill omen.*

A massive impact struck the rear quarter of the assault ship, hard enough to throw Ragnar against the cradle's restraints. His stomach lurched for half an instant as the whole ship seemed to slew sideways. The battle lanterns flickered. In the darkness, one of the Wolf Guard threw back his head and howled like a fiend. Fist and sword clashed against armour, and rough voices barked out battle chants as old as Fenris itself. Ragnar bared his teeth in the close confines of his helmet and felt his blood burn.

Then there was a thunderous roar, and the Thunderhawk shook from stem to stern. A bright red icon flashed a warning but Ragnar already knew what was coming. 'Here we go!' he bellowed, and the assault craft touched down on the battleship's hull with a bone-crushing impact and a scream of tortured metal.

Ragnar rebounded from the cradle restraints and smashed a fist against the quick release. With a murmured benediction, he queried the Thunderhawk's machine-spirit and gauged the position of his forces. Jotun flight had broken formation at the flight leader's order and their high-speed approaches had scattered them in a wide arc across the battleship's dorsal hull. Jotun Four was closest to Ragnar's Thunderhawk, landing parallel to the Wolf Lord's assault ship almost 750 metres away. Jotun Two had landed in the shadow of one of the battleship's massive dorsal lance turrets, well over a thousand metres distant. There was no way to tell by the readout if the assault ship would be able to take off once more. Jotun Three was nowhere to be seen, the Thunderhawk's icon conspicuously absent from the readout.

Ragnar bit back a sulphurous curse. He gestured to Jurgen. 'Ventral breach,' he ordered, and the Iron Priest leapt into action. Slipping out of his assault cradle, Jurgen moved nimbly among the hulking Terminators and knelt before a hatch on the deck in the centre of the bay. The Iron Priest's voice rolled sonorously from the vox-unit of his ornately worked power armour, asking forgiveness from the ancient spirits of the *Dominus Bellum*, and then pronouncing the Benediction of the Fiery Breach as he flipped open an access panel beside the hatch. Jurgen lifted a heavy

lever, and the shaped melta charges attached to the
ventral breaching unit detonated with a leaden *thump*.
There was a shrieking of incandescent gases as the
focused plasma charge drove like a molten spear tip
through more than half a dozen metres of heavy
armour and pierced the battleship's hull.

Moving with the speed and ease of veteran warriors,
the Wolf Guard quickly formed up around the ventral
hatch, ready to jump off. Ragnar keyed open the command channel on his vox-unit. For the moment, he
could tap into the vox-network of Jotun Flight's transports and communicate with his scattered forces. He
knew from experience that would change once he was
inside the hull of the huge warship. 'Strike Team Sur-
tur, status report,' he called.

The company's Wolf Scouts and Leif's Grey Hunter
pack aboard Jotun Two checked in first. 'We're going
in now,' the Wolf Guard pack leader reported. 'I mark
your position at twelve hundred metres. Hogun's pack
is closer. Do you want me and Petur to link up with
the Blood Claws first?'

'You look to your own pack, Leif,' Hogun cut in. The
Blood Claw pack leader's voice was rough-edged with
fury. 'The Blood Claws hunt alone!'

The vehemence in Hogun's voice surprised Ragnar.
The Wolf Guard had proven to be a cold, clear-eyed
warrior, which was why he'd been given command of
the hot-headed Blood Claws in the first place. 'What's
the status of your pack, Hogun?' Ragnar snapped.

'Three brothers are badly wounded. They have
slipped into the Red Dream,' Hogun snarled. Space
Marines, with their enhanced physiology and redun-
dant vital organs, were extraordinarily difficult to kill.

Space Marines in the field who had been incapacitated by their wounds often went into a life-sustaining form of suspended animation until they could receive proper treatment. 'A burst of shells tore through the assault bay,' the pack leader continued. 'The rest of us got away with minor wounds.'

'Does anyone know what happened to Jotun Three?' Ragnar asked.

'They were hit hard, just short of the target,' Leif reported. 'I can't be certain, but I think they overshot and landed on the starboard side of the ship.'

'Have they contacted you?'

'No, lord. It's possible their vox system was knocked out. As I said, they were hit hard.'

That left a pack of Grey Hunters and the company's Long Fangs unaccounted for and possibly dead. Ragnar drew his bolt pistol and considered his options. 'All right,' he said. 'I and my pack will activate our beacons now. Leif, you and Hogun home in on our signal. Petur, take your scouts and see if you can locate Jotun Three. We'll hold here until everyone has linked up. Then we'll head aft to the reactor vault. Now go, and Russ be with you.'

'For Russ and the Allfather!' Leif answered, and the channel went silent.

Satisfied, Ragnar activated his power armour's recovery beacon and instructed his Wolf Guard to do the same. Then he gave Jurgen a curt nod, and the Iron Priest turned a heavy dial on the control panel beside the hatch. With a sharp hiss and a column of scalding steam, the breaching hatch slid open. Ragnar stepped to the edge and peered down into a circular shaft of semi-molten metal that dropped away into darkness.

Baring his fangs in the close confines of his helmet, the Wolf Lord leapt into the shaft.

The drop was longer than he expected. Ragnar fell through the breaching shaft and into a cavernous space beneath, hitting the canted deck twenty metres below with an echoing boom. He landed in a crouch, servos whining, and then leapt to his feet and dashed forward, pistol at the ready. His sword flashed from its scabbard, its diamond-hard teeth whirring to deadly life with a faint, ominous moan.

He found himself in a long, high-ceilinged passageway crowded with debris. Armoured viewports let in the faint gleam of starlight, giving the silent corridor a ghostly cast. Fallen support beams and smashed masonry from toppled statues and broken containers were strewn everywhere. The dust of ages swirled in faint eddies around Ragnar's feet. His armour registered heat and atmosphere, heavy with nitrogen and laced with an acrid stink that set the Wolf Lord's teeth on edge.

The Wolf Priest landed next, power crackling menacingly from his crozius arcanum, and then came the Wolf Guard Terminators in rapid succession. The Terminators faced outwards in a circular perimeter to allow Jurgen and his thralls to lower down their cargo: an armoured case containing a plasma breaching charge. The Iron Priest reckoned that they would need a minimum of three charges to pierce the battleship's reactor cores and destroy the hulk. Ragnar had brought four, just to be safe. Leif's pack had one, Hogun's pack another, and Einar, the Grey Hunter pack leader on Jotun Three, had the spare. With Einar missing, however, they'd lost their safety margin, which Ragnar didn't like at all.

Powerful searchlights cut through the darkness as the Wolf Guard activated their suit lights. 'Ho, lord!' one of the warriors called out. 'Have a look at this.'

Ragnar followed the beam of the warrior's searchlight and saw a curious pile of weapons lying in the dust. Frowning, the Wolf Lord walked over and inspected them. They were crude swords and axes shaped from bulkhead plating, the hide grips tattered and grey. A massive, ungainly firearm, clearly built for something much larger than a man lay nearby. A long, twisted belt of corroded shells lay pooled beneath the weapon.

'Greenskins,' Ragnar growled. 'There were orks on this ship at some point, but what happened to them?'

'The previous owners must have seen them off,' the Wolf Priest replied. '*Someone* turned those turrets on us.'

'Not so,' Jurgen said, lowering the breaching charge carefully to the deck. With a hiss of pneumatics, the Iron Priest's powerful servo-arm retracted against his backpack. 'It could have been an automated response triggered by the ship's machine-spirit,' he said, and shrugged. 'At least now we know the battleship's reactors are still active.'

Ragnar nudged the pile of crude weapons with the toe of his boot. 'Then what happened to the greenskins?' he mused, 'and why were their bodies removed, but their weapons left behind?'

A sense of foreboding crept upon the Wolf Lord, prickling the hairs on the back of his neck. Something was very wrong. He turned and peered warily down the rubble strewn passageway leading aft. Ragnar could feel a chill creeping over him, like a rime of frost

spreading inexorably across the surface of his brain.
He suddenly regretted not having the services of a
Rune Priest at his disposal.

Ragnar keyed his vox-unit. 'All packs report in,' he
ordered.

A hissing screech of static answered. Words came
and went in the torrent of noise. It might have been
Hogun, but Ragnar couldn't be sure. 'Damned
armoured bulkheads,' he muttered.

'Hist!' The Wolf Priest said. 'Did you hear that?'

Ragnar cocked his head and listened, straining his
enhanced senses to the utmost. There! He heard it, a
whispery sound, like wind over broken stones or the
hiss of a distant tide.

Or like the dry clatter of claws, hundreds and hundreds of them, scrabbling along the deck of an ancient
battleship.

They swept up the passageway in a seething wave of
chitin, their armoured shells shining dully in the searchlights. The xenos swarm flowed over obstacles and along
the pitted walls like a swarm of spiders, their four arms
and powerful legs scrabbling for purchase on the slick
metal bulkheads. They were almost as large as Space
Marines, with broad, taloned hands that looked capable
of rending adamantium plate, and armoured carapaces
that shone a mottled green beneath the Wolf Guard's
suit lights. Their heads were bulbous and vaguely
humanoid, each with a leering, fanged mouth and black
eyes as cold as the Abyss itself.

The people of Hydra Hydalis were in far greater danger than anyone imagined.

'Genestealers!' Ragnar snarled, raising his bolt pistol
and firing into the oncoming mass. Carapaces burst,

and torn limbs spun through the air as the mass-reactive shells found their marks. Keening, inhuman shrieks echoed along the passageway, and were lost in the rattling thunder of storm bolters as the Wolves of Fenris answered their foes.

The front ranks of the xenos horde writhed and rippled as streams of explosive shells tore through them, blasting frenzied monsters apart. One of the Wolf Guard stepped forward with a roar and levelled a heavy flamer at the oncoming horde. Scores of shrieking creatures vanished in a seething blast of promethium, but the rest came on, trampling their burning kin beneath the weight of hundreds of clawed feet.

Shouts and gunfire echoed from the forward end of the passageway as well. The xenos monsters had them surrounded. Ragnar caught a glimpse of the Wolf Priest on the other side of the perimeter, directing fire from half the Wolf Guard into the new wave of attackers. A second Terminator opened fire with his heavy flamer, sweeping the forward passage in an arc of all-consuming flame.

A genestealer leapt at Ragnar from high on the starboard wall of the passageway, reaching for the Wolf Lord with its taloned hands. Ragnar pivoted on his left foot and shot the creature point-blank, hurling its shattered body into the oncoming mob. More alien monsters were leaping at him, dropping from the walls or bounding ahead of the oncoming horde. Ragnar's frost blade howled as he decapitated one attacker in mid-leap, and then spun and severed the limbs of another. A fourth monster reared before him like a cobra. Howling his battle lust, Ragnar shot the creature in the face. Then the air filled with mindless, screeching cries as the tide of horrors swept over the Space Wolves.

Claws slashed and rang against Ragnar's armour. Rending talons jabbed like knives, striking hip, shoulder, neck and face. The Wolf Lord's heart hammered in his chest, and his blood seethed with righteous rage. He swept his ancient sword in devastating arcs, splitting torsos, severing limbs and slicing throats. The stink of xenos fluids filled the air, and every blow the monsters landed on Ragnar only enflamed him further. The battle madness was upon him, and he embraced it gladly.

Ragnar's vision narrowed. A howling filled his ears, rising and falling in volume like a spirit of the damned. The sounds of battle blurred, as though echoing from far away. Even the blurring speed of the aliens seemed to slow. A talon found a chink in his armour and bit deep. The Wolf Lord decapitated the monster with a backhanded slash, and then coolly shot three more monsters point-blank. A warning icon at the corner of his eye told Ragnar his pistol was empty. He smashed the butt of the pistol into the skull of another leaping xenos and dashed its body to the deck.

All around him, the Wolf Guard lashed out at the frenzied creatures with fist and blade, their Terminator suits splashed with alien blood. Ragnar glimpsed Jurgen the Iron Priest hurling knots of broken creatures through the air with sweeps of his powerful servo-arm. The Wolf Priest stood at the other side of the circle, laying about with his fiery crozius arcanum and bellowing a fell battle chant in the tongue of Fenris.

A monster leapt at Ragnar from the left. Without thinking, the Wolf Lord stunned the creature with a blow from his pistol and then split it from shoulder to hip with his blood-stained blade. Another, seeing its opportunity, dashed in from the opposite side, talons slashing for Ragnar's throat. Yet before it could reach the Wolf Lord, the monster was torn apart in a stream of storm bolter shells from a nearby Wolf Guard.

Ragnar spun around, seeking more foes to slay, but everywhere he looked he found only the heaped bodies of the fallen. Terminators moved among the enemy dead, smoke rising from the barrels of their storm bolters as they finished off the wounded. Three of the Iron Priest's thralls were dead, their flesh-and-metal bodies ripped apart by alien claws. Jurgen knelt beside the fourth, attempting to repair a damaged leg joint. The Wolf Priest stood off to one side, bloody and indomitable, his Terminator armour limned in lurid red light from still burning pools of promethium.

The Wolf Lord breathed deeply, trying to master the fire burning in his blood. His hands worked of their own accord, dropping the bolt pistol's empty magazine and slapping in another. The howling continued to echo in his ears, a savage, bestial sound, devoid of reason or sanity.

With a chill, Ragnar realised that it was coming over the command channel. It sounded like Hogun's voice.

'Hogun?' Ragnar called over the vox. 'Hogun, answer me!' Abruptly, the howling ceased, but Hogun made no reply. Cursing silently, the Wolf Lord switched channels. 'Leif? Do you read?' Immediately Ragnar heard a response, but it was too garbled by static to make out.

Suddenly the Wolf Priest whirled, raising his storm bolter. 'More scrabbling sounds,' he warned, 'coming from further aft.'

Now that they had been discovered, the genestealers were swarming from their hiding places and seeking out the intruders. It was likely that all of the packs were under attack, and the Blood Claws sounded like they were in dire trouble. If Ragnar didn't act quickly the whole company might be overrun, and the fate of the system would be sealed. 'Follow me!' he ordered, heading down the forward end of the passage in the direction of Hogun's pack. 'Heavy flamers cover the rear. I don't want any of those xenos beasts overtaking us.'

The Wolf Guard fell into formation without a word, surrounding Jurgen and his demolition charge as they moved down the passageway at a rumbling trot. The Wolf Priest loped silently beside Ragnar, peering warily into the gloom. No doubt he'd heard the howls over the vox-net as well, and could guess what they portended.

It had been a long time since Ragnar had heard such a cry from a brother Wolf. Every Space Wolf had to contend with the beast within. The gifts Russ gave to his sons were double-edged, like everything else about Fenris. The strength and ferocity of the wolf could not be tamed, but constantly tugged at its chains, testing the will of its master, and made no distinction between friend or foe. To the wolf, there was only the hunt and the joy of the kill.

Ragnar had travelled almost seven hundred metres down the passageway when he came upon the first xenos bodies. The dead monsters had been burst by bolt pistol shells or split by axe and sword, and the further he went the more numerous they became.

The field of slaughter stretched for almost a hundred metres down the passageway, with dead aliens piled in drifts almost as high as Ragnar's chest. Hogun's Blood Claws had waged an epic fight, driven slowly but steadily backwards by the sheer weight of their foes. Ragnar fought back a wave of dread, expecting to find the torn corpses of the pack somewhere ahead.

Instead, a trio of gore-splashed warriors leapt from behind a pile of alien corpses, levelling their bolt pistols at Ragnar's head. One of the Blood Claws had lost his helmet in the battle, and his eyes were wild with battle lust. Recognising their lord, the Blood Claws lowered their weapons at once and stepped aside. 'Hail, Ragnar Wolf Lord,' the bare-headed warrior cried breathlessly.

'Hail, Bregi,' Ragnar replied, stepping past the warriors. He found himself at a corridor junction, occupied by eight restless Blood Claws. Their armour was battered and rent, spattered with gore from head to toe. They raised their stained weapons in salute, and Ragnar saluted in return. 'What happened here?' he asked.

Bregi stepped forward, head held high. 'We were on our way to meet you, lord,' he said, 'and the cursed xenos were waiting for us. They were hiding in the debris and hanging in the shadows along the walls. Hogun tried to lead us out of the ambush, but there were just too many of them.' The Blood Claw glanced down the passageway, his expression grim. 'They forced us all the way back here, and then they hit us from the junction, too. They broke through our cordon, and then it was every warrior for himself.' The young warrior faced Ragnar. 'I lost count of all the monsters I slew, but for every one I struck down it seemed ten more were waiting to take its place. Then Hogun… he began to howl,' Bregi said, and a haunted look came over him. 'He hurled himself at his foes, slaying half-a-dozen monsters with every sweep of his axe. It was… terrible to behold.'

Ragnar nodded grimly. 'I know of what you speak. What happened then?'

'Hogun fought like a wild beast,' Bregi continued. 'The xenos filth couldn't stand against him. He killed everything he could reach, and then, when there weren't any monsters left to kill, he took to hacking up the corpses. We… we tried to stop him, tried to calm him down, but when Erdwulf and Halvdan laid hands on him he turned and split Erdwulf's skull.' The Blood Claw's gaze fell upon the bodies of his three packmates. 'Halvdan and Svipdaeg fought him, thinking Hogun possessed, and perhaps he was. Hogun lost his helmet in the fight, and I saw the look on his face.' Bregi looked up at Ragnar. 'He was wolf bitten, lord. I saw it in his eyes. He's been lost to the Wulfen.'

'Where is he now?' Ragnar asked.

'He killed Halvdan and Svipdaeg and then ran off down that junction, howling like one of the damned,' Bregli replied. 'He took the demolition charge with him. It was still strapped to his back.'

Ragnar bit back a curse. 'You're pack leader now, Bregi,' he said. 'The Old Wolf will hear of your pack's courage when we return to the Fang. Now see to your men.'

Bregi nodded gravely and turned to his waiting pack.

A terrible howl echoed from the junction corridor. It was a fearsome, hungry sound, fraught with madness and pain.

Memories rose unbidden in his mind, down the long span of years: of the fighting on Charys and the ill-fated journey of the *Fist of Russ*; of Gabriella and his old companions, Torin and Haegr. He saw in his mind's eye the storm wracked plain, and heard the mournful howls of the Wulfen. They had all experienced the curse of the Wulfen-kind on that dark campaign, each in their own way. For a time, they had all known what it meant to be lost.

The Wolf Priest stepped close, his gaze penetrating and inscrutable. 'What now, Wolf Lord?' he asked quietly.

In truth, there was only one thing he could do. 'Tend to the fallen,' Ragnar said. 'I'm going after Hogun.'

ONE
Sealed in Blood

'TWELVE SECONDS TO insertion!' Mikal Sternmark shouted over the vox, his voice rising over the shrieking wind and the thunder of the guns. 'We're entering the flak barrier now.'

As if on cue, a heavy shell exploded close to Berek Thunderfist's drop-pod, peppering its armoured hide with shrapnel, and shaking the Wolf Lord in his restraints like a rat in a terrier's jaws. More shells exploded in rapid succession, like staccato drumbeats against the drop-pod's skin, as the assault force streaked at near-supersonic speed through the capital city's air defence zone.

The Imperial Guard commanders on the ground had assured him that most of the city's anti-aircraft guns had been knocked out of action in the last few weeks. Another blast rang like a hammer blow against the pod's flank, hard enough to rattle Berek's teeth. If this was their idea of light AA fire, by Russ he didn't want to know what a full barrage felt like.

'Hang on, lads,' he said with a fierce laugh, 'here's where the ride gets rough!'

The Chaos uprising was in its fourth month on the planet Charys, an agri-world ominously close to Fenris. Servants of the Ruinous Powers had arisen on dozens of worlds spread across the Space Wolf domains, overthrowing local governments, staging suicide attacks and disrupting vital military and industrial networks. Many of the uprisings had been brutally dealt with by the Space Wolves and local Imperial Guard units, but the speed and ferocity of the campaign had left the Chapter scattered and their resources stretched thin. Elements of the Space Wolves' twelve great companies were in action on more than two dozen worlds, and several important sectors were teetering on the brink of anarchy.

The attacks were anything but random. The Old Wolf Logan Grimnar, Master of the Chapter, had seen that at once. It had begun with a Chaos uprising among the primitive xenos tribes on Hyades, triggering near-simultaneous attacks across vast stretches of space. A complex and devious plan had been set in motion, one that had clearly been in the works for a great many years. The enemy's ultimate objective remained a mystery, but one thing was clear: if the Chaos forces were not stopped soon, the damage inflicted to many of the local sectors could take decades, if not centuries to repair.

Berek and the Old Wolf had studied the pattern of the uprisings for months, looking for the lynchpin of the Chaos campaign. Every indicator pointed to

Charys, which was why he'd brought his entire great company to the agri-world and assumed command of the planetary defences. Within hours of his arrival he'd laid plans for a counter-offensive aimed at driving a spear into the uprising's heart. He and his Space Wolves were the tip of that spear, plunging on trails of fire from the company's battle-barge high overhead.

Battle reports from the planet's surface indicated that two local Guard regiments and the vast majority of the local Planetary Defence Force had forsaken their holy oaths and sworn fealty to the Ruinous Powers. Opposing them were seven loyal Guard regiments shipped in from neighbouring worlds, each of them locked in bitter urban combat to recapture the world's major population centres. Interrogations of captured officers and militiamen pointed to the former governor, Lord Volkus Bredwyr, and his family as the leaders of the revolt. Evidently, Lord Bredwyr and his household had nurtured an obscene cult within the bounds of the governor's palace, from where they continued to issue orders to their followers all over the world.

Berek swore that all that was going to change in the next few minutes.

The capital city of Charys was heavily defended, occupied by one of the rebels' traitor regiments and units of heavily armed planetary militia. Weeks of artillery and aerial bombardment had levelled the city walls and reduced entire districts to smoking rubble, but rebel forces had placed strongpoints at every intersection and turned the narrow streets into mined kill zones. Loyal Guard regiments operating from the nearby starport had only managed to seize a narrow foothold on the eastern fringe of the city, almost a dozen kilometres from the fortress of the governor's palace. The air over the massive, walled compound shimmered with the dark haze of an Imperator-class void shield, proof against the heaviest shells the Guard could throw at it.

As the drop-pods streaked down through clouds of anti-aircraft fire a holo-slate built into the drop-cradle above Berek's head projected a detailed display of the battle unfolding below. Mere minutes before the *Holmgang* launched her drop-pods, the Guard regiments at the edge of the city had begun a fierce offensive, driving hard for the city centre.

Heavy tanks and armoured personnel carriers were assaulting rebel strongpoints, advancing under a steady rain of heavy artillery shells. Dark masses of infantry advanced doggedly in their wake, dashing from one shell hole to the next in the face of intense enemy fire. Lascannon bolts and rocket trails leapt from the rebel positions, and streams of tracer fire raked through the struggling infantry formations. Casualties mounted as the Imperial forces charged across the killing ground. Tanks and armoured personnel carriers exploded in balls of fire, incinerating the hapless squads inside.

The traitors were throwing everything they had at the oncoming troops, and the augurs of the Space Marine vessels overhead took careful note of their positions.

An amber warning icon flashed along the margin of the holo-display as the *Holmgang* and her attendant strike cruisers opened fire. Salvoes of bombardment rounds, each one massing as much as a Leman Russ tank, impacted in a curtain of fire four seconds later, stretching in an arc five kilometres wide in front of the Imperial advance. Rebel strongpoints disintegrated. Entire city blocks vanished in boiling clouds of flame and pulverised ferrocrete. In a single instant of righteous fury, the traitors' defensive line was shattered. Even the Imperial advance faltered for a moment, stunned by the sheer ferocity of the attack. As the Guard units watched in awe, the bombardment shifted, marching inexorably towards the city centre, and the regiments surged forward once more, forcing their way past the shattered rebel positions.

The warning icon flashed an insistent red as the drop-pods neared the terminal phase of their approach, and the second phase of the Space Wolf bombardment began.

'Here it comes,' Berek said, settling deep into his restraints as the icons of five Nova-class escorts in high orbit flashed crimson and unleashed their lance batteries on the shields of the governor's palace. Ravening beams of energy stabbed downwards amid the plummeting drop-pods. One passed so close to Berek's pod that the ionisation caused the onboard lights to flicker, and sent waves of static coruscating across the holomap. The superheated air outside the pod howled like the Stormwolf of legend, and Berek Thunderfist howled along with it.

Five lance beams played across the palace's shields for almost a full second, setting off a ripple of concussive blasts that hammered at the falling drop-pods and rattled the Wolf Lord's bones. The blasts were so intense that Berek didn't even realise the pod's retro thrusters had kicked in until he saw the landing countdown flash on the holo-display. Three seconds later the drop-pod slammed to earth and explosive bolts fired, lowering Berek's assault ramp to the ground. The Wolf Lord hit his quick release and, with a roar, charged into the mouth of hell.

The company's dropsite was a kilometre square parade ground that stretched before the gates of the governor's palace. A hot wind roared across the scorched plain, buffeting the Wolf Lord's bare face and tangling his braided blond hair. Columns of smoke and fire coiled into the sky from the palace grounds and the buildings surrounding the square.

Corpses and parts of corpses littered the parade ground, many burned beyond recognition. Men staggered across the scorched ferrocrete, their eyes glassy with shock and their uniforms blackened by heat. Berek glanced quickly around and saw more than a dozen armoured vehicles arrayed around the square. Some were on fire or had been overturned by the bombardment, but most still appeared functional. The company had dropped right into the middle of a mechanised battalion that had been using the square as a staging area.

Fifty metres away, the rear assault ramp of a Chimera armoured transport dropped, and a squad of stunned rebel Guardsmen scrambled out. Berek turned and raked them with a long burst from his storm bolter. Explosive rounds stitched across the chests of the surprised traitors and flashed along the rear deck of the APC. Before the torn bodies had even hit the ground, the Wolf Lord activated his beacon and keyed the command channel on his vox-unit. 'Blood and thunder!' he roared, sounding the war cry of his company. 'Wolf Guard, to me! All packs, form up and clear the square!'

Even as he spoke, the staccato *thump thump thump* of storm bolters and the more measured fire of boltguns echoed across the square as the Space Wolves leapt into action. Off to Berek's right there was a draconian hiss as a cyclone missile launcher fired, sending an armour piercing rocket into the side of another Chimera. The APC exploded in a huge fireball, and the battle began in earnest.

The four Terminators accompanying Berek in his drop-pod took up positions around their lord, snapping off shots from their storm bolters. One of the Wolf Guard levelled his assault cannon at a charging squad of rebels and tore them to pieces with a two-second burst. Streaks of fire criss-crossed overhead as Deathwind launchers on several of the Space Marine drop-pods went into action. Explosions ripped across the square amid the growing crackle of lasgun fire.

A rocket hissed across the battlefield and struck one of the Wolf Guard standing beside Berek. The krak missile struck the Space Marine full in the chest, knocking him back a step, but the anti-tank round could not penetrate the adamantine breastplate of the ancient Terminator suit. The Wolf Lord caught sight of the rocket team, killed them with a quick burst, and then turned his attention to the disposition of his troops.

Anti-aircraft fire and cyclonic winds had scattered the company's six drop-pods all across the parade field. From where he stood, Berek could see the tops of four other pods, one to the north-west, one to the north and two to the east. 'Aldrek! Where are you?' he called. The Rune Priest had been in the drop-pod containing the rest of Berek's Wolf Guard.

Aldrek responded at once. 'I mark you 300 metres to my east,' he said over the vox. 'We are on our way.'

A loud boom echoed from the edge of the square, and the drop-pod to the east exploded. The voice of Thorvald, one of Berek's Grey Hunter pack leaders, rang out over the command net. 'Battle tank at the eastern edge of the square! I'm taking casualties.'

'We see him, brother,' a gruff voice answered. It was Gunnar, one of the Long Fang pack leaders. 'We're some way off to the west, but we're manoeuvring to line up a shot. Stand by.'

The Wolf Lord nodded in satisfaction. The volume of lasgun fire was increasing, stitching threads of blazing light across the square from every direction, but the company had sorted itself out and was responding decisively to the threat. Berek was just about to order his Wolf Guard forward when the air shook with a roar of dual petrochem engines and a Chimera APC came charging out of the smoke directly at the command squad. The forty-tonne armoured vehicle sideswiped the drop-pod behind the Wolves, toppling it onto its side, and bore down on the Space Marines like an enraged rhinodon. Multi-laser bolts spat from its squat turret, flashing among the Terminators as they scattered to either side of the onrushing war machine. One bolt detonated against the pauldron of Berek's Terminator armour, making his ears ring and leaving a scorch mark on the curved ceramite. The Wolf Lord bared his fangs as he turned to face the APC, his power fist crackling. 'Blood and thunder!' he cried, and met its charge head-on.

Berek gauged the vehicle's approach with an experienced eye. More laser bolts snapped harmlessly overhead as the Chimera drew too close for the gunner to target him. The Wolf Lord raised his storm bolter and rattled off a long burst at the driver's vision block. The explosive rounds smashed into the armourplas, and the driver panicked, slewing the vehicle slightly to Berek's right. At that moment, he stepped forward and smashed his power fist into the APC's right quarter. There was a thunderous detonation. Armour crumpled, partially converted to plasma by the power fist's energy field. The forward axle snapped, hurling a spinning tyre past Berek's head, and the APC flipped heavily onto its left side. Moments later, the rear assault hatch was shoved open, and the bloody survivors of the infantry squad staggered out of the smoking wreck into the Wolf Guard's merciless fire.

'Well struck!' Aldrek cried, raising his gory rune axe in salute as he and four more Terminators jogged heavily out of the swirling smoke. 'Gunnar knocked out the battle tank with his lascannons, and he reports that the traitors are falling back to the east. What now?'

Berek pointed north. 'Forward, to the palace gates,' he cried. 'We have to get inside before the rebels recover from our bombardment and launch a counterattack. If the traitors bring up more heavy armour we'll be overrun before our Guard allies can reach us.' Without waiting for a reply, the Wolf Lord set off at a ponderous run, heading north.

Lasgun fire flickered over Berek's head as he drew closer to the palace walls, growing in volume with

each passing minute. Streams of tracer shells stitched
their way through the smoke as rebel gunners opened
fire with heavy stubbers mounted on the square towers of the palace gatehouse. Missiles hissed through
the air and exploded above the battlefield, showering
the Wolf Lord and his companions with clouds of red-
hot shrapnel.

Berek reached the bulk of his company a minute later,
just a few hundred metres short of the palace gates. Two
of his three Grey Hunter packs had taken cover behind
the burning wrecks of a pair of Chimeras, while his two
Long Fang packs fired at the palace defences from the
rims of a pair of shell craters nearby. As he watched, two
lascannon gunners from Thorbjørn's Long Fang pack tar-
geted the battlements of the leftmost gate tower. The red
beams vaporised a corner of the structure in a cloud of
pulverised ferrocrete, spilling burning bodies onto the
square sixty metres below.

At the Wolf Lord's approach, one of the Grey Hunter
pack leaders rose from cover and dashed over to
Berek. 'Well met, lord,' the pack leader said. 'It appears
we have a problem.'

Berek scowled at the helmeted pack leader. 'What
kind of problem, Einar?' he asked. A few metres away,
one of the Terminators fired a Cyclone missile at the
rightmost gate tower, blasting away a section of its battlements.

'It's the damned gate,' Einar said, nodding his head
towards the palace. 'It's a great deal stronger than we'd
been led to believe. Gunnar and Thorbjørn's lascannons can't scratch it.'

A line of stubber shells marched across the ferrocrete a few metres away and up the leg and chest of

one of the Wolf Guard. The Terminator was knocked back a step by the heavy impacts, but the slugs shattered harmlessly against the heavy armour. The Wolf Guard made a rude gesture with his power fist in the direction of the palace wall, and fired a burst from his storm bolter in reply.

Berek studied the distant gates with his enhanced vision, nodding thoughtfully. 'The former governor had ample time to prepare for this day,' he growled. 'How many melta bombs do you have?'

Einar glanced back over his shoulder at his assembled pack. A lasgun bolt, possibly from a long-las sniper rifle, struck the side of his helmet with an angry *crack*. The Space Wolf appeared not to notice. 'We've got four, and Ingvar's pack has two left.'

'Hand them over,' Berek ordered, and the pack leader began gathering up the heavy plasma charges.

Mikal Sternmark stepped up alongside his lord. 'Going for a walk, are we?' he asked, surveying the killing ground between them and the palace gates.

'The Grey Hunters and Long Fangs will provide cover fire while we take down the gates,' Berek said, gesturing for Einar to hand the charges over to the Wolf Guard. 'Once we're inside, don't waste time clearing the walls or the palace grounds. Aldrek has cast the runes, and believes we'll find Bredwyr in his audience chamber. If we only kill one man inside that palace, it must be him. This uprising has gone on long enough.'

The Wolf Guard answered with growls of assent. 'Lead on, lord,' Mikal said sardonically. 'First man out always draws the most fire.'

Berek threw back his head and laughed. 'Last man to the gate can clean the scorch marks off my armour,' he answered. 'Blood and thunder!'

'Blood and thunder!' the Wolf Guard howled in reply, and they charged for the gates as one.

The Space Wolves were rushing into a storm of enemy fire within moments. Intersecting lines of lasgun fire wove a burning web around the Terminators. Tracer fire arced through their ranks, and explosive shells dug craters the size of feasting plates out of the scorched ferrocrete. Bolters roared as Berek's Grey Hunter packs opened fire at the rebel positions along the walls, stitching chains of red and yellow flashes along the battlements. Lascannon beams and missile trails lanced towards the gatehouse, punching molten craters in the ornately carved stone façade, and spilling curtains of shattered masonry onto the pavement below.

Lasgun bolts and autogun shells rang off the Wolf Lord's armour. A burst of rounds from a heavy stubber struck his left leg, and a bloom of fiery pain caused Berek to stumble. Mikal drew close and reached for Berek's arm, but the Wolf Lord waved him towards the looming gates instead.

An autocannon let off a loud, rattling burst at a Terminator to Berek's right. Red and yellow detonations hammered across the Space Wolf's chest. The Wolf Guard staggered out of the cloud of dust and smoke, his storm bolter still firing despite the three bloody craters punched into his breastplate. After two halting steps, the warrior fell to his knees and pitched over onto his face.

Moments later, the Space Wolves were flattening their bodies against the scarred surface of the palace gates, underneath the arc of the remaining guns along the walls. Many of the Wolf Guard were splashed with blood from numerous minor wounds, but they immediately went to work setting the demolition charges. 'No need to blow the whole gate down,' Berek said through gritted teeth as he probed the wound in his leg. He could feel the shell in his leg, lodged close to the bone. 'Just make us a hole big enough to charge through.'

The breaching charges were ready in seconds. Berek took half of the Terminators to the right of the gate, while Aldrek and the other half went to the left. 'Clear!' The Wolf Lord called out, and when he heard an answer from Aldrek he keyed the detonator.

There was a bone rattling *whump* and a rush of superheated air, and the stink of vaporised metal made Berek grimace. 'Go!' he roared, and the Wolf Guard rushed to the breach.

The melta charges had blown a roughly circular hole three metres across in the thick metal gate, just large enough for one Terminator to pass at a time. Beyond lay a long, rectangular courtyard, bordered by statues of forgotten saints, which the rebels had transformed into a charnel house. Priests and adepts from the local Ecclesiarchy had been brought here and slain, and then hung by chains from the worn, grey statues. A thick cloud of noxious smoke hung over the scene, reeking with strange compounds that seared Berek's nostrils and made his flesh crawl.

An improvised rebel strongpoint made from steel supports, flakboard and bags of ferrocrete stood about twenty metres from the gate. Lascannons and heavy stubbers had been sited there to cover the entrance to the compound, but now the sloped face of the strong-point was ablaze, its surface ignited by molten shrapnel from the melta bombs. Berek dashed forwards, firing bursts from his storm bolter into the roiling fire and smoke. Other Wolf Guard snapped off short bursts with their storm bolters as well, unleashing a hail of deadly fire into the position.

Berek reached the sloped front embrasure of the strongpoint and leapt through the flames, landing next to a heavy stubber and its dead crew. Lasgun fire struck him along the right side, and the Wolf Lord grabbed the stubber by the barrel and hurled it at the squad of traitors who'd shot at him. The rebels scattered out of the way of the spinning weapon, leaving them easy targets for Berek's storm bolter.

A rasping cry from Berek's left brought the Wolf Lord around just as a traitor wearing the tattered uniform of a Guard officer lunged out of the smoke and swung a crackling power sword at his head. Berek deflected the sword with the back of his power fist and shot the rebel point-blank.

The hissing crackle of power weapons hummed amid the smoke and the screams of the dying. Dark shapes flitted through the roiling haze. Aldrek appeared from the smoke like a giant of old, his black beard glistening with spilled blood, and his heavy axe streaming gore. The traitors' false courage broke before the onslaught and they fled in every direction, calling vainly to their newfound gods for deliverance. Those that fled in the direction of the palace were cut down as they ran, reaped like wheat by the blazing guns of the advancing Wolves.

Berek and his men reached the far end of the courtyard in moments. The Wolf Lord climbed the shallow steps of the palace entrance and without breaking stride he smashed his power fist into the ornate wood and metal doors. There was a clap of righteous thunder and the portal exploded inward. Shouts and screams of pain greeted Berek as the Wolf Lord crossed the smoking threshold.

The nave outside the governor's audience chamber was once majestic. Soaring arches decorated with winged saints rose high overhead, their carved hands outstretched towards an octagonal ceiling of coloured armourplas that filled the chamber with shafts of jewel coloured light. Square columns carved with the likenesses of Imperial heroes stood at attention down the length of the chamber, their stern features judging the worth of every soul that strode along the marble floors.

The great space was crowded with a mob of twisted degenerates, gibbering and shouting imprecations to the false gods of the warp. Foul sigils covered the walls and pillars, and many of the carved heroes had been smeared with layers of blood and filth. Naked, rotting corpses lay in heaps at the feet of the columns, their torn faces twisted into masks of horror and despair.

Hundreds of mutants and Chaos worshippers recoiled in shock and anger from the Wolf Lord's sudden arrival. They brandished stained cleavers and chainblades, laspistols and looted autoguns, and the air of the defiled nave shook with their bestial cries. More streamed in from side corridors to the left and right, adding to the mass. It was a sight to shake the heart of even a stalwart hero, but Berek looked upon the shrieking masses and was unmoved. He was one of the Emperor's chosen, a Space Wolf, and he knew no fear.

Berek clenched his crackling power fist and raised it high. His furious voice smote the unbelievers into silence. 'Oathbreakers!' he roared. 'I am Berek Thunderfist! Look upon me and despair! The Allfather knows your crimes and has set his Wolves among you.'

An answering roar echoed Berek from the far end of the nave. An impossibly-muscled, four-armed mutant reared head and shoulders above the rest of the mob and made to answer the Wolf Lord. Berek shot the monster between its three eyes, and with a blood-thirsty howl he leapt among his foes.

The Wolf Lord swept his storm bolter in an arc before him, cutting a vengeful swathe through the packed throng. At such close range the heavy shells tore through two or even three bodies before their explosive tips travelled far enough to detonate. When he'd emptied the weapon's twin magazines he swung it like a club, crushing skulls and smashing ribs. His power fist rose and fell, hurling broken bodies in all directions. Clubs, chainswords and cleavers rained against his ancient armour, but none could find purchase. He was a storm of righteous fury, the embodiment of the Emperor's wrath, and nothing could stand against him.

Aldrek and the remaining Wolf Guard stormed into the nave behind Berek, adding their strength to the battle. Two Terminators stepped to either side of the broken doorway. One launched a pair of Cyclone missiles down the length of the nave, showering the rear ranks of the mob with red-hot shrapnel. The other levelled his whirring assault cannon and unleashed a stream of deadly shells over the heads of his brother Wolves.

Within seconds, the battle had transformed into a slaughter. Even the mutants' fanatical devotion to their new gods was not enough to sustain them in the face of the Space Wolves' fury. They tried to flee, but their large numbers worked against them as they tried to fight their way to the nave's narrow side-passages. They clawed and trampled their kin in their desire to escape, while the Wolves continued their remorseless advance, blood streaming from fist and blade.

By the time Berek reached the far end of the nave there were hundreds of dead rebels heaped in his wake. Aldrek and the Wolf Guard gathered around him, weapons ready. The Wolf Lord eyed the Rune Priest as he reloaded his storm bolter. 'What now, priest?' he asked.

Aldrek took a step towards the audience chamber doors, his hand tightening on the haft of his rune axe. 'I smell the stink of sorcery,' he said. 'Bredwyr must lie within.' He turned back to the Wolves, his face lined with terrible strain. 'There are terrible forces at work in the chamber beyond,' he warned. 'The fabric of reality is... unsettled.'

Berek frowned. 'Unsettled? Speak plainly, Aldrek.'

'This is as plain as I can make it,' the Rune Priest replied, his expression vague and haunted. 'Reality is... shifting, like sand. Forces are mingling, compelled to weave together...' Aldrek shook his head fiercely, trying to drive the image from his mind. 'I cannot explain it. I've never known the like.'

Berek raised his storm bolter. 'Then let us see for ourselves,' he said, and put his power fist to the door.

The portals swung open silently. A wavering nimbus of light washed over the wary Space Wolves, and unseen energies clawed invisibly at their minds.

The Wolf Lord strode forward into the dimly lit chamber. His boots crunched on brittle bones. The entire chamber was littered with human skeletons and cast-off husks of withered skin. The air was hazy with foul incense, streaming from tall, wrought iron braziers placed apparently at random along the room. Sheets of bloody skin had been tacked to the tall pillars by the hundreds, each one carved with intricate patterns of blasphemous runes. It was these runes that filled the room with its tenebrous light.

Berek strode through the detritus of scores of sacrificial victims. His brain felt as though it was on fire. The Wolf Lord passed unheeding through the blasphemous tableau, his gaze fixed dreadfully on the abomination that reared behind the governor's broken throne.

The wall behind the throne was fifteen metres tall and ten metres wide, and in the days of the palace's construction it would have been carved with the likeness of the holy Emperor. Now, the wall was covered in glistening flesh and pulsating organs, stitched together by some form of silver wire that shone like liquid in the sorcerous light. Veins and arteries throbbed, and hearts clenched and unclenched, driving blood through the vile mass. Berek glimpsed naked brains trapped in webworks of palpitating muscle, and eyes rolling in gelid masses of fat. Intestines writhed like snakes across the surface of the towering mass, bound in place by silver wire. Vast and unnatural energies radiated from the thing, like heat from a forge. The abomination was alive, somehow, and on some deep, primal level Berek also knew that it was not some maddened act of depravity. It had been built to serve a very particular purpose.

'Blessed Allfather,' Aldrek gasped, his face turning pale. 'We've found Bredwyr and his entire household.'

Gritting his teeth, Berek raised his storm bolter. 'Then let's finish what he came here to do.'

The Space Wolves fired as one, pouring streams of explosive shells into the horrid mass of flesh. Berek watched with revulsion as the construct writhed beneath the storm of fire. A pink haze of vaporised blood and flesh filled the air around the abomination, but, almost as quickly as they were made, the shell holes sealed shut again.

A wave of unholy power radiated from the construct and swept over the Space Wolves. Vertigo washed over Berek, overwhelming his enhanced senses. It felt as though the room was expanding in every direction, stretching away into the vastness of space. Reeling, the Wolf Lord turned to Aldrek. 'Priest!' he cried. 'Your axe!'

Aldrek had been driven to one knee by the force of the construct's power. His eyes had rolled back in their sockets, and tendrils of smoke curled from the silver and brass connections wired to his skull. And yet, the heroic priest heard Berek's call and nodded. He tried to speak, but only a guttural growl escaped his bloody lips. With a mighty effort, Aldrek rose to his feet, raising his rune axe high, and a black blade carved with blasphemous, glowing runes burst from the Rune Priest's chest.

A towering figure clad in ornate blue and gold armour had appeared behind Aldrek, as though coalescing out of the shadows. The Chaos sorcerer pulled his hellblade from Aldrek's body, and the Rune Priest staggered, blood pouring from his open mouth. With a strangled roar, Aldrek spun about, swinging furiously with his axe, but as he did so two more armoured giants materialised like ghosts to either side of him and drove their swords into the Rune Priest's chest.

More figures were taking shape from the darkness: dreadful warriors clad in baroque versions of power armour eerily similar to those the Space Wolves wore. Berek recognised their blue and gold heraldry at once, and fought back a surge of righteous revulsion and dread. Every son of Russ knew the colours of the Chaos Marines known as the Thousand Sons. Twisted nightmares of muscle and flesh emerged alongside the Traitor Marines, and reached for the Space Marines with glistening, ropy tentacles and fanged mouths.

The ambush had caught the Wolf Guard unawares, but their surprise lasted only an instant. 'For Russ and the Allfather!' Mikal Sternmark cried as the sorcerers and daemons rushed in from all sides, and the air rang with the thunder of bolters and the clash of blades.

Aldrek had fallen to his knees, blood flowing from his wounds. As the sorcerers closed in again, he slashed at one with his rune axe, but the Chaos warrior parried the blow with his hellsword and knocked the axe from Aldrek's bloodless fingers. The Rune Priest howled defiantly at his foes, but the sorcerers laid their hands upon him, and they vanished as swiftly as they appeared, taking Aldrek with them.

Berek Thunderfist let out a furious bellow. 'Stand fast, sons of Fenris!' he cried, blasting a pair of daemons into gobbets of protoplasm. 'Our brothers are coming,' he said, knowing that Einar and the rest of the Grey Hunters could not be far behind them.

'Indeed,' said a silken voice behind the Wolf Lord. 'As a matter of fact, my plan depends upon it.'

Quicker than the eye could follow, Berek spun on his heel, his power fist reaching for the source of the voice, but the gauntlet closed on empty air.

A fearsome impact struck Berek in the chest. Terrible pain, cold and black as the abyss, spread beneath his ribs.

The Chaos sorcerer stood just out of reach. His ornate power armour was wrought with blasphemous sigils of power, and decorated with the writhing skulls of serpentine gargoyles. Terrible, inhuman intelligence burned from the eye slits of the baroque, horned helmet.

With a single, fluid motion, Madox drew the Spear of Russ from Berek's chest. The Wolf Lord felt his strength leave him all at once. His legs failed him, and the Space Wolf fell to his knees.

Madox raised the tip of Russ's spear to Berek's face, showing him the blood dripping from the point of the sacred relic. 'The fate of your Chapter is sealed, Berek Thunderfist,' the Chaos champion said, as darkness filled the corners of the Wolf Lord's vision. 'When you go to stand before your false emperor, tell him that you are the one to blame.' As the sorcerer spoke, his armoured form blurred before the Wolf Lord's eyes, fading from view as if he were a ghost.

The last thing Berek heard was the sound of triumphant laughter, as cold and cruel as Old Night itself.

* * *

A MOANING WIND keened ceaselessly in the crimson temple that Madox had built. Ruddy light seeped from the very stones, and the unnatural wind plucked at the corners of the bloody scraps of skin nailed to the temple columns. The runes inscribed on their surface were black as the void, drawing in the energy that surrounded them.

The blood of the Wolf Lord ran in thin rivulets down the haft of Russ's Spear and across the sorcerer's knuckles. As Madox watched, the insubstantial figures of Berek's Wolf Guard withdrew from sight, dragging the body of their lord through the piled bones and skin that littered the chamber in the physical realm.

Where the governor's throne had stood in the audience chamber, Madox had placed his temple's altar, a single block of black stone carved with runes of power. Offerings covered its surface, gleaming like rubies in the hellish light.

A trio of sorcerers approached Madox, dragging the body of the Rune Priest. The Space Marine still clung to life, despite his terrible wounds. The Chaos sorcerer smiled. 'Hold him up,' Madox commanded.

With inhuman strength the Traitor Marines lifted Aldrek nearly to his feet. Madox placed a taloned gauntlet over the rent in the Space Wolf's breastplate and thrust it within. The Rune Priest stiffened. Pure agony focused Aldrek's gaze on the sorcerer.

Flesh ripped, and Madox tore his hand free. The Rune Priest slumped, eyes glazing in death as the sorcerer showed Aldrek what he held in his hand. 'Now the circle is complete,' he said, and laid the progenoid glands on the altar beside nearly a dozen more.

Aldrek's body fell to the bleeding stones with a lifeless clatter as the sorcerers raised their hands and began to chant. Madox felt the power of the great ritual begin to take shape, and turned to face his master.

Madox held up the Spear of Russ to the blazing eye that hovered in the air before him. 'The end of the Space Wolves is at hand,' he said, showing the Wolf Lord's blood to his dreadful master.

TWO

Identities and Projects

TWO
Alarums and Excursions

THE NARROW BLADE SCORED a thin cut across Ragnar's powerfully muscled chest as he pivoted to avoid the killing thrust. Baring his teeth in a feral snarl, he brought his iron sword around in a blurring arc and chopped down hard on Torin's exposed neck.

It was a blow that would have hacked a normal man's head clean off. Instead, Torin pivoted on the ball of his right foot, nearly too fast for the eye to follow, and Ragnar's heavy blade rang against the Space Wolf's reinforced collar-bone. The dulled sword split the skin in a pressure cut a quarter of a metre long across Torin's chest, drawing a hiss of pain from the older warrior, and filling the air of the practice arena with the coppery scent of blood. At virtually the same instant, Torin's sword swept down and struck lightly at Ragnar's left thigh before the Space Wolf's lunge carried him past his opponent, opening the distance across the sandy training ground.

Dried blood crackled faintly along Ragnar's brow. The enhanced clotting factor in his blood had already stopped the bleeding from the scalp wound Torin had given him seconds before. Both warriors were bare-chested, clad only in loose fitting breeches, torn and stained from dozens of blows. Most Space Marine Chapters preferred to practise their close-combat skills with automated sparring drones or combat servitors, but the Space Wolves kept to the old ways of their home world: man to man and iron against iron.

Both Wolves were covered in angry red weals and shallow cuts. They grimaced at the pain from torn muscles and wrenched ligaments. The wounds sharpened their wits and tested their wills in a way no mindless combat servitor could.

Torin continued to give ground, gliding effortlessly across the black volcanic sand. His iron sword was a little longer and thinner than the heavy broadsword in Ragnar's hand, lending the warrior a slight advantage in speed and reach. The weapon suited him. Torin was tall and lean, almost lithe compared to Ragnar's broad-chested bulk. His blade flickered back and forth through the air, more often than not avoiding directly blocking the younger Space Wolf's more massive blade and leaving Ragnar swinging at empty air. The older warrior's blows were fluid and precise, striking sharply along leg or arm and withdrawing again, as though intended to goad Ragnar into anger rather than strike a killing blow.

If that was Torin's plan, Ragnar had to admit it was working.

The young Space Wolf lowered his head and charged at Torin with a furious bellow. Gauging the distance carefully, he aimed a fierce blow at the older Space Wolf's temple, and then checked the feint at the last moment and reversed the angle of the blow, slashing hard at Torin's thigh. Quick as he was, Torin was still faster. Instead of trying to parry Ragnar's blade or turn aside, he leapt forward and past Ragnar's right side. The sleek blade scored another shallow cut on the inside of Ragnar's right arm.

Snarling furiously, Ragnar spun and lunged for Torin's retreating back, jabbing the blunt tip against his opponent's shoulder blade hard enough to draw a painful grunt from the older Space Marine, but not enough to translate into a killing blow. Torin threw himself forward into a shoulder roll across the black sand, coming up facing Ragnar a few metres away with his sword at the ready. The older Space Wolf's lean face quirked into a faintly mocking grin. 'Good, but not good enough,' he said.

'I came down here to fight, not dance,' Ragnar growled. 'If you'd sit still for half a second you'd be dead.'

Torin's mocking grin deepened. 'A compelling reason not to sit still, don't you think?' he replied.

'Morkai's frozen bollocks,' boomed a thunderous voice from the edge of the arena, 'will you two quit yapping and get on with it?' A massive figure rose ponderously from a stone bench near the arena entrance, brandishing a gnawed leg bone in his knobby fist like a greasy, gristly club. Rich, honey coloured ale sloshed from an enormous drinking horn clutched in Haegr's left hand and splashed over his thick fingers. 'If I were in there I would have killed the both of you and be halfway back to the mead hall!' The huge warrior's bushy red whiskers and bristly eyebrows lent Haegr the appearance of an enraged walrus.

Torin laughed. His voice was light, but his dark eyes never left Ragnar's face. 'Iron sword against ice mammoth haunch? I think I'd like to see you try.'

'Bah!' Haegr exclaimed, pausing to lick the spilled ale from his scarred knuckles. 'The mighty Haegr doesn't play at fighting, Torin. What he fights, he kills. You should know that by now. And if I killed the two of you, who would be left to guard the lady Gabriella besides me?'

The older Space Wolf rolled his eyes in mock disdain. 'Who can argue with wisdom like that?'

Ragnar nearly had him. Just as Torin spoke, he lunged forward, his blade slashing in a blurring figure of eight. For a fraction of a second, Torin appeared to be caught off-guard. He blocked one cut with a ringing blow that sent sparks flying from his sword and barely ducked aside a brutal cut from the opposite angle. Again, his swift blade flicked out, biting painfully at Ragnar's groin, but this time the young Space Wolf kept right on coming, hammering at Torin's head, neck and shoulders. The older Space Wolf back-pedalled furiously, his face growing taut with strain. He was forced to block one blow, and then another. Then a third stroke snapped the thinner blade with a discordant clang. Ragnar's sword continued along its arc and cracked hard against Torin's left cheekbone, knocking the Space Wolf onto his back.

Ragnar leapt forward, stomping down hard on the inside of Torin's right thigh to pin him in place, and then pressing the blunt tip of his blade into the hollow of his opponent's throat. 'This dance is over,' he growled, his hand tightening on the grip of his sword. 'Next time you fight me, try something other than a toy sword.'

Blood flowed in thick streams down Torin's ragged cheek and into his thin moustache. He regarded Ragnar coldly. 'The fight ended five seconds before my sword broke,' he said. 'I killed you, but you were too thick-headed to realise it.'

Ragnar let out a bark of laughter. 'What? That bee sting?'

Torin pushed Ragnar's blade aside and climbed slowly to his feet. He pointed at the spot where his last blow had fallen. 'Femoral artery,' he said. He then pointed to the cut along the inside of Ragnar's sword arm. 'Brachial artery.' Torin jabbed at a fading red mark on Ragnar's abdomen. 'Main pulmonary artery. Even with the clotting factor, I'd have bled you white about two minutes ago.' He turned away and limped over to the broken half of his blade, sticking up from the sands a few metres away. 'You should have paid more attention, my friend. Half a dozen minor blows are just as deadly as one big one.' Torin bent and picked up the battered shard of iron. He frowned, turning it over in his hands. 'I had to have this specially made, you know.'

Torin's cold dissection of the battle drained all the heat out of Ragnar's blood, leaving the younger Space Wolf vaguely shamed. 'You're right, of course,' he said heavily, tossing his notched sword onto the sand.

'Forgive me, brother,' Ragnar said, holding out his hand. 'Give me the pieces of the blade and I'll beg a boon from one of the Iron Priests to have it remade.'

The older Space Wolf shook his head, waving Ragnar's hand away with the broken shard of iron. 'There is nothing to forgive, my friend,' he said. 'The fault is as much mine as yours. I prodded you on purpose, trying to draw out some of the melancholy that's gripped you these last few months.'

'Much as it pains me to say it, Torin's right,' Haegr said, worrying at a piece of gristle with his fangs. 'Here we are back on Fenris, the land of heroes, and all you've done since we got here is mope.'

Scowling, Ragnar turned away, heading for the bench where the rest of his clothes were laid. 'The Chapter is at war,' he said darkly, reaching for his wool and leather tunic. 'We should be out there, fighting alongside our brothers.' Ragnar thought of Sven, his old pack mate, fighting with Berek Thunderfist's great company on Charys. No doubt they were celebrating their victory in the governor's palace even now, while he haunted the stone halls of the Fang like some *nithling*.

'Our place is at Gabriella's side,' Torin said evenly. 'We have a sacred duty to House Bellisarius, Ragnar, now more than ever, after the losses we suffered at Hyades.'

'I hear you, Torin,' Ragnar replied, sitting on the bench and reaching for his dragon skin boots. They were members of the Wolfblade, bodyguards assigned to the Navigator House of Bellisarius by the Great Wolf, in keeping with an ancient pact that was as old as the Imperium. There were never more than two dozen Wolfblade at any given time, and most of those were stationed on Holy Terra, guarding high-ranking members of the Bellisarius line and training their House troops.

Ragnar, Torin, Haegr and six of their brothers had left Terra more than six months ago to accompany Lady Gabriella, one of House Bellisarius's highest ranking Navigators, on an inspection of the House's holdings on Hyades, a jungle world valued for its promethium mines. Once there, however, they had been caught up in the machinations of a Chaos tainted warlord named Cadmus, who had sworn himself to the service of Tzeentch and to the Space Wolves' ancient foes the Thousand Sons. Cadmus's schemes orchestrated a violent battle between Berek Thunderfist's great company, which was patrolling in the region, and a contingent of Dark Angels. The Dark Angels were one of the most secretive of Space Marine Chapters, and nursed a bitter rivalry with the Space Wolves that stretched back thousands of years. The fight that ensued – and Cadmus's own treachery – claimed the lives of their fellow bodyguards, leaving only Torin, Haegr and himself to keep Gabriella safe. Though Cadmus had ultimately been defeated and the Thousand Sons driven off, Hyades was the first spark in the conflagration sweeping across the Space Wolf domains.

Ragnar rose from the bench and reached for his sword belt. The ancient frost blade, a relic borne by the Wolfblade for thousands of years and given to Ragnar by Gabriella was settled comfortably on his hip. 'It's just… if Gabriella isn't safe in the *Fang* of all places, she isn't safe anywhere. The Old Wolf needs every stout sword-arm he can muster and we're being wasted here.'

Torin gave Ragnar a probing look as he settled a heavy bearskin cloak around his shoulders. The months on Fenris had changed Torin somewhat. On Terra the Space Wolf had adopted many of the fashionable airs of the local aristocracy. When Ragnar had first met him, his hair was cut short and his moustache trimmed pencil-thin, in the Terran fashion. Now, his hair was growing out again, and bore none of the scent of perfumed pomade he'd favoured among the Imperial elite. His ability to read people, however, was just as sharp as ever. 'This isn't about doing your duty as a Space Wolf. This is about the Spear of Russ.'

The observation stung Ragnar. Though assignment to the Wolfblade was ostensibly a posting of great honour, most Space Wolves saw it as a form of exile, far from the glory of the battlefield. Ragnar could not see it any other way. He had been sent to Terra by Logan Grimnar after he had lost one of the Chapter's most sacred relics: the Spear of Russ. Once wielded in battle by the primarch, in the glory days of the Great Crusade, it had been kept for millennia at a sacred shrine on the planet Garm, waiting for the day Russ would return for the Last Battle. But an arch-heretic named Sergius had stolen the spear during a bloody uprising on Garm, and Ragnar, then a Blood Claw in Berek Thunderfist's great company, had been among the warriors sent to crush the revolt. After numerous battles, Ragnar came face-to-face with his old nemesis Madox, who had manipulated Sergius into taking the spear in an effort to summon Magnus the Red, his Legion's infernal primarch, into the physical realm.

The foul sorcerer nearly succeeded, but just as Magnus began to cross the threshold from the depths of the warp, Ragnar seized the spear from Sergius and hurled the legendary weapon at the fearsome primarch. The spear struck Magnus like a thunderbolt and the daemon prince was hurled back into the raging maelstrom of the warp. Garm had been saved, but the Spear of Russ had been lost, possibly forever.

He'd had no choice. Ragnar knew this. Even the Old Wolf had once told him that he would have done the very same thing had he been in Ragnar's place. That didn't change the fact that he'd betrayed a sacred oath that the Chapter had sworn to their primarch nearly ten millennia ago. To the people of Fenris there were few things more terrible than an oathbreaker, and the realisation haunted him.

The young Space Wolf shook his head, dragging blunt fingers through his tangled mane of black hair and probing at the cut on his scalp. Unlike Torin or Haegr his square chin was clean-shaven, in the custom of the Blood Claws. A Space Wolf grew his beard only after being accepted into the Grey Hunters or the Wolf Scouts, and those avenues had been closed to him when he'd been sent away to Terra.

'The spear is gone, Torin,' Ragnar said at last. 'I know this. It's just... I haven't been sleeping lately. That's all.'

'Ha! Clearly you haven't been drinking enough,' Haegr interjected, raising his massive ale horn. 'A cask of ale and a good brawl is what you need, Ragnar my lad! Why don't we go to the mead hall and see what we can find, eh?'

Ragnar stole a glance at Torin. The older Space Wolf seemed unconvinced by Ragnar's clumsy evasion. 'I've had enough of waiting, brothers,' he said gravely. 'I'm going to speak to the Old Wolf and demand he send me to the battle line.'

'*Demand?*' Haegr repeated, his expression incredulous. The massive Space Wolf threw back his head and roared with laughter. 'Did you hear that, Torin? The cub thinks to command Logan Grimnar!' Haegr's huge face split in a ferocious grin. 'The Old Wolf will hit you so hard Russ himself will feel it!'

Ragnar felt a flush of anger rise to his cheeks. Before he could reply, however, the vox-bead behind his right ear hummed, and Gabriella's calm, quiet voice filled his head. 'Ragnar, I would have you attend upon me, please.'

The young Space Wolf paused, mastering his temper. He reached back to the vox-bead. 'As you wish, my lady,' he answered grimly. *Perhaps for the last time.* 'Where will I find you?'

'In the Great Wolf's council chamber,' Gabriella replied. 'A ship has arrived from Charys bearing grave news, and there is much to be discussed.'

A cold sense of foreboding prickled the hairs on the back of Ragnar's neck. 'I'll be there at once,' he replied.

Torin watched the change in Ragnar's expression. 'What's happened, brother?' he asked.

The young Space Wolf could only shake his head. 'I don't know,' he replied, 'but I fear it's something terrible.'

WHITE SUNLIGHT FLOODED the Great Wolf's council chamber. The armoured shutters had been drawn back from the tall windows that dominated the east side of

the large room, providing a panoramic view of the
cloud wrapped Asaheim range and the distant, iron-
grey sea. Fenris was swinging close to the Wolf's Eye
once more, ending the harsh winter and heralding the
even harsher Time of Fire. The rising temperatures had
banished the heavy overcast and the clinging mist that
enfolded the Fang for much of the year, and for a short
time Ragnar knew that the seas would be mild and rel-
atively free from storms. The kraken would rise from
the deeps, and the people of Fenris would take to the
sea in their long ships to hunt and to fight. *The Iron
Season*, Ragnar recalled, *a time of feasting and of battle,
of betrothals and births: a time for offering sacrifices to the
gods who watch from the clouds.*

Logan Grimnar was standing before one of those
tall windows as Ragnar entered the room, his wide
hands clasped behind his back as he brooded upon
the unsuspecting world below. The Great Wolf was in
his armour, his shoulders wrapped in a cloak of sea-
dragon scales. Runic charms and wolves' teeth were
woven into the thick braids of his iron-grey hair, and
parchment ribbons from hundreds of major campaigns fluttered like raven's feathers from his scarred
grey and yellow pauldrons. Old and fierce, as
indomitable as the Fang itself, some said that Logan
Grimnar was the greatest living warrior in the
Imperium, and Ragnar could not help but feel awed
by his presence. Nearly a dozen other Space Wolves
stood around the council table, mighty priests or
members of Logan's Wolf Guard, each one a towering
figure in his own right.

At once, Ragnar caught a familiar scent among the fearsome Wolves and searched among the crowded warriors

for its source. Lady Gabriella, Master Navigator of House Bellisarius, sat in a high-backed wooden chair at the far side of the table, studying the assembly over slim, steepled fingers. She wore the dark dress uniform of her House, ornamented with epaulettes and polished gold buttons fashioned with the wolf-and-eye symbol of Bellisarius. Medals and ceremonial braid covered the front of her jacket, proclaiming her personal achievements and the great deeds of her household, and a small pistol and a gracefully curved sabre hung from a belt around her narrow waist. Her long, black hair had been bound up in glossy braids that hung about her narrow shoulders and framed her severe, angular face. A scarf of black silk covered the Navigator's high forehead, concealing the pineal eye that was the source of her psychic talents.

Gabriella turned her head slightly as Ragnar's gaze fell upon her and nodded a curt greeting. Then she rested her hands in her lap and turned her attention back to the Great Wolf.

Ragnar stepped forward and knelt before Grimnar. 'Lady Gabriella said a ship has come from Charys bearing news,' he said without preamble. 'What has happened? Why didn't the astropaths–'

'According to the Lady Gabriella, you encountered the Chaos sorcerer Madox on Hyades,' the Great Wolf said, cutting Ragnar off. 'What did he say to you?'

The question took the young Space Wolf aback. 'We did not meet face to face,' he replied. 'He only revealed himself through one of his minions, just as we were about to leave the planet.'

'And?' Logan growled.

'He said his men were going to kill us,' Ragnar said with a shrug.

Grimnar turned, fixing the young Space Wolf with an icy gaze. 'What of the Spear of Russ? Did he say anything about it?'

Ragnar frowned. 'No, lord, he didn't. The traitor Cadmus, however, claimed that Madox was seeking a relic that was a crucial component of a ritual he sought to perform, a ritual that also depended upon Space Marine gene-seed.' A chill raced down Ragnar's spine. 'This was all in my earlier report. What is all this about?'

'Madox has been sighted on Charys, lad,' spoke a voice beside the council table. Ragnar turned to meet the gaze of Ranek, the great Wolf Priest. 'He has the Spear of Russ with him.'

Ragnar leapt to his feet, startled by the news. 'The Spear!' he said, forgetting himself. *Russ be praised*, he thought, *perhaps all is not lost.*

'This is hardly a cause for celebration, lad!' Ranek snapped. 'Now the full scope of the Chaos incursion becomes clear.'

'How so?' Ragnar asked.

Ranek reached down and touched a rune at the edge of the council table. A hololith mounted in the table-top glowed to life, creating a detailed star map of the sector. Fenris lay near the centre of the map. Systems currently under attack or in revolt shone brighter than the rest. Minor attacks or incursions were coloured yellow, while major attacks were red. Ragnar was shocked to see that more than thirty systems were affected.

'We have been studying the pattern of the Chaos incursion since it began,' the Wolf Priest said, 'trying to ascertain their ultimate objective. Many of the initial uprisings made sense from a military standpoint: forge worlds, industrialised hive-worlds and trade centres, attacks designed to sow confusion and cripple our ability to respond. But many others confounded us.' He pointed to a pulsing red system. 'Ceta Pavonis, an airless rock occupied by gangs of pirates and slavers. Or here: Grendel IV, an old world all but abandoned three centuries ago when the last of its radium mines played out. Even Charys is nothing more than a minor agri-world, with little strategic value other than its proximity to Fenris. Yet, in each of these places there are major uprisings and reported sightings of Chaos Marines.'

Ragnar considered this. 'Diversions,' he concluded, 'meant to draw our attention from the true objective. What else could they be?'

Ranek gave the young Space Wolf an appraising look. 'What, indeed? We wondered much the same thing.' The Wolf Priest shrugged. 'If they were meant as diversions, then our foes chose poorly. There are far more important systems that require our protection. But we know that our enemies are not fools, however much we would like to believe otherwise. There was a plan at work here, but we could not see it at first.' Ranek gestured at the collection of Rune Priests standing quietly around the table. 'The runes were consulted, and they suggested we seek a new point of view on the problem.'

The young Space Wolf turned, pensive. 'Well, I'm not sure how much help I will be, but if you think I can be of use–'

A melodious laugh rose from the far side of the table, and in moments the assembled Space Wolves joined in, breaking the tension in the room. Gabriella covered her mouth with one pale hand, her human eyes twinkling with mirth. 'Ranek was referring to me,' she said, not unkindly. 'He and the Great Wolf thought I might see a pattern where a warrior might not.'

Ragnar fought to control the flush rising to his cheeks. 'Ah, of course,' he said quickly, 'and were you successful?'

Gabriella's angular features turned sober once more. 'Unfortunately, yes,' she said. She turned to Ranek. 'If you will permit me…'

'Of course, lady,' the Wolf Priest said, stepping away from the table.

Gabriella rose from her chair and stepped over to the hololith controls. 'The problem was that everyone was viewing the incursion as a military campaign, not unlike a Black Crusade,' she said. 'As Ranek said, nearly all of the minor targets had military value, but if we just focus on the areas with a major Chaos presence, we are left with this.' She touched a rune and the yellow indicators faded from view, leaving thirteen systems scattered in a roughly spherical arrangement around Fenris.

Ragnar studied each of the systems in turn. 'None of these are major military or industrial targets,' he said, a puzzled look on their face.

'Indeed,' she said, 'but, being a Navigator, another prospect suggested itself to me: what if the systems weren't important because of what they were, but rather, *where* they were?'

Gabriella touched another rune. The hololith drew blinking red lines connecting each of the systems together. Ragnar watched them converge, and his eyes went wide. 'It's a symbol of some kind.'

'Not a symbol *per se*,' Gabriella replied. 'It's a sorcerous sigil, and Charys lies at its centre.' She glanced up at Ragnar. 'Do you remember what the city of Lethe looked like when we left for the *Fist of Russ?*'

Ragnar nodded. 'Fire from the burning promethium lines stretched all across the city. It looked like… well, I remember thinking it looked like a ritual symbol of some kind.'

She nodded. 'That was the ritual symbol establishing Hyades as an anchor point for this larger sigil,' she said, pointing to the blasphemous sign hanging before them. 'Madox has laid the foundation for a sorcerous ritual of enormous proportions. If what you learned from Cadmus is correct, he now has all the elements he needs for the ritual to begin.'

The scope of the sorcerer's plans staggered Ragnar. He looked to the Great Wolf. 'A ship arrived from Charys, bearing news. What has Berek found?'

The Old Wolf's expression turned grim. 'Berek has been gravely wounded,' he said, 'and the Rune Priest Aldrek is believed to be dead.' Logan turned away from the window and stepped heavily to the table. 'When Gabriella revealed the importance of Charys I sent Berek's great company there to bring an end to this monstrous scheme. It appears that Madox was waiting for him. Berek and his men were lured into a trap.' The Old Wolf leaned forward, resting his scarred knuckles on the table's glass surface. His lined face was grim. 'Mikal Sternmark commands the great company for the moment, and he and the Guard regiments continue to fight against the rebels, but warp storms are growing in the region. Soon the system will be isolated altogether, and the Chaos uprisings have scattered our forces across the sector.' The Old Wolf banged his fist on the tabletop. 'Madox and his one-eyed master must have been planning this for decades. They've outmanoeuvred us, and their teeth are at our throats.'

A low growl began to build in Ragnar's throat. Suddenly he was very aware of the blood rushing through his veins and the pounding of his hearts. Every Space Wolf in the room sensed the change. Hands clenched and heads lowered as they caught the scent of the Wulfen.

'Master yourself, young one,' Ranek said in a low, commanding voice. 'Save the wolf's rage for our foes.'

Ragnar struggled to control his rising fury. 'What of your company, Great Wolf?' he said in a choked voice. 'Surely they can turn the tide at Charys.'

'My company is scattered across our domains, bolstering the efforts of the other Wolf Lords who are hard-pressed,' Grimnar replied. 'Berek's company was our reserve force.'

'Send the Wolfblade to Charys, then,' Ragnar snarled, unable to contain himself.

The Old Wolf's fists clenched. 'What, the three of you?' he thundered. 'Do you imagine you'll turn the tide all by yourselves?'

'I'll die in the attempt, if I must!' Ragnar shot back. 'I'd rather lie on a field at Charys than live another day here.'

'Arrogant pup!' Grimnar roared. He straightened to his full height, his fierce presence seeming to fill the entire chamber. He crossed the space between him and Ragnar with a single step, and lashed out with his open hand, cuffing Ragnar on the side of the head. 'I couldn't have said it better myself!'

The Wolves roared with laughter. After a moment, Ragnar joined in as well. Gabriella studied the giants' bloody-minded mirth with an expression of startled bemusement.

'You will have your wish, young Space Wolf,' Grimnar said, clapping Ragnar on the shoulder. 'We are sending every warrior we have left to add their swords to the fight, and Lady Gabriella has pledged her skills to guide our reinforcements safely to Charys,' the Old Wolf said, nodding respectfully to the Navigator. 'Report to Sternmark when you arrive. I'm sure he'll be glad for every stout arm he can get.'

In a flash, Ragnar's anger turned to a fierce, blood-thirsty joy. Death might wait for him on Charys, but so be it, he would face it as a Space Wolf, fighting alongside his battle-brothers. 'The Spear of Russ will be ours once again, lord. On my life and on my honour, I swear it!'

'I hear you, Ragnar Blackmane,' the Old Wolf answered solemnly, 'and Russ hears your oath as well. Spill the blood of our foes and return to us what was lost, and try to set a good example for the lads when you're getting yourself hacked to pieces, eh?'

THREE
Darkness and Ice

THE RUMBLE OF the Thunderhawk's engines drummed
soundlessly across Ragnar's aching bones, rising inexorably to a punishing crescendo as the heavily laden
transport clawed its way into the night sky. He dimly
heard the approaching roar of the engines, the sound
attenuated into a brassy rattle by the thin atmosphere,
and the thick blanket of clouds below the rocky ledge
began to glow a faint blue. The climbing spacecraft
burst through the cloud layer like a spear, riding a column of cyan light into the purple vault of stars where
the *Fist of Russ* awaited. Ragnar tracked its course
through frozen, half-closed lids until it was nothing
more than another fiercely burning speck in the fir-
mament above the great mountain.

Within moments, the last notes of thunder faded,
leaving Ragnar to his silent vigil. He had lost track of
the hours since he'd climbed above the clouds and

settled himself high atop the Fang. Clad only in his woollen clothes and wolfskin cloak, he had knelt in the snow and drawn forth his ancient frost blade. Resting the tip against the frozen ground and placing his hands upon its hilt, he had prayed to the Allfather and to blessed Russ, the First Wolf, until ice crystals clogged this throat and rattled in his lungs. All through the night he waited, his face upturned to the endless expanse of space, hoping for a brush with something he could not rightly name.

For a time after his brief audience with the Great Wolf, Ragnar's spirits had been lifted. The chains of duty had been loosened at last, and fields of war beckoned. More importantly, the Spear of Russ had been spotted on Charys, and for the first time, Ragnar felt that he might have a chance to redeem himself and restore the honour of his Chapter.

However, as the day wore on, and he began preparing his wargear for the journey, his thoughts turned dark once more. The news of Berek's fate at the hands of Madox was a terrible blow, and the picture that the Old Wolf had painted of the overall situation was woefully grim. Restoring those worlds already lost to Chaos would take centuries to complete, if it could be done at all. He'd heard of worlds scoured down to the bedrock by virus bombs and cyclonic torpedoes, once they'd been deemed too tainted to reclaim. Again and again, his mind turned back to that moment in the temple on Garm when he had held the Spear of Russ in his hand. *I threw it away,* he thought, *and everything that came after is because of me.*

He could not help but think of what the Old Wolf had said in the council chamber. *Madox and his one-eyed master must have been planning this for decades.* Could it be true? If so, hadn't he been nothing more than a pawn, pushed and pulled across a vast, invisible board that only the Chaos sorcerer could see? The idea left him sick at heart. It was one thing to strive mightily and fail – at least that was a noble failure, pure in spirit and done with honour – but to dance to the bidding of evil powers... that could not be borne.

So, he had climbed to the highest slope of Fenris he could reach, far beyond the grasp of mortal men, to stare up into the heavens and seek... something, a brush with holiness perhaps, such as he'd felt in the sacred shrine on Garm. He remembered the peace he'd felt then, the sense of rightness that banished pain and weariness and doubt.

Not this time, however. Poised between heaven and earth, fire and ice, Ragnar Blackmane was left with nothing but silence and doubt.

Ice crackled faintly as the Space Wolf slowly bowed his head. His breath no longer left faint wisps of mist in the thin air, having slowed and cooled almost to the point of hibernation. He could hear the sluggish flow of blood through his veins, and the slow, alternating beats of his hearts.

It was several long moments before the buzzing sound of voices registered in his numbed brain. They were approaching from the thick cloud layer, several dozen metres below. Haegr appeared first, broaching the pearly mist like a grey flanked whale. His beady eyes spotted Ragnar at once. 'Ha!' he exclaimed, his booming voice strangely distorted by the altitude. 'I told you we would find him here! That's three kegs of Ironhead Ale you owe me, Torin the Doubter.'

The barrel-chested Space Wolf plodded resolutely up the icy slope towards Ragnar, the heavy armour he wore lending weight and power to his steps. Ice glittered along the shoulders of Haegr's bearskin cloak and dragged down the bristles of his walrus-like moustache, and his cheeks were vivid red. Despite the climb, the huge warrior still carried his massive ale horn in his right hand. Behind him, lighter of step but no less burdened by the savage conditions, came Torin, helmet-less, but wearing an arctic hood that shielded his lean face from the worst of the cold. 'It was two kegs of ale, not three,' the older Wolfblade replied, 'but you won them fairly for a change. How did you think to look here?'

'Mighty Haegr's muscles aren't just in his arms,' he declared, tapping an armoured finger against his skull. 'You saw the look in his eyes when he left the arming chamber this afternoon. When he's in one of his black moods just think of the worst, most inhospitable place a Wolf can get to under his own power, and that's where you'll find him.' The burly Space Wolf climbed onto Ragnar's ledge, and peered sternly at him. 'Been up here all night, by the looks of him. His skin's blacker than an inquisitor's heart.'

Torin slipped past Haegr and knelt beside Ragnar. The older warrior studied him so intently that for a moment Ragnar wondered if Torin thought he might be dead. He took in a deeper breath and spoke, the words coming out in a raspy cough. 'Needed time to think,' he said gruffly. He tried to give Torin a hard look, but his frozen eyes refused to obey.

The older Wolfblade glanced back over his shoulder at the vast sea of cloud below. 'If you'd waited here a few hours longer you'd be watching our Thunderhawk take off and be thinking about how you were going to walk to Charys,' he said. 'Gabriella is taking her breakfast, and wants to be aboard the *Fist of Russ* before daybreak. We tried to call you, but you switched off your vox-bead, or it's frozen solid; I can't tell which at this point.'

Ragnar forced his eyes to close and concentrated on his breathing for a moment. His pulse began to quicken, slowly increasing his body's core temperature. Trickles of water ran from his eyes like faux tears, and froze upon his cheeks. The young Space Wolf clenched his fists around the hilt of the sword and felt ice crackle across his knuckles. When he opened his eyes again he saw that the skin of his hands was blue-black. He would be scraping the dead skin cells away for quite a while. Gritting his teeth, Ragnar climbed to his feet. Fierce pains stabbed through his joints, but he suppressed them with an effort of will. 'I would have come down by dawn,' he grumbled, shaking still more ice from his shoulders.

'Perhaps a note to that effect next time would be helpful,' Torin observed.

Now Ragnar did manage a forbidding glare. 'If I'd done that you would have come looking for me straightaway. I told you, I wanted to be alone.'

'What a bloody stupid thing to say!' Haegr barked. 'A Wolf's nothing without his pack, Ragnar. Even you're bright enough to know that.' He brandished his horn before the young Space Wolf. 'Why, you missed a true hero's feast in the hall last night! There was mead enough to float a long ship, and the eating-board groaned with all the food piled upon it!'

'Which Haegr tried to eat all by himself,' Torin said wryly.

The huge Space Wolf puffed out his barrel chest. 'Don't blame me for your faint heart,' Haegr replied, eyes wide with outrage. 'You could have taken your share at any time.'

'Except that I like my fingers where they are,' Torin remarked wryly. 'I've heard of battle madness before, but feast madness? Were you bitten by a goat at a young age, Haegr? I think you tried to eat the board itself between courses.'

'Don't be stupid,' Haegr shot back. 'I just needed a splinter to get a piece of venison caught between my teeth.'

'That wasn't venison, that was Rolfi, one of the new Blood Claws,' the older Wolfblade replied. He glanced at Ragnar. 'For a while, the cubs just sat and stared at everything that was going down Haegr's throat, but finally Rolfi had enough. He reached for a piece of venison and this great fool tried to take a bite out of him. Started quite a fight. The Claws pulled Haegr down eventually, like a pack of wolves nipping at a bear.'

'And you sat by and did nothing!' Haegr growled, full of dudgeon.

'Not so. I saw my chance and had a fine dinner amid the debris,' Torin answered mildly, and then regarded the young Space Wolf again. 'Did you find what you came here for?' he asked.

Ragnar raised the gleaming frost blade to the starry sky, inspecting the weapon carefully in the faint light. 'No, I didn't,' he said after a moment, and then slid the blade back into its scabbard. 'Perhaps the answer lies elsewhere.'

'On Charys, you mean?' Torin asked.

'Perhaps,' Ragnar said darkly.

Haegr shook his head in exasperation, staring out across the cloudscape. 'You're a good lad, Ragnar, but you think too damned much,' he observed. 'Still, you can pick some fine spots to brood.' The huge warrior spread his arms and sighed. 'By Russ, it feels like we barely got here before we're leaving again,' he said, a touch wistfully, and then chuckled. 'See, now you've got me doing it. I'll be moping about for years when we finally get back to Terra.'

'You're getting ahead of yourself,' Ragnar said. 'We have to win on Charys first.'

'Ha!' Haegr replied, his expression brightening at once. He clapped his hand on Ragnar's shoulder hard enough to stagger the young Space Wolf. 'That's a good one, lad! Haven't you ever heard the old saying? The wolf wins every fight he's in!'

'Every fight but his last,' Ragnar added, his expression grim.

The burly Space Wolf threw back his head and laughed. 'Then Mighty Haegr will live forever!' he roared, raising his ale horn to his lips. He paused, and then lowered the horn and peered into its depths. 'Morkai's black breath,' he cursed, 'my mead's frozen. Let's get below quick. There may be just enough time to thaw it out and get a quick bite to eat before we lift off.'

RAGNAR WATCHED THROUGH the shuttle's viewports as they began their approach to the *Fist of Russ*. The huge warship appeared out of the darkness like a battered fortress, her vast grey flanks bearing deep scars from enemy lances and cratered by salvoes of macro-cannon shells. Her imposing, armoured prow was scorched and pitted by weapon blasts, and her superstructure was a blackened, twisted ruin along nearly half of its length. Smaller repair tenders hovered around the enormous warship, using huge servo-arms and plasma blast torches to replace ruined sections of hull plating. Ragnar's keen eyes picked out swarms of repair servitors climbing like ants over the warship's massive dorsal lance turrets, working furiously to make sure they would be ready for action.

She had once been a Mars-class battle cruiser that had served with distinction alongside the capital ships of Battlefleet Obscuras, nearly fourteen centuries before. In those days she had been called the *Resolute*, but that name fell into infamy when the Arch-Hierophant Vortigern began the Alphalus Insurrection late in the 39th millennium. The petty officers and crew of the *Resolute* had sided with Vortigern and mutinied, murdering the ship's officers and turning the battle cruiser over to the Arch-Hierophant's forces.

For three hundred long years she served as Vortigern's flagship, until Berek Thunderfist's predecessor, the Wolf Lord Hrothgar Ironblade, captured her during the Battle of Sestus Proxima. Hrothgar claimed the ship for his own shortly thereafter, as his previous flagship had been lost, and *Resolute* returned to Imperial service as the *Fist of Russ*. She had fought many great battles since and earned a place of honour in the Chapter's battle-fleet, and it grieved Ragnar to see her in such woeful shape. At Hyades the *Fist of Russ* had faced off against the heavy bombardment cannons of the *Vinco Redemptor*, a battle-barge of the Dark Angels Space Marine Chapter, and then later fought a small armada of Chaos warships summoned to assist Cadmus in the uprising on the planet's surface.

Though she'd survived, and even triumphed, in both battles, the *Fist of Russ* had paid dearly for her victories. Ragnar could see that the warship needed months, perhaps years, to repair all the damage she'd received, but that was a luxury the Space Wolves currently didn't have. All the Chapter's other great ships were already in action, along with their smaller escorts, so the *Fist of Russ* was needed at the battle line once more. Crews from Fenris would continue to make repairs up until the very last minute, returning to their tenders only when the battle cruiser was about to enter the warp.

Ragnar knew that there had been reports of Chaos warships lurking at the edges of the Charys system. He offered a prayer to the Allfather that the repairs would be enough.

'You seem troubled.'

Ragnar turned away from the shuttle's porthole. Unlike the Thunderhawk transports that had ferried the new Blood Claw packs to the *Fist of Russ* during the night, Gabriella was coming aboard the warship on an elegantly appointed personal shuttle from her family's cruiser, the *Wings of Bellisarius*. The young Navigator sat at ease in a curved, high-backed acceleration couch in the shuttle's spacious passenger compartment, her face half-hidden in shadow.

The young Space Wolf cast a glance towards the pilot compartment, where Torin was guiding the shuttle to the warship's starboard hangar deck. Haegr, true to his word, had dashed off as soon as they'd come down from the mountaintop and appeared at the shuttle, just moments before launch, with a huge haunch of meat clutched in one armoured fist. He'd eaten the whole thing, bones and all, before the shuttle had even left the lower atmosphere, and now he sat in the back of the shuttle compartment snoring like an idling Land Raider.

Ragnar considered how to respond. 'The ship has no business heading back to the battle line,' he said after a moment. 'Are you certain you will not reconsider this?'

A faint smile touched the corners of Gabriella's thin lips. 'After everything that you and your Chapter have done for my House?' she replied. 'This is the very least I can do. But you're being evasive. It's not the ship that's bothering you.'

Ragnar folded his arms tightly across his chest. 'Are you peering into my thoughts?' he asked gruffly. The Navigator Houses of the Imperium were some of the most powerful psykers humanity had ever known, and their psychic abilities allowed them to guide ships of all sizes safely through the maelstrom of the warp. Their powers made travel through the Imperium possible for its warships and merchant fleets, and it was the source of their families' enormous wealth and power.

Gabriella let out a small sigh of exasperation. 'Don't be foolish,' she chided. 'When it comes to your emotions you're about as subtle as Haegr,' the Navigator said. 'You've been in a dark mood for the last few weeks,' she continued. 'What is it?'

She spoke calmly and carefully, as she always did, but Ragnar felt a flush of irritation at her persistent questioning. He started to snap at her, lips pulling back from his curved fangs, but caught himself at the last possible moment. *What is wrong with me*, Ragnar thought? He had sworn an oath to serve and protect House Bellisarius. For all intents and purposes Gabriella was no different in authority than Berek Thunderfist or even Logan Grimnar. The young Space Wolf tried to mask his consternation, but gave up with an explosive sigh. 'Honestly, lady, I do not know,' he replied. 'I've been troubled since our escape from Hyades, but my mood has only darkened since arriving on Fenris.'

'I would have thought that returning to your home would please you,' she said.

'Please me?' Ragnar said. 'How could it? My Chapter is at war, and the more I consider it, the more I believe that I am partly to blame.'

'How? By casting the spear into the warp? Ragnar, if Madox had wanted that done, do you honestly think he would have needed your help to do it?'

Ragnar shifted uncomfortably in his seat. 'Well, no, I suppose not, but it troubles me all the same.'

Gabriella sighed and folded her pale hands in her lap. 'Ragnar, I understand what it's like to feel obligated to the people around you, but what's done is done. Be ashamed if you must, but don't wallow in regret. It won't change a thing.'

The young Space Wolf dropped his gaze to the tips of his armoured boots. 'I see your point,' he said reluctantly, 'but lately, I just can't get the thought out of my head. I haven't been sleeping well for days. Lately I've been having strange dreams. I think the spear figures into them, but I can't quite remember what they were about when I awake.' He glanced up worriedly. 'I think Madox may be in my dreams as well. Could he have put some kind of curse on me?'

Gabriella raised an eyebrow. 'A curse? Unlikely,' she said. 'It sounds more like guilt to me.' She gestured gracefully at the massive warship looming large in the shuttle's forward viewscreen. 'Ranek said there was a young Space Wolf Priest leading the Blood Claws we're taking to Charys, perhaps he could help you.'

At the rear of the shuttle, Haegr let out a snort and straightened in his chair. 'A Wolf Priest?' he said fuzzily, wiping drool from his chin. 'I know him, a young lad named Sigurd.'

Ragnar glanced back at the burly Space Wolf. 'How do you know him?'

'He was at the mead hall when those cubs of his stole my rightful share of the feast,' he said indignantly. 'Tried to lecture *me* about discipline and respect! I've got scars older than that pup,' Haegr grumbled. 'He's got a stick shoved so far up his arse I could use him for a hand puppet on feast days,' he said, and then frowned. 'Are we there yet? Mighty Haegr could use a bite to eat to keep at peak fighting condition.'

The rumble of thrusters ebbed as the Bellisarius shuttle began its descent into the battle cruiser's hangar deck. Ragnar found he had one more reason to be concerned about the voyage to Charys.

FOUR
Devils in the Darkness

A LOW GROAN of tortured metal echoed hollowly down
the length of the broad passageway, and Ragnar
thought he felt the heavy deck beneath him tremble as
the *Fist of Russ* was buffeted by energies beyond mortal ken.

They were three weeks out from Fenris, and more
than four days past their scheduled return to real
space at the edge of the Charys system. They had
encountered the first warp storm more than a week
ago, and the intensity of the ethereal winds had only
grown more intense since then. At first, the storms
were almost imperceptible to Ragnar and the rest of
the Space Wolves, but over time the first creaks and
groans began to reverberate through the hull. Now,
the terrible sounds were nearly constant, rising and
falling in volume as the unseen gale wracked the warship's Geller field. There were already scores of hull

breaches in still-damaged parts of the ship. The crew, overwhelmed by the simple day-to-day tasks of keeping the *Fist of Russ* operational, were forced to seal off entire sections of the warship rather than spend precious resources on temporary repairs.

The mood of the crew was tense. Unlike most Space Marine Chapters, which made extensive use of servitors to man secondary crew stations throughout their ships, the Space Wolves preferred human bondsmen to operate their starships. Many of these were former Space Marine aspirants that had fallen short of the enormous demands of training, but were still deemed worthy to serve the Chapter in another capacity. Others were chosen from among the peoples of Fenris specifically because of their skills as ship-handlers. They were among the finest shipmen in any Imperial fleet, but when Ragnar passed them in the corridors of the embattled ship he could smell the acrid scent of fear on their skin. If they didn't find a way through the storms soon, the *Fist of Russ* might not reach Charys at all.

. For their part, the Wolves had grown more restless with every day spent in the confines of the great ship. Despite the battle cruiser's vast size, the individual rooms and passageways took on an increasingly claustrophobic feel, as though the warp storms had a physical weight that pressed in on the ship from every side. The Wolf Priest, Sigurd, kept the Blood Claw packs busy practising boarding drills and mock combats along the length and breadth of the battle cruiser, driving the young Wolves hard, but keeping their minds busy in the process. Ragnar could not help but approve of the Wolf Priest's diligence and dedication, but Sigurd didn't seem to know when to stop. Day-long battle drills would be followed by unannounced inspections or surprise attacks during sleeping hours. Packs were assigned complicated navigation problems to solve within the labyrinthine corridors of the warship, and were not allowed to eat or rest until they were completed. Tempers were growing frayed with each passing day, but the Wolf Priest would not relent. Even Ragnar was growing increasingly irritated about it, and he wasn't even taking part in the training regimen. Torin had approached Sigurd early on in the voyage, offering the services of the Wolfblade, but the older Space Wolf had been coldly rebuffed.

The Wolfblade spent their hours tending their wargear and practising their close combat techniques when the Blood Claws weren't using the training arena. Even Haegr had been persuaded to join, more from boredom and lack of food than anything else.

Sleep continued to elude Ragnar. It had been many weeks since he'd last managed a full rest cycle, and what little sleep he did manage was fraught with strange, fragmentary dreams. Although a Space Marine could function without proper sleep for months at a time if necessary, Ragnar could feel the strain beginning to affect his ability to think and react. He had contemplated approaching the ship's Apothecary for help, or even entering the Red Dream for the duration of the voyage, but the thought of what strange dreams he might encounter in such a state gave him pause.

From time to time, he considered Gabriella's advice about consulting the Wolf Priest for help. As the keepers of the Space Wolves' sacred lore, the Wolf Priests were considered the spiritual heart of the Chapter, and sources of great insight and wisdom. Sigurd, however, was rarely available to anyone outside the Blood Claws, driving himself as hard as, or harder than, his charges, and the one request that Ragnar had left at Sigurd's quarters had gone unanswered. These days, when sleep eluded him, he went to the battle cruiser's bridge and stood watch over the armoured capsule where Gabriella fought to guide the *Fist of Russ* through the warp.

Ragnar intended to return there after the evening meal, for he could already tell that he was too agitated to get any sleep. He had spent the entire day sparring with Torin and Haegr while the Blood Claws practised boarding drills near the bow of the ship, and his body ached in a score of places where his comrades had landed telling blows. He'd kept fighting long past the point of exhaustion, but while his body felt almost leaden with fatigue his mind was tense and agitated. Strangely, even Torin and Haegr seemed to echo the young Space Wolf's mental state. They'd fought just as fiercely as him in the arena, hacking and slashing at one another with silent, murderous intent. Torin brought none of his cunning to bear, reverting back to simple, brutal blows, and even Haegr had little or nothing to say. They padded along silently in Ragnar's wake as they made their way to the ship's mead hall, drawing worried stares from every bondsman that passed by.

The raucous sounds of feasting rolled down the passageway as they approached the mead hall. Ragnar paused, biting back a surge of irritation. The whole reason he'd chosen this time to visit the hall was because normally the Blood Claws were elsewhere. Since the voyage began the Wolfblade had kept their distance from the young Wolves, and the sentiment had been returned in kind. Ragnar had little doubt that Sigurd had painted the Wolfblade as a pack of outcasts and exiles, as many other Space Wolves were wont to do.

'Are you going to stand there all day?' Haegr growled. 'Can't you hear that? The pups are eating our supper!'

Torin sighed, a little exasperated. 'There will be more in an hour or so, you great fool.'

'Then they can wait their turn,' the huge Space Wolf rumbled. 'Pups ought to learn their place, if you ask me. Here we are, three mighty heroes – well, one mighty hero and two fair to middling ones – who deserve their due, and those un-blooded younglings think to snatch the meat and ale from our very mouths. Well, I won't have it!' Puffing out his chest, Haegr pushed past Ragnar and rolled like thunder into the mead hall.

Torin cursed under his breath. 'I must be going mad,' he said. 'Haegr almost made sense there for a minute.' He glanced at Ragnar. 'He's sure to start a fight, you know. On the other hand, I'm almost as hungry as he is. What about you?'

Ragnar almost turned on his heel and headed back to his cell. In the mead hall beyond, the clamour of young voices and the racket of plates fell into a sudden and tense silence. All at once, a surge of irritation washed over Ragnar, raising the hackles on the back of his neck. 'Come on,' he growled, and strode swiftly into the hall.

The hall was full of Blood Claws. At first glance, Ragnar reckoned that all three of the young packs were taking their meal at the same time, something that hadn't happened since leaving Fenris. Shaggy heads hung low over gnawed haunches of meat, and dark eyes surveyed Haegr and his brethren with open hostility. Low growls rumbled across the hall and the air was thick with the scent of challenge, setting Ragnar's teeth on edge.

In older times the warship's mead hall was the officer's wardroom. Now three massive red oak tables were arranged in a rough Y-shape in a room capable of holding easily three times that number. Haegr stood between the two lower tables, his wide hands planted on his hips as he glared back at the Blood Claws. Heads turned to the high table, where the strongest pack typically sat, and the lesser packs would take their cues from them. The pack leader at the high table was a broad shouldered, blond-haired warrior with a hatchet face and hooded eyes. He picked a grox's thigh bone from the debris on the table and cracked it between his powerful jaws, his gaze never leaving Haegr as he sucked out the sweet marrow.

'What in Morkai's name do you want?' he asked with a raspy sneer.

Haegr glanced back at Ragnar and Torin, and gave them a wide grin. 'Now there's a stupid question if ever I heard one,' he replied, his rumbling voice low with menace. 'This is the mead hall, isn't it? We're here to eat and drink our fill, as Wolves ought,' he said, turning back to the pack leader. 'Only you dogs happen to be in our seats.'

More growls rose around the Wolfblade. Ragnar caught Torin, giving him a sidelong glance. He knew that he should say something, a quick word of greeting or an offer to toast the coming battle, but he felt his body responding to the challenge, almost of its own accord. If the cub thought he was the toughest Wolf in the hall, Ragnar was eager to prove him wrong. In fact, he *hungered* for it.

A lean, red-haired warrior to the pack leader's right gave Haegr a wolfish grin. 'I think the walrus is ready for another beating,' he said.

The blond warrior's sneer widened. 'You want to eat? Here,' he said, and tossed the cracked bone at Haegr's feet. 'When you're done you can beg for more. I expect we can find a few more scraps for a bunch of outcasts like you.'

Laughter filled the mead hall. A bone arced from the table to the right and bounced off Haegr's shoulder. A crust of bread flew past, and then a fish head.

Haegr straightened to his full height, his chest swelling like a thundercloud, but by the time he'd opened his mouth to bellow his rage, Ragnar had swept past him in a dozen long strides and reached the high table opposite the pack leader. The blond warrior leapt to his feet, his eyes alight with the promise of battle, and Ragnar slapped him with his open hand hard enough to knock the warrior off his feet.

The pack leader crashed back into his chair and bounced back with a furious snarl, his face twisted with fury. He snatched a carving knife from the table and made to lunge at Ragnar, but the Blood Claw might as well have been standing still. Ragnar chopped his hand down on the pack leader's wrist, breaking it with a brittle crunch of bone, and then backhanded the Blood Claw off his feet.

There was a shout from the pack leader's right and the warrior's red-bearded lieutenant lunged from his chair. The rest of the pack at the high table followed suit, shaking the air with howls of rage, and the mead hall erupted into a wild, wheeling brawl.

The Blood Claws came at Ragnar from every direction, swinging fists, steins or whatever else came to hand. A hurled plate buzzed past his head and a drinking cup shattered against his chest, spraying Ragnar with mead. The young Space Wolf took a step back from the table as the first of the Blood Claws reached him, spoiling the pup's aim as he threw a wild punch at the side of Ragnar's head. Ragnar smashed him to the deck with a bone-cracking punch to the jaw. Another warrior rushed in from Ragnar's right, bent low and aiming to tackle him. The young Space Wolf laid the pup out with an elbow to the back of his head, and then two more warriors crashed into him from the left, driving him off his feet.

The three Space Wolves crashed to the deck with a thunderous clatter of ceramite. Fists rained down on Ragnar, hammering his chest, shoulders and face. One fist raked across his right cheek, opening a ragged cut all the way back to his ear. Snarling, Ragnar grabbed a handful of one Blood Claw's hair and smashed his forehead into the pup's face. The warrior rolled away, momentarily stunned, but the second Blood Claw drove his fist into the side of Ragnar's head. A flurry of bright spots burst across Ragnar's vision, but he shook off the blow with a savage growl and planted his foot against the Blood Claw's chest. Another punch glanced across Ragnar's forehead, and then the young

Space Wolf kicked with all his strength and sent the Blood Claw flying backwards. The warrior hit the heavy oak table and flipped over it, scattering plates and bits of food in all directions.

A heavy chair spun through the air to Ragnar's right and smashed a Blood Claw off his feet. The three packs were fighting the Wolfblade, and battering one another with wild abandon. Ragnar glanced over his shoulder and saw Haegr lift two Blood Claws by the scruff of their necks and knock their heads together. Two other warriors had their arms wrapped around the burly Wolfblade's legs and hips, trying to pull Haegr down, but they might as well have been trying to pull down the Fang itself. Farther off to Ragnar's left, Torin was weaving through the melee like a ghost, felling men with swift, precise blows and picking choice morsels of food off the battered tables as he went.

Ragnar heard the whirring approach of the flung beer mug half a second before it struck. He ducked, letting it pass harmlessly overhead, and glanced back at the high table to see from whence it came. Instead, he saw the red haired Blood Claw just a few steps away, swinging a massive chair in an underhanded blow that was aimed squarely at his face.

Ragnar got his arms crossed in front of his head a split second before the blow struck home. Old oak splintered, driving his heavy vambraces into his face, and the force of the blow sent the young Space Wolf sprawling. He landed in a tangle of splintered debris, blinking blood from his eyes, and his attacker was upon him in an instant, swinging a thick chair leg like an improvised mace.

A heavy blow struck Ragnar high in the chest, and then another landed on his chin. Pain burst across the young Space Wolf's face, and for a split second Ragnar's vision went black. He kicked out blindly and connected with the warrior's side. Then he drew back his boot and drove it against the Blood Claw's left knee. The warrior's leg gave out, dropping him into a painful kneeling position, but before he could react, Ragnar sent the warrior sprawling with a vicious kick to the side of his head.

Ragnar clambered to his feet, shaking his head to try and clear his vision. His keen senses detected someone rushing at him from the left, and he spun to meet the threat. A hand lashed out at him, angling in towards the side of Ragnar's neck, and he barely managed to block it by grabbing his attacker's wrist. With a cold shock, Ragnar felt the prick of a knife-point dig into the side of his throat.

The Blood Claw pack leader let out a wordless snarl and pressed his attack, swinging at Ragnar's head with his free hand. Ragnar let the blow strike home, scarcely feeling the pain. A sudden wave of murderous fury washed over him, and he closed his right hand around the pack leader's throat.

'*Stand fast in the name of Russ and the Allfather!*' shouted a furious voice from the far end of the hall. 'What is the meaning of this?'

Ragnar squeezed the pack leader's throat hard enough to feel the reinforced cartilage creak beneath his fingers. He watched the veins throbbing furiously in the pack leader's face and felt his pulse beneath his palm. At that moment, he wanted nothing more than to tear the fool's throat open.

Dimly, he heard Torin answer. 'Your pups required a lesson in manners, Sigurd,' the older Wolfblade said coldly.

The other voice replied with an iron note of command. 'I think it's the three of you who forget yourselves,' it said. 'Unhand that warrior, Wolfblade, or suffer my wrath!'

Ragnar whirled, dragging the choking pack leader with him. A young Space Wolf, not much older than Ragnar, stood at the far end of the room. He was a handsome youth, with a pale, square-chinned face and sharp, flinty grey eyes. His hair was white-blond, pulled back in a heavy braid that curved around the heavy wolfskin mantle on his shoulders and hung down across his breastplate. No scars marred his close-cropped beard, and his armour, while ancient, showed no sign of recent battle. A massive cross of gold inlaid adamantium, blazoned with a snarling wolf's head, hung from a heavy chain around the Wolf Priest's neck. The crozius arcanum, sacred badge of the priesthood, crackled menacingly in the priest's fist.

The look of fury in the Wolf Priest's eyes took Ragnar aback, extinguishing his rage almost at once. The priests of the Chapter existed apart from the great companies, and in effect were living embodiments of the Chapter's history and traditions. They demanded deference and respect by virtue of their position alone. Even the Great Wolf treated them with the utmost respect. It was what they were trained to do from their first days at the Fang. Without hesitation, Ragnar let the pack leader go, but it was harder to let go of the insult he and his brothers had been dealt. Leaving the pack leader gasping for breath, Ragnar strode towards the young priest. 'Blame the Claw,' he growled. 'He thought fit to challenge his betters.'

'Betters?' the Wolf Priest snapped. Young as he was, he had the look of a prince, and a manner that came from one born to authority. 'Harald has no betters here save for me. This is a hall for warriors, not exiles like you.'

Ragnar's fists clenched. Haegr let out a threatening hiss, and even Torin stiffened at the insult. It was all Ragnar could do not to strike the high-handed priest. 'It is an honour to serve in the Wolfblade, as anyone versed in the Chapter's lore would know,' the young Space Wolf replied with care, 'and we were treated as such in the halls of the Fang.'

The young Space Wolf Priest was unmoved. 'I do not speak of the Wolfblade,' he replied coldly. 'I speak of the three men I see here before me, exiles and out-casts, one and all,' he said. Sigurd took a step closer to Ragnar. 'I know your crimes,' he said. 'I know how you lost the Spear of Russ, the self-same weapon used to strike down your former lord!' His grey-eyed gaze transfixed the young Space Wolf. 'Do you deny it?'

Ragnar trembled with the effort to hold his rage in check. He could not guess what would happen if he gave in to his fury at that moment, and he didn't want the blood of a priest on his hands. 'You know I cannot,' he replied.

'That is so,' Sigurd answered with a grim smile. 'You do not belong here. None of you do. If you would eat, take your meals in your quarters until we reach Charys. You do not belong in the company of true warriors,' the Wolf Priest declared. 'Now get out of my sight.'

For a moment, silence reigned in the hall. No one moved. Sigurd glared implacably at the Wolfblade, merciless and indomitable in his anger. Finally it was Torin who relented. 'Let us go, brothers,' he said coldly. 'Sigurd is right. This is no place for the likes of us.'

The three Wolves filed silently from the hall, each one struggling to contain his rage. Ragnar turned at the doorway, and glared a challenge at the red-faced Harald and his brethren. When he met the pack leader's eyes he saw equal measures of anger and doubt. The young Space Wolf bared his teeth in a snarl. *Try me again and you'll get more of the same, and worse besides,* his look said to the Blood Claws. Then he closed the doors to the hall and stalked alone into the labyrinthine passageways of the warship.

RAGNAR DREAMT OF wolves that walked like men.

The thick, hot air echoed with the snarling of beasts and the sounds of battle. Ragnar could smell spilt blood and the stench of death all around him, and bodies littered the stones at his feet. He saw men and women in bloodstained robes, their bodies torn by tooth and claw, and their lifeless faces frozen in masks of terror.

The wolves wore armour like his own, but they had the faces of savage beasts. They struggled all around him, grappling and tearing at shadowy figures that writhed and lashed at the wolves like snakes. For every one the wolves tore apart it seemed two more rose to take its place. Howls of anger and despair smote Ragnar's ears.

He was standing in a vast chamber, like a ruined temple. Another armoured figure stood at the far end of the room, his face hidden behind a horned helmet. Ragnar didn't need to see the tall spear clutched in the man's armoured fist to know who the figure was. 'Madox!' he snarled, and threw himself at his bitter foe.

His veins turned molten with rage. A guttural growl rose in his throat as he slashed left and right with his keening blade. The ancient sword carved a deadly path through the shadow creatures, but Madox made no move to resist as Ragnar drew closer with each long stride. Ragnar could feel the power swelling in his limbs, his blood-lust quickening his steps until he was little more than a blur.

Voices were calling out to him, shouting warnings he could not understand. None of it mattered; the spear was almost within reach. A howl of triumph rose to his lips as he reached for the sacred weapon, and then his legs seemed to buckle beneath him.

Ragnar collapsed to the stone, his muscles writhing like snakes beneath his skin. The frost blade fell from his hands as his fingers contorted into claws. The only thing that remained constant was his anger, burning as bright as a hunter's moon.

Ragnar fell onto his belly, writhing. He threw back his head and howled in rage, feeling the bones of his face distend, centimetre by centimetre, into a blunt, toothy snout. Snarling, lashing at the air with his talons, he thrashed onto his side and snapped madly at the silent figure of the sorcerer just out of arm's reach.

As he did so, his gaze lit on a pale figure a metre to his right. She lay on the stones beside him, her alabaster face spotted with blood. As she spoke, vital fluids gushed from the terrible bite marks in her throat.

'*The beast waits within us all*,' Gabriella said to him, and then he watched the life go out of her eyes.

HE AWOKE WITH a shout of dismay, lashing about wildly in the darkness with his fists. One hand rang off a thick metal pipe and the violent motion thrust him backwards, causing him to crack his head against a heavy steam fitting. Ragnar collapsed back into a heap, blinking stupidly into the blackness. He had no idea where he was, or how he'd got there.

Asleep, he thought, struggling to make sense of the situation. *I must have fallen asleep*. Within moments his keen eyes adjusted to the gloom, and a second or two later he realised he was in some kind of narrow tunnel, deep within the bowels of the old battle cruiser.

Still blinking, Ragnar rubbed a hand over his face and tried to recall how long he'd been wandering through the ship, a great many hours; that much was certain. The rage he'd felt after the encounter with Sigurd refused to go away, no matter how hard he tried to master it. He'd stalked along the passageways, swearing every vile oath he could imagine to have his vengeance upon Harald and that upstart priest.

The last thing he clearly remembered was deciding to head for the part of the ship where the Blood Claws were stationed, and to lie in wait for Harald's return.

Something like horror washed over the young Space Wolf. Slowly, dreading what he might find, he raised his hands to his face. They were covered in a thick layer of grease and grime, but he smelled no fresh blood on them.

'Blessed Russ,' he sighed. 'What's the matter with me?'

Then a dolorous howl echoed down the conduit, sending Ragnar reaching for his weapons. It was a few moments before he realised that the sound wasn't coming from a living throat, it was the ship's battle klaxon, summoning the crew to their stations.

That was when he realised that the battle cruiser's litany of creaks and moans had fallen silent, and her deck no longer trembled with strain. The *Fist of Russ* had dropped out of the warp at last.

They had arrived at the Charys system, and they were under attack.

FIVE
The Fist of Russ

THE OLD DECKPLATES rang with the tramp of booted feet as the bondsmen crew of the *Fist of Russ* readied the battered ship for combat. The grey uniformed crew raced nimbly past Ragnar as they ran to their stations, but the Space Wolf could not help but see the strain on their faces or smell the fear on their skin. The battle cruiser was in no shape for a fight.

It took Ragnar almost half an hour to find his way to the command deck, high upon the citadel-like superstructure near the aft end of the ship. Blood racing at the prospect of battle and his head still reeling from his strange dream, Ragnar charged past the two bondsmen standing guard at the armoured hatch. The command deck was dimly lit, and despite the high, cathedral-like ceiling the air felt heavy with tension. Officers and midshipmen stood at their stations, consulting brass etched logic engines, and conferring in

99

low voices. Ragnar saw the hunched figure of the Officer of the Deck at the far end of the space as he gripped the edges of the command pulpit and bellowed orders to the bondsmen and servitors of the ship's bridge, half a deck below. The young Space Wolf saw the green and grey orb of Charys filling three-quarters of the high, arched viewports along the bow end of the bridge. They were approaching the world from its night side, and his keen eyes picked out the scattered embers of farming settlements and trade cities burning sullenly across the planet's surface.

A handful of dark, angular shapes hung like cinders above the burning world, limned with pulsing green light from their plasma drives. Raiders, he thought grimly: traitor warships whose crews had sworn themselves to the Ruinous Powers. Some had once been vessels of the Imperial Navy, while others had been built at corrupted forge worlds at the edge of the Eye of Terror. Individually, they were less than a third the size of the *Fist of Russ*, but they were swift, agile craft, and in large numbers they were a threat to the largest battleship.

'What's happening?' he demanded, approaching a small group of senior officers who were standing around the rim of a large hololith table and speaking to Sigurd the Wolf Priest. Among the officers, Ragnar recognised Wulfgar, the ship's master and, half-hidden by the shifting patterns of the holo map, he caught sight of Gabriella. The Navigator's face was paler and more strained than Ragnar had ever seen it, and he could see that she was clenching her fists at her side to keep them from trembling. As near as he could tell, Gabriella remained standing by sheer willpower.

The Wolf Priest whirled around at the sound of Ragnar's approach. Sigurd fixed the young Space Wolf with a baleful glare. 'Return to your quarters, exile,' he snapped. 'The ship is at battle stations. This is no place for the likes of you.'

Ragnar felt a rush of anger so intense that it was all he could do not to throw himself at the arrogant young priest. Several of the ship's officers drew away from Sigurd, their expressions wary. The Wolf Priest's eyes narrowed, his hackles rising in the face of the sudden threat. His gauntleted hand tightened around the haft of his crozius.

Save your fury for the real foe, Ragnar told himself, forcing his body to relax and his fists to unclench. Like it or not, as the highest ranking Space Wolf aboard, Sigurd was the acting captain of the ship, and his word was law. He was bound to heed the counsel of Wulfgar and his officers, but little else. Ragnar wasn't about to bare his throat so easily, however. 'My place is with her,' he said, inclining his head towards Gabriella. 'Where she goes, I go, especially during times of battle.'

Sigurd's aristocratic face twisted into a grimace. He glanced back at Gabriella, and then looked to Wulfgar and the rest of the ship's senior officers as though gauging the strength of his authority. Finally he acquiesced with a curt wave of his hand. 'Very well,' he growled, 'but for the lady's sake alone.'

With an effort, Ragnar nodded curtly to the Wolf Priest and worked his way around the perimeter of the broad table to reach Gabriella's side. As he did so, the young Space Wolf quickly took in the situation unfolding in the air above the hololith. The *Fist of Russ* was less than an hour from entering orbit around Charys, but no less than nine enemy raiders stood in their way. Flickering runes and directional icons on the hololith showed that the raiders were breaking orbit at high speed and heading their way.

Ragnar saw no signs of Imperial ships anywhere in the vicinity. *Where is Berek's fleet?* The Wolf Lord had brought a battle-barge, two strike cruisers and half a dozen escorts to Charys. What could have happened to them?

Wulfgar and two other officers resumed a tense but quiet exchange with Sigurd as Ragnar stood beside Gabriella. The Navigator managed a weary smile. 'You look terrible,' she said.

The comment took him aback. 'I might have said the same about you, lady,' he said quietly, his brows drawing together in a worried frown. 'You suffered much to get us here, it seems. How long have we been in real space?'

Gabriella took a deep breath. Her lips pressed together in a tight line, and Ragnar could sense her disquiet. 'Less than an hour. I brought us in as close to Charys as possible,' she said after a moment. 'It was… difficult. I can't quite explain how.'

'Warp storms?' Ragnar ventured.

'No, nothing like that,' she said, her expression troubled. 'The currents around Charys are fierce, though, like… a vortex, of sorts.'

'A vortex?' the young Space Wolf asked. 'You mean, like a whirlpool?' He knew them well from the craggy coastlines of Fenris, and understood the danger they posed.

'Perhaps,' she said tentatively. She pressed a trembling hand to her forehead. 'I've never encountered

anything like it. It took everything I had to guide the
ship past the tidal forces. A lesser Navigator wouldn't
have stood a chance.'

Ragnar chuckled quietly. 'My lady has spent too
much time in Haegr's company, methinks.'

Gabriella smiled up at Ragnar. 'Save the wry
humour for Torin,' she said. 'But what troubles you,
my Wolf? There is a fey look in your eyes that I've
never seen before.'

Ragnar paused, recalling the wolf dream. What
could he tell her? What would she believe? He didn't
understand it himself. Before he could answer, however, Sigurd's angry voice brought Ragnar's head
around.

'Flee? You expect me to turn tail and run from the
enemy?' the Wolf Priest snarled. Sigurd loomed
angrily over Wulfgar and his officers. 'Where is your
honour, Shipmaster Wulfgar?'

Wulfgar's men bristled at the insult. Though not
Space Wolves, they were men of Fenris still, and such
talk did not go lightly with them. But Wulfgar, the veteran shipmaster, was unmoved. 'There were no reports
of an enemy fleet at Charys,' he said. 'The ship is not
battle-worthy. Most of our repairs are temporary, lord.
A single, well-placed hit could cripple us, leaving us
almost helpless.' The old bondsman leaned forward,
his expression intent. 'We must disengage now, while
we still can. The charts show an asteroid field nearby.
We can hide there and try to come up with another
approach to the planet.'

'And spend days skulking like a whipped dog while
the Thunderfist's company is ground to pieces on the
planet's surface? No. I swore an oath to Logan

Grimnar that I would deliver our reinforcements to Charys without delay, and I will do so if I have to fight my way through hell itself!' The Wolf Priest glanced coldly at Ragnar. 'I'd sooner die than be called an oathbreaker.'

Once again, Ragnar fought to contain a flash of murderous rage. This was not the time or the place to issue a challenge, but for a brief, dizzying moment he found that he did not care.

His hand drifted to the hilt of the frost blade at his hip, but Gabriella gripped his fingers instead. The slight pressure was enough to shock him back to his senses. Ragnar took a deep breath. 'The Wolf Priest's words are ill-chosen,' he said to Wulfgar, 'but nevertheless, he is correct. Our reinforcements are desperately needed on Charys, and even a single day could make the difference between victory and defeat.'

Sigurd gave Ragnar a brief, appraising look, as though surprised at the young Space Wolf's back-handed show of support. Wulfgar listened, and his wrinkled face creased in a deep frown. 'If we must fight our way through then so be it,' he said heavily. 'Load your warriors aboard their Thunderhawks, lord. If our engines fail you may have to launch quickly and fly the rest of the way in.'

The Wolf Priest nodded solemnly. 'Russ is with us, Shipmaster Wulfgar,' he said solemnly. 'Let us bare our blades and begin the battle song!'

'I hear you, Wolf Priest,' Wulfgar answered, and seemed to draw strength from Sigurd's iron conviction. He turned to the officer of the deck. 'Ahead two-thirds!' he ordered. 'Bring us two points to starboard and charge the dorsal mounts! Gun crews fire as you bear!'

THOUSANDS OF KILOMETRES distant, the black-hulled raiders shook off the grip of Charys's gravity with a flare of plasma drives, and swung their rakish bows towards the oncoming Imperial ship. Their hulls were matte black, like dark iron, etched with foul runes that had been sanctified in blood and blessed by the dread hand of Chaos. Gargoyle figures of verdigrised brass crouched atop squat turrets or leered from the armoured mantlets of their towering superstructures, their mouths gaping hungrily. Their viewports gleamed balefully with pale, eldritch light. They leapt from their parking orbits like a pack of jackals and scattered into a loose arc in the path of the oncoming battle cruiser, scanning the void with uncanny augurs and looking for signs of weakness. Gun turrets squealed ponderously on their corroded mounts, training upon the *Fist of Russ* as the range between the two sides decreased.

In response, the distant Imperial ship swung to starboard, showing the raiders her battle scarred flank and her broadside of heavy guns. Along the battle cruiser's dorsal hull, two massive turrets slewed to port, bringing their energy projectors to bear on the incoming enemy craft. Arcs of cyan light crackled and seethed within the huge accumulation chambers of the lance batteries, gathering intensity with each passing moment until the blunt projectors were shrouded in a haze of voltaic wrath. Though the *Fist of Russ* stood alone against the raiders, and her hull was battered and broken, the reach of her guns was longer than most other ships in the Imperial fleet.

The lance batteries fired half a second apart. Twin beams of irresistible force crossed the black gulf in the blink of an eye, converging on the foremost raider in the pack. The first energy lance crashed against the raider's void shield, blazing white at the point of impact and shooting arcs of cyan and magenta lightning across its curved surface. For perhaps a millisecond the powerful shield held, but then the semi-invisible shield flickered and flared as it struggled to dissipate the lance's tremendous power. It failed in a spherical flash of light, like a bursting bubble, and then the second lance beam struck home. It tore the raider open from stem to stern, ripping open its flank like a fiery talon until it penetrated the small ship's reactor decks. The Chaos ship disappeared in an incandescent ball of plasma and radioactive vapour, wreathing its fellows in streamers of purple and magenta fire. The *Fist of Russ* had claimed first blood.

Thrusters flaring, the rest of the pack raced on, plunging through the expanding cloud of debris. Though their main guns were still out of range, the raiders were far from toothless. Three of the Chaos ships surged ahead of the rest, ordering themselves into a rough line abreast. Blackened, pitted blast doors drew back from launch tubes recessed into the ships' angled bows, and a pair of powerful anti-ship torpedoes, each more than forty metres long, streaked towards the battle cruiser on boiling plumes of fiery gas.

'TORPEDOES INCOMING!' SHOUTED one of the tactical officers from his station on the command deck.

Ragnar caught sight of the tense expression on the man's face as he glanced towards Shipmaster Wulfgar.

'Lance batteries switch to antimissile targeting,' the ship's master declared. 'Portside batteries lock on to those torpedo ships and fire at will!' Wulfgar turned to a trio of officers clustered around a set of consoles to his left. 'Ordnance officer! What is the status of our close-in turrets?'

'Defensive guns at sixty per cent to port,' the senior ordnance officer replied.

'Very well,' Wulfgar said gravely. 'At this range they're not likely to miss. Damage control parties stand by!'

THE SIX TORPEDOES fanned out in a broad arc, blanketing the area around the *Fist of Russ*. The weapons were powerful but unguided, their trajectories planned by the infernal logic engines aboard their parent craft. Swift as thunderbolts, they streaked towards the battle cruiser's kilometre-long flank. Though her thrusters were roaring at near full power, for all intents and purposes the Imperial ship might as well have been standing still.

Twin cyan beams lashed through the darkness at the oncoming torpedoes, detonating four of them in globes of nuclear fire. The final pair of deadly missiles slipped past the raking beams and plunged towards the *Fist of Russ*.

At fifty kilometres the battle cruiser's defensive turrets clattered into action, hurling a torrent of energy bolts and explosive shells into the path of the oncoming weapons. A close burst from one shell punctured the fuel tank of one of the enemy missiles and the resulting explosion blew it apart. The second torpedo flew on unscathed, flying by unholy luck through a gap in the ship's flak coverage. It struck the *Fist of Russ* just forward of the portside hangar deck, its nuclear warhead detonating like the hammer of an evil god.

THE ANCIENT WARSHIP shuddered beneath the blow, and a roar like thunder reverberated through the battle cruiser's hull. Men were thrown across the command deck by the impact. Gauges burst and sparks erupted from power conduits on the port bulkhead. On instinct, Ragnar gripped the hololith table to steady himself and wrapped a protective hand around Gabriella's waist. On the bridge deck below, wounded men cried in pain, and a tech-priest cried out a prayer to the Omnissiah.

'Damage control report!' Wulfgar roared from the command pulpit.

'Hull breach from decks thirty-five to thirty-eight at frame 412,' the damage control officer reported. Blood flowed freely from a cut on the bondsman's scalp, and he wiped it away with a savage swipe of his hand. 'Fire on the flight deck!'

'All available crew to the flight deck and commence firefighting procedures,' Wulfgar ordered. The master of the ship turned and addressed Wulfgar. 'I advise you make for the starboard hangars at once, lord.'

Ragnar shot Gabriella a worried glance. The *Fist of Russ* was hit hard, and the battle had only just begun. The Navigator caught his eye and gave a stern shake of her head. The young Space Wolf nodded and raised his head to Wulfgar. 'We stand with you, Shipmaster Wulfgar,' he said. 'Fight on, in Russ's name!'

The ship's master turned back to his task. Ragnar caught Sigurd glancing his way, and was surprised at the Wolf Priest's approving nod.

Off to the right, one of the ship's gunnery officers looked up from his data screen. 'Enemy ships in range of our broadsides!' he said with a vengeful snarl. 'All gun decks report weapons lock!'

'Then give the bastards a taste of hell,' Wulfgar replied.

THE FLANK OF the battle cruiser was limned in red from the molten wound of the torpedo hit. Jets of burning atmosphere vented from the hangar decks aft of the impact site, casting a flickering glow over the dozens of huge gun turrets that swung into action. Macro-cannon barrels elevated into position, aimed by complex gunnery rituals performed by machine-spirits on the battle cruiser's bridge. The enormous weapons fired in sequence, hurling shells the size of land raiders at the oncoming Chaos ships.

Salvoes of explosive shells bracketed the three oncoming torpedo ships, hammering relentlessly against their void shields in staccato bursts of fire. Without warning, the shielding on one of the raiders faltered, and a cluster of shells erupted on the war-ship's rune covered bow and superstructure. One shell tore through the iron decks and found the raider's forward magazine. The resultant explosion ripped the traitor vessel in half.

Half a second later, another raider succumbed, its hull pierced in a dozen places and its superstructure ablaze. The last remaining torpedo ship continued on, its shield overloaded, but otherwise unharmed...

until a cyan bolt from the battle cruiser's lance batteries tore the raider apart.

Nearly half of the raiders were gone, but the rest plunged ahead. They were less than fifteen seconds from entering gun range.

'Two of the raiders are angling aft!' the senior auspex officer declared. 'They're going after our engines!'

'Hard to port!' Wulfgar ordered. 'Show them our bow!' The ship's master chuckled bleakly. 'Maybe if we're lucky one of the blasphemers will try to ram us!' He turned to the gunnery officers. 'Port and starboard broadsides, stand by for salvo fire!'

With a tortured groan of metal, the command deck angled beneath Ragnar's feet as the huge ship swung onto its new course. He could see streaks of red and yellow through the tall viewports as the first enemy shells began hurtling past the struggling warship. Once again, he looked to Gabriella, but her eyes were closed, as though deep in thought or prayer. He thought to ask her once more if she wished to head for the hangar bay, but after a moment's thought he chose to hold his tongue.

The battle would be decided in the next few seconds. If the battle cruiser was doomed they would never reach the hangar deck in time.

Slowly, streaming a trail of frozen oxygen and melted debris, the *Fist of Russ* turned to face her attackers. Wulfgar had timed his move carefully, bringing the warship's heavily armoured prow into position just as the enemy ships hove into range. Macro-cannons and magna bolt projectors spat torrents of fire at the oncoming Imperial ship, bracketing her void shields with an unrelenting storm of explosions. The first layer of shielding failed. Then, seconds later, the inner shield gave way as well. Fierce blasts pummelled the battle cruiser's bow and superstructure, leaving scorch marks against fifteen-metre thick adamantium plate.

Moments later the raiders were plunging past the warship like burning meteors, their weapon batteries still blazing away at their foe. The *Fist of Russ* answered, her broadsides roaring to port and starboard at the swift moving Chaos ships. The nearest raider to port flared cyan under the lash of one of the battle cruiser's lance batteries, before a salvo of macrocannon shells blew it apart.

Scores of explosions ravaged the Imperial ship's flanks. Many were turned aside by the vessel's armour plate, but here and there the enemy shells struck home. One of the battle cruiser's huge lance turrets blew apart, its massive power capacitors detonated by an enemy shell. Hundreds died on the Imperial ship's gun decks as armour piercing shells opened airtight compartments to space.

A raider on the starboard side of the ship was struck by a salvo of heavy shells that collapsed its shields and tore into its thruster banks. The small ship spiralled out of control, trailing a blazing wake of plasma and molten debris until its reactors overloaded moments later in a spectacular burst of light.

Then the surviving raiders were gone, hurtling aft of the *Fist of Russ* and opening the range while the battle cruiser's beleaguered crew struggled to keep the ancient vessel alive.

* * *

FLAMES BILLOWED FROM the bridge, sending clouds of dark smoke roiling over the command deck. Men screamed in terror and pain as the emergency lighting flared to life. Officers picked themselves up off the deck and staggered back to their stations. Ragnar held on to Gabriella and peered warily through the smoky gloom, wishing to the Allfather for a foe he could come to grips with.

The senior damage control officer sang out through the smoke. 'Hull breaches on multiple decks! Dorsal lance battery out of action! Starboard gun decks report heavy casualties. Shields at fifty per cent. Our reactors are stable, but power output is limited.'

'Very well,' Wulfgar replied as he staggered back up to the pulpit. 'Helm! Can we still manoeuvre?'

'Aye, sir,' the chief helmsman replied. 'She's sluggish, but she's still answering the helm.'

'Bring us two points to port,' the ship's master ordered. 'Let's clear our wake and see where those raiders went.'

All starships were blind directly aft, where the roiling wake from their thrusters made sensor returns impossible. Slowly, ponderously, the battle cruiser swung around, streaming twisting ribbons of fire.

The seconds stretched upon the command deck as the ship's augurs searched for the Chaos raiders. Fire-fighting crews were hard at work on the bridge deck, and already the choking smoke was dissipating. Ragnar breathed slowly and evenly, allowing his enhanced respiratory system to filter out the worst of the fumes. He bent low over Gabriella. 'Are you all right, lady?' he asked. 'Shall I call for a medicae?'

'No, no,' the Navigator protested waving a soot stained hand. Her eyes were bleary from the smoke, but her expression was determined. 'The God-Emperor knows they've more serious problems to worry about.'

'Fire-fighting teams on the flight deck say they have evacuated the hangar and vented it to space,' the damage control officer reported. 'The fire is out.'

'Very well,' Wulfgar replied. 'Where are the enemy ships?'

The chief auspex officer looked up from his screen. 'No contacts aft,' he replied, his voice tinged with relief. 'The remaining enemy ships have shut down their augurs and gone silent. They've disengaged!'

A ragged cheer went up from the command crew. 'Belay that foolishness!' Wulfgar bellowed. 'We're far from safe harbour yet. Gun crews and augur teams will remain at their stations. All other crew will report to local damage control stations and lend assistance.'

The ship's officers scrambled to obey. Wulfgar stepped wearily down from the command pulpit and approached Sigurd and Ragnar. Neither of the Space Wolves had moved from their places. Barely four minutes had elapsed since the battle had begun.

Wulfgar bowed his head to the Wolf Priest. 'We've fought our way clear for the moment,' he said grimly, 'but I fear the *Fist of Russ* is crippled, lord. A Thunderhawk can reach Charys orbit in less than three hours. I suggest you and your warriors depart for the planet at once. The enemy could return with reinforcements at any time.'

Sigurd nodded gravely. The young Space Wolf Priest looked around the damaged command deck, apparently stunned by the devastation his orders had wrought. He slowly raised his crozius over Wulfgar's head. 'Praise Russ and the Allfather,' he intoned in a powerful voice. 'You and your crew are to be commended, Shipmaster Wulfgar. It was wrong of me to suggest that a man like you was without honour. The courage of you and your men shames me.' The priest placed his hand on Wulfgar's head and pronounced the Benediction of Iron, an honour normally reserved for members of the Chapter. When Sigurd was finished, Wulfgar looked up at the Wolf Priest in speechless awe, nodded respectfully to Ragnar and returned quickly to his station.

Ragnar watched as Sigurd looked around the damaged command deck one last time, clearly shaken by the fierce battle. When the Wolf Priest's gaze fell upon him and Gabriella, however, his expression hardened once more. 'We will leave for Charys at once,' he snapped at Ragnar. When he turned to Gabriella, his voice was far more moderate. 'Will you accompany us aboard one of our Thunderhawks, lady? It is no longer safe for you to remain aboard, I fear, and it will be some time before the *Fist of Russ* has need of your talents.'

'Your concern is noted, holy one,' Gabriella replied smoothly, 'but I and my Wolves will follow in my personal shuttle.'

'As you wish,' Sigurd replied with a curt bow. To Ragnar, he said, 'Report to headquarters as soon as you've made planetfall.' Then he strode swiftly from the command deck.

Ragnar watched the young priest depart, admiration mixing with outrage. Later, he vowed, Sigurd would answer for his insults to Ragnar's honour. For now, they had a war to fight.

SIX
Unto the Breach

BY ACCIDENT OR a pernicious twist of fate, the enemy rocket attack began just as the landing craft from the *Fist of Russ* began their final approach. Two kilometres north across the cratered and smouldering expanse of the Charys starport, the barrage siren began to wail from the central bunker complex, the notes barely perceptible above the rising shriek of the Thunderhawks' turbines. Seconds later a salvo of rockets roared in from the rebel artillery positions to the east, just as the first assault transport raised its armoured prow and flared in for a vertical landing. The unguided warheads fell at random across the ten-kilometre square starport, detonating amid empty revetments, burned-out warehouses and blackened administration buildings. One came down on the other side of a storage shed less than two hundred metres from where Mikal Sternmark and the assembled honour guard were waiting at the edge of the landing field. The blast hurled chunks of burning flakboard and pulverised ferrocrete into the air with a thunderous explosion. Neither the Space Marines nor the armoured platoon of Imperial Guardsmen seemed to notice.

Roiling clouds of dirt and grit sped in a widening circle as the descending craft touched down in a rough diamond formation at the centre of the landing field, less than a hundred yards away. The hot wind tangled Sternmark's dark hair and pulled at the tattered ends of the black wolf pelt across his shoulders. Needles of pain stabbed along the length of the ugly, ragged wound that marked the left side of Sternmark's head, but the Wolf Guard grimaced stoically into the hot, stinging wind and tightened his grip on the haft of the power axe in his left hand. He'd had little occasion to carry it recently, and he drew comfort from its familiar weight.

He'd carried an entire world on his shoulders for the last three weeks, and now he could gladly set that burden aside. It was one thing to lead men into battle and come to grips with the enemy face to face, Mikal had done that for more years than he could count, and he was good at it. Directing a planetary campaign from a dimly lit bunker, with thousands of troops and tens of millions of civilians to contend with was something else again. Once upon a time, he'd dreamt of rising to the lofty rank of Wolf Lord and holding the fate of star systems in his hands. Charys had shown him the folly of his ambitions. He was a warrior, and a leader of warriors, and he longed to return to the front lines where he belonged.

The ferrocrete landing pad trembled as the transports touched down. Mikal saw with some bemusement that one of the craft wasn't a Thunderhawk at all, but a richly appointed shuttlecraft with the insignia of House Bellisarius emblazoned on its flank. Must be some kind of advance party, he thought, and waited patiently as the transports' assault ramps lowered with a clang and the first troops clattered out into the late afternoon sun.

Dust swirled around the legs of the Space Wolves as they loped onto the ferrocrete and formed up in ranks. Here and there the billows of dust seemed to mask larger, more hulking shapes that stalked menacingly at the corners of Mikal's vision. He shook his head sharply to try and clear it, which only set his wound throbbing again. The hellblade that had struck him during the frenzied retreat from the governor's audience chamber had not been poisoned as far as the company's Wolf Priest could determine, but the injury wasn't healing as it should.

Within moments, three large packs of Space Wolves were standing in ranks before their transports, heads held high and weapons ready at their sides. Blood Claws, Mikal noted with a slight frown. His expression of unease deepened when he saw that none of the warriors bore the heraldry of the Great Wolf on their shoulders.

Movement at the end of the line caught his eye. Mikal saw a Wolf Priest step forward and raise his crozius in salute to the waiting honour guard. The heavy mantle of wolfskin and the bulk of the priest's polished armour made the wearer seem almost childlike in comparison, like a son trying on his father's wargear. After a moment, he recognised the young, aristocratic face. *Sigurd, son of a rich jarl in the Dragon Isles, young and unblooded, Blessed Russ, what is he doing here?*

Off to the west, a heavy drumbeat shook the ground as the Earthshaker batteries of the Imperial Guard fired a counter-battery salvo against the rebel rocket launchers. Nearly a third of the Blood Claws flinched at the sound, weapons jerking in their hands. Sternmark's unease transformed to irritation.

He strode towards the Wolf Priest, lips curling back from his teeth. Silent as a shadow, Morgrim Silvertongue followed in Sternmark's wake, watching the scene unfold with a storyteller's eye. *Marking my every mistake, noting every telling failure,* the Wolf Guard thought sourly. *Every king and hero wanted a fine skald at his side, but pity the warrior whose deeds were not worthy.*

Sigurd watched Mikal approach and smiled, making the sign of the wolf. 'The blessings of Russ and the All-father be upon you, Mikal Sternmark,' he intoned. 'All of Fenris knows of your deeds on Charys, and we have come to add our swords to your own—'

'Where is he?' Sternmark growled.

The Wolf Priest's smile faded. 'I don't... I don't understand,' he stammered.

'Where is the Great Wolf?' Mikal said, still advancing on the young priest. With his terrible wound and his battered Terminator armour, the Wolf Guard was a vision of war incarnate, looming over Sigurd and the front rank of the startled Blood Claws. 'When will he and his company make their landing? Has he been delayed by the space battle?'

Sigurd lowered his crozius, an apprehensive look on his face. 'He… he's not here, lord,' he answered.

'Berek is lord here, not I!' Mikal shouted, suddenly struck with anger. 'I am his lieutenant and champion, and control of this war zone must pass to Grimnar as soon as he arrives.' He took another step forward, teeth bared, his face mere centimetres from Sigurd's. 'Can you tell me when he and his company will make planetfall or not?'

The Wolf Priest blanched at Sternmark's palpable fury, but gamely held his ground. 'He won't,' Sigurd said flatly. 'He can't. The Great Wolf's company is scattered across the war zone, supporting the actions of the other Wolf Lords.'

His answer stopped the Wolf Guard in his tracks. The shock left him painfully aware of the spectacle he'd made of himself. Sternmark fancied he could feel the skald's dark eyes burning accusingly into the back of his neck.

'I don't understand,' he said, not quite able to keep the stricken tone from his voice. 'Did he not read my report? Berek has fallen. Madox is here, with the Spear of Russ. This is where the war will be decided.'

Sigurd nodded, more composed now, but still unable to conceal the look of resentment in his eyes. 'Even so,' he replied, 'the Great Wolf cannot come. We have been sent in his place to aid you in whatever way we can.'

Once again, a tide of anger and despair threatened to overwhelm Sternmark. He shot a look at the waiting Blood Claws and choked back the words that first rose to his lips. *How am I to save our Chapter with three packs of initiates and a boy-priest? Why has the Old Wolf forsaken me?*

Instead, he drew a deep breath and struggled to push his feelings aside. As he did so, he caught sight of another small group approaching the ranks of newly arrived troops. Though distant, he recognised their scents at once.

Ragnar Blackmane, and the Navigator, Gabriella, with Torin the Wayfarer and Haegr the Mountain in tow. What in Morkai's name are they doing here? The answer suggested itself almost at once. *It's the Spear. Grimnar's sent them to reclaim it somehow. Either the Old Wolf is truly desperate, or he knows something I don't.*

Sternmark chose to believe the latter. He'd banked a great deal on the report he'd sent to Fenris, believing that once Grimnar understood how dire things were on Charys, the Old Wolf would gather his warriors and take charge of the campaign. Mikal had clung to that hope for days, knowing he was not up to the task that had been thrust upon him. Now he would have to see things through to the bitter end.

With as much dignity as he could muster, Sternmark turned to the assembled Blood Claws. 'Praise Russ!' he declared. 'Look upon blood-stained Charys, and know that your deeds here will be remembered in the sagas of our Chapter. Glory awaits you, in the Allfather's name!'

The Blood Claws didn't respond for a moment, still stunned by the Wolf Guard's earlier outburst. Then Sigurd raised his crozius and added his voice to Sternmark's. 'For Russ and the Allfather!' he cried. 'Glory awaits!'

Harald, leader of the first Blood Claw pack, took up the cry. 'Russ and the Allfather!' he roared, raising his axe. Within moments the rest of the Space Wolves had joined in, banging their weapons against their breast-plates and howling at the smoke stained sky.

Mikal Sternmark listened to the shouts of his young brethren and fought to master his emotions. Ghostly images played at the corners of his vision: huge, leaping shapes that were neither beasts nor men, and strange, distorted sounds whispered in his ears. The wound, he thought despairingly. That damned hell-blade has laid a curse on me.

He looked to Silvertongue, and caught the skald staring at him with those unreadable eyes of his. Mikal could guess how his own saga would end. Not all the tales ended gloriously. Some ended in tears, or infamy. The thought shamed him, but he resigned himself to it.

Off in the distance, the barrage siren wailed.

THE COMMAND BUNKER was red-lit and stank of unwashed bodies and bile. From what Ragnar could determine, the Guard commander in chief had chosen the starport bunker complex as her headquarters upon first arriving with her regiments on Charys, and what started out as a temporary post became permanent as the campaign wore on. Field cots and piles of empty ration tins in the corners of some of the low-ceilinged rooms suggested that Athelstane's general staff worked, slept and ate at their posts. Judging by the pasty faces and red-rimmed eyes he'd seen on his way inside, Ragnar thought that many of her staff hadn't felt the touch of sunlight in weeks.

That one observation told him all he needed to know about how desperate the situation on Charys truly was.

Athelstane's harried officers all but ignored the new-comers as they were escorted into a small auditorium that had been converted into an improvised situation and planning room. The hard pews had been cleared away, replaced with tables and portable work stations. Harried aides darted between the narrow aisles, carrying flimsy printouts to staff officers who were monitoring battle reports from half a world away. Tense conversations and muted orders rose above the dry clatter of logic engines and vox teletypes. Enginseer acolytes hovered in the corners of the room, muttering prayers and lighting votive candles to keep the data channels open.

Mikal Sternmark led Sigurd, Ragnar and Gabriella across the crowded room to a large, ornate hololith table that had been set up on the auditorium's former stage. There, he introduced them to Lady General Militant Esbet Athelstane. The commander of all Guard forces on Charys was a thin, raw-boned woman with a severe, patrician face and large, dark eyes. Her iron-grey hair was cropped as short as a rank and file sergeant's, and to Ragnar she smelled of leather, amasec and fine machine oil. Athelstane wore the Medallion Crimson among the many campaign ribbons and decorations on her officer's greatcoat, and from the faint sounds of servomotors and pistons, Ragnar reckoned that her right arm and both legs were expertly crafted augmetics.

Athelstane greeted them all with weary professional courtesy, and then introduced an older, balding man in a dark green suit, who reluctantly joined the gathering from a seat at the back corner of the stage. He was taller than the general, with a hook nose and red-rimmed, grey eyes. There was a defeated air about the man; he limped haltingly on his left leg, and his angular shoulders were hunched. As he stepped into the dim light, Ragnar saw that the right side of the man's face and throat was covered in a glistening film of wound sealant, and both hands were wrapped in flexible bandages.

'This is Inquisitor Cadmus Volt, of the Ordo Malleus,' the general said. 'He and his team have been on Charys for the last three years, investigating reports of forbidden practices among the local farming cartels. Since the uprising began, he has advised us on the enemy's capabilities and possible intentions.' From the steely sound in Athelstane's voice it was clear that Volt had been of little use in that regard.

Inquisitor Volt bowed cordially to Gabriella. 'May I ask what brings so esteemed a member of the Navis Nobilite to such a dangerous place as Charys?' he asked.

Gabriella acknowledged Volt with a cool nod and a narrow gaze. The Navigator Houses had a long, antagonistic relationship with the Inquisition. 'House Bellisarius and the Wolves of Fenris have been allies for centuries,' she replied coolly. 'Honour requires that we aid our esteemed friends in whatever manner we are able.'

'Without Lady Gabriella's assistance our reinforcements would never have reached Charys at all,' Ragnar said. 'Turbulence in the warp has all but isolated the system.'

'So we surmised,' Athelstane said with a nod. 'Whatever the enemy is attempting at Charys has taken a fearful toll on our astropaths. We have been awaiting your arrival with great anticipation.'

Both Athelstane and Sternmark looked to Sigurd, and the Wolf Priest picked up on the unspoken cue and began his report of the war council on Fenris. The commanders listened carefully as the Wolf Priest recounted the Great Wolf's deliberations and their subsequent journey to Charys. Ragnar took the opportunity to lead Gabriella to a nearby seat. The Navigator was still somewhat unsteady on her feet, and though she took pains to conceal it, Ragnar could tell that she was deeply unsettled. Gabriella accepted the seat with an absent nod, one hand clinging to his forearm for support.

As strained as her manner was aboard the *Fist of Russ*, it had only grown worse once their shuttle had landed. There was something strange at work on Charys. Ragnar felt it, too, a strange sense of dislocation, as though the world around him had no more substance than a hologram. Shadowy shapes flitted at the corners of his vision, and faint sounds whispered in his ears. The agitation he felt on Fenris seemed magnified tenfold. It was all he could do not to rise and pace across the crowded stage like a caged animal. From time to time, his gaze wandered to Mikal Sternmark's grim face, and he wondered if the legendary champion felt the same as he did.

'Thanks to the Lady Navigator's skill, we emerged very close to Charys, whereupon we came under attack from a force of enemy raiders that had been at anchor in high orbit,' Sigurd continued. 'We had thought to find Berek's fleet waiting there.'

'The enemy has a sizeable naval presence in the system,' Athelstane replied. 'We believe that there was a large armada of raiders hiding within the outer asteroid fields for some time. Since the uprising began, they have been joined by a growing number of escorts and cruisers. Berek's fleet commanded the approaches to Charys for almost a week, and we were able to defeat a number of enemy ground offensives with their support. As the enemy was able to commit more and more ships against Berek's force, casualties began to mount, and it became clear that if they left the system to make repairs, they might not be able to return.' The general glanced briefly at Inquisitor Volt. 'It was decided that the fleet would withdraw to the edge of the system and make what repairs they could. They've remained there ever since, as our force of last resort. Much of the enemy fleet has been drawn off to hunt for them, although groups of raiders have appeared from time to time to bombard our positions from orbit.'

Gabriella straightened in her seat and drew a deep breath. 'How has the enemy managed to communicate with their fleet across the system?'

The general shrugged. 'We don't know. Sorcery, perhaps? That's not my area of expertise.' Once again, she gave the inquisitor a sidelong look. 'Maybe they aren't talking with one another. Their orbital attacks don't seem to coincide with their ground operations as far as we can tell, not that they aren't damaging enough all by themselves.'

'Well,' Sigurd interjected, clearly a little agitated by Gabriella's interruption, 'you've heard our tale. Now, what would you have of us?'

Athelstane rested her hands on the hololith table's smoked glass top and glanced at Sternmark. 'That's an interesting question,' she said slowly. 'We had been led to believe that Fenris would be sending a great deal more troops and heavy weapons to support us. We'd hoped for a spear that we could thrust into the enemy's heart. Instead, it appears that the Great Wolf has gifted us with a handful of brand new knives.'

The bald statement took all of the Space Wolves aback. It wasn't a disparagement, but a cold assessment of the facts. Ragnar saw the Wolf Priest stiffen nevertheless. *This is the second time he and his men have been dismissed as irrelevant,* the young Space Wolf thought, *a hard thing to take, for the son of a powerful jarl.*

When Sigurd didn't reply at once, Ragnar ventured, 'Even a knife can be lethal when used properly,' he said. 'Tell us, how goes the war on the ground?'

'Badly,' Athelstane replied. 'At first we believed the uprising was the work of a small cabal of government officials and officers in the local PDF regiments, but now it's clear that outside forces planned and organised this campaign for many years. More than two-thirds of the planetary defence forces mutinied over the course of a single night. What heavy weapons and vehicles they didn't take they managed to destroy. Bureaucrats in key positions sabotaged the planetary logistical network and crucial emergency response plans. By the time my regiments and I arrived, Charys was almost completely in enemy hands.' She reached down and keyed a control panel recessed into the edge of the table. A holo-map of the planet instantly appeared in the air above the table, showing nearly sixty small cities and townships scattered across the world's vast plains. More than half of the settlements had a skull superimposed over them. They existed in name only, having been abandoned or wiped out by the rebels. The rest showed a red aquila, indicating that they were battlegrounds where neither side could claim total control.

'We managed to establish footholds at a number of points around the planet, but we weren't able to achieve significant gains because we had been misled as to the size of the rebel force and the lack of support we would find on the ground.' The general turned a brass knob and the view switched to an operational map of the capital city. Nearly eighty-five per cent of the districts were red, with only a narrow band of Imperial blue around the outlying sectors to the east that stretched back to the starport outside the city. 'When Berek Thunderfist and your brethren arrived, we attempted a lightning thrust aimed at decapitating the rebel leadership and retaking the capital.' She pressed a stud and a trio of broad, blue arrows leapt from the eastern districts and drove deep into the heart of the city. 'The orbital bombardment and follow-on attacks inflicted very heavy rebel casualties and allowed us to push all the way to the governor's palace.'

Athelstane's expression darkened. 'Unfortunately, the Wolf Lord's attack met with disaster. Sternmark and his warriors managed to break out of the enemy ambush and withdraw from the palace with Berek's body, and then linked up with our lead armoured elements.'

Ragnar glanced over at Mikal. The look in the warrior's eyes was one he knew all too well. He curses himself for retreating, the young Space Wolf thought, and no wonder, but what other option did he have?

'Where is Berek now?' Sigurd asked. 'Does he still live?'

'We think he lingers in the Red Dream,' Sternmark said dully. 'Our instruments detect faint life, but his body will not respond to our priest's unguents and balms. We had hoped that Grimnar would at least send Ranek or one of the senior Wolf Priests to tend to Berek…' The Wolf Guard left the rest unsaid, but the implication was clear.

'What of the palace?' Ragnar interjected.

'Before we could mount another attempt to retake the palace the rebel forces launched a massive counter-offensive,' Athelstane replied. 'This time the rebels were supported by Traitor Marines and packs of daemons. The enemy struck out of thin air, exploiting weak spots in our lines with diabolical skill.' She sighed bitterly, clearly haunted by her failures stemming from that fateful day. 'Fighting raged around the city centre for almost forty-eight hours, but in the end we were forced to withdraw.'

Gabriella leaned forward in her chair. 'How are the Chaos Marines managing these feats of teleportation?'

Inquisitor Volt folded his arms and scowled at the holo-map, as though the secret was somehow hidden there. 'We don't know,' he admitted. 'It's not technological. They appear and disappear like ghosts, coming and going apparently at will, and not just here in the city, but across the entire *planet* as well.' He shook his head in exasperation. 'We've laid wards to protect the starport perimeter from attack. They seem to have worked so far, but the cost of maintaining them is enormous. If I knew *how* the enemy was accomplishing this, I could perhaps devise a better way of countering it, but I can't find a reference to anything like this in my records. The scale is unprecedented.'

Gabriella considered this. 'It is interesting that you mention the notion of scale, inquisitor. I have been studying the efforts of the enemy sorcerers at the subsector level. Perhaps if we were to compare notes, I might be able to give you more insight into the situation.'

Volt stared dumbstruck at the Navigator for a moment. 'That is... unexpected,' he finally managed. 'Of course, I would be happy to hear your thoughts on the matter.'

Gabriella nodded at Volt, and then gestured to Athelstane. 'Please forgive the interruption, general. Pray continue.'

The general keyed another stud, and the blue arrows shrank back from the palace. 'For a time we were able to stabilise our lines with help from the ships in orbit, but once they withdrew the tide turned against us. The enemy has pushed us back bit by bit. The Traitor Marines crack open our lines with precision assaults, and their ground troops pour right through. Berek's company has been divided up among war zones all over the world in an attempt to stem the tide, but all we've done is slow their advance. At this point, we've been driven back to the edge of the city, and there are indications that the enemy is preparing another major offensive.' The holo-map shifted again, returning more or less to the thin blue line at the city's eastern edge. 'Their objective is the starport. If it falls, we lose our one and only air base and supply point. Our regiments will then be isolated and eventually overwhelmed.'

For a moment, Sigurd and Ragnar considered the map in stunned silence. Ragnar glanced up at the general. 'What about the Imperial Navy and the Guard?'

'When I left Corianus with my staff, the lord governor subsector had sent out the call for more regiments,' she said. 'At best, the first units won't get here for another five months, even assuming the Navy can get ships through the local warp turbulence.' She eyed the map grimly. 'We'll be lucky if we can hold out another five days.'

Ragnar walked over to the map table, studying the riot of symbols that depicted the locations of Imperial and enemy units across the city. 'You forget, general, that one ship has already made it through,' he pointed out, 'and, although they are untested in battle, you have almost fifty Space Wolves to add their strength to the fight. Do not be so quick to dismiss us.' He looked pointedly at Sternmark, but the Wolf Guard would not meet Ragnar's eyes.

Athelstane sighed. 'Your courage does you credit,' she said heavily. 'I've had the honour of fighting alongside the Space Wolves several times in my career, and I know very well what you're capable of, but you must understand, even with twice your numbers I doubt we could defeat the forces arrayed against us.'

Ragnar set his jaw and looked the general in the eye. 'You said you wanted a spear to thrust at the heart of the enemy,' he said. He indicated the enemy positions on the map with a sweep of his hand. 'Suppose the Great Wolf had arrived with his company, where would you have employed them?'

The general regarded him appraisingly for a moment. 'For starters, I wouldn't have committed them to the city at all.'

She adjusted a set of dials and the map's viewpoint pulled back until it showed the countryside within sixty kilometres of the city. 'There is a large PDF base approximately twenty kilometres west of the capital. Before the uprising it was the supreme headquarters for the Charys defence forces.' The map shifted, focusing in on a large, fortified military base some five kilometres across. 'We've suspected for some time that the traitor regiments were still using it as their command centre. Naturally, we've bombarded it at every available opportunity, but the base's bunker complex was built to shrug off that kind of attack.'

With another turn of the dial the map zoomed in on the rebel base. Ragnar observed tall, thick perimeter walls sited with dozens of gun emplacements that commanded a flat, featureless killing ground for kilometres in every direction. He saw tank parks and reinforced barracks large enough to hold four or more armoured regiments, defended by Hydra anti-aircraft positions. The central bunker complex alone was over two kilometres across, and Ragnar suspected that it extended even farther underground.

'Once Berek's company arrived we inserted three packs of his scouts into the area around the base to see what we could learn,' she continued. 'Our suppositions proved correct. The rebels were indeed still using it as their headquarters, and recently they have observed the arrival of numerous high-ranking officers and their aides. They are still there, which is why we believe they've been gathered to plan a major series of offensives.'

'And you wanted the Old Wolf's company to destroy this base?' Ragnar asked.

'Not just destroy it,' Athelstane replied. 'We planned a lightning assault to capture the rebel high command and deliver them here for interrogation. Inquisitor Volt assured me he had the means to make the traitors tell us everything they knew.'

Ragnar nodded appreciatively. 'How many enemy troops?'

'A reinforced armoured regiment: at least fifteen hundred troops with heavy weapons and almost forty battle tanks.' She spread her hands. 'We reckoned even Grimnar's great company would have a tough time taking the base.'

The young Space Wolf nodded thoughtfully. 'It's good for you then that we're here instead of the Old Wolf,' he said with a feral grin. 'We'll go in at first light.'

SEVEN
Hit and Run

THE BATTLE CRUISER's brass and steel teleportation chamber rang like a swordmaster's forge as the Space Wolves made ready for battle. The Wolves of Harald's Blood Claw pack congregated in a tight group, checking their weapons and adjusting the heavy load of extra equipment they would be carrying with them on the raid. Most had their helmets off and were talking with one another in low, sullen voices. Ragnar had insisted that the warship's ancient teleporters were vital to the success of the raid, but the Space Wolves hated the thought of placing themselves at the mercy of such an arcane, unreliable device. A few metres away, Sigurd the Wolf Priest stood alone, both hands clasped on his crozius and his head bowed in prayer. Iron Priests and acolytes in full ceremonial vestments moved slowly around the perimeter of the room, checking and anointing the vast network of power couplings and matrix field collectors.

Ragnar stepped through the armoured hatch into the chamber just a few minutes before jump-off. They had returned to the *Fist of Russ*, in high orbit over Charys only a few hours ago, and he'd spent most of the intervening time meditating in his old quarters. A grim sense of foreboding dogged his steps. Although the sense of dislocation had ebbed since leaving the planet's surface, he could not ease the tautness of his nerves or banish the wisps of shadow that flitted at the corners of his eyes.

He could not afford to be distracted once the raid began. Even a moment's hesitation could mean disaster.

The assembled warriors paid Ragnar no heed as he strode across the chamber. He took careful note of Sigurd and the Blood Claws, and then caught sight of Torin on the opposite side of the room. The older Wolfblade was finishing an inspection of his chainsword as Ragnar approached.

'Where's Haegr?' Ragnar asked with a frown.

Torin slid his chainsword into its scabbard and grinned ruefully. 'Where else?'

'Morkai's black breath!' Ragnar cursed. 'If that overfed walrus is late–'

'Peace, brother,' Torin chuckled, raising a gauntleted hand. 'Haegr can be a fool sometimes, but I've never known him to shirk his duty. He'll be here when the time comes, probably clumping along with an ale bucket on his foot, but he'll be here nonetheless.' The older Space Wolf studied Ragnar carefully. 'What's troubling you? I've never known you to get a case of nerves before a battle, even one as risky as this.'

Ragnar shrugged. 'It's nothing,' he began, but stopped trying to pretend when he saw Torin's disbelieving glare. 'Nothing I can explain, at least,' he said grudgingly. 'I don't know, Torin. Truth be told, I haven't felt right since we returned to Fenris. My temper is on a hair trigger, and I feel like I could crawl right out of my skin.' He shook his head savagely. 'Even my eyes are playing tricks on me.'

Torin's eyes narrowed thoughtfully. 'You, too?'

Ragnar froze. 'You mean you feel the same way?'

The older Space Wolf lowered his voice to a conspiratorial whisper. 'Since we arrived on Charys I've been seeing things, like shadows or wisps of smoke, flitting at the edge of my sight.'

'Yes! Exactly!' Ragnar whispered excitedly. He leaned close to Torin. 'Anything else? Did everything planetside feel... I don't know... *unsettled*, somehow?'

'Like nothing was solid or real?' Torin breathed a sigh of relief. 'Thank Russ. I was starting to think I was losing my mind. But wait, you said you were feeling like this back on Fenris?'

Ragnar frowned. 'Well, not exactly. I didn't start seeing things until later, once we'd set off for Charys. On Fenris it was mostly just strange dreams.'

'Dreams about what?'

'Monsters,' Ragnar answered. 'Monsters in the shape of men.'

Torin frowned. 'Monsters... or Wulfen?'

Ragnar felt his hackles rise. 'Does it matter?' he asked.

'Of course it does,' Torin answered. 'Have you talked to the Wolf Priest about it?'

'Even if I'd thought of it, there was no time to talk to Ranek,' the young Space Wolf replied.

'What about Sigurd?'

Ragnar snorted. 'Don't be stupid. We're just a bunch of *nithlings* as far as he's concerned. The only things I plan on sharing with him are my fists.'

The older Wolfblade shook his head. 'Don't be so quick to judge him, Ragnar. Yes, he's a bit of an idiot, but we all were at that age. He still thinks he's the son of a jarl, not a young priest who's just earned his crozius. He's unsure of his authority and overwhelmed by the role he's been thrust into. Basically, he's terrified of failure.' Torin looked pointedly at Ragnar. 'Sound like anyone you know?'

'I'm not sure what you mean,' the young Space Wolf growled.

'Fine, consider this instead: Sigurd wouldn't have been raised up unless Ranek and the other priests saw some potential in him. Talk to him about the dreams. Give him the benefit of the doubt, and perhaps he'll learn to do the same for the rest of us.'

Ragnar thought it over. Finally, he shrugged. 'All right,' he said, 'as soon as we get back, provided we don't get blown to pieces in the meantime.'

Torin grinned and clapped Ragnar on the shoulder. 'That's the cheery soul I used to know. Trust me on this, brother. I know what I'm talking about.'

The young Space Wolf turned and surveyed the chamber once more. 'Is that so? Then where is Haegr? We jump off in thirty seconds–'

A booming laugh rolled down the passageway outside the chamber. Haegr's bristly, grinning face appeared in the hatchway, his massive drinking horn clutched in one great fist. 'Mighty Haegr is here!' he roared, sloshing a bit of frothy ale onto the deck. 'Draw your swords and beat your shields, sons of Fenris! Battle and red glory await!'

For a moment, it looked as though Haegr wouldn't be able to force his bulk through the narrow hatchway. Iron Priests and acolytes hurried over to help, but the huge Space Wolf paid them no heed. First one foot, then the hand bearing the ale horn, then a hip the size of a boar's flank and a torso half again as large as a mead cask, and with a grunt and a creak of metal, Haegr squeezed sideways into the room. Still grinning, he took a long draught from his ale horn and licked the froth from his whiskers. 'Next time I see the Old Wolf,' he said to Ragnar, 'remind me to tell him we need bigger ships.'

FAR BELOW, ON the surface of the embattled world, the first stages of Ragnar's plan were swinging into motion.

At Gorgon-4, an Imperial Guard firebase five kilometres east of the starport, a vox teletype began to clatter in the company commander's blockhouse. The sound jolted the vox operator awake, dragging him from a pleasant dream about a girl he used to know back home. Rubbing his bleary eyes, the young Guardsman read off the script as it printed and confirmed by the message header that it had been sent to the proper unit. Then he tore the flimsy copy from the machine and dashed out into the trenches to find the artillery officer.

The vox operator found the battery commander sipping lukewarm recaff from a tin cup as he watched the sun start to rise through the smoke-stained horizon to the east. The officer, a veteran of many campaigns, took the proffered script without a word and read the orders between sips. His dark eyes widened a bit as he saw the time stamp on the page, and he turned to rouse the gun crews with a stream of leathery curses.

Within minutes, the long barrels of Gorgon-4's Earthshaker batteries rose into the sky. Six hundred kilo shells had already been fed into the guns' open breeches, and bare-chested Guardsmen were still blinking sleep out of their eyes as they wrestled propellant bags from their armoured caissons.

Still watching the glow on the eastern horizon, the battery commander slowly raised his right hand. All along the line, the gunnery crews scrambled clear of the gun carriages. Each gunnery sergeant in the battery checked his gun, checked his elevation, checked his crew and then shot his right hand into the air.

The battery commander smiled in satisfaction. At that exact moment, the first rays of the sun broke through the haze.

'Fire!' he cried, dropping his arm, and the eight heavy guns roared. Thunder shook the earth to the north and south as five other firebases added their guns to the barrage.

FIVE KILOMETRES WEST, the vox-units crackled in the cockpits of Mjolnir Flight. 'Mjolnir Lead, this is Echo five-seven. Green light – repeat, green light. Good luck and good hunting.'

Ten pilots and their crews straightened in their jump seats and put away their pre-flight checklists. They had been wakened in the dead of night, briefed and taken out to their birds an hour before dawn. Now wide awake, they reached for the throttles and brought idling turbojets to a full-throated roar.

One by one, eight Valkyrie gunships and two Thunderhawk assault transports rose heavily from their revetments and headed off to the west. They would be over their target in just twelve minutes.

BACK ABOARD THE *Fist of Russ*, the Iron Priests and their acolytes filed one by one from the teleportation chamber. An unearthly hum began to fill the air, sinking deep into Ragnar's bones.

'Form up!' Ragnar ordered, drawing his bolt pistol and sword. The Blood Claws fell silent at once, separating into three teams as Ragnar had planned. Three of the Claws trotted over to join Ragnar, Torin and Haegr. Raising his crozius, Sigurd moved quickly to the head of another team of five Claws. Harald stood ready with the remaining six members of the pack. There were no dark looks, no challenges or recriminations. Whatever Sigurd or the Blood Claws thought of Ragnar and his companions, none of it mattered now. They went to war as battle-brothers, as their forebears had done since the dawn of the Imperium.

Sigurd the Wolf Priest turned to his brethren and began the Benediction of Iron. One of the Blood Claws clashed his axe against his breastplate and started his battle-chant, singing of salt waves and splintered shields in a low, rumbling voice.

Haegr threw back his head and drained his ale horn in a single draught. Foam dripping from his whiskers, he gave his companions an enormous grin. 'By Russ, these are the moments that make a man's blood sing!'

he roared, laughing like a drunken god. 'Try to keep up with mighty Haegr if you can, little brothers, lest he claim all the glory for himself!'

Chainblades growled to life. Power weapons crackled and moaned. Bolt pistols rattled as shells were driven home, and then the teleporter activated with a searing flash of light.

THERE WAS A moment of terrible, blind dislocation, and in the space of a single heartbeat the Space Wolves found themselves near the southern edge of the sprawling rebel base, caught up in a storm of fire, thunder and steel.

Ragnar staggered and dropped into a crouch as the earth shook beneath the Imperial barrage. Heavy shells howled overhead, falling across the rebel base with thunderous detonations and tall pillars of dirt and smoke. They were well within the base's defensive walls, perhaps two hundred metres from the broad ferrocrete bunkers of the tank park. The mangled wreckage of a staff car blazed brightly nearby, its passengers scattered in smoking pieces for a dozen metres around the impact site. No one else could be seen. The base's garrison had run for the shelters the moment the barrage began.

Red-hot shrapnel rang off Ragnar's armour. He ducked his head and shouted at the top of his lungs. 'Go for objective one!' he shouted into the cataclysmic storm. 'Go!'

Without hesitation, the three teams of Space Wolves separated, charging off into the howling storm of shells. They had to deal with the anti-aircraft batteries first. Their air support would be over the base in less than ten minutes.

It was General Athelstane's comment about bombarding the PDF base that had given Ragnar the idea. Despite his protestations, he knew full well that the Blood Claws stood no chance facing the base's garrison in a conventional fight. Dealing with them one element at a time, however, was another matter. One pack, he reckoned, would be enough for what they had to do. Any more and they risked taking unnecessary casualties from their own artillery fire. As it was, there was a good chance that some of them would be caught by an unlucky blast, but that was a risk Ragnar was willing to take.

There were three large Hydra anti-aircraft batteries situated around the base, consisting of four quadruple cannon mounts and a high-power auspex unit. Ragnar chose the battery furthest from the insertion point as his team's objective. The Space Wolves dashed through the pall of smoke and dirt, navigating more by memory than sight. Concussions smote at them with invisible fists, and steel fragments whizzed past their heads. Ragnar heard Torin grunt in surprise and pain, but a quick glance showed that the older Wolfblade was still running alongside him. Bright blood leaked from a shrapnel wound in his arm.

They covered the three kilometres to the battery in just over three minutes. The gun mounts were in concrete revetments arrayed in a diamond around the central auspex unit and barrage shelter. Ragnar signalled to his men, and the warriors peeled away and headed for the guns, leaving him to take care of the battery's crew.

He vaulted a slit trench connecting two of the batteries and ran to the low ferrocrete bunker in the centre. Pulling a grenade from his belt, he put his armoured boot to the bunker's steel hatch. The door crumpled and fell inward on the third kick.

Bolts of blue light snapped out of the interior of the bunker, detonating against his breastplate. One shot sizzled past his head, close enough to leave an angry welt on his cheek. Ragnar fired a pair of wild shots from his bolt pistol and ducked to the left of the door as he chucked the grenade inside. A chorus of shouts was silenced by a sharp *bang* as the grenade exploded. Moving quickly, the young Space Wolf dashed into the smoke filled bunker and made certain the occupants were dead before heading back outside.

By the time he was finished the four gun mounts were wrecked. Ragnar waved to his men and keyed his vox. 'Objective one-one clear,' he shouted.

'Objective one-two clear,' came Sigurd's reply.

'Objective one-three clear,' Harald answered a moment later.

Ragnar nodded in approval. So far, so good. 'Go for objective two!' he called.

The Space Wolves converged on the centre of the base from three different directions, heading for the garrison's cluster of barrage shelters. Two and a half more minutes elapsed. According to the plan, the Imperial barrage was about to lift.

Ragnar and his men reached the first of the barrage shelters. Each one was a low, ferrocrete bunker capable of holding a hundred men, with a reinforced steel door and a set of narrow vision slits running along their flanks.

A hundred traitors versus five Space Wolves, Ragnar thought, taking cover to the right of the door. Those were odds he could deal with.

He motioned to a pair of Blood Claws. The Wolves ran to the door, one of them detaching a heavy melta charge from his backpack. Working quickly, they attached the charge's magnetic clamps to the door and keyed the timer.

The bunkers' ferrocrete construction made them strong enough to shrug off a direct hit from an Earthshaker round. It also made them strong enough to channel the blast of a melta charge instead of bursting apart and dissipating it. Ragnar had seen what melta charges did to the crews of enemy tanks. He expected a similar result here.

With a hollow *thump* the charge detonated, vaporising the steel door and hurling it inwards as a plume of incandescent plasma. The concussion wave struck the far end of the bunker and rebounded through the open door with a thunderclap of superheated air. Grinning fiercely, Ragnar signalled his warriors, and they swept inside, hunting for survivors.

They didn't find many.

RAGNAR'S MEN CLEARED fifteen bunkers in just under four minutes. By the time the last Imperial shells landed across the enemy base its garrison had been almost completely destroyed.

The three teams linked up again on the west side of the central bunker complex. A quick head count showed that three Wolves were missing. Two had been unlucky running through the barrage, and one Blood Claw had got over-eager assaulting the bunkers and had stepped in front of a rebounding concussion wave. He lay inside a bunker awaiting extraction, deep in the Red Dream.

A chorus of petrochem engines growled off to the west, on the other side of the bunker complex. The tanks would be rolling out of their shelters soon. The faint roar of jet engines off to the east told Ragnar that the traitors were about to be in for a brutal surprise.

'Here's where the fighting begins in earnest,' Ragnar told the assembled Space Marines. 'We don't know how many troops are inside the central complex, but Russ knows they'll put up a stiff fight. Expect anything,' he said. 'You've all got maps of the complex loaded into your memory cores. If you get separated, fight your way to the vault or head back outside for extraction. Kill everything that gets in your way.'

The Blood Claws growled in assent. Ragnar glanced at Torin and Haegr and nodded. 'All right, let's go.'

They ran to the western side of the bunker, emerging like vengeful spirits out of the smoke and haze. Autogun fire and bolts of energy snapped out at them from the bunker's firing slits, but the enemy was too startled to draw beads on the fast-moving Wolves. Two Blood Claws ran ahead and started fixing their last demolition charge to the western bunker doors. They keyed the timer just as Ragnar and the rest of the force arrived.

The concussive blast buffeted Ragnar and his companions from ten metres away, checking his headlong charge for half a step. Then, with a howl, he plunged into the searing heat and smoke beyond the gaping doorway. The young Space Wolf found himself in a short narrow corridor, emerging after a few moments into a large, square room that reeked of hot metal and burned flesh. A squad of rebel stormtroopers had been formed up inside the room. At least three of them had been caught by the force of the blast and torn apart, while the rest were hurled like rag dolls against the stone walls. Ragnar burst upon them just as they were staggering to their feet. Their sergeant let out a yell and shot the young Space Wolf full in the chest with his hellpistol. The crimson bolt cracked harmlessly against the ancient ceramite breastplate. Ragnar hacked off the sergeant's left arm and head with a backhanded swipe of his frost blade, and then shot two more troopers as they tried to flee from the room.

Another sharp concussion rang from the bunker walls as Haegr stepped to Ragnar's left and smashed two more rebels to bits with a swing from his thunder hammer. The last surviving stormtrooper threw down his hellgun and raised his hands in surrender. Torin stepped into the room and shot the man in passing. They were going to have enough trouble with prisoners as it was.

Two corridors led out of the entry room, heading left and right. Ragnar recalled the maps he'd studied of the bunker layout, looked to Sigurd and pointed left. The Wolf Priest, his pale face speckled with fresh blood, nodded and led his and Harald's teams down the corridor. There were two staircases in the complex that led down to the lower level where the vault was located. They would work their way across the bunker to the stairs on the west side, while Ragnar and his companions fought their way to the closer staircase. That way they could ensure that none of the rebel commanders got past them if they decided to flee.

Shots and lasgun bolts whipped through the entry room from the right-hand corridor as rebels opened fire on Sigurd's team. Ragnar pulled another grenade from his belt and hurled it down the passageway. A second before it detonated, he nodded to Haegr, and the burly Wolf charged into the wake of the blast. Screams and brutal thunderclaps echoed down the corridor, punctuated by the Space Wolf's booming laugh.

Ragnar readied his bolt pistol and dashed off after Haegr, running past broken bodies and shattered weapons that littered the passageway floor. The massive Space Wolf was ploughing ahead like a stampeding mastodon, crushing any resistance in his path. Ragnar and his men charged, more than once, into a bloodstained room, and found themselves fighting stunned guardsmen, who Haegr had simply overrun and left behind.

They caught up to Haegr several long minutes later, at a four-way junction deep within the complex. The huge Wolf had his back against the wall near the corner of the junction, wrapped in swirling tendrils of smoke. The smell of ozone and shattered stone filled the air.

Haegr looked over at his battle-brothers as they approached. Ragnar saw that the right side of Haegr's face was red and blistered, and half of his unruly whiskers had been burned away. 'Mighty Haegr is unusually nimble for one of his heroic girth,' he grumbled, 'but these tight corridors make it hard to dodge plasma fire.'

'Like shooting fish in a barrel,' Torin said tightly. He glanced at Haegr. 'Sorry. More like spearing whales.'

'Must I do the foe's work and thrash you myself?' Haegr said. 'That would be tragic, would it not?'

'Where is the plasma gunner?' Ragnar said.

Haegr jerked his head to the left. 'Around the corner, about twenty metres,' he replied, 'and he's not alone. Looks like another squad of storm troopers is covering the staircase.'

The young Space Wolf nodded. 'Did you try any grenades?'

Haegr blinked at him. 'Grenades. Yes. A good idea,' he agreed.

Torin rolled his eyes. 'What did you do? Eat yours?'

The burly Wolf glowered at Torin. 'The mighty Haegr prefers to look the foe in the eye before ending his life, not cowering behind a cloud of shrapnel.'

'Meaning your thick fingers can't work the grenade dispenser,' Torin said drily.

Haegr shifted uncomfortably. 'Yes, well, possibly that, too,' he growled.

Ragnar couldn't help but chuckle. 'Now I know why the pair of you were sent to Terra,' he declared, shaking his head. He sheathed his sword and drew a grenade from Haegr's belt. Thumbing the fuse, he tossed it around the corner. Immediately, a hail of fire chewed along the length of the stone wall and ricocheted across the junction. Seconds later the grenade went off, and Ragnar spun around the corner, firing as he ran.

The young Space Wolf saw at once that Haegr had neglected to mention the barricade a few metres down the corridor.

A barrier of layered flakboard had been erected across the width of the passageway, and his grenade had left a scorch mark at its feet. The stormtroopers taking cover behind it were just popping back up from behind cover as Ragnar started his charge. Scarlet bolts of hellgun fire burst across his breastplate and pauldrons, leaving scorch marks across the ceramite plate. He saw the rebel plasma gunner pop up and level his weapon. Ragnar brought his pistol around and shot the man in the head.

Another bolt detonated against his thigh, and Ragnar felt a jolt of pain as the shot burned through his armour. He stumbled, and then redoubled his pace, charging headlong at the enemy barrier while he dragged his frost blade from its scabbard.

Two more shots struck his midsection as he leapt over the barrier. Ragnar's frost blade flashed and two storm troopers toppled in a welter of blood. He landed on a third rebel, driving the soldier to the floor before shooting him in the neck. Ragnar spun to the right, slashing downward with his sword and slicing another screaming trooper in half.

The remaining stormtroopers fell back, snapping off shots from their hellguns as they went. Drunk with battle lust, Ragnar stalked after them. He shot the closest man in the head. Then the crowd before him parted, and he was facing a sergeant with a glowing power sword in his hand, and a trooper with a hissing flamer levelled at Ragnar's chest.

There were two loud booms behind Ragnar, and a pair of heavy rounds hissed past the young Space Wolf's head. The first shot struck the man with the flamer in the shoulder, and the second tore through the trooper's throat. The stormtrooper spun to the right, his finger tightening on the trigger, spraying his comrades with a stream of liquid fire.

Ragnar dodged to the right, away from the flames, and the storm trooper sergeant rushed forward, slashing at the young Space Wolf's chest. Ragnar caught the glowing sword on the diamond-hard teeth of his frostblade and ripped open the rebel's chest with a back-handed blow. The survivors fled down the hall, firing wildly as they went, abandoning their post at the head of the staircase to Ragnar's right.

The young Space Wolf looked back the way he'd come and saw the rest of his team rushing up to join him. Haegr was out front, smoke curling from the barrel of his bolt pistol. Ragnar scowled at the burly warrior. 'You could have warned me about the barricade,' he growled.

'Barricade? You mean this pitiful thing?' Haegr drew back a foot and kicked the layered flakboards apart. 'I thought it was just a pile of rubbish.'

Shaking his head, Ragnar gave the wound in his leg a cursory check. Finding nothing serious, he bent and picked the flamer and plasma gun off the bodies of the dead stormtroopers. 'Take these,' he said, passing them over to two of the Blood Claws. 'Flamer up front. Let's go.'

The Blood Claw with the flamer nodded curtly and stepped to the head of the staircase. The iron rungs receded into darkness.

A breath of cold air rose up from the depths, smelling of old stone and lingering rot. Ragnar bared his teeth and slapped the lead Blood Claw on the shoulder. Slowly, cautiously, they began their descent.

EIGHT
Descent into Darkness

THE IRON STAIRS rang as the Space Wolves made their way into the command bunker's lower level. With a draconic hiss the flamer spat a stream of burning promethium down the length of the dark staircase. Ruddy orange light pushed back the cave-like shadows for a moment, revealing a steep descent to a ferrocrete landing and a switchback leading farther down. Teeth bared, the lead Blood Claw clambered slowly down the stairs with Ragnar and the rest of the team close behind.

Bolt pistol trained over the Blood Claw's right shoulder, Ragnar strained his senses to the utmost, listening for tell-tale signs of ambush. In the distance, he thought he could hear the crash and echo of gunfire, but the stone walls of the bunker made it hard to gauge where the sound was coming from.

Once again, a cold wave of vertigo swept through him, and the young Space Wolf fought to control his balance on the narrow stairs. Shadow shapes flitted at the corners of his vision, further disorientating him. Ragnar growled softly and forced himself to concentrate on the feel of the weapons in his hands and the presence of the Blood Claw in front of him as they made their way down the stairs.

Ragnar signalled for the lead Wolf to halt at the bottom of the first staircase. They listened in the gloom. Faint sounds reached Ragnar's ears. Was it whispering, or the faint scrabble of claws on metal? Whatever it was, the sound was coming from around the corner of the staircase. Ragnar signalled to the Blood Claw, who nodded and swiftly thrust the flamer around the bend. An all-too-human scream of horror was quickly swallowed in the flamer's hissing roar.

The Blood Claw held down the trigger for a full second before drawing back out of the way. Ragnar swept past, bolt pistol levelled, and pumped shells at the burning, flailing forms writhing on the staircase. He advanced into an inferno, killing men with shots to the head and chest or ending their agonies with a sweep of his blade. Power packs and ammunition cooked off all around him, filling the narrow space with thunderous detonations and deadly ricochets. Behind him, the rest of the team swept down in Ragnar's wake, eager to come to grips with the foe.

There was a small landing at the base of the stairs, piled with smouldering corpses. In the dim firelight, Ragnar's keen senses picked out an open doorway to the left of the landing. As he approached, he heard the distinct double *click* of a pair of grenades being primed, and the twin silver canisters were lobbed through the doorway at his feet. A lesser man might have panicked. Ragnar simply knocked them back the way they'd come with a sweep of his armoured boot. They detonated less than a second later, close enough to pepper him with bits of searing shrapnel, but the effect on the rebels in the chamber beyond was far worse.

Ragnar charged through the doorway into the reeling squad of rebel troopers, knocking two men off their feet with bolt pistol shots before slashing into the rest with his frost blade. The room was nearly pitch-dark. Ragnar's keen senses caught the ultrasonic whine of thermal-vision goggles and marked the locations of the rebel Guardsmen in the stroboscopic flashes of their weapons. Light burst from a lasgun to his right, sending a beam point-blank into Ragnar's breastplate. The flash revealed a snarling Guardsman little more than a metre away, his sunken cheeks crudely carved with blasphemous sigils. Ragnar spun on his heel and lashed out with his sword, eviscerating the soldier with a sweeping cut.

A shotgun went off, spraying his right shoulder and the side of his face with lead pellets. Ragnar howled in fury and fired a round in the direction of the flash, hearing the meaty sound of the shell striking home in the rebel's chest. As Ragnar drove deeper into the room a chainsword slashed in from the left, glancing off his left pauldron and tearing open his chin. Without hesitation, the young Space Wolf tore upwards with his keening frost blade, severing the rebel's arm near the elbow.

There was another flash, this time behind Ragnar, as Haegr fired at another target. The young Space Wolf glimpsed the rebel who'd struck him, reeling away, blood jetting from his shorn arm. Another traitor cowered on the floor near the far wall, his blood spattered hands pressed to his face. Ragnar shot them both for good measure.

Thunder and man-made lightning burst again and again in the confined space. Guardsmen thrashed and spun, hammered to the ground by bolt pistol shells. Within moments, the survivors broke and ran, loosing ragged volleys of lasgun fire as they fled down an adjoining passageway to the north.

Ragnar heard Haegr and Torin step to the mouth of the passageway and fire on the retreating troops. The young Space Wolf stood near the centre of the dark room and tried to get his bearings. He swayed unsteadily on his feet. Strange smells assaulted his senses over the reek of propellant and the stink of ruptured organs. The hairs on the back of his neck prickled. Somewhere, impossibly far away, he thought he heard a howl.

The rest of the team spread out into the room. In the darkness, Haegr chuckled cruelly. 'The fools should have stayed put,' he said. 'I've never met a man who could outrun a bolt pistol shell!'

'There's a room at the far end of the passageway,' Torin cut in. 'I can see some sort of faint, purple glow.'

Sorcery, Ragnar thought. That had to be the source of his hallucinations. Madox and the Thousand Sons served the dreaded Changer of Ways, a vile god of madness and illusion. Now, it appeared that the rebels were turning to their unholy patrons for help against the implacable Wolves.

Ragnar peered around the dark room, struggling to focus. Time was running out. Beyond the danger of whatever sorceries the rebels were trying to invoke, the extraction flight would be over the base, circling and strafing any traitor vehicles that emerged from their shelters. They couldn't remain for long. If they weren't back on the surface within a few minutes, there wouldn't be anyone waiting to take them back to base. He didn't want to try his odds fighting his way back on foot with half a dozen enemy prisoners in tow.

The young Space Wolf tried to summon the maps of the bunker complex to the forefront of his mind. He knew that the vault adjoined the main war room on this level, but how many passageways connected to it? The spilled blood in the room made it difficult to think. Ragnar started to pace, fighting the urge to charge off into the gloom in search of something to kill. Sounds echoed in the darkness. A howl seemed to echo from another passageway to the south.

'Did you hear that?' he hissed.

To Ragnar's surprise, Torin answered at once. 'I did. It could be Sigurd or the other team. If they're pinned down, we're the only ones in position to reach the vault.'

Ragnar stifled a curse. Torin was right. He was letting his imagination get the better of him, and time was wasting. He worked his way past the fallen bodies of the rebel soldiers and reached the mouth of the north passageway, where he too could see a dim, purple glow pulsing slowly at the far end. As he passed Torin, he whispered, 'Is there anything else you feel? Do you see shadows?'

'Yes,' Torin whispered back, 'perhaps worse than before, but let's worry about that later. For now, let's just get down this corridor.'

Ragnar nodded to himself. He shouldered his way alongside Haegr and checked the ammo load for his pistol. Satisfied, he focused on the light in the distance and set off at a loping run with the rest of the team behind him.

They passed through half a dozen small rooms along the way, cluttered with debris and devoid of life. As they drew closer to the pulsing, ethereal light, Ragnar could feel the invisible tides of sorcery washing over him in waves of oily filth. A strange, acrid stench burned in his nostrils and set his teeth on edge. Buzzing, atonal notes echoed in his ears, growing louder with each step he took.

Distracted as he was, Ragnar didn't notice the flakboard barrier until he was within three metres of the end of the passageway. The enemy had laid boards over the doorway to well above human height, their grey sides reflecting the shifting purple light from the ceiling of the room beyond.

Ragnar slowed his pace at once. 'Barrier ahead,' he said gruffly, his voice sounding tinny and distorted over the infernal buzzing in his ears. 'We'll get the plasma gun–'

Haegr laughed. The sound was deep and guttural, like the growl of a bear. 'A barrier for you perhaps,' he growled, 'but not for mighty Haegr!'

The huge Space Wolf charged right at the slabs of flakboard, his thunder hammer ready in his hand. With a bloodthirsty shout, he crashed against the barrier. The flakboard exploded inward in a shower of debris, falling apart so easily that Haegr stumbled forward with an awkward shout into a hail of gunfire and a chorus of excited cries.

'Morkai's black breath!' Ragnar shouted angrily, and then chased off after Haegr. Shouts and war cries echoed after him as Torin and the Blood Claws took up the chase.

Sharp blasts of thunder rang from the walls of the chamber as Ragnar charged through the doorway and found himself in the bunker's expansive war room. Situation tables and logic engines had been over-turned or moved to create defensive positions across the wide, rectangular room, and more than a score of huge, burly figures stood or crouched behind their barricades and unleashed a storm of fire upon Haegr and Ragnar both. Beyond them, at the opposite side of the war room, Ragnar saw a pair of gleaming steel doors: the entrance to the bunker's emergency vault.

Stubber shells whipped through the air around Rag-nar or rang off his ceramite armour. One gouged a fiery path across the side of his head before ricochet-ing off his thickened skull. Tracer fire criss-crossed around him in a deadly web of shells. A few metres away, Haegr had crashed against the face of an upended hololith table and was smashing at the trai-tors on the other side with his crackling, blood smeared hammer. Bullets sparked and howled off the curved surfaces of his armour, though Ragnar saw where almost half a dozen rounds had left red-rimmed holes in the burly warrior's arms, waist and legs. The hits didn't seem to slow Haegr in the least.

A heavy blow struck Ragnar in the left arm, and fiery pain blossomed just above his elbow. Snarling, the young Space Wolf turned and blasted away at the rebels taking cover behind the barricades to his left. A huge figure reared up behind a broken logic engine.

Ragnar caught sight of a twisted, misshapen hunk of gleaming muscles and a scarred lump that might once have been a human head. The mutant turned its beady red eyes on Ragnar and levelled a short-barrel heavy stubber at him. Roaring, the young Space Wolf charged at the mutant, blazing away with his bolt pistol. Shell after shell rocked the monster, blowing gory holes through its massive arms and torso, but the mutant refused to die.

Its heavy stubber hammered at Ragnar, spitting a stream of tracer rounds at the onrushing Space Wolf. Hammer blows struck Ragnar in the chest and abdomen, but the blessed armour plate held against the heavy stubber rounds. Howling like a beast, Ragnar leapt onto the toppled logic engine and buried his blade in the monster's cartilaginous skull. Sickly grey and yellow matter spewed from the frost blade's whirring teeth, but the mutant refused to die. It howled and thrashed, throwing down its smoking gun and reaching for Ragnar's blade. Horrified, Ragnar shot the monster twice in the face and dashed its blasphemous corpse to the floor.

Howling, gibbering figures rushed at the young Space Wolf from every direction. A Guardsman with a skinned face swung a chainsword at Ragnar's left leg. Ragnar parried the stroke with his frost blade and kicked the onrushing rebel in the head, bursting it like a melon. Another mutant, this one wearing the tattered uniform of a PDF staff officer, wrapped a long, barbed tentacle around Ragnar's left ankle and with surprising strength hauled the Space Wolf off his feet. He landed heavily, smashing his head and shoulders against the metal and glass case of the logic engine before rolling, senseless, to the floor.

For less than half a second he was too stunned to move. Sounds rolled like surf in his ears: shouts, gunshots, screams and thudding blows. A blade of some kind smashed into Ragnar's back again and again, grinding off the armour. Figures crowded above him; a gun went off, the round burying itself in his backpack. Then a tentacle squirmed wetly around his throat and began to squeeze.

Ragnar roared like a wounded beast and lashed out with his whirring blade, shearing through ankles in an arc around his head. Mutants shrieked and toppled like felled trees, bleeding their lives out onto the floor. Ragnar used the impetus of the swing to flip onto his back, his bolt pistol hammering at the foes still looming above him. Three mutants reeled backwards with smoking holes in the backs of their heads. The tentacle around Ragnar's throat came away with a spasmodic jerk.

An upended table nearby exploded in a blue ball of plasma, scattering flaming debris across the room. Two mutants staggered away from the explosion, blinded and firing wildly into the melee. Battle chants and bloodthirsty cries rang from the stone walls as the Blood Claws in Ragnar's team charged into the fray. Ragnar caught sight of Haegr carving a gory path through a knot of struggling mutants, bursting them apart with earth shaking blows from his hammer. A shadow passed across the young Space Wolf's vision, but this time it was Torin, leaping nimbly over a barricade of smashed logic engines and opening the throats of the mutants hiding behind them.

For a moment, the room seemed to spin. Ragnar felt as though he was falling, but then he heard a guttural voice snarl into his ear. *'Watch your head!'*

Something in the tone of the voice galvanised him. Ragnar rolled to the left, just as a roaring chainblade smashed into the ferrocrete where his head had just been.

Heart racing, Ragnar threw a blind swing behind him as he lurched to his feet. His frost blade swept through empty air, and then he heard the chainblade's throaty rasp, and a terrible blow struck him in the back of his left thigh.

The pain was immense. For a brief, agonising instant, Ragnar could feel the teeth of the chainblade tearing through his flesh. He staggered, but his sacred armour sensed the impact and locked his left knee-joint to keep him upright. Snarling in agony, the young Space Wolf spun on his immobilised leg, barely warding off a second blow aimed at his neck.

He found himself staring at an enormous, hyper-muscled mutant, wielding a two-handed chainsword in its clawed fists. Ragnar recognised the weapon at once: it was an eviscerator, a ponder-ous but devastating weapon favoured by would-be martyrs in the Guard's Ecclesiarchal auxiliaries. The young Space Wolf realised that the leering mutant was wearing the tattered remains of a priest's home-spun robes. An Imperial aquila, once the priest's most prized possession, hung upside-down on a necklace of body parts strung around the mutant's bull-like neck.

The mutant gibbered a stream of blasphemies and pressed its attack. The eviscerator was a clumsy weapon in human hands, but the muscle bound trai-tor wielded it like a willow-switch. Ragnar blocked one powerful blow after another, knowing that if his defence failed, even for a moment, the mutant would hack him in two.

A blurring stroke leapt at Ragnar's face. The young Space Wolf blocked the eviscerator in a shower of sparks, and shot the mutant in the left knee. The monster staggered, bellowing through a mouth full of pointed teeth, but it pressed its attack without pause.

The mutant charged forwards, slashing across Ragnar's left pauldron and leaving a deep gash in the ceramite. A lightning-fast return strike nearly took off half the young Space Wolf's face. Ragnar shot the mutant twice more, once in the belly and once in the groin, and this time, when the mutant lurched beneath the impacts, the young Space Wolf lashed out with his frost blade and severed the traitor's left hand at the wrist. Hot blood spurted onto Ragnar's face as the mutant howled in agony, and the young Space Wolf rushed in to finish off the traitor, but the former priest dropped its weapon and seized Ragnar's sword wrist in a vice-like grip.

Ragnar felt servos whine under intolerable pressure as the mutant closed its fist. The cuff of his gauntlet began to deform under the pressure. Bones grated in his wrist. Ragnar put the bolt pistol to the mutant's head and pulled the trigger, but the weapon was empty.

The mutant looked into Ragnar's eyes and hissed cruelly. Ragnar felt a wave of panic as the bones in his wrist and arm began to splinter. It was as though a wild beast came howling up from deep in his breast. With a savage growl, Ragnar leapt forward and buried his teeth in the mutant's over-muscled neck.

He bit deep, feeling flesh and cable-like muscle tear within his powerful jaws. Blood, hot and bitter, filled his mouth. The mutant shrieked, pummelling Ragnar with the stump of its left arm, but the young Space Wolf wrenched his head left and right, widening the wound and digging for the pulsing arteries buried within the neck.

Ragnar could feel the heat of the mutant's heart-blood. He hungered for it, longing to feel it spilling in a flood over his gaping jaws. It was the purest, most vivid thing he'd felt in his entire life. For a fleeting instant, Ragnar was gone. What remained behind was something raw and elemental: a wolf in name and deed.

He tore out the mutant's throat, and then he started to feed.

NINE
Wolf-bitten

A POWERFUL BLOW smote Ragnar on the side of the head. The force of it knocked the young Space Wolf onto his side, but he was back upright in moments, showing his red slicked fangs and crouching protectively over his kill. Sigurd's pale face appeared before him, blood spattered and severe.

'*By the holy name of Russ the Primarch I take your soul into my hands, Ragnar Blackmane!*' The priest's voice trembled, but the words were powerful, infused with the strength of centuries of faith. Ragnar blinked, drawing back from the image of a wolf's skull amulet that Sigurd brandished before his eyes.

'*The wolf cannot have you! Your heart is not yours to give, but belongs to the Allfather, now and forever more! Remember your oaths, son of Fenris! Remember who you are!*'

The words were like the tolling of a bell inside his head, cold and bright and irresistible. He fell heavily onto the floor, shaking his head dazedly.

After a moment, Ragnar's vision cleared. Sigurd the Wolf Priest loomed above him, his wide eyes fearful, but his expression hardened into a mask of determination. His Iron Wolf amulet was clenched in one gauntleted hand.

Ragnar could feel blood trickling over his lips and staining his breastplate. A shudder passed through him. The young Space Marine rose to his knees with an effort, and as he did so he noticed the bloody figure sprawled beside him. Ragnar looked down at the mangled corpse of the former priest and felt a wave of horror and revulsion crash down upon him. Blessed Russ, he thought despairingly, I'm wolf-bitten.

'Forgive me,' he said hoarsely, unable to tear his eyes away from the gaping wound in the mutant's throat.

'Forgiveness is earned in battle,' Sigurd said coldly. 'Stand and fight like a man, Ragnar, not an animal.' The Wolf Priest brandished his crozius before the young Space Wolf. 'Just as Russ overcame the wolf inside him out of love for the Allfather, so too must you rise above the beast within. Now get up. The foe awaits.'

Nodding, Ragnar lurched to his feet. The battle in the war room was over. Sigurd and the remaining Blood Claws had arrived and overwhelmed the remaining traitors as Ragnar struggled with the huge mutant. Smoke and the stench of burned flesh hung in the air, and the bodies of the traitor Guardsmen lay in bloody heaps behind their makeshift barricades. Harald and his pack-mates stood among the carnage, clutching their weapons and watching the exchange between Ragnar and Sigurd with wary, fearful eyes. It was all Ragnar could do not to hang his head in shame.

A heavy blow to the shoulder nearly knocked the young Space Wolf off his feet. Haegr loomed over Ragnar, chuckling deep in his throat. 'You call that a bite? Mighty Haegr would have taken that monster's head off with a single snap of his jaws!'

The huge Space Wolf's laugh was infectious. Soon, every warrior in the room was laughing along with him, but for Sigurd and Ragnar.

'You want something to chew on, come over here and try your teeth on this,' Torin said, pressing his fingertips to the cold steel doors of the vault. 'Our time is almost up, and the Allfather alone knows what they're up to inside.'

Ragnar rubbed his chin with the back of his hand and turned to Sigurd. 'Have you got any charges left?'

'Two,' the Wolf Priest said, and nodded to Harald. The Blood Claw pack leader waved a pair of his men forward, and they began setting the charges against the door.

Harald turned to Sigurd. His eyes passed over Ragnar, as though afraid to see what lurked within the young Space Wolf's gaze. 'We're sure to kill everyone inside when these go off,' he said.

'No,' Ragnar replied, shaking his head as he reloaded his pistol. 'These doors are doubly reinforced, designed to protect the general staff in the event of a major attack. More likely the shockwave will rebound back on us, so I suggest standing well off to either side of the door.'

The battered and bloodied Space Wolves quickly took up positions around the vault. Ragnar could still feel the sickly wash of unclean energies rippling from within. He nodded to the Blood Claw waiting at the threshold. The warrior keyed the fuse and leapt clear.

Sure enough, a tremendous concussion shook the entire room, throwing the armoured warriors back against the stone walls and sending clouds of broken debris flying through the air. When the smoke cleared, Ragnar leapt forward, weapons ready, and found a hole melted through the thick steel doors just wide enough for a Space Marine to fit through. He threw himself into the gap while the metal edges were still red-hot, with Torin, Haegr and Sigurd just a few steps behind him.

The vault was a small redoubt, with a narrow, thick-walled passageway beyond the molten doors that opened into an octagonal chamber barely ten metres across. Two bodies, charred almost beyond recognition, were sprawled on the stone floor at the far end of the passageway. Beyond them lay a scene of bloody pandemonium.

There were perhaps twenty officers and staff aides crammed into the chamber, shouting and babbling desperate pleas to their newfound gods. Their ornate uniforms were torn and stained where they had dug into their flesh with ceremonial knives, and their faces were painted in fresh blood. More blood had been spilled on the floor. A young orderly, little more than fifteen, had been dragged to his knees and slit from ear to ear, and the red flood that had poured from his narrow throat had been used to paint a blasphemous circle in the centre of the room. It was towards this terrible sigil that the rebels directed their pleas, their gore-stained hands outstretched in abject worship. As Ragnar charged into their midst he saw a ghostly figure take shape within the sigil. It was a towering form clad in ancient, baroque armour of blue and gold, its edges inlaid with blasphemous sigils, and its curved plates decorated with charms and fetishes of bone and withered skin. Flickering purple flames glinted hungrily in the oculars of the Chaos champion's horned helmet, fixing Ragnar with a glare of eternal malice. In one hand, the sorcerer held a sword made from tooth, horn and soulless, black iron. Flames leapt hungrily in the palm of his other hand, hissing and spitting in the dank air.

For a fleeting moment Ragnar's heart leapt with bloodthirsty joy at the thought that he'd come face-to-face with Madox himself. Yet there was no glint of recognition in the sorcerer's strange eyes as he raised his blazing hand and called out a horrific string of syllables in a raw, hateful voice.

A howling torrent of pink and purple fire burst from the sorcerer's hand, aimed right at Ragnar's chest. The bolt struck one of the rebel officers a glancing blow as it passed, and the traitor dissolved right before the young Space Wolf's eyes. Cursing fearfully, Ragnar threw himself to the side and the sorcerous flame struck his right pauldron a glancing blow. He heard the ceramite hiss and *scream* beneath the blast, scattering molten droplets upon the floor. The bolt continued on, missing Haegr by a hair's breadth and crashing into the onrushing form of Sigurd.

The sorcerous flames washed over the Wolf Priest in a chorus of thin, unearthly howls and a crackle of

brittle thunder. Two Blood Claws to either side of the
priest were thrown to the floor by the blast, but Sigurd
was unmoved. The flames curled away from the
rosarius that the Wolf Priest held before him, and he
called out in a powerful voice, 'Traitor! Servant of false
gods! I abjure you, warrior of the Thousand Sons!
Look upon the sons of the Wolf and despair!'

The Thousand Sons Chaos Space Marine laughed at
the Wolf Priest and uttered a stream of vile curses that
caused the rebel Guardsmen to fall thrashing to the
floor. Baring his teeth, Ragnar gathered his courage
and charged at the unholy warrior, snapping off shots
with his bolt pistol as he went.

Explosive rounds detonated harmlessly against the
champion's breastplate and helm, leaving scarcely a
mark on the ensorcelled armour. Undaunted, Ragnar
stepped close and unleashed a storm of deadly blows
with his master crafted frost blade, fully intending to
chop the Chaos Space Marine to pieces.

Not a single blow found its mark. Whether by sorcery or pure, deadly skill, the champion blocked or
evaded Ragnar's every move. The huge figure moved
like quicksilver, seeming to anticipate the young Space
Wolf's attacks, and countering them with disdainful
ease. At one point Ragnar sensed he'd found an opening in the sorcerer's guard and nearly found himself
impaled on the champion's unnatural blade.

A shadow flowed into Ragnar's field of vision to his
left. Torin was there, catching the sorcerer's blade
against his chainsword. Sensing an opportunity, Ragnar lunged forward with a slashing cut to the
champion's shoulder, but the Chaos Space Marine fell
back, dodging the blow.

Shouts and battle cries echoed in the confined space as the rebel troops reared up from the stone floor like beasts, and threw themselves at the Space Wolves. Dimly, Ragnar heard Sigurd repudiating the traitor Guardsmen in a loud, sonorous voice over the roar of chainblades and the bark of laspistols. Then a mountainous form loomed to the young Space Wolf's right and unleashed an earth shaking blow upon the Chaos champion. Haegr laughed as the sorcerer leapt backwards out of the path of the falling hammer. 'That's it, traitor! Dance like a maid!' he roared. 'You can't match blows with mighty Haegr!'

The sorcerer's hateful gaze never wavered, however, as he fell back, step by step, across the chamber. Ragnar counted the steps and gauged their distance to the far wall. He'll have his back up against the bricks in a few more metres, he thought, pressing his attack, and the bastard's too good not to know it, too. He's trading space for time.

A flash of understanding nearly stopped Ragnar in his tracks. 'Ambush!' he cried out, just as the air seemed to thicken and tear like rotted parchment, and a host of gibbering horrors appeared in the Space Wolves' midst.

Something heavy and rank landed wetly behind Ragnar and uttered a piping, lunatic cry. Fearful of turning his back on the deadly Chaos Marine, the young Space Wolf pivoted on his back foot and thrust out his pistol at a writhing column of pink and purple flesh. The daemon's four thorny tentacles wrapped around Ragnar's arm and chest, and the column of muscle contracted, hauling the young Space Wolf towards the creature's serrated beak.

Ragnar cried out as the black beak gaped mere centimetres from his skull. Then he felt the lash of another set of tentacles around his neck and waist, and he was jerked to a painful halt. Yet another daemon had trapped him in its talons, and now the two unholy creatures gibbered and squawked at one another as they vied for his flesh.

An entire pack of tentacled horrors filled the octagonal space, snapping and lashing out at everything that moved. As Ragnar struggled, he saw a pair of rebel Guardsmen torn to pieces in a messy spray of blood and entrails. Sigurd reeled within the grasp of a trio of snapping monsters, thick purple ichor smoking from the crackling edges of his crozius. The Blood Claws were beset on every side, but Harald stood in their midst, holding the burning husk of a daemon in his power fist and shouting a rallying cry to his men.

Growling angrily, Ragnar squeezed the trigger and the bolt pistol bucked in his hand, blowing a smoking hole in the daemon standing before him. Shrieking, the monster recoiled, drawing its tentacles still tighter. The daemon behind Ragnar pulled back just as fiercely, and the young Space Wolf felt the bones in his neck creak from the strain. With a savage curse, he lashed out with his free hand, and the frost blade slashed through two of the tentacles that bound him. Ichor gushed over Ragnar's armour as the daemon in front of him unwrapped its remaining tentacles and tried to slither away. Immediately, the young Space Wolf was hauled backwards towards his second assailant, but Ragnar levelled his bolt pistol and fired twice more at the wounded daemon, blasting its head apart in a shower of dissolving flesh. Then he spun in mid-air, levelling his frost blade and impaling the daemon that had been so hungry to draw him into its embrace. The rune-marked chainsword tore through the daemon's abominable form, causing it to discorporate into a cloud of foul, clinging mist.

Ragnar twisted as he fell, landing hard on his back and skidding across the stone floor. His bolt pistol came up, seeking targets. The entire chamber was filled with a riot of struggling, slashing bodies, and the crash of battle roared surf-like in his ears. The light inside the chamber seemed to pulse and shift. Shadows flitted at the corners of the young Space Wolf's eyes, but he muttered a prayer to Russ under his breath and focused on the battle at hand.

He caught sight of a Blood Claw grappling with a snapping, strangling daemon a few metres away and put a bolt-round through the monster's nominal head. Another warrior went down beneath the thrashing tentacles of a pair of purple horrors. Ragnar pumped shell after shell into the daemons' muscular bodies until the Space Wolf managed to tear his sword-arm free and hack one of the monsters in half.

A severed head bounced across the floor. The face was masked with blood, but Ragnar knew from the scent that it was one of Harald's battle-brothers. Some distance away, the young Space Wolf saw Haegr pull a lashing, snapping daemon from his chest with one broad hand and smash it against the wall beside him. Another monster darted in, bloodstained beak clashing hungrily, but the Wolfblade crushed it with a downward sweep of his massive hammer.

Another daemon erupted in a gout of purple ichor. Harald raised his dripping power fist in triumph, his fangs glinting in the faint light. Then Ragnar saw the monster rising like a snake behind the pack leader, its tentacles rearing back to strike.

Ragnar drew a bead on the daemon, and a dark shadow fell over him. He heard the rasp of ancient armour and the hungry sweep of the Chaos champion's blade as it drew back for the killing blow.

In a split-second, the young Space Wolf made his choice. Commending his soul to the Allfather, he fired an explosive round past the pack leader's head and into the daemon's gaping beak.

Shadows danced above his head. Metal crashed against metal, and Ragnar heard a rumbling, liquid growl.

Blood pounding in his temples, Ragnar faced his attacker, only to find the sorcerer grappling with a huge Space Wolf in scarred, gunmetal-grey armour. The warrior fought the champion bare-handed, one powerful hand gripping the sorcerer's sword wrist, while the other closed inexorably around the Chaos Marine's throat.

There was wiry grey fur matted along the back of the Space Wolf's hands. Ragnar caught a glimpse of curved, black talons, and then he noticed the shaggy mane and the strange shape of the warrior's head.

The Space Wolf sensed Ragnar's eyes upon him. He glanced back at Ragnar, furred snout wrinkling as his lips pulled back in a bestial snarl.

Cursing wildly, Ragnar hurled himself to the right, rolling away from the struggling figures. In moments, he clambered unsteadily to his feet and whirled around, weapons raised, but the struggling warriors were gone. They had simply vanished, as though they'd never existed.

Bolt pistols hammered, the shots echoing from the walls. Chainswords sang their harsh battle song, tearing through unnatural flesh, and then, abruptly, the only sound was the panting of exhausted men and the pained breaths of the wounded.

The stone floor seemed to sway beneath Ragnar's feet. Numb with shock, he surveyed the blood spattered chamber. Harald and half a dozen Blood Claws were still on their feet, their eyes wide and their armour splashed with gore. Three others knelt or lay among the bodies on the floor, wounded grievously but still alive. Two battle-brothers would not rise again, their bodies ripped apart by tentacles and snapping, serrated beaks.

Haegr knelt by Torin's prone form a few metres to Ragnar's left. The older Wolfblade was struggling to rise with Haegr's help, despite a deep wound in his hip.

A feeling of dread settled in Ragnar's stomach as he began to inspect the dead. Every one of the rebel officers had been torn apart by daemons or melted by sorcerous flames.

Of Sigurd, there was no sign. The young Space Wolf Priest was gone.

THEY RODE BACK aboard the Thunderhawks in silence, each warrior lost in his own grim thoughts. Harald had suggested looting the war room of every bit of useful information they could find, and they dragged away makeshift boxes full of maps, data-slates and memory cores. As they loaded up their wounded and dead, however, the Wolves could not help but feel that they had failed.

Ragnar reported to Mikal Sternmark while the raiding party was still in the air, apprising him of what had happened. The loss of Sigurd was an exceptionally hard blow to Sternmark, recalling as it did the ambush at the governor's palace a few weeks earlier. Ragnar accepted full responsibility for what had happened in the bunker, lauding the courage of Harald and his pack as well as his fellow Wolfblades, but he wasn't sure Sternmark paid attention to any of it.

The return flight took them low over the southern outskirts of the city, and it was obvious to everyone on board that the forces of the enemy were on the move. Plumes of blue-black petrochem exhaust hung in a poisonous haze over the cratered transit ways leading into the capital, as regiments of infantry and armour moved towards the tenuous Imperial lines. White flashes stuttered and strobed beyond the hills west of the city as rebel gun batteries pounded the eastern rim of the capital. More than once the Thunderhawks and their Valkyrie escorts had to dive behind broken ridges or weathered hilltops to evade rebel anti-aircraft rockets or gun positions, and it was more than an hour after dust-off before the assault ships reached friendly lines and could land at Charys starport.

They disembarked in the middle of another rocket attack, carrying their seriously wounded brothers to the port's medicae facilities through a storm of fire and shrapnel. Torin wanted no part of the packed and chaotic field hospital, with its exhausted chirurgeons and outdated equipment. He insisted his wound was minor and would heal quicker on its own. 'I'd rather lie down in the dark somewhere like a wounded hound than risk getting my limbs cut off by some drunken bone-cutter,' he declared, and his protests grew so vehement that even Haegr shrugged his broad shoulders and relented. Of course, they hadn't the faintest idea what to do with the older Wolfblade, so finally Ragnar and Haegr turned around and carried him back to the Thunderhawk.

Once they'd settled Torin back in the same suspensor-web he'd lain in on the flight out of the PDF base, Ragnar left Haegr to watch over their battle-brother and headed to the command bunker to report to Athelstane and Sternmark. On the way there he thought to check with Gabriella and ensure that she was safe, but the memory of what he'd done back at the rebel base was still painfully fresh in his mind. I'm as much a danger to her as the enemy is, he thought in despair, wondering what was going to happen to him now.

Every Space Wolf struggled with the wolf inside him. The gifts of the Canis Helix made them into peerless warriors, but such savagery was two-edged. The wolf within was always testing its limits, seeking escape in the fire of battle to rend and tear until its appetite was sated. Once the wolf had got its teeth in a man, there was no turning back, so far as Ragnar knew. Little by little his mind slipped away and his body succumbed to the influence of the helix's bestial influence. Sometimes there were Wolf Lords who took one of the Wulfen into battle with them, but most often the wolf-bitten were given into the care of the Wolf Priests and taken from the Fang, never to fight for the Chapter again.

Now he understood from whence his dreams had come, and why he had been feeling so strange of late, but the realisation gave him little comfort. He would probably be dismissed from the Wolfblade, he reasoned, and without a Wolf Lord willing to speak for him, this campaign would doubtless be his last.

Ragnar gritted his teeth and pushed such thoughts from his mind. For now, there was a battle to be fought and won.

The young Space Wolf found an open crate of field rations in the command bunker, and forced himself to eat. It had only been a few days since he'd last had a meal, but focusing on his body's mundane needs kept more troubling thoughts at bay. The ration paste also helped kill the taste of blood that still lingered in his mouth.

'WE SHOULD HAVE expected this all along, after the ambush at the governor's palace,' Sternmark said bitterly. 'What I want to know is how they knew when we were going to strike?'

The Wolf Guard was pacing along the back wall of the bunker's war room, gauntleted hands clasped tightly behind his back. Sternmark's face was fierce and brooding, his dark eyes darting from Ragnar to Athelstane and back again. The Guard general sat in a nearby camp chair, fixing the situation holo with a dark stare. From the beleaguered look on her face Ragnar suspected that she hadn't slept in days.

Ragnar stood at parade-rest at the foot of the table opposite the general. He raised his scarred chin and addressed them both. 'I don't believe it was an ambush at all,' he said. 'If the rebels wanted to lay a trap for us at the base they could have done it easily enough without putting their generals in the crossfire.'

'At this point I'm starting to have my doubts that they were generals at all,' Athelstane said with a frown. She gestured at the holo with a gloved hand. 'Their planned counter-offensive hasn't skipped a beat. Reconnaissance imagery shows that the traitors have moved another forty thousand men into the city since daybreak, and they'll be in a position to hit us by tomorrow. The Emperor alone knows how we're going to stop them.'

Ragnar shook his head. 'You didn't see the looks on their faces when we broke into the vault. Those men were high-ranking officers, all right, and they were desperate to escape,' he said. 'They had painted some kind of symbol on the floor. It looked like they were calling for help, honestly.'

'Yet the Chaos champion and his daemons killed those same men during the fight,' Sternmark pointed out. 'If the champion killed the army commanders, who then is leading the counter-offensive?'

The young Space Wolf shrugged. 'The Thousand Sons themselves, I would think,' he replied. 'We know this world is the lynchpin to their entire campaign. I can't imagine that they would trust a cabal of Guard officers to defend it.' He glanced uncomfortably at Athelstane. 'No offence, ma'am.'

Athelstane brushed the remark aside with an impatient wave of her hand. 'If the Thousand Sons are commanding the planet's defence, where are they? They must have a base somewhere on the planet, correct?'

'Not necessarily, I'm afraid.'

Heads turned at the sound of Gabriella's voice. The Navigator and Inquisitor Volt stood at the edge of the former stage, their arms piled with dusty books. She looked to the Inquisitor, who nodded and addressed the general. His face was pale and grim.

'We think we know where the Thousand Sons are striking from,' he said. 'If we are right, we are all in far greater danger than we imagined.'

TEN
Tripwire

'IT WAS LADY Gabriella who provided the key,' Volt said quickly. The inquisitor shuffled up onto the stage and spread his weathered books on the situation table. The holo image above the table warped into a storm of rainbow hued static as Volt covered many of the hololith's projector eyes.

'What's all this about?' Athelstane asked, unable to conceal a note of irritation in her voice.

The inquisitor didn't seem to hear the general at all. 'As focused as I was on events here on Charys, I failed to pay close attention to reports from the other affected worlds across the subsector,' Volt said, fumbling with his trembling, bandaged hands at the iron lock and hinge securing one of the tomes. The book's cover was smoke stained and charred along the edges, and one corner of its heavy, cream-coloured pages was spotted with red.

'A… a campaign of this size, with so much preparation, it should have been obvious that there were deeper patterns in play,' Volt said, almost to himself, as he rifled through the thick pages. 'The diversionary attacks, yes, and the choice of targets… Ah! Here,' he said, gripping the bottom of the open book with both hands and turning it around so that Athelstane and Sternmark could see. 'This is what I'm talking about.'

The general and the huge Space Wolf leaned over the table. Volt had opened the book to a page covered in hand lettered High Gothic script. Spread across the pages was a vast, intricate circle, inscribed with dense patterns of blasphemous runes. Athelstane caught just a glimpse and turned away, making the sign of the aquila and muttering a prayer under her breath. Sternmark raised his eyes and studied the inquisitor carefully.

'This is not the symbol I saw in the governor's palace,' he said.

'No, not at the palace!' Volt snapped, his grey eyes blazing. He turned and beckoned to Ragnar. 'You were at Hyades, were you not? Tell me what you see.'

Frowning bemusedly, Ragnar stepped over to the table. The lines etched in red across the page burned into his mind, calling up a memory of the tense shuttle flight off the beleaguered Imperial world. He glanced from Volt to Gabriella. 'It's the symbol we saw burning over the capital city,' he said.

'Aha!' Volt said, pleased to hear the young Space Wolf's confirmation. 'This is what is known as a cornerstone, an anchoring sigil designed to shape the boundaries of a much larger occult symbol,' he said. 'In my time, I've seen them spread across the hab blocks of a small hive city, even once across the breadth of an entire island.' He traced a finger across the surface of the page. 'Only once in history has anyone attempted such a feat on an *interstellar* scale.'

Volt turned his attention to the remaining books on the table, searching through them impatiently. Gabriella stepped forward quietly and handed over a battered tome from the top of her stack. The inquisitor looked up with a grunt of surprise and took the volume with a mutter of thanks. 'It happened around thirteen hundred years ago,' he said, flipping quickly through the ancient pages. 'A traitor named Arsenius Talvaren tried to open a permanent gateway to the Eye of Terror, centred on Holy Terra itself.'

Athelstane, Sternmark and Ragnar shared incredulous looks. The general shook her head. 'Obviously, he failed,' she said.

'Obviously, yes,' Volt replied. 'The attempt was doomed almost from the very start, but the madman's underlying theory was *entirely sound*, from an arcane standpoint.' He paused at a particular page, reading closely, and then nodded to himself. Volt looked up from the book. 'Lord Sternmark, come here and take a look at this for a moment,' he said. 'Tell me if this is more familiar to you.'

The powerful champion moved slowly around the perimeter of the table, a look of dread settling like a mask over his features. He looked down at the book, and grimaced at once. 'It is similar,' he admitted, 'very similar.'

'So you're telling me that the traitors are trying to pry open the Eye of Terror?' Athelstane asked, her stoic expression tinged with concern.

Volt snapped the tome shut. 'No, not this time,' he said. 'Talvaren, the mad genius, overreached himself. He could not master the forces necessary for such a feat, and even if the Inquisition hadn't stopped him on Luna, the demands of the ritual would have destroyed him.' The inquisitor glanced at Sternmark and the general. 'Here on Charys we're dealing with forces that are altogether more powerful and sophisticated.'

'Then what, pray tell, are they attempting?' Athelstane asked, her patience clearly nearing its limit.

'A bilocation,' Volt said gravely. 'A... link, if you will, between Charys and a daemon world within the Eye.'

The lady commander rubbed her brow with an augmented hand. 'I thought you just told me that wasn't possible,' she growled.

Lady Gabriella cleared her throat diplomatically. 'A co-location is not the same as a conduit,' she said, setting her books on the table. 'Because the Eye of Terror is a location where the warp spills into physical space, the notion of distance and time within the region is fluid,' she said. 'This is the same reason why we use the warp to travel between the stars.'

'Yes, yes, I know all that,' the general said with an impatient nod.

'Well, think of the warp as a fast-flowing river,' the Navigator continued. 'A person could either walk along the bank to get from one town to another downstream, or he could leap into the water and be rushed there at a much faster rate. Now, what Talvaren tried to do was create a tributary of that river, allowing the water to flow from the Eye of Terror directly to sacred Terra, a tremendous feat that had little chance of success.'

Gabriella reached into her belt and removed her vox-unit. 'We think Madox is trying to strain the fabric of reality around Charys and create a shadow of the world inside the Eye of Terror.' She extended her hand slowly, edging the rounded vox-unit into the projector field of the hololith. As the object occluded the edge of the projection field it created an oval shaped dark patch in the shimmering, distorted map.

Sternmark glowered at the shadow before him. 'The Eye of Terror is hundreds of parsecs away,' he protested. The Eye was a vast stellar region within the Segmentum Obscuras, where the Chaotic energies of the warp bled into the physical universe. It was a realm of horror and madness, an eternal battlefield where the worshippers of Chaos warred for the favour of their uncaring gods. After the Horus Heresy, the Traitor Legions of the Warmaster Horus fled into the Eye, where they continued to plague the Imperium with deadly raids and ruinous Black Crusades.

'Remember that within the warp there is no notion of space or distance,' the Navigator said. 'A location can be fixed by will and ritual alone, and Inquisitor Volt suspects that a series of daemon worlds within the Eye are maintaining cornerstone sigils to stabilise the shadow world as well. The sigil within the governor's palace provides the glue that conjoins the two worlds.' She turned to Ragnar. 'It's this ritual that is causing the strange turbulence in the warp I spoke of.'

Ragnar nodded thoughtfully. *It also explains the sense of dislocation Torin and I felt, and perhaps even the hallucinations.* 'Then the Thousand Sons are simply stepping between worlds when they attack us.'

Gabriella nodded. 'Yes, exactly.'

'But to what end?' Athelstane demanded. 'I'm going to assume that what you just told me is possible, but even so, surely pulling it off would have to consume enormous resources.'

'Yes, indeed,' Volt nodded. 'We can't even speculate on what the traitors had to do in order to create the cornerstones within the Eye, but it's obvious that they devoted many years and a huge investment of effort to arranging the rituals across this subsector.'

'Then what do they stand to gain from all this?' the general asked.

'Several things,' Volt replied. 'First, it gives them a secure base of operations from which to pursue their efforts on Charys. They can strike us anywhere, at any time, and retreat to safety without fear of pursuit. It also allows them to tap into the limitless power of the Eye to fuel their sorcery.'

'But what's their objective?' Athelstane snapped. 'That's the one piece of information I need, inquisitor. If I know what they're after, I can try to counter it.'

Ragnar remembered the war council back on Fenris. 'The runes say that the Thousand Sons have a plan to bring about the downfall of our entire Chapter,' he said. 'That's why Madox is here.' And the spear as well, he thought.

Inquisitor Volt looked sidelong at Ragnar. 'As to what their ultimate goal is, neither I nor Lady Gabriella can say,' he continued, 'but we do know that the heart of the enemy's power lies not on Charys, but upon its shadow twin within the Eye.'

'Then that is where we must strike,' Ragnar said at once.

Athelstane interrupted with a harsh bark of laughter. The bitter amusement died at once as she saw the look on the young Space Wolf's face. 'You're serious,' she said incredulously. 'But... that's not possible.'

Volt glanced at Gabriella. 'We think it is,' the inquisitor said, gesturing to her. 'Please explain.'

Gabriella nodded. 'The *Fist of Russ* made orbit not too long ago,' she began. 'Shipmaster Wulfgar reports that she has sustained severe damage, but her warp drive is intact. We could place a strike team onboard and use the ship to enter the warp.' The Navigator took a deep breath. 'Providing we activated the drive close to the planet, the ship would cross the barrier into the immaterium at the point where the shadow world is anchored.'

The general interjected with a peremptory sweep of her hand. 'Now, forgive the interruption, my lady, but I know enough about warp travel to know that the ship is surrounded by a force field that keeps it isolated from the immaterium–'

'The Geller field, yes,' Gabriella said. 'It projects a pocket of reality around a ship travelling through the warp that keeps the forces of Chaos at bay. Naturally, we would have to deactivate it before making the attempt.'

Athelstane was struck speechless. Finally she stammered, 'That would be suicide.'

'Normally, yes,' Gabriella agreed, 'but not in this case. Just as the co-location causes some of the warp to spill over into the physical realm, the reverse would apply to the shadow world. There should be a pocket of stable reality around the planet strong enough to keep the ship from being destroyed outright.'

'*Should*,' Athelstane echoed. 'All of this is theory. You haven't one shred of proof that any of this is true.'

Volt raised his chin. 'It fits the evidence at hand,' he replied archly.

'I can only take your word for that,' Athelstane replied. 'My experience doesn't help much in matters like these, but I *do* know what will happen if you've guessed wrong and you head off into the warp without a Geller field. You, the ship, and everyone on board will be destroyed.'

Mikal Sternmark folded his arms and glowered thoughtfully at the books scattered across the situation table. 'I'll gather the Wolf Guard,' he said, 'plus a pack of Grey Hunters and Einar's Long Fangs. We could–'

'No lord, you can't,' Athelstane declared. 'I won't let you do this.'

Sternmark slowly turned to the general. 'You forget yourself, lady commander,' he said coldly. 'You have no authority over the Sons of Russ.'

Athelstane rose to her feet and stared up at the towering Space Wolf. 'Perhaps not,' she said, 'but you swore an oath to protect the people of this world, and without you Charys is most assuredly lost. Every squad you pull out of the battle line makes our defence that much more precarious. Are you willing to risk losing an entire world for the sake of a suicidal gamble like this?'

'What other choice do we have?' Sternmark shot back. 'Volt is right. The Thousand Sons can strike our lines at will, and there are no reinforcements coming. At best, we're just delaying the inevitable. Better to strike a blow against the enemy than sit in our holes and let them come for us!'

'And what if they're wrong?' Athelstane said. 'If that ship hits its warp drive and there's no stable pocket of reality on the other side, you'll have thrown away not just your life, but *millions* of others as well. Make no mistake, without you and your men we won't last twenty-four hours once the rebel counter-offensive begins.'

'Send the Wolfblade,' Ragnar interjected. The words burst from his lips before he fully knew what he was saying. 'Us and Harald's pack as well.'

Sternmark shot Ragnar a disdainful look. 'What, thirteen of you against Madox and the Thousand Sons?'

Inquisitor Volt spoke up. 'Actually, I was thinking along much the same lines,' he ventured. 'It is unlikely that the enemy is expecting this kind of attack, and a small force would have a better chance of avoiding detection.' He spread his bandaged hands. 'Of course, given the situation, I would assume command of the expedition. My skills will be able to further protect the strike team and lead it to its target.'

The Wolf Guard regarded Volt balefully for a moment, and then relented with a curt nod. 'There's still the matter of the warp turbulence,' he said. 'How do you plan on getting past that?'

Volt turned to Gabriella. She raised her head and said calmly, 'The mission will have need of an expert Navigator. Otherwise the ship could be hurled deep into the Eye and meet with disaster.'

The Wolf Guard's eyes went wide. 'No,' he said, 'I can't allow this.' He glanced at Ragnar and Volt for support. 'Lady, surely you can see that this mission is a forlorn hope at best. Even if everything goes as planned and the mission is a success, the survivors will face the full wrath of the Thousand Sons. With an attacking force this small, no one is going to survive.'

Gabriella only nodded. 'I understand, lord, and I appreciate your concern, but just as the lady commander has no authority over you or your men, neither do you hold any sway over me.' She met the Wolf Guard's eyes and gave him a faint smile. 'Rest assured, the Navis Nobilite are no strangers to sacrifice in the name of the holy Emperor.'

Sternmark thought it over. 'The Old Wolf will have my hide for a rug when he hears about this,' he growled, but he threw up his hands in surrender. 'All right. Make your preparations to depart,' he said. 'Ragnar, I'll leave it to you to give Harald the good news.'

Ragnar bowed his head to Sternmark, and with a worried glance at Gabriella he took his leave. The Navigator sketched a bow to Athelstane and the Wolf Guard. 'I'll contact the *Fist of Russ* and inform Shipmaster Wulfgar of our plans,' she said, and departed as well.

Sternmark watched them go while Inquisitor Volt gathered up his scattered tomes. Finally he sighed. 'I hope you know what you're doing,' he growled.

'As do I,' Volt answered. He straightened and fixed the Wolf Guard with a commanding stare. 'It's time we contacted the *Holmgang*.'

THE BLOOD CLAWS weren't at the staging area near the starport's command complex, and none of the headquarters staff seemed to know where they'd gone. Ragnar wasn't all that surprised, but the discovery irritated him nonetheless. As more enemy rockets plunged like arrows across the cratered expanse of the starport, Ragnar was reduced to tracing his route back to the Thunderhawk they'd flown in, and then tracking Harald's pack by scent.

He finally found them in an isolated supply bunker not far from the Thunderhawks' armoured revetments. Ragnar followed the trail down a shallow ferrocrete ramp that led to an open doorway in the bunker's flank. Two Blood Claws posted as sentries rose silently to either side of the interior doorway as the young Space Wolf stepped inside.

The bunker had been emptied out long ago, and the pack sat on the bare floors in the gloom, tending weapons and making field repairs to their armour. The three men that they'd taken to the field medicae unit had either been released or they'd decided to release themselves. They rested against one of the ferrocrete walls, letting their enhanced constitution and their armour's medical systems tend to their injuries.

Harald was sitting with a pair of packmates, cleaning and checking their weapons when Ragnar appeared. The pack leader glanced up and his face darkened into an angry scowl. 'What in Morkai's name do you want?' he snarled.

Ragnar strode purposefully into the bunker. The two Blood Claws to either side of him closed in quickly, intending to bar his way, but he stopped them in their tracks with a steely glare. 'I bring tidings from Mikal Sternmark,' he declared. 'We're going back into action.'

He sketched out the planned expedition quickly and concisely, entertaining no questions from Harald or his packmates. As he spoke, the Blood Claws shared disbelieving looks that only turned grimmer as the inquisitor's plan took shape.

When he was done, Ragnar turned back to Harald and planted his hands upon his hips. 'If you have something to say, pack leader, now is the time,' he said. He could see the challenge building behind Harald's eyes, and part of him hoped that the Blood Claw would try to do something about it.

'Who is commanding this expedition?' Harald asked. 'The last time you led us, we lost our Wolf Priest and a third of our pack. Surely Sternmark isn't about to place us in your hands again.'

The rest of the Blood Claws were silent, glaring angrily at Ragnar. The young Space Wolf bared his teeth. 'There's an inquisitor on the planet, a man named Volt. He'll be leading the force.'

Harald snorted in disgust. 'First an exile, then an inquisitor. By Morkai, we're an ill-fated bunch,' he told his men. They growled their agreement. The pack leader sneered at Ragnar. 'Next thing you know, that damned three-eyed maid of his will try her hand at us.'

'Get up,' Ragnar said coldly.

The pack leader smiled. 'Well, well,' he said. 'Struck close to home, did I?'

'I said *on your feet*.' Ragnar took a step forward. 'Take your beating like a man, not grinning up from the floor like a dog.'

Harald leapt off the floor with a snarl, blue fire crackling between his fingers as he activated his power fist. Startled shouts filled the bunker as the rest of the pack threw their bodies between the two men and tried to push them apart.

'Enough!' yelled Harald's second, the red-haired warrior called Rolfi. He grabbed Harald by the front of his armour and shook him. 'No challenges during war time! That's the Old Wolf's law!'

Harald pushed himself away with a snarl, but anger still smouldered in the pack leader's eyes. 'When we return to Fenris, then,' he declared, pointing at Ragnar with his crackling fist. 'You're going to answer for Sigurd, exile. That I swear.'

Ragnar shook off the men gripping his arms like a bear shakes off a pack of hounds. 'Let Sigurd speak for himself,' he shot back. 'I for one choose to believe he still lives.' He glared savagely at the assembled Wolves. 'Muster for battle at Thunderhawk Two in an hour,' he said. 'We're going to go and get him.'

Ragnar turned and headed for the doorway. He paused at the threshold, and looked back over his shoulder at Harald. The pack leader was still surrounded by his men, gazing angrily at the young Space Wolf's back.

One fight at a time, Ragnar thought, and stepped out into the sunlight.

THE GUARD'S POWERFUL VOX transmitters were only a short walk from the bunker's situation room. Inquisitor Volt led the way, with Sternmark pacing only a few steps behind him. The stormtroopers stationed at the door shouldered their hellguns and admitted them without a word.

Inside, Volt surveyed the crowded room. Half the space was given over to humming vox consoles, where soldiers hunched over flickering cathode screens and read off messages from sheets of flimsy parchment passed from the war room across the hall. The rest of the dimly lit room contained rack upon rack of

transmitters, receivers and power supplies. The stink
of ozone hung heavy in the cramped space. Nodding
in satisfaction, he dismissed the on-duty vox
operators and tech-priests with a murmured
command. When the door had shut on the last of the
men, the inquisitor walked over to the central console
and began adjusting the frequency controls on the
system's orbital relay.

Sternmark put his back to the door and folded his
arms. For once he was glad not to have the watchful
eyes of the skald boring into his back. A sense of
despair gripped him. He could not shake the feeling
that the situation was spiralling out of control and
nothing he did could alter its course. 'You don't have
to do this,' he said grimly.

'It is now or never,' Volt replied, fine-tuning the frequency. 'You said it yourself. There is virtually no
chance that any of us will return from this mission. I
must set things in motion before we depart–'

'That's not what I meant,' Sternmark said. 'It's too
premature to call for Exterminatus.'

Volt turned to face the dour Space Wolf. 'Do you
think I'm doing this lightly? I've been an inquisitor
for a hundred and fifty years, and do you know how
many worlds I have condemned? *None.* Not a single
one.' The inquisitor took a step towards Sternmark,
his bandaged hands trembling. 'There was always
another way to deal with the traitors and save the
innocent, *always*. We… we always found a way.' He
took a deep, shuddering breath. 'But not this time.
The enemy was too well prepared. We worked for
years, slowly penetrating the governor's household
and the PDF hierarchy, but they were aware of us

the entire time. When the traitors finally revealed themselves my... friends... were the first to die.' Volt's face grew haunted, his gaze turning inwards as he relived that bloody night in the capital. He shook his head. 'Now... there's nothing left. If we don't succeed on the shadow world, then it's only a matter of time before your positions are overrun.' Volt regained his focus with a start, like a man waking from a nightmare. 'We have to be prepared for that eventuality.'

Sternmark tried to formulate a reply, but the inquisitor turned his back on the Wolf Guard and keyed the transmitter. '*Holmgang*, this is Citadel,' Volt said, using the code name for the planetary headquarters. 'My authorisation is five-alpha-five-sigma-nine-epsilon. Please respond.'

For several long moments nothing emerged from the vox-unit except for the ghostly hiss of static. Then, faintly, a voice replied. 'Citadel, this is *Holmgang*. Countersign is gamma-alpha-seven-four-omicron-beta. What is your message?'

The battle-barge and her surviving escorts had been hiding out in the asteroid belt for weeks, powered down and maintaining vox silence to avoid detection. Volt had insisted that the ships be held in reserve once it had become clear that losses were mounting against the Chaos fleet. The barge's powerful barrage cannons and cyclonic torpedoes were a force of last resort in the event that the Imperial defenders on Charys were overwhelmed.

Volt took a deep breath and invoked the wrath of the Holy Inquisition. 'Implement Tripwire,' he said. 'Acknowledge.'

Silence hung heavy in the air as the signals crossed the void. Finally, the voice replied, 'Tripwire acknowledged. *Holmgang* out.'

The inquisitor slowly reached up and switched off the transmitter. 'Mark the hour,' he said to Sternmark. 'From this day forward the all-clear code must be sent at exactly the same time.' He turned back to Sternmark, and his expression was bleak. 'If you or Athelstane fail to send the code, the ship's master will assume that the headquarters has been overrun, and by order of the Inquisition, Charys will die.'

ELEVEN
Into the Storm

THE SHELLS FELL from orbit with a rumbling, clattering roar, passing high overhead and falling beyond the horizon to the west. White and yellow flashes lit the undersides of the thick clouds of billowing smoke above the capital, and a roll of man-made thunder sent a shiver through the ground beneath the Space Wolves' feet.

An early dusk was coming on as the strike team finally began to board their ships and rendezvous with the *Fist of Russ*. Their departure had been delayed more than four hours by rocket attacks and a surprise air raid by a squadron of rebel Valkyries late in the afternoon. Fires were still burning out of control at the fuel depot on the other side of the starport, and several of the Guard's aircraft had been damaged or destroyed. Rocket attacks had continued over the course of the afternoon as well, making repair work hazardous. It was clear to Ragnar and the rest of the Wolves that these were the opening stages of the coming enemy offensive.

The delays were further compounded by Shipmaster Wulfgar, who, upon receiving his orders from Sternmark, insisted on evacuating the cruiser of all non-essential personnel and transferring the ship's supply stores down to the planet. The off-loading took more than three hours, during which time the battle cruiser's surviving weapon batteries bombarded rebel positions in and around the capital. Wulfgar wanted to do as much as he could for the embattled defenders while he had the chance, and no one, not even Sternmark, sought to gainsay him. No one said it aloud, but everyone knew that once the *Fist of Russ* broke orbit and entered the warp, there was little chance the crippled warship would ever return.

A grim mood hung like a storm cloud over the Wolves of Harald's pack as they queued up to board Thunderhawk Two. Thunderhawk One, where Torin had chosen to rest and recuperate from his wound, had been hit during the air raid and badly damaged by enemy bombs. Though the injured Wolfblade had managed to put out the fire raging in the assault ship's fuselage, the damage was so extensive that the Thunderhawk had been put out of action. Smoke stains still smudged the older Wolfblade's lean face, giving him a dark, glowering mien as he limped around the exterior of the Bellisarius shuttle on a pre-flight inspection.

There was a scent in the air, something thin and acrid that cut through the smell of burning petrochem and flakboard and set Ragnar's hair on end. He could see by the hunched shoulders and hooded eyes of the rest of the Wolves that they felt it, too, all but Haegr, who seemed serenely oblivious of everything but the grox thighbone he had between his teeth. Something's got under our skin, he thought, watching the Blood Claws climb aboard their waiting assault ship a few dozen metres away. *Something's burning in the blood.* The thought perplexed him, but he found himself strangely assured that he wasn't the only one in an ill humour. *It's not just me, not just the wolf inside. Surely the curse can't be clawing inside each of us.*

Gabriella seemed troubled as well, in her own way. She arrived at the shuttle silent and withdrawn, clad in partial carapace armour drawn from the Guard's meagre stores. She walked with great care across the tarmac and up the ramp into the shuttlecraft, as though burdened by the unfamiliar weight of breastplate and greaves. Ragnar had stood at the bottom of the ramp, immobile as a statue, and she passed him without a word or a sideways glance. He'd long since gone over every argument he could think of to dissuade her from joining the expedition, and not one of them seemed sufficient. It was her right, indeed, her duty, to place her life in harm's way for the good of the Imperium, and yet he could not help but feel as though he and his brothers had failed her somehow. It should never have come to this, Ragnar thought darkly.

Inquisitor Volt arrived, a short while later, disembarking from the armoured squad bay of a scarred Chimera APC. He emerged alone from the idling transport, carrying nothing more than a battered leather book case in one hand and a scabbarded sword in the other. Polished armour gleamed from beneath the folds of his dark, red robes, and the unmistakeable bulge of a bolt pistol rested upon his hip. Ragnar saw at once that the war gear had been made with Volt in mind, but the inquisitor bore it awkwardly. He reminded Ragnar of an aged veteran, long past his prime, who'd put on his old gear for the first time in a great many years. Another salvo of heavy shells rattled overhead as Volt strode across the tarmac, and he turned to mark their passing as they fell upon the far-off capital. Ragnar watched the man stare contemplatively at the distant horizon for several long minutes. Then the inquisitor raised his hand, as though in farewell. With that, he straightened and resumed his course in a swirl of crimson robes and nodded wordlessly to Ragnar as he joined Gabriella inside her shuttle.

Torin completed his check of the shuttle's thrusters, and limped over to Ragnar. His armour had been patched where the sorcerer's hellblade had torn through his hip, but the pale line of the chemical weld showed how large the wound had actually been. His voice was a husky growl, no doubt from the clouds of toxic smoke he'd inhaled fighting the fire. 'She took some fragments during that air raid, but she'll fly,' he said, 'providing Haegr hasn't managed to put on any more weight since we've been here.'

Haegr cracked open the end of the bone with his granite-like molars. 'If I have, I can work it off in a few moments by giving you a good thrashing,' he said idly.

Torin gave his battle-brother a wolfish stare, and for a moment it looked as though he welcomed the chance for a fight. The sight startled Ragnar. 'Head inside and start up the engines,' he said quickly. 'I want to launch as soon as Harald's men have boarded.'

The older Wolfblade nodded, almost sullenly, and then nodded at something past Ragnar's shoulder. 'Sternmark's coming,' he rasped, and headed up the shuttle ramp.

Bemused and deeply unsettled, Ragnar turned to see half a dozen Wolf Guard striding purposefully through the smoke towards the strike team. Sternmark led them, his helmet tucked beneath his arm and his long, black hair unbound. He seemed a different man, Ragnar thought at once. Gone were the troubled expression and the hunched, almost defeated look that he'd had inside the command bunker. Out in the open air, with guns pounding and enemy shells flying overhead, the Wolf Guard held his head high and there was a fell look in his dark eyes. He strode through the fury of war like a hero of legend, the true son of a hard and warlike people. Some of Harald's pack caught sight of Sternmark and called out his name, raising their chainblades in salute. Ragnar did so as well, drawing his frost blade free and lifting it to the sky. Even Haegr tossed his splintered bone hurriedly aside and gripped the haft of his thunder hammer.

'Mikal Sternmark, lord and captain, hail!' Ragnar called in a deep, powerful voice.

Sternmark nodded gravely to the warriors and returned their salute with a raised fist. 'There is no lord here but Berek,' he said, 'I am only his sworn man, acting in his name.' He stopped before Ragnar and called out to the nearby Blood Claws. 'Harald! Come here!' At once, the pack leader broke into a run, covering the few dozen metres between them in moments. He arrived with a clatter of armour and the faint whine of servomotors, bowing his head respectfully to the Wolf Guard. Ragnar lowered his sword, suddenly very conscious of the silent figure of Morgrim Silvertongue, the company skald, watching the proceedings from the rear of the group.

'I am heading for the front line soon,' Sternmark said without preamble. 'The enemy offensive has begun, and every warrior will be needed to hold the traitors at bay.' He paused, a frown momentarily creasing his brow as he struggled for the proper words to say.

After a moment, he continued, 'The survival of Charys depends upon you. If the Rune Priests speak true, the fate of the entire Chapter rests upon your shoulders as well. Whatever evil our foes are working you must somehow destroy it, no matter the cost.'

Harald's expression turned sombre. This was the first time he'd heard of the priests' dire predictions regarding the future of the Chapter. 'No matter the cost,' he echoed. 'You have my oath upon it.'

'And mine,' Ragnar said.

Sternmark nodded. 'I am no priest, so I have no benedictions to offer you. Nor am I a lord, to gift you with gold rings or titles. I can only give you this,' he said, offering his hand, 'and wish you good hunting.'

They clasped forearms in silence, warrior to warrior, as more rockets howled overhead. Ragnar was last, and Sternmark gripped his arm a moment longer. 'Fight well,' he said quietly. 'If we do not meet again, know that you are redeemed in the eyes of Berek's company.'

Ragnar understood what Sternmark intended. *He sends me off to die with honour,* he thought, and was moved. Yet he shook his head. 'No,' he answered, 'not yet, not until the Spear of Russ is returned to Garm. That is my oath to the Great Wolf.'

The Wolf Guard smiled grimly and nodded. 'So be it,' he said. 'Russ will know your deeds, even unto the depths of the warp.' Sternmark took a step back and saluted the two Wolves one last time. 'Until we meet again, brothers, in this life or the next,' he said. As he started to turn away, the Wolf Guard caught Haegr's eye. 'And if you get to the Halls of Russ before me, save me a sip of ale and a crust of bread, will you?'

Haegr watched the Wolf Guard and his retinue stride off, his brow furrowed in consternation. 'Now what do you suppose he meant by that?' he mused aloud.

NOT FAR FROM the starport's command bunker, the warriors of Berek's company had taken their fallen lord and laid him in state like a king of old, clad in gleaming armour and stretched upon a table of stone. His blond hair was unbound, and but for the deathly pallor of his face, Berek Thunderfist might have been sleeping, lost in red dreams of glory. His scarred power fist was laid across his chest, and his helm, which the Wolf Lord almost never wore, had been dug out of his arming chest and set by his side.

Twin braziers burned low inside the abandoned bunker, one at each end of the long table. When it became clear that the Wolf Priest's salves and incense did nothing to rouse their stricken lord, Sternmark had the censers removed and the braziers put in their place. He'd lit the wood fires himself, as his people had done on Fenris for thousands of years. The orange fire threw martial shadows against the thick walls. In the weeks since Berek had fallen, his warriors had heaped their war trophies around their lord's feet. Swords and axes, pistols and rifles, skulls of mutant and human alike filled the space around Berek nearly to ceiling height, and more were arriving every day.

A single Wolf Guard stood vigil over the fallen lord. It was all the company could spare in these desperate times. Old Thorin Shieldsplitter filled the doorway with his fearsome bulk, barring the way with his two-handed power axe. He had been the company champion before Mikal, and now he bowed his head and stepped aside as Sternmark approached to pay homage to his lord.

He entered the bunker alone, hard footsteps echoing strangely in the crowded space. The faint crackling of the fire and the smell of wood smoke reminded Sternmark of home, and for the first time in months he found himself thinking of Fenris, so many light-years away.

Sternmark approached the bier carefully, set his own helmet upon the floor, and slowly drew Redclaw. The ancient, rune-etched blade gleamed in the firelight as he rested its tip on the floor and sank to one knee. For a long time he stared at the blinking status runes flickering from an exposed access panel on Berek's armour. The Wolf Lord still clung to life, so faintly that the armour's powerful systems could only barely detect it. On Fenris, perhaps, something could possibly have been done, but here, on Charys, all they could do was wait, and they were nearly out of time.

The Wolf Guard cast his eyes downward, to the blinking red telltale of the melta charges set beneath the bier. If the starport perimeter was ever breached and the Imperial defenders overrun, then Thorin's last duty was to hit the detonator and ensure that their lord would never become a trophy for the enemy.

A sense of inevitability hung over Sternmark. It was like riding a longship into the teeth of a storm and perching atop a towering wave, waiting for the moment when the prow would start to dip and the terrifying plunge would begin. *Death comes for us all, sooner or later*, but it was not death that the warrior feared. A part of him welcomed the coming foe and the brutal simplicity of battle. When the swords sang and blood flowed, a man's decisions meant life or death for him alone, not uncounted thousands half a world away.

What Sternmark feared was the stain of failure, and the realisation that he was not worthy of the challenge laid before him.

'Why?' he said softly, his hands tightening on the hilt of his blade. 'Why me?'

'If not you, Mikal Sternmark, then who?'

Sternmark leapt to his feet. For the briefest instant he thought it was Berek's voice that he heard, but then he recognised the smooth, practiced tones of Morgrim the skald. Sternmark felt his cheeks burn with the shame of his confession. He whirled, teeth bared, and saw Morgrim standing silently just within the bunker's entrance. His expression was unreadable as ever, but his eyes were sharp and clear.

Watching me. Marking my every mistake.

White hot rage boiled in Sternmark's breast. The weight of the sword felt good in his hands, and then he saw that the two of them were alone. I could kill him now, he thought wildly. My shame will die with him.

He took a single step forward... and then realised what he was doing. 'Blessed Russ!' he cried, wrestling with his revulsion and rage. He glared at Morgrim, furious at himself and the skald besides. 'No wonder you skalds are called stormcrows,' he growled, 'always sticking your beaks where they don't belong!' With a conscious effort Sternmark slammed Redclaw back into its scabbard. 'What will you say of this moment, I wonder?'

Morgrim cocked his head curiously. 'I will tell of a hero and a dutiful warrior who spent his hour before battle paying homage to his lord,' he said. 'What did you imagine I would say?'

'Don't lie to me!' Sternmark roared, once again feeling the rage claw through him. A vision danced before his eyes of the skald thrashing on the bunker floor, his eyes wide and his hands pressed to the shredded ruin of his throat. The Wolf Guard shook his head savagely, trying to drive the image from his mind. Blessed Russ, he thought, what is wrong with me?

'Do you think I haven't seen you these past few weeks?' Sternmark shouted. 'Dogging my steps and noting every false move I've made? Do you think me blind to the way you judge every decision I make?'

The skald's eyes narrowed. 'It's not my place to judge you,' he said carefully. 'My duty is to bear witness, and remember the deeds of our company.' He spread his hands. 'Do you think I do this out of spite, or for an evening's entertainment? No. I remember all the deeds of our brothers so that when times are desperate and our leaders are in need of advice, I will be able to help.'

'And now you've got a fine tale of a man's failure!' Sternmark shouted. 'If you manage to survive my blunders here on Charys you'll have a cautionary tale for the next lord who comes along.'

'What blunders are those?' Morgrim asked, and the sincere interest in his voice gave Sternmark pause.

The Wolf Guard groped for the right words. 'This... this looming *defeat*,' he said, clenching his fists. 'Nothing I've done here has stemmed the tide one whit, and you well know it. We're about to be overrun. Berek's great company is about to die, and *the blame is mine.*'

Morgrim did not answer at once, instead tugging thoughtfully at his beard. Finally, he said, 'Do you imagine Berek could have done any better?'

'Of course!' Sternmark snapped. 'How many battles has he won? How many times has he led us against impossible odds and stood triumphant?'

'Five hundred and thirty-seven.'

Sternmark frowned. 'What?'

'You asked how many battles Berek's won, and I told you, five hundred and thirty-seven. That's major battles, of course. We don't concern ourselves with skirmishes or raids unless they lead to something noteworthy.'

'Are you *mocking* me, stormcrow?' the Wolf Guard asked, incredulous.

'By the Allfather, I'm not!' Morgrim said with a laugh. 'Think on this: in five hundred and thirty-seven battles, do you not imagine that Berek had occasion to feel the exact same way you do now?'

Sternmark glowered at the skald. 'Why don't you tell me?'

'Morkai's black breath! Of course he did,' Morgrim replied. 'Paxos VI; Manes Primus; the whole of the damned Lucern Suppression,' he said, ticking them off with his fingers. 'And those are just the most recent ones. That's the burden of command, Mikal Sternmark: holding the lives of your brothers in your hands and knowing that no matter what you do, they could still die. Sometimes the enemy is stronger, or more clever, or just luckier. You can only do the best that you can, and the rest is up to fate.' The skald walked past Sternmark and stood next to the bier. 'Berek is a fine lord and a mighty warrior,' he said, 'but he still walked into an ambush in the governor's palace.' He shrugged. 'Perhaps he would have done things differently, perhaps not. Every light fails in time,' the skald said. 'Battles are lost. Heroes die.'

Sternmark looked down upon his stricken lord. 'I failed him, Morgrim.'

'No,' the skald replied, 'you never shirked from your duty. What man can do more?'

The Wolf Guard considered this, and found he only had one answer. He bent and picked up his helmet, turning its battered shape over in his hands. 'When the time comes we can fight and die like Wolves,' he said softly.

'And so we shall, brother. So we shall.'

The Fist of *Russ* limped away from Charys at half power, trailing a glittering stream of leaking air and coolant in her wake. Her augurs swept the void, searching for signs of danger, while the skeleton crew aboard prayed to the Divine Emperor that they would find none. Her shields were weak, only half her guns worked, and all but one of her port thrusters were out. The crippled battle cruiser wouldn't last long against a determined group of raiders, but the young Navigator on board told them not to worry. The voyage, she assured them, would be a short one.

Smoke still stained the bulkheads on the warship's command deck, and the air still smelled of burned wiring and scorched flesh. Tech-priests walked in solemn circles across the deck, swinging censers and intoning damage control catechisms. Shipmaster Wulfgar was alone on the deck, save for a handful of his senior officers. Their faces were grim as they went about their tasks, calling out orders with an almost funereal solemnity. Every one of them had volunteered for the mission. Sailors down to their bones, they had refused to give up the ship.

Shipmaster Wulfgar stood at the command pulpit, his hands gripping the lectern before him as he looked out over the bridge, below. He had been reading passages aloud from the *Lexicanum Imperialis* as the ship sailed on through the endless night, but he had fallen silent as Gabriella had climbed quietly inside the Navigator's vault. Torin and Haegr took positions at either side of the vault's adamantium hatch, as though their presence could somehow shield the Navigator from harm. Ragnar understood how they felt. The young Space Wolf caught Volt's watchful eye, and the inquisitor gave him a nod. Ragnar took a deep breath and moved quickly to Wulfgar's side.

The ship's master turned slightly at Ragnar's approach. Despite the added height of the pulpit, the bondsman was still a few centimetres shorter than the towering Space Wolf. Ragnar saw a pair of faded picts laid across the illuminated pages of the *Lexicanum*: a young boy in a bondsman's black tunic, grinning up at the imager, and a woman, tall and severe, wearing the armoured coveralls of an engineer. Wulfgar's right hand settled protectively over them as the young Space Wolf approached.

'The engine decks report ready,' Wulfgar said. 'We are merely awaiting word from the Navigator to commence jump. The Geller field has been shut down.'

Ragnar nodded slowly. 'I understand your concerns, Shipmaster Wulfgar,' he said, 'but I trust the Lady Gabriella with my life. If she and Inquisitor Volt say that there is a world on the other side, then there is.'

Wulfgar began to speak, but thought better of it and simply nodded instead.

'She also says that there is little chance we'll find any hostile forces above the planet's surface,' Ragnar continued, 'so our arrival should go unchallenged.' He looked Wulfgar in the eye. 'So you should have no problem completing the jump cycle and returning back to real space as soon as the strike team is deployed.'

The master of the ship turned fully about to face the young Space Wolf. 'That would be your death warrant,' he said. 'It takes many hours to recharge a warp drive under optimal conditions. You'd be dead before we could return to get you, providing we could even find our way back to the proper time and place.'

Ragnar nodded. 'But the ship – and her Navigator, our solemn charge – would be able to escape.'

Wulfgar studied Ragnar for a long moment. 'You've talked this over with the inquisitor?'

'I have. We are all agreed.'

The ship's master sighed, and then nodded solemnly. 'So be it. May the Allfather protect you all.'

Ragnar nodded solemnly, secretly relieved that he'd at least found a way to place Gabriella out of harm's way. The Thunderhawk carrying the strike team could deploy within minutes of reaching the shadow world. Gabriella wouldn't even need to leave the safety of her heavily armoured vault.

A red telltale began flashing on a screen set into the lectern. Wulfgar knew its meaning with a glance. 'Signal from the Navigator,' he said, turning back to the pulpit. He drew a deep breath and cried out across the bridge. 'All hands, stand by to jump!' As an afterthought, he glanced over his shoulder at Ragnar. 'You'd best find something to hang on to. Russ alone knows what will happen when we engage the drive.'

Ragnar looked dubious. 'And holding on to a stanchion is going to help?'

The ship's master shrugged. A faint grin touched one corner of his mouth. 'It can't hurt.'

Ragnar thought it over and shrugged. It was bad enough that they were going to leap headlong into the warp without protective shielding; there was no sense tempting fate any further. He stepped over to one side and closed his hands around the railing overlooking the ship's bridge.

Moments later the jump siren began its shrill cry. 'Stand by!' Wulfgar shouted. 'Stand by... *jump!*'

Without warning, a howling wind tore across the command deck, cutting deep into Ragnar's bones. The massive battle cruiser pitched and yawed like a long-ship in the teeth of a gale, her massive superstructure groaning against the strain. Lights and strange, reflected shapes flowed like oil through the cathedral-like viewports of the bridge. The air curdled. Men screamed in terror, or ecstasy. Ragnar felt the unbridled desecration of Chaos crash over him like a wave and called out to the Allfather for deliverance.

As if in answer, the howling, groaning storm simply ceased. Ragnar staggered, clutching desperately at the rail as his body tried to compensate for the sudden shift in motion. A sense of unreality passed through him. For a moment he feared that his hand might pass through the metal rail as though it were made of smoke. Just like Charys, he thought.

The air tasted strange on Ragnar's tongue. He looked around and saw men sprawled upon the deck. Two of the tech-priests were in convulsions, sparks flying from their augmented eyes and foam speckling their lips. Even Torin and Haegr were on their hands and knees, shaking their heads drunkenly from the shock of the brief transit. Inquisitor Volt was climbing slowly to his feet, his mouth working in a silent prayer.

Red light flooded through the viewports, thick as congealed blood. Ragnar brought his head around and forced his eyes to focus on the realm beyond the stricken ship. He saw the dark curve of a world, like a sphere of ebon glass. Skeins of purple lightning ravelled across its surface, silhouetting vast, arrowhead shapes drifting like leviathans high above the shadow world.

The sky was full of Chaos ships.

TWELVE
No Matter the Cost

THE LAST SALVO of the rebel barrage landed right on target, bursting along the entire length of the Imperial barricades blocking the Angelus Causeway. Huge siege mortar rounds and Earthshaker cannon shells blew gouts of pulverised ferrocrete and structural steel dozens of metres into the air and turned human bodies into clouds of blood and vaporised flesh. Ten metres to Mikal Sternmark's right, a bunker made of salvaged masonry and quick-setting ceramite compound took a direct hit and vanished in a cloud of grey smoke and razor-edged shrapnel. Guardsmen manning firing positions to either side of the bunker were tossed into the air like broken dolls, their armour melted and their clothes alight.

Nearly three weeks of constant shelling had turned the once-prosperous commercial district that lined the causeway into a nightmare landscape of gutted buildings and smoking, debris-lined craters. The causeway itself passed through the centre of the Imperial lines. Fed by four major transit lines, the broad, six-lane road was made to ferry the produce of Charys's sprawling agri-complexes into the arms of the mercantile syndicates at the nearby starport. Columns of local granite had been raised along the entire length of the causeway, topped by severe-looking angels bearing the scales of commerce or the upraised sword of war. Nearly all of the angels had been destroyed during the long weeks of combat: all save one, who seemed to tower defiantly over the right end of the Imperials' defensive line, his sword raised to strike down the Emperor's foes.

The defenders had built their barricade from the carcasses of the bombed-out buildings that lined the causeway. Heavy slabs of ferrocrete had been dragged into place by cargo walkers brought up from the starport, and engineering teams had gone to work constructing firing steps and gun pits out of masonry and layers of flakboard. The line of fortifications stretched for a full kilometre, from one side of the causeway to the other. An entire regiment, the Hyrkoon Grenadiers, one of Athelstane's veteran units, had been ordered to hold the causeway at all costs. A full platoon of Leman Russ battle tanks had been assigned to support the defenders, their squat, blocky turrets rising threateningly from ferrocrete revetments built just behind the barricade. From their firing steps, the defenders could see for almost two kilometres down the wide, flat causeway. It was an ideal killing ground, one that any sane commander would dread having to cross, but it also stretched from the city like an out-thrust spear, reaching right for the heart of the Imperial forces on Charys. If the enemy forced open the causeway they could reach the star-port in little over an hour.

Sternmark had no doubt that the causeway would be the traitors' main objective. He and his Wolf Guard had joined the surviving members of Einar's pack just as the first enemy shells had begun to fall. Now, amid the deafening thunder of the rebel bombardment, his enhanced senses detected a different timbre to the impacts landing on the far side of the barricade. Stern-mark placed a boot on the firing step and raised his head above the lip of the stone embrasure. A thick wall of grey vapour was swelling silently across the concertina wire and tank traps laid before the barri-cade, fuelled by the bursts of dozens of rebel smoke rounds. At the same time, the roll of artillery blasts dwindled, and beyond the wall of smoke Sternmark heard the distant growl of petrochem engines and the war-shouts of the rebel host.

A grim smile touched the corners of the Wolf Guard's soot stained face. He keyed his vox-unit. 'Here they come!' he called out, both for the benefit of his battle-brothers and for the platoons of Guardsmen huddled against the fortifications to Sternmark's left and right. 'Stand ready!'

Shouted orders echoed thinly along the barricade as sergeants broke the spell of the enemy barrage with a shower of fiery curses and got the men onto their feet. The long, grey line seemed to swarm with darkly coloured beetles as the grenadiers scrambled onto the parapet and readied their weapons. The cries of wounded men rang shrilly through the air, mingled with angry shouts and the piping notes of officers' whistles. Not far from Sternmark one of the Leman Russ battle tanks started its engine with a throaty roar, its turret tracking slowly from left to right as its gunner sought targets beyond the curtain of smoke.

Frantic activity swirled about Sternmark's towering figure. A priest staggered from a makeshift shelter no bigger than a penitent's cell, furiously chanting the Litanies of Extermination. A young grenadier, barely old enough to serve, clambered over the debris behind the barricade and picked through the body parts of his dead comrades in search of spare power packs for his squad mates. A trio of soldiers grappled with a tripod-mounted autocannon, struggling to lift it back into position after it had been dislodged by a shell impact. More grenadiers raced past the towering Space Wolf from shelters further to the rear, and climbed awkwardly onto the firing step. Rifles were checked. Some men laid grenades on the chipped stone parapet where they would be close to hand. Bayonets were pulled from their sheaths and locked in place. A tall, cadaverous-looking sergeant strode quickly along the line, eyeing the grenadiers' preparations with a practised eye.

Volleys of crackling red las-bolts began lashing their way through the smoke, detonating against the stone barricades or buzzing angrily overhead. Bursts of shells kicked up puffs of dust or ricocheted crazily off the edges of the parapet. The roar of the engines was closer now, as well as the demented howls of the rebel infantry.

Sternmark closed his hand around Redclaw's hilt and drew the great blade from its scabbard. Sunlight played along the mirror finish of its edge and the runes carved along its length. He held the sword up and rested his forehead against the flat of the blade. Then he closed his eyes and offered up prayers to Russ and the Allfather. When he was done he thumbed the sword's activation rune and felt the familiar hum of its power field sweep reassuringly up his arm. A sense of calm settled like a mantle onto the Wolf Guard's shoulders. For the first time in almost a month, the anger and frustration that had gripped him at the command bunker receded from his mind. On the verge of battle, he felt whole once more.

Looking left and right, he could just see Haakon and Snurri. His battle-brothers were a hundred metres to either side, and the Wolf Guard and Einar's pack was stretched thin along the entire length of the barricade, ready to lend their strength to any breach in the line. Sternmark considered keying his vox and shouting words of encouragement to his brothers, but nothing came to mind. He had never been much good with words, and besides, what was there left to say? While he'd been driving himself mad with route maps and logistical tables they had been out on the front lines, doing the work of warriors. They knew what was at stake far better than he did.

Ahead, the smoke was thinning. Sternmark could see the dark shapes of Chimera APCs heading down the causeway towards him, their multilasers and heavy bolters spitting fire. Platoons of infantrymen ran along in their wake, snapping off wild shots with their lasguns as they advanced.

Bolts of energy tore through the air around Sternmark, and the Imperial defenders opened fire, unleashing a storm of energy bolts and deadly shells into the ranks of the oncoming enemy. A Chimera was struck by a lascannon beam and lurched to a stop, smoke pouring from its burst hatches. Men staggered and fell as lasgun beams or heavy stubber shells found their marks. The foe pressed on, drawing closer to the barricades with each passing moment.

Sternmark raised his sword heavenward and began the battle chant of his ancestors. Looking up at the iron-grey sky he thought of Ragnar, and wondered if the young Space Wolf and his companions were still alive.

THE FLEET OF Chaos ships turned upon the *Fist of Russ*, trailing glittering arcs of grave-light from their thrusters as they broke orbit, and closed on the Imperial battle cruiser like a swarm of hungry sea drakes. Bolts of pulsing light stabbed from the weapon batteries studding the hulls of the Chaos ships, but their aim was wide and the first salvoes streaked harmlessly into the battle cruiser's wake.

'Helm, hard to port!' Shipmaster Wulfgar roared from the command pulpit. His voice was calm and assured, but the bondsman's knuckles were white as he gripped the edges of the lectern. 'Ahead full! All batteries fire as you bear!' The master of the ship glanced at Ragnar, and then turned and fixed his engineering officer with a commanding glare. 'Run the reactors at one hundred and twenty per cent.'

The engineering officer paled, but nodded nevertheless. 'Reactor at one-twenty, aye,' he confirmed, 'but the containment wards won't hold for long.'

'Very well,' Wulfgar replied, as the battle cruiser started her turn. Deep, groaning sounds echoed aft from the engineering decks as the warship increased power, her tortured superstructure suffering under the strain. Thunder rang through the deckplates as the first of the enemy salvos struck home against the warship's weakened shields.

Ragnar's mind raced as he studied the nearby plot table and studied the flashing lines marking the courses and positions of the Chaos ships. The *Fist of Russ* was turning its armoured prow to the oncoming enemy ships, but within moments the battle cruiser would be surrounded and vulnerable. His worried glance fell on the still-sealed Navigator's vault. Then he addressed the ship's master. 'We can be at the hangar deck and launch our Thunderhawk in ten minutes,' he said. 'Alter your course and open the range, Shipmaster Wulfgar. We can slip past the Chaos ships in the confusion and make planetfall.'

Wulfgar glowered at the young Space Wolf. 'You wouldn't last ten seconds, lord,' he said with a snort. 'We've got to get you as close to the planet as we can before you launch, or they'll blow you apart.' Greenish light flickered through the high viewports as an enemy salvo flashed past the battle cruiser's bridge. Wulfgar turned back to the command lectern. 'Once we're through and you're on your way, we'll come hard about and jump again. With Loki's luck we'll still be in one piece when we come out on the other side.'

A series of deafening blasts battered the port bow of the stricken battle cruiser. Men were thrown to the deck by the impact. Only Ragnar's speed and strength kept him upright, although his grip creased the command deck's metal rail. A bloom of orange and red swelled in slow motion on the port side of the warship, just aft of the armoured prow. Ragnar saw molten hull plating streak like meteors down the length of the battle cruiser and tumble into the void.

'Shields have failed!' cried the ship's deck officer. 'Augurs report an enemy ship dead ahead, coming about on a collision course! We have to come about–'

'Steady as she goes!' Wulgar roared back as he pulled himself to his feet. The ship's master pressed a hand to a cut, smearing blood across his forehead. 'Dorsal lance battery, fire at will!'

Ragnar could see the Chaos ship now, a distant, arrowhead shape, glimmering with pale, unnatural light. It lay squarely in the battle cruiser's path, firing bolt after bolt at the Imperial ship's prow. The young Space Wolf shook his head. 'A single lance won't be enough, Shipmaster Wulfgar,' he said.

'So now you're a ship master, lord?' Wulfgar snapped, but he gave the young Space Wolf a fierce grin. 'They suspect what we're doing, and they're moving to stop us. If we alter our course even a single degree it will make the task of reaching orbit that much harder.' The bondsman shook his head. 'No. We'll plough right through that bastard if he doesn't bear away. You have my oath on it!'

A cyan flare from beyond the viewport showed that the battle cruiser's remaining lance battery had gone into action. The arcs of voltaic force leapt across hundreds of kilometres in the blink of an eye, and flared in a raging storm against the shields of the onrushing Chaos ship. The battery charged and fired again within seconds, and once more the powerful beam weapon battered against the still-glowing curve of the enemy cruiser's void shield, until it failed in a blaze of light.

More explosions battered the flanks of the Imperial ship. Sparks showered from a power conduit along the starboard bulkhead, and alarms began to wail across the command deck. Wulfgar quickly checked the readouts on the command lectern, and his expression turned grim. 'Engineering, increase reactor output to one hundred and thirty-five per cent. Helm, bring us to ramming speed.'

The *Fist of Russ* was almost completely surrounded and taking fire from all sides. Her surviving batteries answered, and the space around them was so dense with enormous ships that every shot found a target. Macro cannon shells smashed aside enemy shields and blasted deep craters in the flanks of the Chaos ships. One cruiser sheered abruptly to starboard, streaming molten debris from a blast that had smashed its command deck. Its sudden manoeuvre carried it directly into the path of another Chaos ship, and the two collided in a spectacular eruption of blazing plasma, and shorn hull plating. However, deprived of her shields, the damage to the ancient battle cruiser was mounting swiftly. Fiery explosions rippled along the length of her hull, and she bled ragged streamers of burning oxygen that tangled in her wake.

Then, like a wounded bear, the *Fist of Russ* surged forward, her surviving thrusters blazing. Caught unawares by the sudden change of speed, many of the enemy salvoes fell harmlessly behind her as she bore down on the lone enemy vessel in her path. The two ships closed the distance rapidly, still blasting away at one another with their remaining weapons. Lance fire had wrought terrible damage along the Chaos ship's bow, and the battle cruiser's armoured prow and superstructure had been repeatedly cratered by high-energy bolts.

The Chaos ship swelled in the battle cruiser's forward viewports. 'Sound collision!' Shipmaster Wulfgar cried. 'For Russ and the Allfather!'

Ragnar had just enough time to grip the command deck rail with both hands and check to make sure that Gabriella was still sealed in her vault, before the two ships collided.

Though the *Fist of Russ* was burned and broken, she was still a massive ship, weighing tens of millions of tonnes. The armoured prow of the battle cruiser struck the cruiser's bow and split it open like a rotten fruit. Crumpled hull-plates and shorn bracing beams burst outward from the impact, propelled by a cloud of superheated metal and escaping gas. The Imperial ship tore through the cruiser from stem to stern, plunging like an iron tipped spear thrust by a wrathful god.

The wounded battle cruiser suffered too. Ragnar was thrown hard against the deck rail and the air reverberated with the groan of tortured metal and the scream of tearing hull plates. Several of the bridge officers were thrown forward by the impact, hurled over the deck rail and onto the bridge crew below. Sparks exploded from a pair of overhead conduits, and then suddenly the lights went out. Ragnar heard screams of pain and terror, and the deck trembled with powerful explosions from deep below decks.

Then, with a flare of multicoloured light, the Chaos ship's reactor exploded, wreathing the forward end of the battle cruiser in fire. The *Fist of Russ* shuddered, and Ragnar felt an ominous tremor pass along the warship's battered keel. Then, all was silent, save for the faint cries of the wounded.

Red emergency lighting slowly illuminated the command deck. A faint haze of acrid smoke hung in the air. Ragnar surveyed the deck in the dim light and was amazed to find many of the crew still at their stations, working hard to keep the warship in the fight. Shipmaster Wulfgar still stood at the command pulpit, bent with pain, but quickly scanning the readouts on the lectern before him. 'Damage report,' he ordered in a raspy voice.

'We are on emergency reserve power,' the damage control officer replied. 'No one is responding on the engineering deck, but indications are that the reactors have failed. There are reports of multiple fires below decks, but most of our damage control stations are not responding.'

Wulfgar nodded. 'What about the hangar decks?'

The damage control officer checked his gauges. 'Both hangar decks report ready, though I don't know for how much longer.'

Ragnar listened to the exchange and felt a cold ball of dread settle in his stomach. 'What does this mean, Shipmaster Wulfgar?' he asked, even though he already suspected he knew the answer.

Wulfgar slowly straightened and addressed the young Space Wolf. His face was pale, and a trickle of blood leaked from the corner of his mouth. 'It means we've gone as far as we're able,' the bondsman said. 'Take your lady and make for the hangar deck as fast as you can. There's not much time.'

Ragnar felt a surge of desperation. He glanced back at the Navigator's vault and saw that the armoured containment system was already starting to cycle open. 'But the jump–'

The master of the ship shook his head. 'We can't make the jump now that the reactors have failed.' Wulfgar replied. 'Now go, lord! Get to the surface and do what you came to do. We'll cover you for as long as we can.'

Ragnar bared his teeth in a silent snarl. 'I'll take your engineering officer and we'll try to reach the reactors. We can make repairs–'

'No,' Inquisitor Volt said. His voice was sombre, but there was cold steel in his tone. 'Shipmaster Wulfgar is right. We must reach the shadow world and confront Madox, or all of this is for nothing.'

A growl of anger welled from Ragnar's throat, but he knew that Volt was correct. Hard discipline asserted itself, and the young Space Wolf nodded curtly. 'I understand,' he told the inquisitor, and then nodded his head respectfully to Shipmaster Wulfgar. 'We'll take our leave of you, master,' he said. 'Inform Harald to load his men and stand by for launch.'

'I will,' Wulfgar said. Then, the bondsman reached forward and extended his hand. 'It has been an honour to serve, lord.'

The young Space Wolf shook his head. 'No, Shipmaster Wulfgar, the honour has been ours.' He clasped the master's bloodstained wrist. 'I shall tell the Old Wolf of your deeds,' Ragnar said. 'You have my oath on it.'

The bondsman smiled, and then straightened his tunic and turned away. He studied the pages of the book propped on the lectern before him, and began to read aloud in a strong, clear voice. '*For if the Emperor is with me, who may stand against me...*'

Ragnar turned to Inquisitor Volt, and the old man nodded silently. Torin and Haegr were already escorting Gabriella to the lift at the rear of the command deck. His heart heavy, the young Space Wolf hurried to join them.

THE DECKS BENEATH the battle cruiser's bridge were a hellish realm of fire, smoke and twisted wreckage. Torin salvaged an emergency air supply from the body of a damage control technician and gave it to Gabriella, while Haegr and Ragnar took turns forcing their way past the worst of the debris. More explosions hammered at the hull of the dying battle cruiser, and with every passing minute Ragnar feared that they would not reach the hangar deck in time.

Yet luck was with them once they were within a few decks of the hangar bay. They made it past the worst of the fires and quickly regained their bearings. The many days Ragnar had spent wandering the lower decks of the huge ship paid off, and he was quickly able to lead the party down a series of maintenance accessways that brought them directly to the waiting Thunderhawk. Harald had the engines idling as the group burst onto the deck, and Volt gave the order to launch as soon as they were aboard.

Ragnar struggled to reach the Thunderhawk's command deck as the assault ship roared down the launch platform and into a storm of enemy fire. The Chaos fleet had come about and was blasting away at the *Fist of Russ*. Ragnar saw at once that the battle cruiser's main thrusters had been reduced to a twisted mass of metal, and her dorsal superstructure had been all but ripped apart. Fires glowed like sullen coals in the deep wounds along the warship's flank.

The horizon spun crazily as the pilot rolled the assault craft and pulled away beneath the Imperial ship. Ragnar gripped nearby stanchions for support and kept his eyes on the dying battle cruiser the entire time, bearing witness to its final moments.

She went down fighting, her guns still defiantly answering the enemy barrage. Ragnar saw an enemy cruiser burst apart under a punishing strike from the battle cruiser's lance battery. Then an enemy shell found one of the Imperial ship's magazines. The *Fist of Russ* disintegrated in a massive chain reaction, a fitting pyre for her heroic crew.

Ragnar took a deep breath and looked through the forward viewports at the ominous curve of the ebon world. 'How long until we make planetfall?' he asked.

'Forty-five minutes, lord, give or take,' the pilot replied, his voice subdued. 'I'll keep the wreckage between us and the enemy ships until we're well out of range.'

Ragnar nodded. With the *Fist of Russ* destroyed, there would be no escape from the shadow world for any of them. Wulfgar and his crew were only the first among them to die.

Setting his jaw, Ragnar forced such thoughts ruthlessly from his mind. They had a mission to perform. Beyond that, nothing else mattered.

He was just about to turn and head back into the troop compartment when a warning telltale began to blink on the augur officer's panel. The crewman leant forward, twisting a series of dials.

'Russ preserve us,' the bondsman said, reading the icons on the screen. 'I have multiple contacts launching from the enemy ships. They look like fighters!'

Ragnar swallowed a curse. 'Full power!' he snapped at the pilot. 'Get us on the deck as fast as you can!'

Thrusters flaring, the assault ship dropped like a thunderbolt towards the shadow world. Behind them, the first of the sleek attack ships was already passing through the battle cruiser's debris field and starting to dive.

The hunt was on.

THIRTEEN
World of Darkness

'I COUNT TWENTY – no, thirty – contacts, closing fast!' the Thunderhawk's augur operator cried, his eyes glued to the phosphorescent display screen. The bondsman's gloved hands played with the augur unit's tuning knobs. 'At present speed they'll be in range in seven seconds,' he calculated.

'Very well,' the assault ship's pilot replied calmly. He reached up and keyed his vox-mic. 'Gunners, look alive! Contacts at six o'clock,' he said, alerting the four crewmen manning the weapon stations in the compartment beneath the command deck. As an assault ship meant to carry troops into hostile landing zones, the Thunderhawk traded speed and manoeuvrability for weapons and armour. Along with a massive forward firing battle cannon and a pair of lascannons, the Thunderhawk also mounted four twin-linked heavy bolters on remote hardpoints. Two of these hardpoints were mounted beneath each wingtip, allowing them to fire both forward and aft. Ragnar felt the vibration of the hardpoint gimbals and the clatter of the autoloaders as the two mounts swung about and began tracking the incoming Chaos fighters.

Ragnar's grip tightened on the stanchions to either side of the command deck's hatch. He hadn't counted on the possibility that the cruisers circling above the shadow world could carry attack craft as well. 'How long until we make planetfall?' he asked, eyeing the lightning-streaked curve of the ebon planet.

'Twenty minutes, more or less,' the pilot answered tersely. 'Setting up the proper re-entry angle is going to be tricky at this speed.'

'We'll be lucky to last twenty seconds,' the young Space Wolf growled. His hearts were hammering in his chest, and he thought he could feel the blood hissing in his temples. It took every ounce of will not to lash out, to feel something break and bleed in his hands. He closed his eyes and forced the Wulfen from his thoughts. The red tide seemed to ebb somewhat, after a moment, leaving his mind a little clearer.

'Is there any sign of a city on the planet's surface?' Ragnar asked. 'If this planet is truly a mirror image of Charys, there must be a shadow version of the capital as well.'

The pilot shook his head. 'I don't see anything but lightning,' he replied, and then glanced back at the augur operator. 'Otto, switch to navigational surveyors and sweep the planet.'

'What about the enemy ships?' the operator asked, looking up from his screen with a panicked expression on his sallow face.

'Forget about them!' the pilot snapped. 'You heard the lord. Find me a city down there.'

Swearing under his breath, the augur operator jabbed at a set of runes on his control panel, and the display screen shifted to a new set of oscillating lines. Frowning, the bondsman adjusted a series of knobs, and studied the pulsing readouts. 'I'm picking up small collections of ground structures at wide intervals. They fit the profile for agri-combines,' he said. 'Hard surface reflections from transit lines, but nothing... wait!' he leaned forward, gently twisting a pair of brass dials. 'Looks like a hard set of returns bearing zero-one-five, right at the planetary terminus. There's your city.'

The pilot nodded and brought the assault ship into a shallow turn to starboard. 'Lining up on zero-one-five and starting our descent,' he said, reaching up and adjusting a set of controls on a panel over his head. The Space Wolf looked over his shoulder at Ragnar. 'Good news, lord. The city is right at the edge of our glide path. We can touch down near the outskirts without adding any more time to our descent.'

Ragnar nodded. 'And the bad news?'

As if on cue, streams of seething energy bolts filled the darkness around the Thunderhawk, and the assault ship rang with a series of heavy blows along its fuselage. Warning icons flashed amber on the techpriest's control panel, and the crewman began to recite the Litany of Atmospheric Integrity as he frantically jabbed at damage control runes. At the tips of the assault ship's wings, the twin-linked heavy bolters went into action, barking out stuttering bursts that reverberated through the Thunderhawk's armoured frame as the high-speed dogfight began.

The enemy fighters were sharp and angular, like shards of polished obsidian. Faint, greenish light glowed from their angled cockpit viewports, giving the ships a sinister, insect-like appearance. They descended on the larger Thunderhawk in a swirling, chaotic swarm, blasting away at the Imperial ship from a dozen different angles. Energy bolts burst across the assault ship's wings, fuselage and tail, wreathing it in a web of small explosions that ate away at the Thunderhawk's dense armour plate. The assault ship side-slipped abruptly left, and then right, trying to spoil the attackers' aim, but it wasn't enough to fully evade the storm of enemy fire.

Red tracer rounds slashed through the enemy formation in response as the Thunderhawk's heavy bolters returned fire. A pair of Chaos fighters blew apart in clouds of glittering fragments and glowing plasma. The shattered fighter craft dissolved in the ebon world's upper atmosphere, consumed by arcs of sorcerous lightning, but there was still more than a score of attack ships dogging the battered Thunderhawk's tail.

A powerful impact struck the assault ship's port side, causing the craft to slew sideways for a dizzying instant before the pilot could regain control. 'Number one engine is hit!' the tech-priest cried out. 'Pressure indicators are spiking!'

'Hold it together for another few minutes,' the pilot shot back. Another blast hit the nose of the attack craft just beneath the cockpit, limning the pilot's helmeted head in lurid green light. 'I'm going to increase our angle of descent and see if I can get the bastards to back off. Hold on!'

The Thunderhawk steepened its dive, coming into the planet's turbulent atmosphere at a sharper angle and increasing the speed of its re-entry. At once, the leading edges of the hull began to glow red with friction build-up. The Imperial vessel trembled like a ship in a summer gale, but her reinforced superstructure held against the strain. Several of the enemy fighters sharpened their dives as well, but their hunger for destruction proved their undoing, as the heat and turbulence tore their hulls apart. The rest of the swarm fell back, unable to match the assault ship's dangerous descent.

'Well, that bought us a minute or two,' the pilot shouted over the thunder of re-entry. The heat inside the cockpit was intense, and the assault craft shuddered violently as it plunged towards the planet's surface. More and more warning icons flashed an insistent red on the tech-priest's display.

Ragnar held on for all he was worth. It was clear that the pilot was pushing the Thunderhawk to the edge of its performance envelope and possibly beyond. 'Will this get us on the ground any faster?' he shouted.

To the young Space Wolf's surprise, the pilot threw back his head and laughed. 'Oh, aye, lord! One way or another, it surely will.'

They were close enough to the planet's surface for Ragnar to make out dark oceans and broad continents studded with mountain ranges. There were no lights that he could see, but the shape of the land masses was a perfect reflection of Charys as near as he could tell. All this just to facilitate a single ritual, Ragnar thought with a terrible sense of awe. He truly grasped the sheer scope of Madox's plans, for the first time, and felt something akin to dismay. He thought of the handful of Space Wolves in the troop compartment behind him and wondered how they could possibly challenge something so vast. *Who are we to overcome an entire world?*

The answer was obvious. We are sons of the Allfather, Ragnar thought, just as Madox once was. Whatever the traitor can bring to bear against us, we are its equal.

The Thunderhawk flashed past a rocky coastline, plunging towards the dark surface of the world like a fiery comet. Vast plains stretched beneath the descending craft. Ragnar was amazed to see the outlines of enormous agri-combines, their subdivided crop zones radiating like the spokes of enormous wheels more than a thousand kilometres across. The young Space Wolf could just make out the towering granaries and equipment hives at the hub of each combine, where legions of farm servitors would shuttle back and forth like bees to tend their carefully monitored crops.

Within minutes, the fierce shuddering began to subside as the assault ship passed through the upper atmosphere and dived through a dark sky empty of clouds. A torrent of green bolts slashed downward from high and to starboard. The daemon ships were closing the range once more. Ragnar eyed the multitude of warning runes flashing on the tech-priest's screen to his left. 'How long?' he asked.

'Otto?' the pilot said.

'Surveyor shows the city dead ahead at five hundred kilometres,' the augur operator replied. Then, suddenly, he straightened in his seat. 'Wait – I'm getting something–'

Bursts of green energy bolts howled down around the Thunderhawk from high and to starboard. The pilot muttered a curse. 'Never mind, Otto. I see them.'

'No! There's something else!' the operator exclaimed. He fumbled for a set of dials and adjusted them carefully, his head cocked intently to one side. 'I... I'm getting a signal on the vox. It sounds like one of our recovery beacons.'

The pilot looked back over his shoulder at Ragnar. 'How is that possible?'

Bolts impacted across the assault ship's wings and fuselage in a string of sharp detonations. The Thunderhawk shuddered beneath the blows and seemed to plummet downward for a vertiginous instant before coming under control. Ragnar leaned close to the augur operator. 'Can you get an identity code from the beacon?'

Otto shook his head. 'I can barely hear it at all,' he said, pressing a hand to his headphones. 'There's a lot of atmospheric interference—'

Another thunderclap smote the aft section of the transport, throwing the crew against their restraints. An alarm buzzed shrilly on the tech-priest's panel, but Ragnar was oblivious to everything but the signal that the augur operator was receiving. 'Can you isolate its location?' he asked.

The bondsman shook his head. 'I can get a bearing and an approximate distance,' Otto replied, shouting over the explosions battering the Thunderhawk. 'It... it looks like three-five-five degrees at about eighty to a hundred kilometres. That's deep in a range of low mountains on the far side of an agri-combine right ahead.'

Before Ragnar could ask further, the sound of the assault ship's engines changed pitch and the Thunderhawk slewed violently to starboard. The tech-priest let out a sharp cry. 'Number one engine's failed!' he said.

There was another stomach clenching drop as the assault ship fell like a stone. Both pilot and co-pilot wrestled with the controls. 'Increase power to number two,' the pilot ordered, his voice tense with strain. 'Can you restart number one?'

'No chance,' the tech-priest shouted back, 'turbine's seized!'

Ragnar was thrown forward as the Thunderhawk's nose dipped into a steep dive. The pilot was trading altitude for speed, trying to keep his ship in the air for as long as possible. The young Space Wolf clung to the stanchions and watched the ground rushing towards them through the cockpit viewports. He could see the pale ribbon of a transit route crossing the plain below them, pointing to the outskirts of the agri-combine that Otto had mentioned.

The Thunderhawk began to shudder violently. 'Controls are getting sluggish,' the pilot grated. 'Where's my hydraulic pressure?'

A flurry of energy bolts surrounded the diving assault ship, and multiple hits slammed into the Thunderhawk's tail and wings. The wingtip heavy bolters returned fire with a roar, but then there was a loud explosion aft and the world seemed to spin out of control.

'Number two engine's hit!' the tech-priest cried, and then lapsed into a desperate prayer to the Omnissiah.

'Well, that's it then,' the pilot said, his voice surprisingly calm as the horizon spun beyond the cockpit viewports. 'Cut power to number three! Hurry!'

The co-pilot threw himself against his restraints, reaching desperately for the throttle levers. Ragnar saw that the Space Wolf wasn't going to make it.

Praying to Russ, the young Space Wolf pulled himself towards the pilots' controls. Fighting hard against the G-forces pinning the crew into their seats, he pushed his armour's systems to the limit and strained forward with his right arm. The tips of his fingers brushed the steel throttle lever and drew it back far enough to get a solid grip. Ragnar wrapped his fingers around the lever and pulled back with all his might, nearly tearing it from its housing.

The howling wail of the engine fell silent. All Ragnar heard was the whistling wind and the impassioned prayers of the tech-priest in the few seconds before the assault ship slammed into the ground.

ANOTHER WAVE OF flesh and steel bore down on the Imperial positions at the Angelus Causeway. Clawed feet scrabbling for purchase, a huge mutant heaved itself up the shifting mound of bodies at the foot of the barricade and reached for Mikal Sternmark. Beady red eyes glittered with hate from within thick, pasty folds of fat, and the entire lower half of the creature's doughy face was nothing but a massive set of powerful jaws and a lashing, serpentine tongue. One clawed hand gripped a shock maul, of the type that Arbites riot troopers often carried, and its bloodstained tip crackled with lethal energies. A pack of lesser mutants swarmed behind the massive creature, armed with a collection of laspistols, slug throwers and gory chainblades. They howled encouragement to their leader and scrambled along in its wake, eager to sweep over the Imperial defences and slaughter the soldiers on the other side.

Sternmark met them with a bloodthirsty shout, smoke curling from bolter and blade. His bare face and ornate armour were covered in blood and grime, and his fangs shone red in the fading light of day. The traitors had hurled wave after wave of assaults against the barricade over the course of the day. Burning vehicles and the bodies of the dead stretched for almost a full kilometre down the causeway, but each attack had brought the rebels a few hundred metres closer to the Imperial positions. Four times the enemy troops had attempted to scale the barricade, and four times the Space Wolves had driven them back.

The Wolf Guard levelled his storm bolter at the oncoming creature and fired a burst into its chest. Mass-reactive rounds punched clean through the mutant and felled a pair of gibbering monsters behind it, but the lantern jawed monster only roared in bloodlust and kept coming. It swung its shock maul at Sternmark's head, but Redclaw blurred through the air to meet it. There was a sharp *crack* of electrical discharge and a blue-white flash as the ancient power weapon cut the maul in two. Teeth bared, Sternmark brought the heavy blade down in a diagonal cut, slicing through the mutant's shoulder and deep into its chest. Ichor flowed thickly from the wound. The creature snarled and snapped at the Wolf Guard, still trying to climb onto the top of the barricade, but its strength failed it all at once and it collapsed onto its face just short of its goal. The mound of dead now rose half a metre higher than it had before.

More of the mutants climbed over the corpse of their fallen leader. Las-bolts detonated across Sternmark's chest and shoulders, and a slug left a crease along the side of the Wolf Guard's right cheek. Sternmark tore his sword free of the mutant's corpse and split one of his attackers from groin to chin. Another tried to scramble past him, dragging a grenade from its belt, and he shot it point-blank in the chest. An arm came up, levelling a laspistol at his face. With a backhanded swipe of his blade, he severed the limb, and smashed the screaming foe off the barricade with a blow from the butt of his storm bolter.

Sternmark whirled in place, seeking more enemies to slay, but after a few moments he realised that he was alone among the dead and dying. Looking out along the causeway, he saw figures in tattered Guard and PDF uniforms retreating back into the smoke, chased by las-bolts and bolter fire from the Imperial defenders. The last of the mutants who'd tried to challenge him had stumbled back down to the base of the mound and were running for their lives.

The Wolf Guard threw back his head and howled at the red-stained skies. All along the line, a ragged chorus of voices joined his, celebrating the glory of the kill. The enemy had been broken for a fifth time and hurled back in disarray. Watching their fleeing figures, Sternmark felt the blood burn in his veins, and his mouth gaped in a wolfish grin. The urge to give chase, to fall upon the terrified enemy and tear out their throats was almost too much to bear.

He took a step down onto the slippery mound of corpses, then another. Sternmark could almost feel the rushing wind of the chase against his skin.

There was a buzzing in his ears, like the whine of a biting fly. Sternmark frowned, pressing a hand to his ear. Belatedly, he realized that he'd dropped his empty storm bolter, and he was tottering uneasily atop the shifting mound of the dead.

The last of the retreating traitors disappeared into the smoke. Slowly the tide of bloodlust ebbed, flowing restlessly into the back of his mind, and the buzzing in his ears resolved into words. 'My lord! What are you doing?'

Sternmark turned, as though in a dream. One of Einar's pack members stood a few metres away atop the barricade, a bolter and a bloody chainsword hanging loose in his hands. The warrior's silver-blond hair was braided, as was his bloodstained beard. It took a moment for Sternmark to dredge the young warrior's name from the red surf pounding in his brain. 'Sven?' he asked. 'What are you doing here?'

The young Space Wolf shifted uncomfortably. 'I'm here to report, lord.' He raised his bolter. 'My pack fired off the last of our ammunition in the last wave, even the rounds we gathered from Einar and Karl.'

'Einar? Karl?' Sternmark glared at Sven, trying to make sense of what the Grey Hunter was saying. 'What's happened to them?'

The question took Sven aback. 'Karl was killed during the third attack,' he said. 'A mutant with a meltagun got too close to the barricade.'

'And Einar?'

'Deep in the Red Dream. An eviscerator took his right arm and most of his shoulder, but he bloody well killed the traitor that did it.' Sven eyed the Wolf

Guard with concern. 'We reported this over the vox. Is your system malfunctioning?'

'You tend to your wargear, brother, and I'll attend to mine,' Sternmark snapped. 'Who is in charge of the pack now that Einar is down?'

Sven paused, unsettled by the vehemence of the Wolf Guard's rebuke. 'By rights, that would be Freyr–'

'But Freyr isn't here making the report, is he? You're acting pack leader now, Sven. Return to your brothers and prepare for the next attack. I'll speak to headquarters about resupply.'

'I...' Sven's eyes widened. 'Lord, are you certain you are well?'

'Well enough,' Sternmark growled. His eyes narrowed in challenge. 'Do you think I've chosen poorly, brother?'

'No, lord!' Sven took a step back, clearly uncertain how to proceed. After a moment, the young Grey Hunter bowed his head in submission and backed away, his expression troubled.

Sternmark turned away, searching for his storm bolter among the dead. He found the weapon atop a trio of fallen grenadiers and bent to retrieve it. It felt clumsy and awkward in his hands. He fumbled with the magazine release for nearly a full second before he managed to drop the empty clips. Only the iron conditioning of many decades of campaigning kept him from hurling the weapon away in frustration.

The temptation stunned the Wolf Guard. Sternmark shook his head fiercely, as though trying to break the grip of a terrible dream. Shadowy forms flitted at the corners of his vision. He whirled, trying to focus on them, but saw only the bodies of the dead, stretching as far as he could see along the length of the barricade. The battle tanks that had supported the defenders were blackened hulls, destroyed by rebel suicide attacks or artillery strikes over the course of the long day.

He realised, dimly, that he had no idea how many of the Guardsmen were still alive, or where their commander was. He'd last spoken to their commander… was it after the second attack, or the third? Sternmark couldn't be certain. The regiment could be on the verge of retreat, leaving him and his battle-brothers to hold the causeway alone.

Sternmark looked left and right, searching for the Wolf Guard who'd accompanied him to the barricade. Rage and shame boiled inside him, making it difficult to think. 'Cursed,' he growled bitterly. 'This damned world has cursed us all.'

Rebel artillery howled overhead, crashing behind the Imperial positions. A chorus of battle cries rose from the rebel lines as the traitors resumed their attack.

RAGNAR AWOKE TO the dull ache of broken bones. Lines of pain pulsed across his forehead and down his face, almost as far as his jaw, and he tasted the coppery tang of blood in his mouth.

Lightning flashed beyond his closed eyelids. Ragnar blinked, and then carefully opened his eyes. He was lying on his back, staring up at a dark sky devoid of stars. The air smelled dry and musty as a tomb, tinged with the acrid stink of burning synthetics.

Two shadowy figures loomed over the young Space Wolf. One knelt closer. Lightning flickered across the empty sky, revealing Torin's angular face. The Wolf-blade peered with worry at Ragnar's face, and then broke into a wry grin. 'See? I told you he was still alive,' Torin said to the second figure. 'Lucky for us his face absorbed most of the impact.'

With a deep breath, Ragnar pushed up onto his elbows. The fractures across his face and skull caused him to grimace in pain, but he could tell that the bone was starting to knit together already. He glanced up at the second figure and realised it was Harald. The Blood Claw pack leader scowled disdainfully at Ragnar and turned away.

The Thunderhawk was a twisted pile of wreckage a few dozen metres away, half-buried in a furrow of scorched earth that stretched for nearly three-quarters of a kilometre behind the mangled wreck. Somehow, the pilot had managed to crash-land the assault ship along the grey ribbon of roadway that he'd spotted during their descent. Twisting columns of black smoke rose from the wreckage. The cockpit of the Thunderhawk was burst open, its viewports shattered and the metal bracings peeled apart. The assault ship's port wing had been torn away during the crash, and the starboard wing jutted crookedly from the wreckage. Three warriors from Harald's pack were attempting to disassemble the remaining wing's heavy bolter hardpoint under the watchful gaze of the Thunderhawk's tech-priest. Four other figures in heavy flight suits were unloading a number of small packs and other survival gear from an open hatch on the assault ship's fuselage.

Torin followed Ragnar's gaze. 'We had to tear open the cockpit with Harald's fist to get you out,' he said.

'The pilot and co-pilot died in the crash, and the augur operator was dead by the time we pulled him out.'

Ragnar nodded painfully, realising sadly that he'd never learned the heroic pilot's name. 'Any other casualties?' he asked.

'Not yet, thank Russ,' the Wolfblade said, glancing up at the empty sky. 'We heard the enemy fighters fly overhead a few times as we were trying to cut our way out of the ship, but they were gone by the time we made it outside.'

'Lady Gabriella?' Ragnar inquired.

Torin indicated a spot off behind Ragnar with a curt nod of his chin. 'Haegr is watching her,' he replied gravely. 'She's not doing too well.'

His pain forgotten, Ragnar clambered quickly to his feet. Gabriella was sitting just a few metres away, her legs drawn up and her head resting on her knees. Haegr loomed protectively over the Navigator, his thunder hammer held at the ready. Inquisitor Volt knelt beside Gabriella, speaking to her in low tones. The rest of Harald's Blood Claw pack formed a security perimeter some way off, diligently scanning the surrounding terrain for signs of danger.

Ragnar approached the Navigator carefully and sank down into a crouch next to Inquisitor Volt. The inquisitor paid the young Space Wolf no mind. His head was bowed and he was reading from a small book resting in his bandaged hands. With a start, Ragnar realised that Volt was *praying*, reciting a litany in High Gothic that he'd never heard before. He sensed it was being done for Gabriella's benefit, but he could not follow the specifics.

Leaning forward, Ragnar spoke softly to Gabriella. 'Lady? Are you well?'

At the sound of his voice, the Navigator raised her head. Gabriella's pale face was smudged with soot and grime, and her expression was one of pure anguish. Her scarf was gone and her black hair hung loosely about her face. In the centre of her forehead the Navigator's pineal eye burned like a tiny star, stunning Ragnar with its intensity.

'I can feel it,' she said in a stricken voice, 'lines of terrible power stretching into the physical realm, anchored by the suffering of millions. The fabric of space turned inside out, warped by the will of...' A look of horror passed across her face. 'I cannot say it! I dare not say it! Blessed Emperor preserve us!'

'The Emperor is with us,' Volt told her, his voice trembling with conviction. 'His sacred light shields us, and he has set his Wolves to watch over us. Be strong, Gabriella of Bellisarius,' he said, and laid a hand gently on her arm. 'What can you tell us of the ritual our foe is planning?'

'Planning?' Gabriella said. 'No, not planning, *performing*. It has been going on for some time. I can hear their voices in my head, whispering terrible things. Whatever the ritual portends, it is nearing its culmination.'

Volt squeezed her arm compassionately and glanced at Ragnar. 'It is worse than I feared,' he said quietly, but it was unclear if he was speaking about the ritual or the effect it was having on Gabriella. 'There isn't much time left.'

Ragnar nodded gravely. 'Lady, we need to get moving,' he said, as gently as he could. 'Can you walk? One of us can carry you if need be–'

'I can walk,' Gabriella said forcefully, though the strain of what she was feeling was painfully apparent in her eyes. 'I can do whatever I must.'

'Then rest for a few moments more,' Ragnar replied, and turned to Volt. 'Do you have any idea where we are?'

Volt closed his book of devotions and nodded, surveying the dark plain that surrounded them. 'We're about a hundred kilometres due south of the capital,' he said, and then pointed to the roadway. 'This is one of the main transit routes linking the southern agri-combines. It leads right into the heart of the city.'

Ragnar scowled at the news. Time was of the essence. The Space Wolves could cover a hundred kilometres in less than seven hours at a forced march, but there was no way that Gabriella, Volt or the bondsmen would be able to manage such a pace. 'The roadway is too exposed,' he said to the inquisitor. 'The enemy fighters have gone for now, but I expect that something will arrive to search the wreckage before much longer.'

Volt nodded. 'I fear you're right.' He put away his book and then gestured to the north, where the grey stripe of the roadway bisected a dark green band that stretched across the horizon. 'We'll head for that agri-combine. It's much smaller than most, but the crops will give us some cover for at least twenty kilometres.'

Ragnar shook his head, bemused. 'What does a shadow world deep within the Eye of Terror need with crops and agri-combines?'

'It's the law of correspondence,' Volt said. 'The shadow world has to be an exact geographical copy of Charys for the co-location to work.'

'All right,' Ragnar said. 'What about the mountain range beyond the combine? If we follow it instead of the roadway, how close will it take us to the city?'

Volt pursed his lips thoughtfully. 'We could follow them to within ten kilometres of the city's south-west districts,' he said, 'but it would be rough going.'

Ragnar nodded. 'Then that's what we'll have to do.'

'What's this?'

Ragnar and Volt looked up at the sound of Harald's voice. The pack leader had arrived with his three Blood Claws and the surviving Thunderhawk crew in tow. Two of the warriors carried the heavy bolters stripped from the assault ship on improvised shoulder slings. The tech-priest and the assault ship's gunners were carrying stubby lascarbines in their hands and had bulky survival packs on their shoulders.

Harald glared down at Ragnar. 'You're not in command here, exile,' the pack leader said. 'No one's taking orders from you.'

A shadow fell across Harald as Haegr leaned forward, his hands tightening around the haft of his hammer. 'Shall I thrash some sense into this pup, brother?' he asked.

Harald bristled at the threat. 'I'd like to see you try,' he said, baring his fangs.

'That's enough,' Volt snapped, rising to his feet between the two warriors. The Wolves stood head and shoulders above the old man, but the inquisitor's tone was hard and unyielding. 'Ragnar isn't in command of this expedition, but *I* am, and we're heading for the agri-combine. Harald, assemble your men. I want two of your Wolves on point and one covering each flank, understood?'

The pack leader stared down at Volt for a long moment, and Ragnar thought for an instant that Harald was going to challenge the inquisitor. Then, just as suddenly, he nodded an acknowledgement and began calling out orders to his men.

Volt began to gather up his gear without comment, as though nothing had happened. Haegr held out a hand to Gabriella and helped the Navigator to her feet. Torin appeared quietly out of the gloom. Only Ragnar noticed the older Wolfblade sliding his pistol back into its holster. The two warriors shared apprehensive looks.

'Not a good beginning,' Torin said softly, as the band prepared to move out. 'Harald's only barely holding it together.'

Ragnar glanced thoughtfully to the north. 'Aren't we all,' he replied.

FOURTEEN
The Lost

DISTANCES WERE DECEIVING on the vast, dark plains of
the shadow world. When they'd set out from the crash
site, Ragnar had reckoned they were only a few dozen
kilometres from the edge of the agri-combine, but an
hour later they still seemed no closer to their objective. The Space Wolves loped along at a tireless,
ground-eating pace, their eyes restlessly scanning the
horizon for signs of enemy activity. The bondsmen,
accustomed as they were to the physical regimens of
the Fang, kept up the pace without complaint.
Inquisitor Volt and Lady Gabriella did the same, but
Ragnar could tell that they were beginning to tire.
Their scents were bitter, laced with crippling fatigue
poisons. Gabriella in particular was suffering greatly
after the difficulty of the warp transit, yet she held her
head high and never slowed. Ragnar followed along in

her wake, waiting for her to ask for help or to catch her up in case she should stumble.

He could hear the labouring beats of her heart, drumming a desperate counterpoint to the rhythmic cadence of her feet. When he breathed, he could taste the warmth of her skin and feel the heat of her blood on the tip of his tongue. Since he'd set foot on the shadow world his senses had become incredibly sharp. An almost electrical charge galvanised his blood and banished the weariness from his limbs. It felt as though he could run forever under this starless sky, pacing along in Gabriella's wake and listening to the beat of her heart, waiting for her to stumble.

The surge of pure, soulless *hunger* that gripped him nearly took Ragnar's breath away. For a fleeting instant he could imagine her throat within his jaws and taste the hot rush of her blood. He staggered, bile rising in his throat, and fell out of step with his brothers.

The rest of the pack loped past Ragnar, all except for Torin, who slowed his pace and came up alongside the young Space Wolf. The older Wolfblade's expression was full of concern, but Ragnar waved him away with a savage sweep of his hand. 'Keep your distance brother,' he said hoarsely. 'I… am not myself.'

'I know, brother,' Torin replied quietly. 'I can smell it. Your scent is changing as the Wulfen grows in strength.'

'Russ preserve me,' Ragnar said, his hearts clenching in horror. He looked out across the featureless plain and for a fleeting instant he was tempted to run as fast and as far from his brethren as he could. 'I can't believe Harald or the others haven't noticed.'

'The reason is simple,' Torin replied, his voice grim. 'They can't tell the difference because it's happening to all of us.'

Ragnar scowled at Torin, thinking for a moment that he was being mocked, but then he saw the look in the older Wolfblade's eyes. Behind the concern there was a cold, desperate glint, hinting at the inner struggle going on inside the warrior. Ragnar suddenly noticed the tension gripping Torin's lean frame and caught the older Wolf's scent. There was a musky undercurrent that immediately set the young Space Wolf's teeth on edge. Instead of his battle-brother, Ragnar saw only another predator and a potential rival.

The sudden realisation struck Ragnar like a physical blow. He reeled away from Torin, his lips pulling back in a feral snarl.

Before he could react further, Torin's voice pulled Ragnar back from the brink. 'Peace, brother!' he said quickly, stepping forward and gripping Ragnar's wrist. 'Master yourself, or all of us are lost.'

Ragnar clenched his jaws and fought against the beast that threatened to suborn him. He focused on Torin's unwavering gaze and the steadying grip of his hand, and after a moment the fire in his blood subsided. When he could speak again he asked, 'How can this be, Torin? How is this possible?'

The older Wolfblade could only shake his head helplessly. 'I do not know,' he said. 'I've sensed the changes ever since we landed here. Even Haegr is being affected to some degree.' Torin grinned fleetingly. 'If we're not careful he might try to eat us all.'

The attempt at humour was lost on Ragnar. 'I've never heard of so many Wolves succumbing at once,' he said.

'Nor I,' Torin replied. 'At first I thought that the planet was affecting us – we are somewhere in the Eye of Terror, after all – but you were feeling the curse when we were still on Fenris.' The older warrior's shoulders slumped. 'I should have seen it then and brought it to Ranek's attention, but you can be so damned melancholy sometimes.' He sighed. 'Forgive me brother. I failed you.'

Ragnar shook his head ruefully. 'This is no fault of yours, Torin. You told me to speak to Sigurd aboard the *Fist of Russ*, but I was too stiff-necked to seek him out when I had the chance.' A thought occurred to the young Space Wolf. 'Could it be me?' he asked. 'Could I somehow be affecting the rest of you?'

Torin's brows knitted thoughtfully. 'Honestly, I don't know. I've never heard of such a thing, but who knows? Perhaps that's why the priests cull the Wulfen from the companies and isolate them.' After a few more moments' thought, he shook his head. 'No, if that was true then Haegr and I would have been affected ere now. Something else is causing this.'

Ragnar thought it over, and was forced to nod in agreement. 'That's a pity,' he said grimly. 'If I thought I could stop this by putting a bolt pistol to my head I would do it.'

'Don't be stupid,' Torin snapped.

'You wouldn't say that if you felt the same way I do,' Ragnar said. 'I'm becoming a danger to Gabriella, Torin. The thoughts that are going through my head…'

'I can guess,' the older Wolfblade replied. 'Don't worry, brother. I won't let you harm her. You have my oath upon it.' He sighed. 'Honestly, it's the younger ones I'm worried about. Harald and his packmates don't have the experience we have. They could succumb to the Wulfen and never know it until it was too late.'

Ragnar nodded gravely. 'I hear you, Torin. We can only pray to the Allfather that our oaths will sustain us long enough to deal with Madox and his infernal master. After that...' he shrugged.

'Aye,' Torin said. 'The rest is up to the Fates.'

The two Wolfblades had fallen several dozen metres behind the rest of the group. Ragnar nodded to Torin, and they began to pick up the pace. As they did so, Ragnar caught a hint of motion out of the corner of his eye. With a flash of irritation and a shake of his head he dismissed the phantom image, until he saw it again, streaking across the starless sky from the east.

'Hostile aircraft,' Ragnar bellowed. 'Take cover!'

The Chaos fighters howled across the plain less than fifty metres above the deck, opening fire the moment the Space Wolves began to scatter. Streams of green energy bolts raked along the dark ground and left melted craters in the surface of the roadway. The Space Marines reacted with blurring speed and years of experience and training, seeming to dance effortlessly among the streams of fire. One of the bondsmen wasn't so lucky, however. Two bolts took him high on the chest and shoulder, blowing the gunner apart.

Ragnar caught a glimpse of Haegr pushing Gabriella and Volt to the ground and placing his considerable bulk between them and the attacking ships. The two enemy fighters streaked overhead and split up, arrowing skyward on pillars of ghostly fire. An arc of red tracers fanned the air behind the southerly fighter as one of Harald's Blood Claws opened fire with his salvaged heavy bolter. The Chaos ship made a tight roll, avoiding the explosive shells, and disappeared into the darkness.

'Move, move!' Ragnar yelled, rising to his feet. The dark green border of the agri-combine appeared to be only a few hundred metres away. It wasn't much, but it was the only cover he could see for kilometres. 'Run for the fields! Go! Haegr, get Gabriella moving.'

The Blood Claws started moving at once, heavy bolters sweeping from horizon to horizon in smooth, controlled arcs. Haegr lifted Gabriella bodily to her feet, and then Volt as well, sending both running full-tilt down the roadway with the surviving bondsmen close behind. Torin fell into step beside Ragnar. 'Scout flight, you reckon?' he asked.

'Scouts or escorts,' Ragnar said, searching the sky. 'We'll know for sure in the next few minutes.'

The Chaos fighters made their second pass from the north-east, appearing without warning over the fields ahead. As bolts of energy tore through the pack of Wolves, Harald's gunners stopped in their tracks and filled the air with tracer fire. A burst of shells stitched a line of small explosions along the length of one of the attack craft. It roared overhead, trailing a ribbon of smoke and flame, and then went into an uncontrolled spin and crashed into the earth half a kilometre away.

Las-bolts chased vainly after the second fighter as the bondsmen vented their rage at the enemy ships. Ragnar gripped his bolt pistol and was tempted to loose a few pointless rounds, just for spite's sake. One of the Blood Claws was reeling, clutching at the melted stump of his left arm and cursing at the sky.

Ahead, Harald and his packmates had come to a halt before a knee-high barrier of pale metal that marked the outer boundary of the combine. Volt and Gabriella stood in their midst, staring motionless at the rustling fields beyond.

Ragnar charged past the smoking heavy bolters and made straight for Gabriella. He could almost feel the second fighter rolling in for a third pass, straight down the roadway behind them. 'What in the Allfather's name are you waiting for?' he snarled. 'We've got to get under cover–'

Gabriella turned to him, and the look of horror on her face stopped Ragnar in his tracks.

A dry, whispering sound rose from the dark fields as the vast fields of the agri-combine rustled in the wind. Except, Ragnar suddenly realised, there was no breeze blowing against his face.

The tall, dark green stalks ordered in neat ranks beyond the barrier looked like gene-crafted corn at first glance. Long, drooping leaves, dozens of them on each stalk, trembled and whispered against one another, as though fearful of the Space Marines' presence.

Lightning split the sky to the east, painting the glossy leaves in pale, green light. Each leaf bore a human face, distorted into a mask of terror and pain. As Ragnar watched, the lips of each face moved in a silent scream or a plea for release.

'Blessed Russ!' Ragnar hissed. 'What in the Allfather's name is this?'

'A harvest of damnation,' Volt said gravely. 'These are the sacrifices that made this dark world possible. Field after field of them, stretching for thousands of kilometres all across the planet.'

'We have to burn them,' Harald said hoarsely. 'Our flamers–'

'Our flamers are not enough,' Ragnar said, 'and right now we need them.'

Then the heavy bolters began to roar again, and streaks of ghostly fire hissed past the stricken Blood Claws. Ragnar whirled and saw a stream of green bolts marching up the roadway towards him. 'Into the field!' he roared. 'Now!'

Raising his bolt pistol, Ragnar began walking towards the oncoming fighter, aiming and firing one shot after another as the Blood Claws began to scramble over the barrier. If the enemy fighter pilot wanted a target, he was going to give it one.

The attack ship was low and level, just a few dozen metres above the roadway. It plunged through a web of tracer fire, its cannons blazing. The two Space Wolf gunners blazed away at the Chaos ship just ahead of Ragnar. One of the Blood Claws was struck full in the chest by one of the energy bolts, blowing a hole the size of Ragnar's fist clean through the young warrior. The gunner staggered, and then sank to one knee, but the Blood Claw kept firing.

A volley of bolts filled the air around Ragnar. One glanced off his left pauldron and burned a molten furrow through the ceramite plate. The blow knocked the young Space Wolf back a step, but he continued to fire until his pistol's magazine was empty.

'Ragnar! Get back here!' Torin called from the combine's metal barrier.

The mortally wounded Blood Claw toppled forward, his hand still closed around the firing lever of his heavy bolter. Hits were beginning to register across the hull of the oncoming fighter however, as the surviving gunner found the range. Howling his defiance, the gunner stepped into the middle of the roadway, right into the attack ship's path.

Ragnar glanced back at the barrier. Torin was there, beckoning with his blade. 'Come on!' he shouted over the hammering blasts of the heavy bolter.

Explosive shells burst in staccato flashes across the nose and glowing viewports of the Chaos ship. Suddenly there was a larger blast farther aft, and the attack craft was haloed in a nimbus of burning gas and electrical discharges. The ship seemed to stagger in midair, and then plummeted like a thunderbolt towards Ragnar and the Blood Claw gunner.

Ragnar saw the danger at once, but the gunner continued to fire at the diving craft. 'Run!' the young Space Wolf yelled at the Blood Claw, but the gunner didn't seem to hear. He was still firing, the barrel of his heavy bolter glowing red with heat, when the fighter smashed into the roadway and crushed him beneath its skidding, tumbling bulk.

Cursing, Ragnar spun on his heel and raced for the combine's metal barrier as quickly as he could. He could hear the grinding, crashing screech of the attack ship disintegrating along the roadway behind him, growing closer with every passing second. At the last moment, Ragnar gathered his strength and leapt for the barrier. Something hard and unyielding smashed into his back the moment his feet left the ground, cracking his backpack and hurling him through the air. Tumbling, he struck the dark earth hard and rolled for several metres, flattening the morbid stalks, and digging furrows into the ground.

The attack ship spent the last of its energy against the combine's metal barrier, scattering steaming debris across the dreadful field. Twisted hunks of red-hot metal landed all around Ragnar, the pieces hissing against the dark ground. Within moments, Torin was at his side, all but dragging the young Space Wolf to his feet. 'I saw more thrusters burning off to the south,' Torin said. 'They're coming this way. Looks like those two were escorts after all.'

Ragnar climbed to his feet. His hands seemed to move of their own accord, dropping the empty bolt pistol magazine and slapping in a fresh one. 'Where's Gabriella?'

'Somewhere in this cursed field,' Torin replied, glancing warily to the south. 'She's with Haegr and Volt. The inquisitor told everyone to make for the buildings to the north.'

The young Space Wolf scowled at the news. 'We can't afford to get hemmed into a static defence,' he said. 'We've got to stay on the move or we'll be over-whelmed.'

'Tell that to Volt,' Torin said ruefully.

'First things first,' the young Space Wolf replied, breathing deeply of the dry, musty air. He tasted Gabriella's scent and felt his pulse quicken. 'Let's go find them.'

The two warriors dashed deeper into the sacrificial field, forcing their way down narrow rows carved between the dark green furrows. Slick, waxy leaves slithered against the plates of their armour and across their faces. When they brushed against his ears Ragnar thought he could hear the plaintive whispers of the souls trapped within.

He focused instead on the sounds of pounding feet echoing from the field in a wide arc ahead of him. It sounded like the Blood Claws had fanned out, or perhaps they had simply been separated by the field's endless, identical rows. Ragnar keyed his vox-bead and his ears were filled with a harsh, atonal sound, rising and falling like the howl of a demented wolf. He called to Haegr or Volt, but got no reply. He gave up after a few tries and concentrated instead on loping after the Navigator's scent.

Ragnar heard the approaching ships before he saw them, a rising crescendo of shrieking thrusters coming in low from the south. A dark shape roared overhead. Ragnar glanced up at a black, angular hull that glistened like polished iron and was studded with rows of curved spikes and jagged blades. Open portals gaped like mouths along the underside of the ship, and the young Space Wolf saw armoured, red-eyed figures crouching at their rims.

The assault ships thundered past Ragnar in a staggered line four abreast, riding boiling plumes of smoke and steam. More than a score of dark shapes leapt from the speeding craft, falling like stormhawks on shrieking pillars of superheated air. Ragnar saw at once that they were Chaos Space Marines, but their desecrated suits of power armour were fitted with bulbous, turbine-driven backpacks. They carried ornate bolt pistols and chainswords in their hands, and long trophy cords strung with human scalps hung heavily at their waists. The young Space Wolf recognised them with a surge of frozen dread: Chaos Raptors, the shock troops and flesh hunters of the Traitor Legions. They plunged like arrows into the field around the running

Wolves, filling the air with their bloodcurdling shrieks.

Angry howls and the crack of bolt pistols echoed among the shifting stalks as the Raptors closed in from all sides. Ragnar howled a challenge of his own and drew his frost blade from its scabbard. Just as the rune-marked blade whirred into deadly life a dark shape burst into the narrow row ahead of the young Space Wolf. The Raptor spun on his heel, his trophy lines fanning out in a dreadful display as he brought his weapons to bear.

The Raptor's bolt pistol boomed and a mass-reactive shell flattened against Ragnar's breastplate. Snarling, the young Space Wolf broke into a full run, snapping shots at the foe as he came. The bolt pistol shells rang harmlessly off the Raptor's armour, and an answering shot ricocheted from the side of Ragnar's knee. With a fierce shout, Ragnar raised his sword and slashed at the Raptor's neck, but the Chaos warrior was a blur of motion, parrying the stroke with a sweep of its chainsword. Sparks flew from the clash of blades, but the attack was only a feint. Ragnar took another step forward, put his bolt pistol against the Raptor's left eye and pulled the trigger. The heavy shell burst the helmet apart, and Ragnar leapt over the foe's collapsing form.

Sounds of confused fighting echoed all around Ragnar as he tried to focus on Gabriella's scent. Las-bolts hissed through the air, and stray bolt-rounds carved paths through the dense rows of sacrificial stalks. Off to Ragnar's right, a man screamed in agony and a volley of wild las-bolts tore through the air. Bolter rounds rang off armour to the young Space Wolf's left, and then came the unmistakeable sound of a chain-blade rending flesh.

Gabriella's scent was growing stronger. She was close by, and Ragnar's pulse quickened when he realised that her trail led into the midst of a fierce battle that was raging just ahead. He was so intent on the sounds of battle that he didn't see the Raptor coming, until it leapt at him through a screen of rustling stalks to his right.

A chainsword roared through the air, slicing through the tall, green plants and scraping against Ragnar's right pauldron. The blade's whirring teeth sliced open the skin along his jaw, cutting the young Space Wolf to the bone. He whirled, bringing up his frost blade, but the Raptor blocked it with its snarling blade and raised his bolt pistol for a shot at Ragnar's unprotected neck. But before either Wolf or Raptor could react, a slim blade was buried deep in the attacker's neck. The Chaos warrior collapsed in a flood of steaming ichor as Torin pulled his sword free.

There was a sound like a thunderclap a few dozen metres ahead, and a bellow like that of an enraged bear. 'That would be Haegr,' Torin said with a grin. Ragnar nodded curtly and broke back into a run.

Within moments, they found themselves at the edge of a trampled clearing of sorts, where blades, bodies and tramping feet had flattened a rough circle within the blasphemous field. Gabriella, Volt, and Haegr stood back to back in the centre of the clearing, shooting and swinging at the pack of Raptors that encircled them. Bodies lay everywhere. Half a dozen armoured Chaos warriors were sprawled across the dark earth, close to the broken bodies of two of the

Thunderhawk's gunners and Harald's one-armed Blood Claw. At the far end of the clearing the Thunderhawk's tech-priest was on his knees, choking for breath as he pressed red-stained hands to his torn throat. Haegr was trying to reach the mortally wounded bondsman, keeping the Raptors at bay with mighty sweeps of his thunder hammer.

Inquisitor Volt levelled his bolt pistol at one of the Raptors and fired. The shell took the armoured warrior square in the chest, and powerful blessings worked into the ammunition punched right through the armoured breastplate and consumed the man inside in a sheet of silvery flames. The inquisitor's armour burned bright with the glowing tracery of potent wards, and his unsheathed sword glimmered with pale blue lightning, similar to a Rune Priest's blade. A Raptor's gun barked, and a slug smashed into Volt's shoulder, knocking the old man off his feet. Three of the Chaos warriors rushed forward, leaping high on jets of shrieking air and plunging like falcons upon their prey.

To Ragnar's horror, Lady Gabriella rushed to protect the fallen inquisitor. She levelled a sleek-looking silver pistol at the lead Raptor and fired an indigo-coloured beam that burned a glowing hole clean through the armoured foe. The warrior collapsed with a screech, but before his companions could react, the Navigator slashed at them with a sweeping stroke of her sabre. The master crafted power blade glimmered like white-hot steel as it sliced through the legs of one Raptor and cut the thigh of the other. The wounded Raptor let out a sharp hiss and staggered backwards, shooting Gabriella twice in the chest. She pitched backwards and fell without a sound.

Ragnar charged into the clearing with a wild howl, sword ready and bolt pistol blazing. Two Raptors toppled, their throats blown apart by mass-reactive shells, and another had its chest split open by a stroke from the young Space Wolf's blade. Torin followed in Ragnar's wake, snapping off precise, deadly shots at the foemen near Gabriella's prone form.

Two Raptors spun around at the Wolves' sudden assault and slashed at Ragnar. The young Space Wolf took their raking blows against his battle worn armour, and struck off their heads with a single sweep of his sword. He stepped past their collapsing bodies and buried his sword into the side of another onrushing Chaos warrior. The Raptor's sword raked at the side of the young Space Wolf's face and cut deep into his neck before his lifeless form sank to the ground. Ragnar hurled the Raptor's body away, and with two more steps he reached the Navigator's side.

His enhanced senses told him at once that she was still alive; he could hear her heartbeat hammering in her chest. She sat up with a grimace, letting go of her sword and pressing her hand to the two slugs that had flattened themselves against her breastplate. 'I'm all right,' she said breathlessly. 'Help me up.'

Taking her at her word, Ragnar lifted Gabriella to her feet, while Torin helped Inquisitor Volt. Haegr whirled around, raising his stained hammer, and then his beady eyes widened as he recognised his brothers. 'Torin! Ragnar! Where the devil have you two been? I've been fighting the whole damned horde single-handed!'

'Never mind that now,' Ragnar snarled. 'How much farther to the buildings at the centre of the combine?'

Haegr straightened, peering over the tops of the sac-rificial plants. 'Three hundred metres or so,' he said. A stray bolt-round whickered past the Wolf's shaggy head, causing him to duck down again.

'Let's go,' Ragnar said. 'I'm on point. Torin on the left, Haegr on the right. Lady Gabriella, Inquisitor Volt, you're in the middle. Now move!'

They set off once more down the narrow lanes between the sacrificial stalks, weapons held ready. The fighting seemed to be tapering off, and howls echoing back and forth from the fields ahead told Ragnar that at least some of Harald's pack still lived. As they ran across the remainder of the field, they stumbled over more trampled scenes of carnage, strewn with blood and scorched earth from the Raptor's jets.

Ragnar and his companions came upon Harald and his warriors all at once, nearly falling over them as they crouched behind a metal barrier at the north end of the field. The pack leader was studying the complex of darkened buildings ahead. Lightning flickered, banishing the shadows around the structures for a tan-talising instant.

Harald shook his head. 'Gunther thought he saw movement behind one of those buildings, but with all the lightning it's hard to be sure.'

'Well, we can't stay out here,' Volt said hoarsely. 'We need to get somewhere defensible before those ships come back again.'

'No, we need to keep moving,' Ragnar said flatly. 'If we hole up in these buildings the enemy will sur-round us and wear us down. Time and numbers are on their side.'

'We agree on that much at least,' Harald growled.

The old inquisitor studied the buildings almost wistfully. Ragnar sensed that the man was exhausted, and Gabriella was not in much better shape, but Volt finally nodded. 'All right, we stay on the move,' he said, and then pointed at the buildings. 'We'll cross the compound and disappear into the field on the other side. That's the most direct route to the mountains north of us.'

Ragnar and Harald exchanged glances and rose to their feet as one. Weapons sweeping the open ground beyond the barrier, the Space Wolves emerged warily from the field. Lightning glittered across the surface of their ice-blue armour and on the whirring teeth of their chainblades.

The buildings were low, ferrocrete bunkers, most of them built to house the agri-servitors that tended the fields, plus a generator station and a logic hub. Four tall granaries towered from the centre of the compound, rising more than forty metres into the air. There were no lights, nor were there doors set in the buildings' doorframes or glass panels in the windows. Evidently, the structures alone were enough to make Madox's geomancy possible.

Ragnar surveyed the battered group that emerged from the depths of the sacrificial field. None of the Thunderhawk's gunners or its tech-priest had survived, and three of Harald's pack were gone. Counting Volt, Gabriella and the Wolfblade, there were only twelve souls left against the might of an entire Traitor Legion.

It will be enough, Ragnar thought grimly. It will have to be enough.

They moved quickly and quietly down dark lanes between the empty structures. Ragnar felt his hackles rise as he watched the open doorways for signs of movement. The lightning played tricks on his eyes, hinting at movement down the dark side-streets.

Within a few minutes they had reached the foot of the towering granaries, and the lanes widened to a large ferrocrete plaza, where the agri-servitors could load and unload grain from the huge silos. Moving cautiously, the Wolves advanced across the open space.

Their boots echoed hollowly across the ferrocrete as they stepped into the midst of the towering granaries. Lightning flashed silently overhead. On impulse, Ragnar looked up at the arcs of unearthly light, and saw the silhouettes of horned helms and hulking shoulders ringing the tops of the four silos. 'Ambush!' he cried, raising his bolt pistol, but it was already too late.

The Raptors leapt from their perches atop the silos and dropped heavily among the surprised Wolves. Ragnar guessed that there were perhaps a score of them, attacking the group from all sides. They had been the true threat all along, he realised. The Raptors dropped into the field had been like hounds, driving the prey into the trap.

One of the attackers landed next to Gabriella, but was struck by Torin, Haegr and the Navigator almost simultaneously. Ragnar sighted on another Raptor a few metres away and shot the warrior through the neck. Then a pair of attackers rushed at him from the left, firing as they came. One shot smashed into his hip and another took him high in the shoulder, flattening against his armour, but nearly knocking him from his feet.

The sounds of fighting and the cries of wounded Wolves echoed from all sides. Ragnar howled a challenge at the oncoming Raptors and prepared to die like a son of Fenris.

He shot the first warrior between his red eyes, and then parried the sweeping stroke of the second foeman. The Raptor reversed its stroke in a blur of motion and slashed downwards at Ragnar's knee. The snarling chainsword found a gap in his armour and bit deep, grating across the bone. The young Space Wolf snarled and hacked downwards, slicing off the foeman's sword-hand at the wrist.

Then there was a flash of light, and a terrible, burning impact smashed into the side of Ragnar's head just above the temple. He heard a roaring sound in his ears, like a howling wind or the pounding of a stormy surf, and then he realised he was falling.

Ragnar landed face down on the ground, blood pouring from the wound in his head. Sounds of fighting raged above him. There was a crack of thunder and a shouted oath, and then the roaring filled his ears once again.

No, not roaring, howling, like a huge pack of Fenrisian wolves on the hunt.

The sound set Ragnar's blood hissing in his veins. He struggled to get his legs underneath him so that he could stand. He blinked, discovering that he could no longer see out of his left eye.

Something heavy fell on top of him. With a slurred curse, he shoved at the thing, grasping dimly that it was the riven corpse of a Raptor. Ragnar rolled awkwardly away from the thing and found himself lying on his back.

A dark silhouette loomed over him. Teeth bared, Ragnar tried to raise his sword, but the figure laid an armoured boot across his wrist and pinned it to the ground. The young Space Wolf raised his bolt pistol, only to find that his gun hand was empty.

The howling continued all around him. Lightning flashed, and in the flickering light Ragnar saw that the figure above him was cased in dark grey power armour similar to his own. Yellowed skulls and leather cords strung with long, curved fangs hung from the warrior's belt, as well as ancient tokens of iron etched with the runes of his people. A red wolf's head snarled fiercely upon the warrior's scarred right pauldron.

The warrior was huge, easily as large as Haegr. His broad shoulders were covered in a black wolf pelt, and his iron grey hair hung in two thick braids that draped heavily across his rune worked breastplate. His shaggy beard was still black as jet, however, and the eyes that shone beneath the warrior's craggy brow were yellow gold, like those of a wolf. In one hand he gripped a mighty, single-bearded axe, its curved blade marked with the scars of countless grim battles. Fell runes were carved into the dark metal, and it crackled with unseen and deadly energies.

When the figure spoke, his voice was cold and hard as the glaciers of Fenris, full of power and old beyond reckoning. To the young Space Wolf it sounded like the voice of a god.

'You must be Ragnar Blackmane,' the warrior said. 'We've been looking for you.'

FIFTEEN
The Company of Wolves

A BATTLE CANNON shell howled high overhead. The rebel tank gunner had been overeager and had fired too early, missing the fleeing Imperial troops by hundreds of metres. Grenadiers shouted and screamed at one another as they ran pell-mell down the debris choked causeway. Tracer fire from heavy stubbers and volleys of lasgun fire raked through the retreating soldiers. Men writhed, clutching at their wounds, or fell lifelessly to the ground.

Panicked grenadiers flowed in a dark tide around the impassive figures of Mikal Sternmark and his four Wolf Guard. The presence of the armoured giants was the only thing keeping the Imperial retreat from becoming a total rout. The Wolves moved at a stolid, measured pace, facing back the way they'd come and cutting down rebel squads that pressed too close.

'Haakon!' Sternmark called, levelling Redclaw at the rebel tank nosing its way among the squads of enemy troops a hundred metres behind them. The Terminator to Sternmark's right stopped in his tracks, raising the targeting module in his hand, finding the range to the target, and then loosing one of his few remaining Cyclone missiles. The antitank round streaked down the causeway with a hissing, spitting roar and detonated against the front of the battle tank's turret. Concussion and shrapnel scythed through the infantry surrounding the tank, and the Leman Russ lurched to a sudden halt. A good shot, but Sternmark couldn't be certain whether it had knocked the tank out or not.

They had held the barricade beneath the towering angel for much of the day, throwing back no less than ten bloody assaults before they had been forced to withdraw under a storm of tank and artillery fire. By pure, evil chance a shell had struck the defiant angel at the start of the last barrage, blowing it apart and showering debris on the weary defenders below. Superstitious to a fault, the beleaguered grenadiers had taken it as an omen.

Surrounded by hundreds of their dead comrades and facing an apparently inexhaustible tide of enemy troops, the surviving regimental officers ordered a general retreat just as the rebels renewed their attack. Sternmark watched helplessly as the first squads began to stream away from the ruined barricade, but he knew from experience that there was no rallying the broken troops now that the withdrawal had begun. Instead, he formed the battered platoons around him into a rearguard, and sent Sven's pack racing down the causeway as fast as they could to form a second line of defence ahead of the retreating Guardsmen. He'd had no contact with the young Grey Hunter since. Sternmark could only pray to

Russ that Sven had been successful. They were less than a kilometre from the edge of the city. If the rebel troops made it into the open terrain beyond the city there would be no stopping them from reaching the starport.

Sternmark caught sight of a rebel lascannon team struggling to haul their weapon into firing position, and cut them down with a burst from his storm bolter. The rebels responded with a hail of wild lasgun fire that burst across Sternmark's Terminator armour and pitted the ferrocrete roadway. The Wolf Guard ignored the flickering barrage, casting a quick glance over his shoulder to gauge the terrain along their path of retreat. Sternmark caught sight of a massive pile of rubble a hundred metres or so away. A building had collapsed onto the causeway, laying a natural barricade almost two-thirds of the way across the road. Armoured figures peered over the top of the debris pile, awaiting the approach of the rebel troops. They'd reached the second line of defence.

Mikal keyed his vox-unit. A shrill squeal of static filled his ears. The rebels had been trying to jam the Imperial vox-net since morning. 'We're holding here!' he called. 'Fall back and take position behind the debris pile!'

The Terminators raised their swords or power fists to show they'd received the order as they continued to fire at the advancing rebel troops. The first grenadiers were already swarming over the rubble or running around the far end of the pile. Sternmark fired another burst at the traitors and turned to run for the barrier. His mind worked furiously as he studied the terrain and tried to work out the best way to organise its defence. He could put his Wolves along the rubble pile to keep the infantry at bay and keep the grenadiers behind the barricade, out of the line of fire but ready to hit the flank of any attackers trying to force their way around the far end.

There was a loud boom and a battle cannon shell crashed against the debris pile, blowing a deep crater in the jumble of ferrocrete and steel. The Leman Russ was back in action, its treads clanking as it resumed its advance. Sternmark grimaced at the sting of shrapnel along the side of his face, and clambered up the jumbled slope of stone blocks and twisted girders. As he reached the summit, the Leman Russ fired again, blasting another crater in the barrier and showering him with a rain of dirt and stone.

Sternmark leapt over the summit and skidded down the other side until he was out of the line of fire. He found Sven and the two remaining members of his pack crouching behind the largest pieces of stonework they could find. The young Grey Hunter had acquired a Guard-issue meltagun at some point, and Sternmark was startled to see the two warriors beside Sven carrying hellguns instead of their blessed bolters.

'Where are your weapons?' the Wolf Guard snapped.

Sven shifted position to show his bolter stowed in its travel clip beside his suit's backpack. 'Ran out of ammunition hours ago,' he said.

'Why in Russ's name didn't you report it?'

The Grey Hunter looked bewildered. 'I did, lord,' Sven said, 'back at the barricade, just before the eighth bloody wave hit! Don't you remember?'

Sternmark shook his head angrily. The truth was that he couldn't recall. Everything seemed to be blurring together in his mind, dissolving into a jumble of half-formed images. The red tide in the back of his mind washed everything else away.

'Never mind!' the Wolf Guard snarled, turning away angrily to survey the state of the barrier's defences. He hoped to find at least a few hundred grenadiers and some heavy weapons dug into positions angling away from the barrier. With enough troops and a little luck, he thought, they could hold until nightfall, long enough to get some more ammunition sent up.

The only Guardsmen he saw, however, were the members of his rearguard, still retreating farther down the causeway. Sven and his two battle-brothers were alone on the barricade.

Shock and anger played across Sternmark's blood-stained face. 'Where are they?' he asked Sven. 'Where are the grenadiers? I ordered you to form a second line–'

Another explosion cut Sternmark off, raining more debris down on the beleaguered Wolves. 'We tried to form a line here,' Sven shouted back, 'but the regimental commander received orders from his superior to fall back to the starport.'

'The starport?' Mikal said incredulously. As he spoke, his four bodyguards appeared around the end of the barrier, still firing at the oncoming troops. Heavy stubber fire from the advancing tank rang off their armoured breastplates, scattering glowing red tracers in all directions. Sternmark waved his warriors back around the end of the barricade and out of the line of fire. Then he skidded to the bottom of the debris pile and keyed his vox-unit once more. 'Citadel, this is Asgard!' he shouted into the pickup. 'Citadel, this is Asgard! Do you read me?'

Sternmark strained to hear a response over the screech of the rebel jamming signals. Several seconds passed before he heard a faint reply.

'Asgard? Where have you been?' Athelstane asked angrily. 'We've been calling you for the past three hours.'

The Wolf Guard ignored the question. 'Why did you order the grenadiers back to the starport?' he shouted. 'We can't hold the causeway without them.'

'The causeway is already lost,' Athelstane shot back. 'The rebels broke through our lines four kilometres east of your position and have split our forces in two. If we don't pull back to the starport now our troops in the city will be surrounded and destroyed. That includes *you*, Asgard.' It was hard to tell over the jamming, but Sternmark thought the anger in Athelstane's voice had subsided a bit. 'There are reports that Chaos Marines have been sighted in the city, and we've lost contact with several of your packs scattered across the planet.'

Sternmark felt his blood run cold. 'Lost contact? What do you mean?'

'I mean they aren't answering our signals, much like you,' the general replied. 'You need to get back here right away, Asgard. Things are getting out of hand.'

Cursing bitterly, Sternmark switched off the vox-unit. The rumble of the rebel tank engine and the squeal of its treads were very loud now, sounding as though it was just a few dozen metres away on the other side of the barrier. He could hear the hoarse shouts of the traitor Guardsmen and the gibbering cries of the mutants in their midst as they raced for the barrier.

Mikal checked his storm bolter. He was down to his last magazine, and it was reading half-empty. His fellow Wolf Guard stood close by, ever courageous and resolute, but he knew that they must be nearly out of ammunition as well. Nevertheless, he was tempted to remain where he was, to make a stand at the barrier and fight to the last.

If the rest of the line had held, he wouldn't have hesitated, but what would it achieve now? Sacrifice was second nature to the Adeptus Astartes, but not without good reason. A final battle here would just be a waste of good men and precious wargear.

Still the red tide rose within him, demanding release. It promised nothing save spilled blood and dead foemen, and Sternmark longed to surrender to its embrace. I am no leader of men, he thought angrily. I'm a warrior, a wolf wrought of ceramite and steel.

Atop the barrier, Sven and his battle-brothers nodded to one another, and then went into action. The three Grey Hunters moved as one. The warriors with hellguns popped up and rapid fired into the approaching traitors, while Sven took careful aim with his meltagun. There was a draconic hiss of superheated air as the assault weapon fired, and a thunderous explosion sent the rebel tank's turret spinning into the air. Screams and shouts of alarm rang from the other side of the barrier as the Grey Hunters dropped back into cover and slid down the slope to the waiting Terminators.

'That took care of the tank!' Sven said with a feral grin. 'There must be a few hundred rebels left, though. What shall we do, lord?'

Sternmark gripped Redclaw's hilt and fought against the wolf inside him. 'We retreat,' he said grimly. 'We're falling back to the starport. The battle in the city is lost.'

* * *

RAGNAR BLINKED HOT blood from his eyes and bared his teeth at the bearded giant looming above him. A chorus of lusty howls filled his ears and set his mind to reeling. He could feel the curse of the Wulfen responding to the throaty cries. 'Who in the name of Russ are you?' he growled, letting the frost blade slide from his hand.

The giant narrowed his yellow eyes. 'Who am I?' he said, his voice rough edged with menace. 'I'm Torvald the Reaver, of Red Kraken Hold, and with this axe I've slain gods and men.' He raised the fearsome weapon in his hand and showed the gleaming edge to the young Space Wolf.

Ragnar could feel challenge in the giant's voice, like a blade against his skin. His blood seethed, and the Wulfen gripped him, body and soul. This time, he didn't try to stop it.

His empty sword hand closed around Torvald's ankle and pulled with all the wild strength of the Wulfen behind it. In the same motion, Ragnar rose up and drove his other hand against the side of the giant's hip. The speed and ferocity of Ragnar's attack took the giant by surprise. His heavy cloak flaring like dark wings, Torvald fell forward onto his knees. Swift as a shadow the young Space Wolf came up behind him, grabbing a handful of the giant's hair and pulling his scarred head back to reveal the corded muscles of the Reaver's throat.

Angry howls and bestial cries shook the air. Dark shapes rushed at Ragnar from all sides, and he glimpsed huge, swift forms in gunmetal grey armour with luminous, lantern yellow eyes. Lightning flickered across the empty sky, revealing shaggy heads and blunt, toothy snouts. Long, black talons glinted as the massive wolf-men lunged for Ragnar.

The world seemed to tilt beneath the young Space Wolf as the monsters closed in around him. These were the beasts that haunted his dreams and had fought the daemons in the command bunker at Charys! He let go of Torvald and staggered backwards, struggling to think. A low, animal growl rose in his throat, and the pack of wolf-men answered, snarling and snapping their fanged jaws.

'Be still!' shouted a clear, strong voice. 'In the name of Russ and the Allfather, be still!'

The wolf-men paused, hanging their heads and sniffing the air cautiously. The voice echoed strangely in Ragnar's head. He turned around, seeking its source, and his knees buckled beneath him.

A figure in familiar power armour was striding towards him through a press of hulking wolf-men, as a lord might move among his hounds. Lightning glimmered on the warrior's golden hair and the iron wolf amulet hanging from a heavy chain around his neck.

Sigurd the Wolf Priest approached Ragnar, his crozius arcanum held high. 'Remember your oaths, Ragnar Blackmane,' he said sternly. 'Master the wolf within you and stay your hand. We are all brothers here.'

The words seemed to echo strangely, as though from a great distance. Ragnar blinked his one good eye and looked for Gabriella, but all he found was darkness.

FIERY PAIN BLOOMED in Ragnar's head, dragging him roughly back to consciousness. He snarled, shaking his head, but an armoured hand closed fiercely around his jaw and held him fast.

Blinking furiously, Ragnar opened his crusted eyelids and saw Sigurd's pale face looming above him. He was lying on his back, surrounded by crouching figures. Faces swam into focus. Torin and Haegr watched the Wolf Priest work, their expressions guarded. Gabriella's face was bleak and etched with strain.

It was Haegr's hand that gripped him. Torin leaned close. 'Hold still a moment more,' he said to Ragnar. 'He's almost done.'

There was another bright flash of pain, but this time Ragnar was able to blunt it with the mental rotes he'd learned at the Fang. He felt a trickle of blood seep down the side of his head as Sigurd leaned back and inspected the blood-stained tip of a bolt pistol round. 'You must have a head made of solid ceramite,' the Wolf Priest growled. 'Still, you're lucky the shot hit at an angle, or it would have blown your brains out.'

Torin chuckled. 'No worries there, priest. That slug would have had to rattle around in Ragnar's head like a dice before it hit anything important.'

Sigurd offered no argument, tossing the bullet aside with a frown and digging a couple of metal jars from a pack at his belt. 'The shot hit you just above the left eye,' he said as he began applying the healing balms to Ragnar's wound. 'Are you having any trouble with your vision?'

Ragnar struggled to focus his thoughts. Visions of an axe-wielding giant and snarling wolf-men loomed like ghosts in his mind. 'I had some trouble before,' he said absently, 'but that might just have been the blood. I'm fine now.'

Sigurd nodded curtly, but his expression was dubious. He pressed a wound sealant to Ragnar's forehead, and rose to his feet. 'Watch him closely,' the Wolf

Priest said to Haegr and Torin. 'I expect we'll be on the move very soon.'

Grimacing, Ragnar rose to his elbows as Sigurd turned on his heel and strode away, picking his way over the broken bodies of Chaos Raptors that littered the ground between the towering granaries. He saw Harald and his pack mates a few metres away, crouching beside Inquisitor Volt, checking their weapons and speaking to one another in low voices. Hulking forms stalked silently around the edges of the open space, sniffing warily at the empty sky. Ragnar caught the scent of the wolf-men and felt his hackles rise.

Ten metres away, Torvald stood with his axe raised to the sky. Lightning flickered upon his upturned face. The giant's eyes were open, but they glimmered green, like Gabriella's pineal eye, and Torvald's face was set in an expression of grim concentration.

Ragnar struggled to make sense of the scene. 'What in Morkai's name is going on here?' he muttered.

'We've fallen into the pages of a legend,' Torin said reverently, 'one that stretches back ten thousand years.'

The young Space Wolf scowled. 'What are you talking about?'

'Don't mind him,' Haegr said. 'I haven't understood a single thing he's said since the battle ended. If I didn't know any better I'd say he took the head wound instead of you.' The burly Wolfblade surveyed the scene of carnage and shrugged. 'The Raptors ambushed us. I'm sure you remember that part. But before mighty Haegr could put them to flight, Torvald and his... warriors... raced out of the shadows and tore our foes to pieces.'

'But who are they?' Ragnar asked, still haunted by the images in his mind's eye. 'They are clearly sons of Fenris, but the armour and insignia–'

'They haven't been seen since the Heresy,' Torin said, 'not since Leman Russ descended on Prospero to wreak his vengeance on the Thousand Sons.' He shook his head in wonder. 'They're part of the Lost Company, Ragnar, the Thirteenth.'

Haegr let out a snort. 'Listen to him. He thinks he's a skald, now.'

'Perhaps I was, once upon a time,' Torin said archly. 'There's more to life than just eating and fighting, you shag-eared lummox.'

'But what are they doing here?' Ragnar interjected. 'And how did Sigurd come to be with them?'

Torin shrugged. 'You'd have to ask them, brother. Sigurd wouldn't tell us a thing, and I gather Torvald is using his powers to hide us from our foes.'

'He's a priest, too?' Ragnar asked dumbly.

'Not just a priest, Ragnar. Torvald was one of the *first* Rune Priests,' Torin replied. 'He fought alongside Russ during the Great Crusade. Imagine that!'

'And you pitched him into the dirt as if he was a bare-chinned aspirant,' Haegr said, slapping Ragnar on the shoulder. 'That was well done, little brother! He's lucky he didn't try to shake his axe in my face. I might have bitten it off and spat it at his feet!'

The young Space Wolf paid Haegr no mind, staring instead at the huge wolf-men patrolling around them. 'They're all wolf-bitten,' he said, 'even Torvald. He has the mark of the Wulfen in his eyes.'

'According to the sagas, Magnus and the Thousand Sons escaped our wrath on Prospero by retreating through a portal into the warp, but Russ wasn't about to let them escape so easily. He ordered the Thirteenth to give chase, and they disappeared into the fading portal, never to be seen again.' Torin shook his head ruefully. 'It's a wonder any of them are alive at all.'

'Ten thousand years,' Ragnar echoed, trying to make sense of all he'd heard. 'What does Torvald want of us?'

'Not Torvald, he's here at the bidding of his lord, Bulveye. Sigurd said we're to head up into the mountains to meet with Bulveye and the rest of his warband. I expect we'll learn more when we get there,' Torin said.

Ragnar met Torin's eye. 'How do we know we can trust them?' he asked.

The question surprised Torin. 'They're our brothers, Ragnar!'

'Even so, they've spent ten millennia at the mercy of the warp,' the young Space Wolf countered. 'Who can guess what their motives are now?'

Torin shifted uncomfortably. 'We'll know soon enough. Torvald and his Wulfen mean to take us into the mountains, and I don't think we have much choice in the matter.' The older Wolfblade rose abruptly to his feet. 'Besides, we're not exactly unblemished ourselves.'

Ragnar watched, bemused as Torin stalked away. Haegr shook his head and rose to lumber after his long-time friend. The young Space Wolf turned to Gabriella, a questioning look on his face. 'What did Torin mean by that?'

The Navigator looked at Ragnar for a long moment, and then reached out and lightly touched his cheek. 'It's your eyes,' she said, a weary sadness in her voice, 'they're yellow-gold now, just like Torvald's.'

* * *

AT THE SAME moment, many leagues across the shadow world, a crescendo of pain and suffering rose within the walls of the crimson temple as the energies of the great ritual approached a critical mass. A thousand sorcerers and initiates knelt on the stone floor of the cavernous hall, their hands outstretched to the altar of black stone and the bloody scraps of flesh that lay upon it. Their lips were cracked and bleeding, their throats raw and their eyes seared shut by the awful energies emitted from the burning eye that hung like a blasphemous sun above the sacrificial stone.

Hellish light fell upon Madox. He could feel the terrible favour of his primarch resting like a fiery mantle upon his shoulders. The sorcerer lord stood before the great altar, leading the intricate ritual in a cold, implacable voice. In one hand he gripped the stolen Spear of Russ, and it was through this sacred icon that Madox channelled the force of his unholy spell. It was the fulcrum upon which the ritual would act. Without it, the great spell would have been for naught.

Madox felt the minds of the lesser sorcerers in the room, each one shaping a specific part of the malediction that he would channel into the spear. The elements were slipping inexorably into place, like the workings of a vast and terrible engine. He could sense the moment approaching and his voice swelled with triumph.

The Space Wolves had carried the seeds of their own destruction from the very beginning. Very soon those seeds would bear bitter fruit.

SIXTEEN
Red Tide Rising

TORVALD THE REAVER drove the Wolves hard, leading them out of the dismal fields of the agri-combine and towards the slate coloured mountains to the north at a dead run. Despite his age, the Rune Priest was fleet as a deer. Ragnar and the other warriors had to push themselves in order to keep up. During the first hour the dark green fields of the combine were just a faint line on the horizon, and the empty plains were giving way to low, rounded foothills of dark stone and lifeless earth.

Inquisitor Volt and Gabriella managed to keep the pace for the first half hour, but the exertions they'd endured after the crash of the Thunderhawk quickly took their toll. The older Volt faltered first, his pace slowing and his breath coming in ragged gasps. He stumbled, on the verge of collapse, but two of Harald's Blood Claws closed in on either side of the inquisitor

and slipped their arms around his waist, carrying him
along just as they would a crippled pack-mate.
Gabriella lasted almost half an hour longer, but the
sound of her pained breathing made it clear that she'd
driven herself well beyond her physical limits. Before
she could falter Haegr came up behind her and
scooped the Navigator up in the crook of one arm,
like a father might carry a child. Gabriella hung limp
in the burly Wolfblade's embrace, too exhausted to
manage much in the way of protest.

The Wulfen, no less than fifteen of them, Ragnar
was shocked to discover, loped along easily beside the
warriors. They moved with a swift, fluid gait, clawed
hands swinging and shoulders hunched, their wolf-
like heads held low as if to sniff for signs of danger.
Their armour was dented and scarred from centuries
of hard use, and Ragnar saw that many of their suits
had been patched with scavenged parts. He couldn't
be certain, but some of the replacements looked to
have been taken from the suits of slain Chaos
Marines. Their strength and speed were incredible, but
there was little intelligence in their golden eyes save
for the fierce cunning of a predator. When Ragnar met
their flat stares he felt his hackles rise with an instinc-
tive challenge, and more, a sense of mutual
recognition.

Is this my future? Ragnar brooded over the notion as
they raced across the twilit plain. He thought of Torvald. The Rune Priest was wolf-bitten, but for all that
he seemed capable of holding the curse at bay. There
must be a way, the young Space Wolf thought. He
couldn't bear the notion that he was a prisoner to his
fate.

There was only one person he could think of who could answer his questions. Gritting his teeth, Ragnar picked up his pace and sought out Sigurd the Wolf Priest.

Sigurd ran in the midst of Harald's Blood Claw pack, just a few metres behind Torvald. The younger warriors had gravitated around the priest since his unexpected return, like iron to a lodestone, and they glared belligerently at Ragnar as he worked his way into their midst.

The Wolf Priest noted his approach with a single, forbidding glance. 'What do you want, exile?' he said.

Ragnar gave the priest a sidelong glare. 'All of us are exiles now, priest,' he retorted. 'Our ship was destroyed, so there's no chance of ever returning home to our Chapter and kin.'

Sigurd said nothing at first, although the priest's stiff, silent demeanour told Ragnar that his point had hit home. Finally he said, 'We saw the battle unfold above the shadow world, but could only guess at the outcome.'

'The *Fist of Russ* is gone, and many brave men are feasting in the Halls of Russ now,' Ragnar said gravely. 'We detected a signal as we tried to make planetfall. Was that yours?'

'Yes,' Sigurd said. 'Bulveye was against it, but I thought it worth the risk. Lookouts spotted the aerial battle and the fires of your crash, and Torvald volunteered to search for survivors.' The priest spread his hands. 'The Wulfen caught your scent and led us to the agri-combine just in time.'

'It seems that the Wulfen saved you as well,' Ragnar said thoughtfully. Memories of the confused melee in the rebel command bunker flashed through his mind. 'The last I saw of you, you were surrounded by daemons.'

Sigurd gave Ragnar a hard look, but reluctantly nodded. 'It was a grim battle,' he agreed. 'They came upon me all at once, rising out of the aether like ghosts. This world we're on lies across Charys like a shadow, allowing them to step between the two at will.'

'I know,' the young Space Wolf replied. 'Inquisitor Volt and Lady Gabriella unravelled the mystery, which is what led us here in the first place.'

The Wolf Priest nodded in understanding. 'The daemons seemed to take particular interest in me for some reason. Perhaps a priest makes a better trophy than a mere warrior,' he said ruefully. 'I struck down several of the abominations, but to my shame the rest of them overwhelmed me. They pinned my arms and somehow dragged me back across the threshold into this nether realm.' Sigurd nodded to the towering form of the Rune Priest just ahead. 'But the foul creatures didn't realise they were being hunted. Torvald and the Wulfen ambushed the Chaos sorcerer and his daemons even as they ambushed us.'

Ragnar remembered the sight of the towering Wulfen grappling with the Chaos sorcerer in the vault beneath the rebel command bunker. 'So Torvald and his warriors can cross between the worlds as well?'

Sigurd frowned. 'Were that possible, I would have returned to the battle straightaway,' he snapped. 'No, the crossing is affected by sorcery. Sometimes it's possible to be caught up in the spell and drawn across the threshold, but only for a moment.' He shrugged. 'The Wulfen pulled down the sorcerer and tore him apart,

and Torvald turned his axe upon the daemons beset-
ting me. When the battle was done I tended their
wounds as best as I could, and they treated me as one
of their own.'

'But how did they come to be here?' Ragnar asked.
'Torin says the Thirteenth Company was lost during
the time of the Heresy.'

'Lost?' Sigurd seemed astonished by the notion.
'Bulveye's company was never lost, Ragnar. When a
Wolf Lord is slain a new one is raised up to take his
place. The same is true for the great companies, but a
place for the Thirteenth remains at the table of the
Great Wolf back on Fenris, as though they are
expected to one day return. Think on that, Ragnar. The
Thirteenth Company was sent into the Eye of Terror
by Russ, and for ten thousand years they have continued their mission, regardless of the cost.'

The thought was a sobering one. Ragnar studied the
grey, featureless mountains ahead and tried to imagine wandering them for ten thousand years, until
Fenris was nothing but a distant memory. Unbidden,
he felt the wolf within him stir. 'Their honour has cost
them dearly,' he said.

'Honour always does,' the Wolf Priest replied.

For a while, they ran on in silence. The footfalls of
the Wolves were like a heavy drumbeat across the
sloping plain, beating out a war-song in time to the
baleful lightning overhead. Ragnar considered his
words carefully.

'How does a man come to be wolf-bitten, Sigurd?'

The Wolf Priest shot Ragnar a sharp look, but
abruptly relented as he met the young Space Wolf's
golden eyes. He considered the question for a

moment before he replied. 'All of us have the wolf in our blood,' he said. 'It sharpens our senses and gives us the glad rage of the berserker in battle, but like any wild thing it tests its bonds constantly, waiting for the chance to break free.'

Sigurd stared thoughtfully at a pair of Wulfen loping silently along beside Harald's pack. 'It is a constant struggle between man and wolf,' he said, 'and not every soul is strong enough to keep the beast at bay.' The priest laid a hand on the Iron Wolf amulet at his breast. 'We bind the beast with sacred oaths to Russ and the Allfather, and we of the priesthood purify our battle-brothers with rituals and devotions to strengthen their resolve. For most, that is enough.'

'Yet not enough for Bulveye and his warriors.'

Ragnar expected a pious retort from the young priest, but when Sigurd spoke, his voice was surprisingly compassionate. 'It is not our place to judge these warriors,' he said with conviction. 'Even the ancient Dreadnoughts must sleep between times of war, lest they succumb to their feral natures. How hard must it be to keep one's soul intact after a thousand years of war, much less *ten*?' The Wolf Priest shook his head solemnly. 'It is a testament to their courage and honour that they have endured as long as they have.'

The young Space Wolf nodded thoughtfully. 'But… is there no way to restore them?'

Sigurd stiffened slightly. Ragnar was straying into the proscribed territory of the priesthood. 'The transformation is a gradual one,' he said guardedly, 'but once begun, the process is inexorable. As the wolf within gains power, it exerts physical changes on the body.' He gestured to the Wulfen nearby. 'Much depends on the will and the faith of the warrior. The degradation can be halted, sometimes indefinitely, but it cannot be undone.'

The priest's words sent a chill through Ragnar's veins. 'Gabriella says that my eyes have changed colour,' he said numbly. 'How much longer do I have?'

Sigurd frowned. 'Truly, I do not know,' he said reluctantly. 'Again, it depends upon the warrior. The process begins slowly, but accelerates as the wolf gains power.'

'How slowly?' Ragnar asked.

The Wolf Priest glowered at Ragnar. 'Are you trying to shame me with my lack of experience?' he snapped. 'I confess I do not know for certain. The curse usually strikes initiates hardest, because their minds are still adapting to the changes taking place within them. Once a warrior becomes a full-fledged battle-brother... the curse takes years for the transformation to take hold.'

'Years?' Ragnar exclaimed. 'But I felt nothing before I returned to Fenris, just two months ago!'

Sigurd stared sharply at the young Space Wolf. 'That's not possible,' he said. 'Even with an initiate, it takes at least a year for the first changes to make themselves known.'

'If I were wolf-bitten a year ago, Ranek would have known it,' Ragnar declared, 'and I would have never been sent to Terra to serve House Bellisarius.'

The young priest thought it over, and his expression began to darken in consternation. 'It's true,' he said at last. 'Something else must be at work here, but I confess that I don't know what it could be.'

Ragnar nodded. 'Perhaps Bulveye or Torvald can tell us,' he said, daring to hope that things were not as hopeless as Sigurd suggested.

'Perhaps,' the priest allowed. 'We should reach the Wolf Lord's camp in a few more hours. I expect we'll learn a great deal then.'

They reached the first, wood-fringed foothills south of the grey mountains not long afterwards, and Torvald led the Wolves along the winding track of a dry streambed until they were hidden within the walls of a narrow, stony defile. Their pounding footfalls echoed crazily from the rocky walls as their course led north and east from one canyon to the next. The trail doubled back more than once, and without a pattern of stars to navigate by Ragnar soon lost track of where they were.

Within an hour Ragnar began to pick up the faint scents of other Wolves, and reckoned they were approaching the perimeter of the camp. His experienced eyes scanned the slopes of the rocky canyons through which they passed, but if there were sentries observing their approach he couldn't detect them. Then, abruptly, the canyon sloped steeply upward and the path narrowed to a cleft in the stone barely wide enough to admit the broad Space Marines.

Ragnar felt a prickling sensation race across his skin as he worked his way through the pass. Once through the cleft he quickly scanned the close-set walls of the defile that surrounded him and saw a pair of iron bars that had been driven into the stone on either side of the pass. Skulls and iron tokens carved with runes hung from each of the bars, and a wave of invisible power radiated from them.

'Those are way-posts, part of Torvald's system of wards,' Sigurd explained as he emerged from the cleft behind Ragnar. 'They confound attempts to locate Bulveye's camp using sorcery.' The Wolf Priest gazed upon the way-post with a mixture of awe and superstitious dread. 'Torvald and his kin have learned a great deal during their long campaign in the Eye.'

The path to Bulveye's camp had been carefully chosen, the approach forcing the Wolves to travel single-file and climb a steep, rocky approach into a high, sheer-sided canyon. At the southern end of the canyon, Ragnar saw the first of Bulveye's warriors: a pair of men crouching in the shadow of a boulder, covering the entrance to the canyon with a pair of plasma guns. Both warriors wore cloaks of tanned hide that had been covered in dirt and dust, and their motionless forms allowed them to blend in perfectly with their surroundings. Like Torvald, their long hair was thick and braided, and their beards hung halfway down their patched breastplates. They said nothing as the rescue party climbed past, studying them with cold, lupine eyes.

A little farther up the canyon a massive boulder had been rolled into a narrow place, creating a kind of dog-leg to prevent a clear line of fire into the area beyond. More warriors stood guard on the other side of the boulder, brandishing old, worn bolt pistols and ancient, rune carved blades. Their armour was decorated with intricate runes and carvings of battle scenes or voyages, and there were skulls or other battle trophies hanging from their broad belts. The warriors stared at Ragnar and the newcomers with frank but wary interest, stealing sidelong glances at one another and communicating in subtle gestures or nods.

More than a dozen metres further up the canyon they came upon a series of well-worn but serviceable wilderness shelters built alongside the rock walls. The camp looked as if it had been occupied for some time, and many of the shelters were marked with recent war trophies such as daemon talons and damaged pieces of blue and gold armour. More than a score of yellow-eyed warriors sat outside the shelters, cleaning their weapons or making repairs to their gear. On the surface, it looked no different from any other Space Wolf field camp that Ragnar had seen... except for the wary, challenging stares of the battle-brothers and the sense of history that stretched like an invisible tapestry across the camp and its inhabitants.

He'd felt such a thing once before, back when he was but a young lad plying the salt oceans of Fenris. His longship had been blown far off course during a storm, and they'd put in at a small island in search of fresh water. There they stumbled onto the camp of a small band of their clansmen who had been stranded there by a similar storm two years before. Ragnar still remembered the first time he'd set foot in their camp, and how the survivors had stared at him like a pack of wild dogs. They had lived in another world altogether since they had been lost, and their experiences had forged a bond that no one else could understand, much less share. It was a world in which he and his clansmen could not ever fully belong, and Ragnar felt the same sensation as he walked among the warriors of the Thirteenth Company.

They passed silently through the small camp and headed up to the far end of the canyon. Just off to the left, Ragnar was surprised to find a pack of huge, Fenrisian wolves stretched out in front of the entrance to a large cave. The wolves raised their shaggy heads as Torvald and the Wulfen approached, and the smallest of the pack rose onto its paws and loped into the darkness beyond the cave mouth. Torvald raised his axe, signalling for the party to halt, and went inside without a word. The Wulfen sank onto their haunches, some closing their eyes to rest while others dragged scraps of flesh from pouches at their belts and tore at them with their powerful jaws.

Harald's Blood Claws lowered Inquisitor Volt carefully to the ground. The old man spent several long minutes fishing a metal vial from his pack. He opened it with trembling hands and drank its contents in a single swallow. A little further away, Haegr set Gabriella on her feet. Though obviously tired, the Navigator was studying the Wulfen and the grim little camp with wide-eyed interest.

Ragnar slowly turned in place, surveying the canyon and its strange, forbidding inhabitants. He reminded himself that despite the differences between them, they were bound by the same oaths and the same world. The Thousand Sons were still their implacable foes, and Ragnar had no doubt that they would be able to count upon Bulveye and his warriors when the time came to strike at the heart of Madox's grand scheme. For the first time since crashing upon the shadow world, the young Space Wolf felt a spark of real hope.

Suddenly, a sharp cry echoed from the rocky walls. Ragnar whirled to see Gabriella stagger and fall to her knees, her hands pressed tightly to her face. Fierce green light from her pineal eye flared between her pale fingers.

'Lady!' Ragnar shouted, rushing to the Navigator's side.

The young Space Wolf had nearly reached Gabriella when a wave of sorcery buffeted him like an unseen wind. Its terrible energies sank through his armour and deep into his flesh, setting blood and bones afire. A cry of terrible agony tore its way past Ragnar's lips as he collapsed to his knees.

Dimly, he was aware that he was not alone. Harald and his Blood Claws had fallen too, and were writhing upon the ground. Even Haegr was down on one knee, his eyes screwed shut with pain.

Ragnar closed his eyes as another wave of agony wracked his body. His muscles roiled beneath his skin, and his flesh crawled. He tasted blood in his mouth, and then he was aware of nothing but a chorus of hungry, bestial howls filling the air and a red tide rising up to swallow his mind.

THE AIR ABOVE the rolling plain hissed with bolts of lascannon fire, and rumbled with the thunder of heavy guns. Pillars of black smoke rose into the sky from the burning hulks of tanks and armoured personnel carriers, painting the western horizon the colour of old blood.

Rebel troops had reached to within half a kilometre of the Charys starport before their offensive ground to a temporary halt. Outnumbered and outgunned, the

Imperial defenders had managed to retreat in good order despite constant artillery barrages and furious assaults. The causeway linking the capital city to the starport was choked with bodies and wrecked vehicles, testament to the desperate rearguard action fought by the Twentieth Hebridean Foot and the Tairan Irregulars, two of Athelstane's veteran units. The tattered colours of the regiments fluttered in the rough wind blowing over the causeway, surrounded by the bodies of their fallen colour guard. Both units had died to a man, holding back the traitors' armoured assault long enough for the rest of the Imperial units to reach the port's fortified perimeter.

Now the frenzied rebel troops found themselves under the guns of the starport's defenders, forced to march across hundreds of metres of open ground covered by mines, anti-tank guns and artillery batteries. After two bloody assaults, the traitors were forced to pull back out of range until their heavy artillery could be brought forward to pound the Imperial positions.

Just over a kilometre from the beleaguered defenders, the first batteries of rebel guns were being rolled into position by the light of the dying sun. Barechested gun crews strained and cursed as they unlimbered heavy, stub-nosed siege mortars and tried to roll them into position along the reverse slope of a low, treeless hill. Other crews took pry-bars to squat, wooden crates containing the massive high-explosive shells. Within the hour they would be ready to fire the first salvoes.

The gun crews were exhausted, and they'd grown careless with the promise of impending victory. No sentries were posted to watch the surrounding terrain, so there was no one to take note of the eight armoured figures observing the battery from a copse of trees a hundred metres to the west.

Mikal Sternmark flexed his armoured fingers around the hilt of Redclaw and tasted the scents of the enemy troops. 'Ammunition?' he asked of his men.

Sven eyed his two packmates. 'Jurgen and Bors can shoot those bloody flashlights for another month before they run dry,' he said, scowling at the hellguns in the Wolves' hands. He checked the power meter on his meltagun. 'And I've got one shot left.'

Haakon cleared his throat. Several pieces of shrapnel had lodged in his neck over the course of the afternoon, leaving him hoarse. 'I'm out of rockets,' he grated. 'Bjørn, Nils and Karl are down to five rounds each.'

'Grenades?' the Wolf Guard asked.

Sven shook his head. 'Not since that fight back at the crossroads.'

Sternmark nodded, although he couldn't honestly say he remembered which fight Sven was talking about. The day had blurred into one long, deadly pursuit. They would retreat a few hundred metres, lay an ambush for their pursuers, and then strike, kill as many as they could and retreat to the next ambush point further down the road. The Wolves had left hundreds of dead traitors and wrecked vehicles in their wake, until finally they'd eluded their pursuers inside the drainage network at the edge of the city.

They could have slipped into the low hills south of the capital, lain low until nightfall, and then crept past the rebel positions under the cover of darkness and into safety behind the Imperial lines, but

Sternmark would be damned before anyone said he slunk back to camp like a whipped dog.

The red tide was rising. He could feel it pressing against the backs of his eyes, and he welcomed it.

'We'll advance in standard skirmish formation,' he told his men, and then pointed with his bloodstained blade at a team of gunners who were fixing fuses to a trio of waiting shells. 'Sven, when we're in range, you put your last shot right there.'

Sven let out a low whistle. 'Pull the trigger and eat dirt. Aye, lord.'

The Wolf Guard ignored the Grey Hunter's impertinence. He was already moving, gliding swiftly from the shadows beneath the trees.

They raced across the low ground in moments, unnoticed by the labouring artillery crews. Sternmark measured the distance with a predator's eye, and then nodded to Sven and sank to one knee. Without hesitation, the Grey Hunter raised the meltagun to his shoulder and fired.

The three heavy shells detonated in a single, earth shaking blast that staggered the kneeling Wolves, and pitched Sven onto his back. For a single instant, the slope of the hill was painted in fiery orange. Then a shower of earth and smouldering pieces of flesh fell in a dark rain around the rebel battery.

Sternmark was on his feet before the flash had completely faded, charging among the stunned and wounded artillerymen. Redclaw flashed and hummed, splitting torsos and severing arms. A handful of gunners staggered to their feet and ran, screaming curses. Hell-guns barked, and their smoking bodies tumbled to the ground. Within seconds, the slaughter was complete.

The Wolf Guard studied the guns. One of the mortars had flipped onto its side, but the rest seemed unscathed. 'Sven, you and your brothers right that mortar,' he said. 'Bjørn, Nils and Karl, fetch more shells.' He pointed to the summit of the hill. 'Haakon, you'll spot for targets.'

The Wolves leapt into action at once, realising Sternmark's plan. Haakon strode swiftly up the slope while the other three Terminators pulled apart more crates and hefted mortar shells like oversized boltgun rounds. Within moments, they were being fed into the breeches of the six waiting siege mortars.

'Targets?' Sternmark called.

Haakon peered over the slope. 'A motorised battalion between us and the starport,' he said, raising the targeting surveyor in his hand. 'Range six hundred and fifty to seven hundred metres.'

Sven and his packmates raced between the mortar tubes, dialling in the range. When they were ready he raised his hand to Sternmark. The Wolf Guard smiled coldly.

'Fire.'

The mortars went off in a staggered volley, spitting half-tonne shells high into the air. They screamed like the souls of the damned, and Sternmark threw back his head and howled along with them. By the time the first shells burst among the unsuspecting rebels Sternmark had crested the slope and was charging towards the foe.

Haakon had guided the shells right onto their target. The rebel unit had been assembling behind another line of low hills, their trucks and armoured cars massed in a disorderly knot behind the highest ridge line. Now the vehicles were smashed to pieces or tossed around like children's toys, spraying burning fuel across the blackened earth. Bodies and pieces of bodies lay everywhere, and wounded men tried to crawl or stagger away from the scene of carnage.

The Wolves raced among them, slashing and striking without mercy. Sternmark scythed his way through the screaming traitors, his teeth bared at the smell of hot blood. Las-bolts crackled through the smoky air. Once, an infantryman lurched upright, struggling to aim a meltagun with a pair of charred hands, but Nils blew him apart with the last of his storm bolter shells.

Sternmark found the battalion commander trying to climb out from under a pile of bodies, and struck off his head with a casual swipe of his sword. Enemy return fire was intensifying as the survivors recovered from the shock of the barrage. He spied almost a platoon of soldiers retreating farther south, firing wildly at the warriors of Fenris.

Snarling, the Wolf Guard made to pursue the fleeing traitors, but Sven let out a yell. 'The way is clear, lord!' he said, waving his chainblade from the summit of the next hill. 'We're fifteen hundred metres from the starport.'

Sternmark paused. For a moment he couldn't make sense of what Sven was saying. His bodyguard rushed up to surround him, firing well-aimed shots into the retreating traitors. Mikal tasted the blood of his foes upon his lips and eyed the fleeing rebels hungrily.

Somewhere, off in the distance, he felt a tremor, like the fall of a heavy shell or the first drumbeat of a coming storm. It tugged at him, making his veins tremble like plucked wires and catching the breath in his throat.

Mikal turned, seeking the source of the thunder. Haakon gripped his arm. 'What are your orders, lord?' he asked in his rough voice.

Sternmark struggled to focus on Haakon's face. He could sense the rebel troops escaping, drawing further away with every passing moment, and longed to run them down. 'We…' he began, struggling to pull the words from the red tide in his mind. *Chase them. Drag them to the earth and tear open their throats.*

Haakon frowned, worried. He, too, seemed to feel something strange in the air. 'The men are waiting, lord,' he said.

'The men…' Sternmark echoed. He breathed deeply, and then nodded towards the slope. 'Right. Let's go.'

The Wolves fell in behind their leader as he marched stolidly up the slope. At the summit he saw the broad expanse of the starport spread before him and the killing ground littered with the dead. Energy bolts and tracer fire sped back and forth across the corpse choked field as Imperial troops and rebel forces along the causeway traded volleys.

Sven eyed the field warily. 'A quick and easy run for once,' he said.

The Wolf Guard shook his head savagely. 'I've done enough running for one day,' he growled. 'From here, we walk.' And, raising his ancient blade to the sky, he started forward.

For ten minutes, the Space Wolves strode across the smoking plain, in full view of both sides. Redclaw caught the light of the setting sun and her blade shone like an evening star, drawing the eye of every soldier within sight. Almost at once, rebel gunners opened fire on the slowly marching warriors, but the las-bolts and stubber fire flew wide of their targets. Sternmark did not alter his pace in the slightest, his head straight and his stride measured. A chance shot cracked against his side, but his armour held and he missed not a single step.

By the time they reached the middle ground between the two sides, the Wolves could hear the cheering from the Imperial fortifications. Return fire stabbed out at the rebel troops, providing cover for the heroic Space Marines, and lone voices called out encouragement to Sternmark and his men. More shots flashed through the knot of bloodstained warriors. The rebels were firing grenades at long range, sending hot pieces of shrapnel ringing against the Wolves' flanks. A missile streaked from a rebel position to the south, but its aim was poor and the shot fell short.

Three hundred metres. Two hundred and fifty. A shot from a heavy stubber smashed into Sternmark's hip, shattering against the armour and sending splinters into his leg. Mortar rounds whistled overhead, smashing into the earth ahead of the Wolves like burning fists.

'Nice day for a walk!' Sven shouted into the din. A las-bolt cracked against his leg, and he brushed irritably at the scorch mark it left. 'Pity about the bugs, though!'

They were climbing the long slope up to the first of the Imperial entrenchments. Sternmark could see the grimy, cheering faces of the troops, calling out to him from their firing positions. They were less than a hundred metres away.

He faintly heard the clatter of treads far off to the west, and a lusty shout went up from the rebel positions. Then, too late, he heard the hollow boom of a battle cannon.

The world seemed to slow to a turgid crawl. Sternmark's senses grew supernaturally sharp. He could feel the rumble of displaced air as the heavy shell arced towards them. Pulverised rock and bits of dirt rang off his armour like tiny chimes as he turned, looking back towards impending doom.

The shell was a dark, thumb-shaped smudge in the air, spinning lazily as it fell. Next to him, Sternmark heard Sven draw in a sharp breath.

'Allfather protect us,' the Grey Hunter said, and the world vanished in an eruption of earth and flame.

SEVENTEEN
The Wolf King's Hall

SHOUTS AND BESTIAL snarls shook the air of the narrow canyon. Fists and blades clashed against ceramite plate as warriors clawed at their breasts in rage and pain. Ragnar howled in helpless fury, his fingers digging deep furrows in the lifeless earth. It felt as though his body was tearing itself apart from the inside out. His muscles writhed like maddened snakes, constricting around his reinforced bones and bending them with the strain. His eyes burned and his teeth ached to their roots, and it felt as though a swarm of stinging insects was crawling hungrily beneath his skin. Ragnar pitched forward and smashed his forehead against the lifeless ground again and again, trying to drive out the awful sensations with jolts of pure, honest pain.

The Wulfen snarled hungrily within him, setting its teeth deep in his bones. Ragnar tore clumsily at his armour, as though he could reach in and rip the beast from his body. The tips of his fingers ached fiercely, and mindless with rage, he tugged at the gauntlets with his teeth, trying to pull them free.

Voices were shouting all around him, but he could not make any sense of the words. Wolves snapped and snarled, clashing their fearsome jaws. The air was thick with the acid reek of anger and the sweet, heady smell of blood.

Something small crashed against him, and soft blows beat at his chest and face. A thin, piping sound reverberated in his ears. Shaking his head savagely, Ragnar gripped the flailing object and heard a gasp of fear. Breath ghosted against his face, and his eyes opened in surprise.

Gabriella's face was centimetres from his, her expression stern, but her eyes shining with fear. His hand was closed tight around her upper arm, hard enough to crack the carapace armour she wore.

She drew back her hand and slapped him hard across the face. The gauntlet came away slick with blood.

'Ragnar!' she cried, her voice sharp and faintly trembling. 'Listen to me! This is dark sorcery, and it feeds on conflict! The more you fight it, the stronger it grows! Don't struggle. Do you hear me? Let it wash over you like a wave, and then it can't affect you!'

The words echoed strangely in Ragnar's ears. He tried to grasp them, but they slipped from his mind like quicksilver. Every nerve was aflame, and he felt as though he was coming out of his skin.

Gabriella struck him again, and he tasted fresh blood on his lips. Ragnar bared his teeth at the blow, and his hands seemed to move of their own accord.

He grabbed the Navigator by the hair and wrenched back her head, stretching the tendons of her pale neck.

'*Ragnar, no!*' Gabriella cried, her eyes widening in terror.

Fangs glistening, the young Space Wolf lunged for her throat.

A shadow fell over Ragnar at that moment, and an armoured fist closed around his neck like a vice. His lips scarcely brushed Gabriella's skin before he was hauled into the air and shaken like a newborn cub. A powerful voice, deep and sonorous, cut through the cacophony around the young Space Wolf and snapped his tormented mind into focus.

'Forget those soft words little brother, and fight the beast for all you are worth! You must struggle against the wolf in all its forms, as the primarch himself commands. That is the first oath of our brotherhood, and without it we are lost!'

Ragnar twisted his head to see who had seized him. He found himself staring down at a giant of a man, straight from the most ancient tapestries of the Great Wolf's Hall at the Fang. The warrior was tall and lean, cased in ornate armour wrought during the glory days of the Great Crusade. His pauldrons were edged in gold and finely carved with scenes of battle, and the pelt of the largest wolf Ragnar had ever seen was stretched across the man's broad shoulders. Trophies from a hundred campaigns decorated the warrior's breastplate or hung from his wide belt: fearsome skulls and cloven helms, medallions of gold and silver, polished scales and plaques of raw iron. In his left hand the warrior gripped the haft of a fearsome axe, wrought from a metal blacker than the night. Runes glittered like frost across its surface, and it exuded a cold nimbus of dread that chilled Ragnar's very soul. Unlike his kin, the warrior's head was bald, and his blond beard was close-shaven. Fierce blue eyes glittered like chips of polar ice beneath a grim, forbidding brow.

'Leman gave us the blessings of the wolf so that we would never be defeated by our foes,' he said, 'but his gifts come with a price. As we are born to battle, so are we called to prove our worth time and again, through strength, courage and guile. *War within. War without. War unending.* That is how we live, little brother. That is who we are.' The warrior shook Ragnar once more, as if to emphasise his point. 'I am Bulveye, axe man of the Russ and lord of this warband,' he said. 'Do you hear what I've said to you?'

Ragnar gritted his teeth and drew a deep breath as he summoned the catechisms of self-discipline he'd been taught as an aspirant. By force of will, he dampened the sensations wracking his body and struggled to clear his troubled thoughts. 'I… I hear you lord,' he said after a moment. 'I hear and obey.'

Bulveye nodded in approval and set Ragnar on his feet. The sheer force of his presence seemed to still the chaos sweeping through the camp. He paid no mind to Gabriella at all, turning his full attention to Haegr and Torin. 'What of you, brothers?' he asked, his eyes narrowing in appraisal.

Torin sank to one knee before the giant. His face was wracked with pain, and his eyes had turned yellow-gold, but a brief smile caused his moustache to twitch. 'I am no stranger to this fight, my lord,' he said breathlessly. 'The wolf may howl, but I am unmoved.'

'And you?' the warrior asked, turning to Haegr.

The burly Wolf puffed out his broad chest. 'The mighty Haegr fears no one!' he declared. 'Not even Haegr himself!'

Ragnar was cheered by his fellow Wolfblade's bravado, even as he saw signs of terrible strain around Haegr's eyes, but then he heard a bestial snarl off to his right, and saw that not everyone had been as fortunate as they.

Harald and his Blood Claws, all of them little more than aspirants, had suffered the worst under the sorcerous onslaught. Their faces were distended, already lengthening to form wolf-like snouts, and their skin was darkening with a fine pelt of fur. They crouched like beasts within a circle of the Thirteenth Company's Wulfen, snapping and snarling whenever the older beasts drew too close. Many of the warriors had tugged their gauntlets free and slashed at the air with thick, curved talons.

The sight stunned Ragnar, and a prayer to the Allfather came, unbidden to his lips. At that moment, the warrior that had been Harald glanced up and met Ragnar's eyes. The young Wulfen threw back his head and uttered a single howl of despair.

Bulveye looked upon the cursed warriors and shook his head sadly. 'Where are you, young priest?' he called.

Sigurd emerged from the pack of stricken Blood Claws. The Wolf Priest's face was ashen with grief. His eyes, once dark, were now a deep yellow-gold.

'Here I am, lord,' he said sombrely.

Bulveye nodded. 'Tend to your brothers, priest,' he said quietly. 'The first hours are always the hardest.'

Sigurd nodded, a bleak look upon his young face. Then he turned, spreading his hands, and began to chant a litany that Ragnar had heard only once in his time with the Chapter. It was the Litany of the Lost, a mournful observance for those who had been taken by the Wulfen.

Another, smaller figure elbowed his way through the snarling mob of wolf-men. Inquisitor Volt looked feverish with shock and fatigue, his eyes wide and his seamed face taut with strain. He caught sight of Ragnar and Lady Gabriella and rushed to their side. 'What has happened?' he demanded, falling to his knees beside the stunned Navigator.

Gabriella reached for the old inquisitor's arm like a drowning man clutches at a storm-tossed spar. Her pineal eye still burned brightly in her forehead, and her face was as white as chalk. 'A wave of psychic force,' she gasped. 'So much power, so much *hunger*, flowing like molten iron through the aether.'

'The ritual,' Volt said. He turned to stare at Harald and his monstrous packmates. 'Blessed Emperor,' he whispered, his voice filled with dread. 'They've completed the ritual. We're too late.'

The Navigator's gaze drifted back to Ragnar once again, and a look of horrified realisation drained the last of the colour from her face. 'You would have killed me,' she said, her voice leaden with anguish. 'Had it not been for Lord Bulveye, you would have torn out my throat!'

Ragnar stared speechlessly at the Navigator, struck dumb by the enormity of what he'd nearly done, but the Wolf Lord spoke.

'Allies we may be, Lady Bellisarius, but we are not tame dogs to sniff at your heels,' Bulveye said sternly.

'Even a loyal wolf bites if provoked. You and your people would do well to remember that.' He fixed the inquisitor with his steely gaze. 'The lady I know by the heraldry she wears,' he said. 'Who are you?'

Volt rose to his full height and met the Wolf Lord's eyes. 'Inquisitor Cadmus Volt of the Ordo Malleus,' he said coolly.

Bulveye's craggy brows knitted in consternation. 'Inquisitor?' he asked. 'Is that anything like a remembrancer?'

The old man was taken aback by the Wolf Lord's reply. 'Certainly not,' he stammered.

'Good. Then I won't have to feed you to my wolves,' Bulveye replied gruffly. 'Now tell me of this ritual.'

The old inquisitor recovered his composure quickly and shook his head. 'First, tell me what this is,' he said, pointing to the Wulfen. 'At first, I thought your warriors had been twisted by exposure to the warp, but now I wonder if this is something deeper. The Inquisition has long suspected that there were flaws in the Space Wolf gene-seed. Is this true?'

The Wolf Lord's eyes narrowed coldly. 'I was wrong,' he said quietly. His hand drifted to the pistol at his hip. 'It appears I'll have to kill you after all.'

'It's the curse!' Ragnar snarled, overcome with horror and shame. 'I can feel it, like a hot coal buried in my brain. Madox has cast a spell to awaken the Wulfen in all of us.' He stared up at Bulveye. 'Even you, my lord! Surely you must feel it as well.'

The Wolf Lord set his jaw stubbornly, but there was a glimmer of doubt deep in his eyes. 'How do you know that thrice-cursed fiend, Madox?' he asked.

'There is a blood feud between us,' Ragnar answered. 'He has stolen the Spear of Russ, and I have sworn an oath to get it back.'

The news struck the Wolf Lord like a physical blow. 'Morkai's teeth!' he snarled, his eyes widening. He turned, seeking out the hulking form of the Rune Priest. 'Torvald! Did you hear–'

'No need to shout,' the Rune Priest said, making his way through the crowd of warriors towards Bulveye and Ragnar. 'The pup speaks the truth, lord. I've told you for some time that the air here stank of sorcery, and now I know why. I curse myself for a fool for not suspecting it sooner.' The bearded warrior gave Bulveye a meaningful look. 'And now these tidings of Madox and the spear. You see? The runes did not lie!'

'They may not have lied, but they tell their truths sidewise,' Bulveye said. He raised his head to the empty sky, and for an instant Ragnar saw an enormous weariness etched into the lines of the Wolf Lord's face. Then it was gone, so quickly that the young Space Wolf could not be certain he'd seen it at all, and Bulveye surveyed his warband with a commanding gaze.

'Torvald, summon the pack leaders,' the Lord of the Thirteenth Company said. 'It's time we held a council of war.'

FOR A FLEETING instant, Mikal Sternmark was gripped by the jaws of a dragon. Fierce heat and a thunderous concussion buffeted him, and red-hot shrapnel raked at his face and neck. He staggered beneath the blow, but did not fall.

A shower of dirt and stone rained down all around him. Smoke curled from the surface of his Terminator armour, but he was still alive, and Redclaw still pointed defiantly at the sky.

It took several long seconds before Sternmark understood that he'd been spared. He looked around, dazed, and saw the stunned figures of his bodyguards, all of them battered and bloodied, but nevertheless alive. Among them, Sven and his battle-brothers were picking themselves up off the ground and looking off to the east in amazement. The battle cannon shell had landed just a few metres short of its intended target, gouging a deep, smouldering crater in the ground behind the Wolves.

Moments later the first cheer went up from the Imperial lines. A priest who'd been watching the scene from a nearby gun pit clambered atop the trench line and raised his arms to the sky. 'The Emperor protects!' he cried, and soon the Guardsmen took up the cry as well.

'The Emperor Protects! The Emperor Protects!' The shout echoed across the killing field, and men took heart again after the bitter retreat from the capital.

One by one, the Wolves turned and walked the last few metres into the Imperial fortifications. Sternmark waited until the last, his sword still gleaming in the sun's dying light. Then he turned his back on the traitors of Charys and joined his brothers in the trenches.

Sven and the others were waiting for him, surrounded by a ring of awestruck Guardsmen. The Wolves were joking with one another, the raw edge to their laughter betraying the tension of their brush with death. There was something almost feral in their wide eyes and rough-edged voices, raising the hackles on Sternmark's neck. His scalp prickled, and it felt like a swarm of hungry insects had crawled beneath his skin. 'Take half an hour to eat and replenish your ammo,' he snapped, 'then return to the line.'

The Wolves were startled by the harsh edge to their leader's voice, prompting a chorus of deep growls and a narrowing of eyes. For a fleeting instant, the air was charged with tension. Sternmark's hand tightened on the hilt of his blade, but then a powerful voice broke the deadly spell.

'That was boldly done, my lord,' Morgrim Silvertongue called as he moved through the throng of admiring troops. 'When you disappeared earlier in the day we feared you had been lost.'

Sternmark turned to the skald as though in a daze. The red tide was rising once more, threatening to overwhelm the last vestiges of reason he had left. His hands and fingertips ached, and abruptly he felt smothered inside the weight of his Terminator armour.

A sharp challenge rose to the Wolf Guard's lips, but it was Sven who spoke first. 'Another few moments and we might well have been, Silvertongue,' the Grey Hunter said grimly, and then pointed out across the killing ground. 'Look.'

Sternmark turned. Something was happening along the rebel lines. The very air seemed to thicken and deepen in hue, and purple lightning flickered above the traitors' heads. Cries of adulation and terror echoed across the killing ground as shifting, luminescent forms appeared among the rebel Guardsmen.

From the gun pit nearby the regimental priest made the sign of the aquila and began the Litany of Detestation in a harsh, trembling voice. Men clutched their weapons and pressed themselves fearfully against the packed-earth walls of the trench lines as hundreds of daemons howled a chorus of blasphemous curses at the Imperial defenders.

Still worse to Sternmark was the clashing, rhythmic sound of armour, rising and falling like a dirge beneath the cacophonous, otherworldly cries. He stepped to the trench parapet and studied the rebel positions carefully until he spied the first glimmer of blue and gold.

They towered over the cringing traitors in their baroque armour, their boltguns held at port-arms in perfect unison as they marched towards the battle line. Rebel soldiers flinched from the sound of their dreadful tread, parting like smoke before the Thousand Sons' inexorable advance. The heads of the towering warriors turned neither left nor right. No human curiosity shone from the glowing depths of their ornate helms. Their bodies had been consumed by sorcerous fires thousands of years ago. Nothing remained inside those armoured shells but spirits of pure, immortal hate and murderous skill. Fell sorcerers marched alongside the ghostly Chaos Space Marines, driving the warriors onward with fierce oaths and imprecations to their abominable god.

Sternmark counted almost two hundred of his Chapter's arch foes. In all his years of campaigning he'd never seen so many of the spectral troops assembled in one place. Even without the howling daemons and rebel battalions at their command, they could crush the starport defenders in an implacable, armoured fist.

Morgrim joined the Wolf Guard at the parapet. 'It seems you arrived not a moment too soon,' he said quietly.

'I wonder if the rabbit thinks the same thing as he sticks his head into the snare,' Sternmark hissed. He found himself thinking of his fallen lord Berek, and the melta charges laid beneath his bier. The cold demands of duty focused his mind somewhat, helping him ignore the awful sensations wracking his body. He bared his teeth, tasting the strange scents around him. 'How many of our brothers remain?' Sternmark asked.

The skald folded his arms thoughtfully. 'It's hard to say,' he answered. 'We've Gunnar and Thorbjørn's Long Fangs here at the starport, as well as half of Thorvald's Grey Hunters.' He paused, his lips pressing into a grim line. 'But we've lost contact with the rest.'

'Lost contact?' Sternmark gave the skald a hard look. 'What does that mean? Are we being jammed planet-wide?'

'There is some jamming, yes,' Silvertongue replied, 'but some packs have simply stopped responding to our calls. We aren't sure what's happened to them.'

'Not sure?' the Wolf Guard snarled. 'They're dead, Silvertongue. What other explanation could there be?' Sternmark brought his fist down on the ferrocrete parapet, sending up a spray of broken fragments. The rage was rising within him once more, and it was getting harder and harder to find a reason to fight it. He looked out across the killing field. 'What are they waiting for? Let's get to the bloody business of the day and be done with it!'

Silvertongue eyed the Wolf Guard warily. 'I expect they are still waiting for their heavy artillery,' he said. 'We have enough heavy weapons left to make a frontal assault very expensive, and before he left Inquisitor Volt instructed the priests to lay a series of wards that will keep the daemons at bay.' The skald peered closer. 'My lord? Your eyes... they've changed–'

The Wolf Guard seemed not to hear him. 'Wards?' he spat. 'Those won't last long with all those sorcerers out there.'

'Aye, that's true,' Silvertongue replied carefully, 'but we only need a few more hours.'

Sternmark glared at the skald. 'What in Morkai's name are you talking about?' he demanded.

Something in the Wolf Guard's face took Silvertongue aback. He recoiled slightly from Sternmark, as though suddenly confronted by a snarling Fenrisian wolf. 'I... I thought you'd been informed,' he said quickly. 'Lady Commander Athelstane has ordered every available ship made ready for launch. She believes that there are enough transports still able to fly to evacuate the entire starport in one go–'

'*Evacuate?*' Sternmark spat, the word bitter on his tongue. 'She would have us abandon our honour and slink away like whipped dogs?'

He staggered, overcome with fury. The red tide surged, angry and wild, and swallowed him up entirely.

Silvertongue shouted something, his voice urgent, but the Wolf Guard did not hear. He was gone, running like a shadow ahead of the crimson sunset towards the distant command bunker.

* * *

Bulveye led Ragnar and his companions into the dimly lit cave, setting his wolves to guard its threshold once more with a quick gesture and a few whispered commands. Beyond the entrance, the cave narrowed quickly into a long tunnel that meandered for several dozen metres into the side of the mountain. To Ragnar's keen night vision the passageway seemed shrouded in twilight. Veins of dark ore ran in serpentine paths through the rough stone walls, and runes of warding were chiselled at every corner to foil the questing spirits of their foes.

Finally they came around another narrow turn, and Ragnar's eyes narrowed at a sudden blaze of firelight. The passageway emptied out into a large, high-ceilinged cavern almost twenty metres across, laid with furs and rough stone benches in the style of a lord's feasting hall. The warriors of the Thirteenth Company had felled some of the strange trees that dotted the foothills at the base of the mountain and had piled the logs in a crude pit at the centre of the cavern. The wood burned without sound or smoke, giving off a fey, otherworldly blue light.

At the far end of the cavern, ailing servos creaked and whined, and a pair of careworn servitors struggled upright at their master's arrival. Bulveye turned and addressed the newcomers sombrely. 'Enter my hall with the blessings of the Allfather,' he said, and beckoned to the servitors.

The Wolf Lord welcomed them according to the ancient tradition, with handclasps, bread and salt. The gesture was both strange and oddly reassuring. Custom and tradition are all they have left, Ragnar mused, as Bulveye bade them sit by the fire, and then strode off to a far corner of the cavern. He returned with guesting gifts: a gold ring for Gabriella and iron daggers for her Wolfblade. The weapons had been forged on Fenris, Ragnar noticed, and beautifully made.

Another piece of home, he thought, turning the blade over in his aching hands. He realised, for the first time that he would never see Fenris again, and a terrible melancholy stole over him.

A few moments later the first of the pack leaders filed into the cavern. They were silent, implacable figures, marked by ten millennia of warfare: the pauldrons of a World Eater champion sat on the shoulders of one warrior, while another wore the breastplate of a fallen lieutenant from Abaddon's infamous Black Legion. They wore cloaks of daemon hide or necklaces of hellhound teeth, and the twisted skulls of those they'd slain were spitted on iron trophy spikes jutting from their backpacks. The pack leaders took their places around the fire, each according to his position within the warband, and they spoke quietly amongst themselves as they waited for the council to begin.

Sigurd stole quietly into the hall shortly afterwards, his expression solemn. Rather than take a seat among the warriors he kept to the shadows at the back of the hall, arms folded, and deep in thought.

Ragnar stole a glance at Torin and Haegr. The two warriors were silent and withdrawn, their eyes hooded and shoulders hunched as they fought their silent struggles with the beasts beneath their skins. Beyond them, Inquisitor Volt and Gabriella sat on a bench to themselves. Volt was sitting ramrod-straight, his gaze moving constantly around the cavern, while the

Navigator sat with her arms tightly folded across her chest, lost in some tormented reverie.

Torvald was the last to arrive, striding slowly past the fire and taking a seat at Bulveye's right. The Rune Priest surveyed the assembled warriors and nodded. Then he struck the cavern floor thrice with the butt of his axe. 'The blessings of the Allfather be upon you, brothers,' he said in the silence that followed. 'Our foes gather before us, calling us to battle. Ere the swords sing and the blood flows, hear what our lord has to say.'

Bulveye surveyed each of the warriors seated around the fire. 'It was Torvald's runes that led us to this place,' he said. 'He consulted the Fates, and when he took his hand from the leather bag, he was holding Tyr's Rune, the Rune of the Spear.'

One of the warriors let out a sullen growl. 'Yet when we got here, what did we find? A host of enemies and the shadow of an Imperial agri-world,' he said. 'If he was here we would have found him by now–'

'We have been here for some time, trying to puzzle out the riddles of this place,' Bulveye interjected sharply, throwing a warning look at the pack leader. 'Now our distant kin have arrived, with answers to some of the questions we seek.' The Wolf Lord nodded to Ragnar. 'Tell us how you and your brothers came to be here.'

The young Space Wolf eyed his companions and rose uneasily to his feet. As quickly and succinctly as he could, he related the events on Hyades and the Chaos uprising around Fenris, and then told the grim tale of the battle for Charys and their desperate foray to the shadow world. 'The heart of Madox's ritual lies here,' he said, 'within a great temple at the centre of the shadow city to the north.' He paused. 'Inquisitor Volt can tell us more about what our enemy intends.'

Ragnar gestured to the old inquisitor, who raised his head with a scowl and rose slowly to his feet. 'The enemy intends nothing less than the perversion of the Space Wolf gene-seed,' Inquisitor Volt declared. 'And in so doing, the Thousand Sons will inflict a wound upon the Imperium from which it may never heal.'

Bulveye glowered at Volt. 'How can you be so certain of this?'

'How? The evidence is sitting right here, before your very eyes!' Volt pointed to the Wolfblade. 'See how they have been changed already by Madox's spell?' He cast an accusatory stare at each of the warriors seated around the fire. 'You all feel it, don't you? Madox is reaching into the very core of your being, warping you from the inside out!'

'You speak of nothing that I and my brothers have not struggled with for ten millennia!' Bulveye growled. 'The warp twists everything it touches.'

'Do not dissemble, lord!' Volt snapped. 'We have no time for denials or deceptions! You saw what happened to Harald and his warriors. Has the curse Ragnar spoke of ever struck so quickly before? Somehow I doubt it.' The inquisitor turned to Sigurd. 'Come here, priest. It's your duty to safeguard the souls of your battle-brothers. Tell us then, are these transformations normal?'

The Wolf Priest stiffened at the mention of his name. Slowly, reluctantly, he stepped forward into the firelight. His eyes were yellow-gold, like two brass coins. 'No,' he said gravely, 'they are not.'

'There!' Volt snapped. 'You hear it from one of your own priests. Lady Gabriella felt the initial wave of sorcery as the ritual reached its culmination. That energy has crossed the aether into the physical realm, where it will wash over Charys and then down the sorcerous anchor lines until it charges the vast sigil that Madox painstakingly built.' The inquisitor began to pace, his hands clasped tightly behind his back. 'The Chaos uprising was both a cover and a lure to draw the Space Wolves within reach of the sigil,' he said. 'As the sigil becomes charged, every one of the great companies will be affected; even Fenris will be caught within the web of power.'

Sigurd scowled at the inquisitor, but he took a deep breath and spoke. 'The aspirants will succumb first,' he said, 'then the younger warriors. The senior pack members will hold out for some time, I expect, but slowly, they too will be overwhelmed. In the end, perhaps even the great Dreadnoughts beneath the Fang will awaken in the darkness and howl for innocent blood.'

Pandemonium broke out as pack leaders leapt to their feet, shouting angry oaths or denouncing Volt as a liar and a blasphemer. Bulveye sat in silence, brooding darkly over the news. Finally Torvald rose to his feet and raised his axe high. Lightning crackled from the blade and a sharp thunderclap deafened everyone in the cavern. '*Sit down!*' the Rune Priest commanded, and the pack leaders reluctantly obeyed. Then Torvald addressed Volt directly. 'What you are talking about would require enormous amounts of psychic power,' he said.

'Naturally,' Volt replied. 'That is why Madox and his lord had to perform the ritual here, in the Eye of

Terror. They can draw upon the warp to fuel their sorceries, and then channel those energies through the sigil around Charys. No one, not even Grimnar himself, could resist such a spell for long.'

'And then?' Torvald asked.

Volt's expression became a mask of dread. 'Then blood will flow across a dozen worlds,' he replied. 'The Wolves will turn upon the sheep they once swore to protect. I expect millions of Imperial citizens will die, and that would be just the beginning. The Inquisition would declare the Space Wolves *excommunicae traitoris*, and then there would be war.'

Ragnar felt his guts turn to ice. Volt was right; the Inquisition would spare no effort to hunt the Wulfen to destruction. Virus bombs would fall upon Fenris, and those that did not flee to the outer reaches of the galaxy, or into the Eye of Terror, would be slain. Of course, the Wulfen would not go meekly. By the time the war was over, entire sectors would lie in ruins. The Imperium would need thousands of years to rebuild, provided its foes did not decide to take advantage of humanity's weakened state and move against it.

'Now we know why the Chaos cultists were taking the progenoid glands from dead Space Marines on Hyades,' Ragnar mused. 'Madox needed Space Wolf gene-seed for his ritual.' He frowned as another thought struck him. 'But what of the Spear of Russ? What does he need with that?'

Volt shook his head. 'I've been wondering about that myself, and I can only speculate at this point,' he said. 'I believe that Madox required a relic of great significance to bind the ritual to your Chapter. The spear

– tainted with the blood of Berek Thunderfist, a Wolf Lord – is the fulcrum for Madox's ritual.'

Once again, the cavern erupted in wild shouts as Bulveye's warriors reacted to the news, and this time it took the Wolf Lord himself to end the tumult and bring the council back to order. 'It is no surprise that Madox would have chosen the spear for his diabolical spell,' Bulveye told Volt. 'For we Wolf Lords swore our allegiance to Leman upon that self-same weapon and formed the great companies of our Legion. The most binding oaths of our brotherhood were wrought with it.'

The news stunned Ragnar. Did Logan Grimnar or the priests at the Fang realise the spear's importance, or had its true significance been lost over the course of thousands of years?

'But how did Leman lose his spear?' one of the pack leaders cried. 'It's inconceivable!'

'Morkai's black teeth!' Torvald swore, shaking his head. 'He was constantly losing the damned thing. You may not remember any more, but *I* do.' The Rune Priest pointed to Bulveye. 'Do you recall the time he drank all that stormwine on Sirenia and tried to throw the bloody spear at the moon? Took us four days to find it afterwards.' He chuckled ruefully and grinned at Ragnar. 'Truth be told, he hated that big boar-sticker, but the Allfather gave it to him as a gift, so he was stuck with it. He dragged it out for ceremonies, and then he'd stick it in a corner somewhere and forget about it. Drove his huscarls mad.'

'Never mind how he lost the spear,' Bulveye said, turning his attention to Volt. 'You said this sigil had to charge itself before it reached full power. Does that mean we can stop the ritual before it is too late?'

'Yes, I believe so,' the inquisitor replied. 'We must find a way to reach the temple at the centre of the city and wrest the spear away from Madox. Without that focus, the ritual energies will dissipate.'

Ragnar clenched his hands around Bulveye's iron dagger. He could feel his fingertips changing as thick talons began to take root. 'What about our brothers who have already succumbed?'

'If the ritual is disrupted before it causes too much corruption to the gene-seed, they may revert to normal,' Sigurd said, 'but every moment brings us closer to the point of no return.'

The young Space Wolf leapt to his feet. 'Then we must attack at once!'

Ragnar was greeted with loud roars of approval from the pack leaders, but Bulveye glowered at the warriors. '*Shut up*, for the Allfather's sake!' he bellowed. 'We've been watching the enemy come and go from that city for a long time. It's more than a day's march away, and the streets are guarded by an army of cultists and Thousand Sons.' The Wolf Lord paced in front of the fire. 'If we had the whole company here we could just charge right down their throats and *dare* the bastards to stand in our way, but there is only us.'

'What can we do, then?' Ragnar asked.

The Wolf Lord studied the faces of his pack leaders, and then stared thoughtfully into the cold flames. 'We must bring the enemy here,' he said.

EIGHTEEN
Wolf's Honour

THE FIRST HEAVY shells began to fall on the Imperial defences as Mikal Sternmark reached the command bunker complex. No barrage siren wailed this time as the earth shaking blasts pounded the fortifications to the east. The augur crews and communications staff were loading all the equipment they could carry on a trio of heavy cargo haulers as Sternmark came charging out of the twilight. Soldiers and technicians scattered out of the Space Wolf's path, intent on making good their escape from the impending rebel assault. The stink of defeat hung heavy in the air, stoking his rage even further.

No sentries remained to challenge Sternmark at the command bunker's entrance, but the narrow passageway beyond was filled with a procession of near-panicked Guardsmen carrying boxes of documents and crates of equipment. They recoiled before the grim, blood-spattered visage of the Space Wolf, flattening themselves against the ferrocrete walls as best they could to allow his armoured bulk to pass.

The burning beneath his skin had turned to a sharp, pulsing ache that reached down into his bones. Sternmark tasted blood on his lips, and a steady, agonising pressure was building behind his eyes. He lashed out like a maddened beast as he lurched down the corridors of the bunker, gouging craters in the reinforced ferrocrete with blows from his armoured fist.

A technician was hurrying out of the war room with a portable logic engine in his arms as Sternmark arrived. The man froze at the sight of the wild-eyed giant, and the Wolf Guard hurled him backwards into the chamber with a brutal shove. He hit the floor with a crash and a shout of pain, his arms still wrapped protectively around the precious machine.

Most of the equipment in the large chamber had already been removed, and a score of soldiers and staff officers were hard at work unhooking and packing up the rest. Heads turned at the sudden commotion, and the frenetic buzz of conversation in the room fell silent. Several of the Guardsmen took one look at Sternmark's horrific appearance and surreptitiously laid their hands on their lasguns.

Lady Commander Athelstane was standing on the stage at the far end of the room, surrounded by half a dozen of her senior officers. The men were carrying despatch cases bulging with maps and data-slates, and looked ready to depart at a moment's notice. They all turned at the Wolf Guard's sudden arrival, hands drifting to the butts of their laspistols.

Athelstane scowled at the blood-stained Wolf. 'Have a care with my equipment,' she said coldly. 'Those logic engines are difficult to come by.'

Sternmark bristled at the general's cynical tone. 'What is the meaning of this?' he demanded.

'I should think the meaning would be obvious!' Athelstane snapped. 'The enemy has driven us from the capital and is preparing for a final assault against the starport. Now, I must concern myself with preserving as much of my command as possible while there is still time. If you'd bothered to answer any of my vox transmissions you would have known about this hours ago.'

'You're fleeing from the enemy!' Sternmark roared. The savagery in his voice stole the colour from the Guardsmen's faces, but Athelstane was made of far sterner stuff.

'Have a care, sir,' she warned. 'I'm not in the mood for insults.'

Sternmark stalked towards the stage, his power blade gripped tightly in his hand. The pain in his head made it hard to think. It felt as though his very skull was being warped by the pressure. He lashed out with a clenched fist and smashed a table to pieces. Startled, the Guardsmen scattered out of his way and raised their weapons.

'Where is your honour?' Sternmark growled. The words were barely intelligible, as the Wolf Guard's lips stretched taut over prominent fangs. 'Our troops are dug-in. We have heavy weapons, and my men are well supplied–'

'How many of your men are left?' the general shot back. 'We haven't been able to contact anyone beyond the capital since mid-afternoon. My men are exhausted, and their vaunted heavy weapons are nearly out of ammunition. There's nothing more we can do here except die,' she said, 'and I won't waste the lives of good soldiers on a lost cause.'

Athelstane nodded curtly to her officers and checked her chronometer. 'It's almost time to check in with *Holmgang*,' she said. 'I was going to request that they return to Charys and cover our withdrawal, and then they can bombard the starport and the capital with everything they've got. We can at least make the enemy pay for massing so many of their troops in one place.'

She led her officers down off the stage and approached the Wolf Guard. 'Now that you're here, I could use your help convincing the *Holmgang* to support the withdrawal plan.' As the general drew closer, her eyes narrowed and she studied Sternmark's face closely. 'What's happened to you?' she said with a curious scowl. 'There's something wrong with your eyes–'

'*I cannot let you do this.*' The Wolf Guard's voice was little more than a deep, liquid growl. Redclaw fell with a discordant clang to the war room floor as a wave of agony swept over Sternmark. '*Better death than this.*'

His words gave way to a terrible howl. Sternmark pressed his hands to his face and felt the bones beneath his skin start to shift.

'Blessed Emperor!' Athelstane cried. 'He's suffering some kind of attack.' She turned to her men. 'Go and fetch a priest, quickly!'

'*It is too late for priests!*' the Wolf Guard snarled. Sternmark's head came up, his face distended into a toothy snout. Powerful jaws gaped at the stunned general and her staff. *'Cursed!'* he howled. *'I am cursed!'*

Guardsmen screamed at Sternmark's bestial transformation and brought up their guns. Bolts of energy detonated harmlessly against the Wolf Guard's Terminator armour.

Sternmark's body moved with pure, animal instinct, surging forward and smashing two of the Guardsmen across the room with blows from his powerful fists. Bones shattered. Men cried in mortal pain, and the scent of blood hung in the air.

Lady Commander Athelstane uttered a blistering curse and reached for the hellpistol at her hip. She fumbled open the holster flap and pulled the weapon free just as the Wulfen's teeth closed around her throat.

HALFWAY ACROSS THE Charys star system the *Holmgang* and her escorts drifted silently through the icy void. For weeks the battle-barge had played a deadly game of cat and mouse with Chaos ships in the asteroid field at the system's edge, but *Holmgang's* wily master reversed his course and slipped unnoticed through the enemy cordon. Since then the Space Wolf ships had been gliding on a parabolic course back towards the embattled agriworld, growing closer with every passing day.

The ship's master and his lieutenants gathered at *Holmgang's* signals room and eyed the minutes ticking away on the chronometer set above the vox station. Tripwire required at least three command officers present to confirm receipt of the scheduled signal. There could be no room for error with the fate of an Imperial world hanging in the balance.

The minutes ticked away. No one spoke. The silence in the signals room was broken only by the quiet hum of the vox-units and the ghostly whisper of static. At the appointed time the officers raised their heads to the crackling vox-speaker and listened.

They waited while the seconds passed, and their faces turned cold and grim. A full minute passed, and then another, until finally the ship's master could wait no more. With solemn ceremony he stretched out his hand and pressed a switch. The vox-unit fell silent.

Within the hour the orders were transmitted to the rest of the fleet. Thrusters glowed to angry life, and the Space Wolf ships put on speed. Belowdecks, Iron Priests garbed themselves in leaden robes and began the Rites of Atomic Redemption, unlocking the great seals that would waken the ship's cyclonic torpedoes. There was little time to waste.

The *Holmgang* would reach Charys in less than four hours.

BULVEYE'S PLAN WAS simple and direct. After issuing a few curt commands to Torvald, the Rune Priest left the cavern to set events in motion. Then there was nothing left to do but wait.

The Wolves passed the time in the same way as their ancestors of old, telling tales of the campaigns they had fought and the foes they had bested. Bulveye and his warriors spoke of the Great Crusade and the battles they had fought alongside Leman Russ. Their stories were told in the old tongue of Fenris, shaped in the chanting cadences of the ancient sagas. Ragnar learned of lost civilisations and long-dead races. Bulveye was a gifted storyteller, and painted vivid tales of fiery combat drops and titanic land battles, of desperate struggles and heroic stands fought for the sake of a young and hopeful Imperium.

They spoke of Russ himself, not the blessed Primarch Russ, but the black haired, flame eyed warrior who was more wolf than man. They spoke of his rough manner and intemperate heart, of his wild oaths and petty rivalries, of his melancholy nature and his merciless rage. 'He drove us all to distraction,' Bulveye said ruefully. 'I remember one time when he'd got Horus so worked up I thought they were going to come to blows. The Allfather got between them, and Leman punched him full in the jaw.'

Ragnar's eyes widened. 'What happened then?'

Bulveye laughed. 'The Allfather hit Leman so hard he was unconscious for a month. Spent the rest of the campaign flat on his back aboard the battle-barge.'

One of Bulveye's pack leaders, a warrior named Dagmar, shook his head and chuckled. 'That was the quietest month we ever had,' he said, and his companions laughed along with him.

'Leman didn't speak to the Allfather for almost a year, but eventually they came around,' the Wolf Lord said with a grin. 'That was how they were, like a jarl and his sons, always squabbling about one thing or another, but they never forgot the ties of blood and kin.' Bulveye paused, and his smile faded. 'Well, not until the end.'

Torin leaned forward, resting his elbows on his knees. His eyes shone yellow in the cold firelight, and there was a troubled look on his face. 'The legends say that Russ sent you into the warp to finish what was begun back on Prospero.'

'Is that so?' Bulveye replied conversationally, but there was a guarded look in his blue eyes. 'That sounds like an interesting story. You will have to tell it to me sometime.'

Silence fell around the fire. Ragnar glanced sidelong at the Wolf Lord. 'You came to this world because Torvald cast the runes and drew the Spear,' he said. 'What were you expecting to find?'

The Wolf Lord considered the young Space Wolf for a long moment. 'You've already answered the question,' he said carefully. 'I came looking for the spear, and now you've helped me find it.'

'It wasn't just the spear, though, was it?' Ragnar said. 'You had no idea that Russ has been lost for ten thousand years, and that he'd left his spear behind on Garm. You expected him to be here.'

Bulveye gave Ragnar a wolfish smile. 'Leman is no more lost than we were,' he replied. 'I don't know where he's gone, but I do know this: he swore an oath to us a very long time ago, and one day he will keep it.'

'How can you be so sure?' Torin asked.

The Wolf Lord chuckled. 'Because, little brother, Leman of the Russ was a scoundrel and an axe-bitten fool at times, but he always kept his word, regardless of the cost.' Bulveye held out his right hand. 'When last we met, he clasped my wrist and swore that one day we would meet again.' The Wolf Lord lowered his arm and stared into the ghostly flames. For a fleeting instant Ragnar saw the terrible weariness once again in the warrior's blue eyes. 'In time, that day will come.'

A faint clatter of armour drew the attention of the assembled warriors. Torvald had returned to the cavern, and now strode quickly into the firelight. 'It's done,' he said curtly, returning to his bench.

Ragnar scowled at the cold, blue flames. 'How can you be sure the Thousand Sons will take the bait?'

'Because we've been a dagger in their side for ten millennia,' Torvald answered. 'Their sorcerers are always sniffing at our trail, waiting for the slightest mistake that will give our presence away. Now I've given them one. I allowed the wards concealing the camp to go out, for the briefest instant, before energising them again.'

'But how can you be certain they noticed the lapse?' Ragnar persisted.

The Rune Priest let out a snort. 'Who do you think we're fighting here, little brother? Of course they noticed!'

'And they will send every warrior and daemon they can muster,' Bulveye added.

'Then why are we still here?' the young Space Wolf asked in exasperation.

'Why, to fight them, of course,' Bulveye answered. 'If their warband arrives and finds the camp deserted, they'll suspect a trick and return to the city as quickly as they can.' The Wolf Lord raised his ebon axe and laid it across his knees. 'So, we'll let them spring their trap, and keep the devils busy while you fight your way into the temple and get back Russ's spear.'

The news stunned Ragnar. He glanced quickly at Haegr and Torin, noting their looks of shock. He'd expected that Bulveye and his more experienced warriors would claim the privilege of confronting Madox and reclaiming the artefact. 'This is a great honour, lord,' he managed to say.

'It's nothing of the kind,' Bulveye replied irritably. 'I'd like nothing better than to tear Madox apart with my bare hands, but if I'm not seen here with my troops the enemy might still see through our ploy.' He stared appraisingly at Ragnar and his companions. 'As far as we can tell, Madox doesn't know any of you are here. That's why you're staying in this cave until the attack is well begun.'

Ragnar's brain was whirling, trying to puzzle out the hidden elements of the Wolf Lord's deceptively simple plan. 'If we're still here when the attack begins, how in Morkai's name are we supposed to reach the city undetected?'

The Wolf Lord's eyes glittered with cold amusement. 'By the Allfather, you ask more questions than a Blood Claw!' he said. 'Suffice to say that we've got a few secrets that not even the Thousand Sons suspect.' He beckoned to Sigurd. 'Gather your charges, priest, and bring them here,' he commanded. 'We will not have much longer to wait.'

Sigurd nodded silently and left to find Harald and his packmates. After he had gone, the Wolf Lord turned back to his guests with a faint smile. 'Now, little brothers, speak to us of distant Fenris. Tell us tales of our home.'

Ragnar was taken aback by the sudden request. He'd never considered himself a storyteller, and as he felt the eyes of Bulveye and his pack leaders focus on him, his mind went utterly blank. An awkward silence hung in the air as the young Space Wolf groped for something worthwhile to say, but then Torin drew a deep breath and began to speak. At first his voice was rough and awkward, tainted by the beast inside him, but as he spoke of the tall cliffs and crashing salt waves of the islands, a change came over him. His tone grew stronger and more polished, falling into the smooth cadences of a skald, and the old warriors listened, rapt, as he told them of all that had transpired since the days of the Heresy.

Bulveye and the warriors were shocked to hear of all the changes that had befallen the Imperium in their absence. Their expressions turned grave as they heard how their glorious Legion had been reduced to a mere Chapter in the wake of Horus's rebellion, and they glanced thoughtfully at one another when they learned of Russ's departure. But the tales that gripped the warriors most of all had nothing to do with wars or strife. They wanted to hear of their homeworld, of the heaving seas and the tall mountains, of the Time of Ice and the Time of Fire. They asked how the fishing was off the Kraken Isles, of which clans had prospered and which had disappeared over the course of the centuries. They asked after villages and peoples that had vanished ages past, of legends that no one could now recall. Ragnar listened and watched the old Wolves, and saw the sense of loss etched on their faces.

Before long Sigurd returned, leading a shuffling pack of wary beasts that had once been men. Ragnar watched them gather around the priest a respectful distance from the fire, and heard the priest speaking to them in low, soothing tones. Inquisitor Volt and Gabriella had retreated from the circle, and sat cross-legged on a pile of rugs at the far end of the cavern. The Navigator's head was bowed and her eyes were tightly shut. For a moment, he considered going to her, but then he remembered the look of horror on her face when she'd glimpsed the Wulfen inside him. We are all of us forsaken, he realised bitterly. All of us have lost our way.

As Torin spun his tales, Haegr ran his wide hands over his whiskered face and glowered into the fire for some time. After a while he reached a decision and began rummaging quietly through the field bags attached to his waist. Slowly, carefully, he drew out a squat cylinder the size of a melta bomb and cradled it in his lap. Then he reached over his shoulder and drew forth his great ale horn.

Ragnar faintly heard the hiss of escaping air and thought nothing of it at first. Then he noticed a palpable change among the warriors sitting around the fire. The old Wolves were leaning forward, their expressions intent. Even Lord Bulveye had stopped listening to Torin and was watching Haegr's every move.

By this point Torin had noted the change as well, and his story came to a halt. Haegr, meanwhile, set the empty cylinder on the stone floor and started to raise the foaming horn to his lips.

'Is that ale?' asked Dagmar, licking his lips. His voice sounded almost reverent.

'Aye,' Haegr replied with a broad grin. 'Good, brown Iron Islands ale, tapped from the kegs in the Fang's deep cellars,' he said proudly. 'I've been saving this one for a special occasion, and this seems like the time! Bringing it all the way from Fenris was a saga all by itself, I can tell you.' He raised the horn to the warriors. 'Skoal!'

'We haven't had a drop of ale in six thousand years,' Bulveye mused, eyeing the ale horn appreciatively.

'Six thousand three hundred and twenty-two years, eighteen days, six hours and twenty-one minutes,' Dagmar said, 'give or take.'

Haegr froze, the rim of the horn touching his lips. His eyes flicked from one thirsty face to the next. 'Well, I suppose I could offer you a taste,' he said reluctantly, 'just a swallow, you understand–'

'That's fine!' Bulveye said, reaching eagerly for the horn. Prying it loose from Haegr's fingers, he raised it high. 'Drink deep, lads! The next taste we get will be in the Halls of Russ! *Skoal!*'

'*Skoal!*' the warriors cried, rising from their benches and crowding around their lord. Haegr watched the frenzy with a stricken grin frozen on his face.

Muffled thunder rolled down the winding tunnel, followed by the faint howl of wolves. Bulveye and the warriors froze, their celebrations forgotten. Then came another rumble, this one staccato and sharp edged, like the hammering of a heavy bolter.

'It has begun,' the Wolf Lord said.

NINETEEN
The Forlorn Hope

Sven crouched low and ran along the trench line, clambering over the twisted bodies of Guardsmen as bolter and missile fire crashed into the firing position he'd just left. Rebel artillery continued to fall, unleashing a storm of shrapnel and churning the earth behind the Imperial lines. The blasts strobed angrily in the darkness, painting the shattered fortifications in lurid colours and long, jagged shadows.

The Grey Hunter worked his way along the trench for a dozen metres, and then popped up and swept his bolter across the crowded killing ground.

The massed assaults by mobs of rebel troops had finally ground to a halt, and scattered platoons of infantry and bands of howling mutants crept their way forward metre by metre over the bodies of their fallen cohorts. Sven caught a small squad of traitors just as they rose from a smoking shell-hole and cut them down with a one-handed burst from his bolt-gun. Twelve rounds left, he thought, keeping the count in his head as he ducked to avoid the storm of return fire that clawed at the battered parapet.

Another salvo of shells crashed into Sven's section of the line, nearly pitching him forward onto his face and showering him with dirt and broken ferrocrete. The Space Wolf heard a fierce oath further down the corpse-filled trench, and saw a hulking, armoured figure on his knees, one hand pressed to the side of his neck. Teeth bared, the young Grey Hunter scrambled over to the wounded Space Wolf.

It was Gunnar, one of the company's Long Fang pack leaders. Bright red blood streamed between the old Wolf's fingers and spattered his dirt covered breastplate. Sven's eyes widened at the sight. 'How badly are you hurt, brother?' he asked, shouting over the roar of enemy shells.

Gunnar grimaced and spat a stream of blood onto the ground. 'I've had worse,' he grated, showing red-stained fangs. A krak missile slammed into the parapet directly over their heads, silhouetting their faces in yellow and orange. Both Wolves ducked as more fragments hissed over their heads. 'I don't think they like us very much,' Gunnar observed.

Sven couldn't help but grin. 'Must have been something I said,' he quipped. 'Where is the rest of your pack?'

'Thorin and Mikkal are fifteen metres back that way,' the pack leader said, jerking his head in the direction of the trench line to his left. 'I don't know where Ivo or Jan got off to, but they'd best hope the enemy finds them before I do!'

Sven shook his head. 'I've lost track of Jurgen and Bors as well,' he said. 'One minute they were with me, and the next...'

Gunnar nodded. 'I know,' he replied, tentatively pulling his hand from the wound in his neck. 'I thought Ivo and Jan might have heard the withdrawal order and pulled back. My vox isn't working.'

'Neither is mine,' Sven admitted. 'Not a single thing is going right, if you ask me.'

'Have you seen Sternmark?'

'He went charging off to the command bunker two hours ago and I haven't seen him since,' Sven answered.

The Long Fang growled deep in his throat, and then rose above the parapet and fired off a quick burst. Screams echoed up from the killing ground. 'Now would be a good time for Berek to get off his death bed and sort things out,' Gunnar said as he dropped back into cover.

'Not likely,' Sven muttered. He readied his bolter and waited for the storm of return fire to pass. Movement from further down the trench caught his eye. 'Someone's coming,' he said, pointing at the armoured figure swiftly working its way towards the two Wolves.

Gunnar peered warily at the approaching figure. 'That's Silvertongue,' he noted. 'Maybe now we'll get some damned answers.'

The skald looked in no better shape than they were. Streaks of blood and soot covered his long face, and shallow craters across his breastplate and pauldrons showed the impact of heavy calibre shells. 'Have either of you seen Sternmark?' he asked as he reached the two Wolves.

Sven and Gunnar shared a sidelong look. 'We were hoping you had,' the Long Fang admitted.

'Not since he headed off towards the command bunker,' the skald replied. 'His Wolf Guard is holding about a kilometre of the trench line back behind me, but I haven't been able to find anyone else besides you two.'

A rocket made a banshee wail right over the Wolves' heads, nearly close enough for Sven to reach out and touch it. 'There's something strange going on,' the Grey Hunter yelled. 'What's happened to the withdrawal? I thought we were pulling back to the ships?'

'Athelstane was supposed to give the order more than an hour ago,' Silvertongue replied. 'Some of the Guard units have already pulled back–'

'Pulled back?' Gunnar spat. 'They're retreating all along the line! If we don't do something soon this is going to turn into a rout!'

As ill fate would have it, screams and shouts of terror rang out along the Imperial line. In the fiery light of the rebel bombardment Sven caught glimpses of dreadful, sinuous forms rearing up from the trenches and scattering torn pieces of meat that moments before had been men.

'Morkai's teeth!' the Grey Hunter cried. 'The wards! The bloody wards have fallen!'

Battered, reeling figures were scrambling and crawling out of the trenches, firing wildly at the unholy monsters that had appeared in their midst. The Guardsmen had finally reached their breaking point, pushed past the point of endurance after a long day of blood, steel and flame.

Then, a dreadful, rolling drumbeat rattled from the depths of the killing ground. Fleeing soldiers staggered or spun about, torn by precise bursts of mass-reactive shells.

The three Wolves eyed one another grimly. They knew that sound and what it portended.

Sven popped up over the parapet and searched for targets. Down in the killing zone marched a thin line of figures cased in blue and gold.

The Thousand Sons strode like iron gods past the cowering rebel troops. Eldritch fires blazed from the oculars of their ornate helms and leaked from the joins in their ancient armour, and their rune-etched weapons spat streams of death at the fleeing Guardsmen.

Breathing an oath to the Allfather, Sven laid his sights on one of the advancing warriors and fired a quick burst. Detonations crackled along the foeman's breastplate and blew a fist-sized hole through its helmet. The Chaos Marine staggered, fires licking from the wound, but the warrior brought its weapon around and returned fire in the same motion.

A stream of cursed shells dug craters from the parapet, and burst along Sven's right pauldron. With a blistering curse, he ducked back into cover, absently smearing blood from a shrapnel wound across his cheek with the back of one hand.

Gunnar stole a look over the lip of the trench, and ducked back as another volley of shells tore into the parapet. 'We'll wait until they hit the trench line and give them a taste of our blades,' the Long Fang declared.

Morgrim Silvertongue shook his head. 'We three aren't going to stop this,' he said. 'The Guard regiments are in full retreat and our brothers have been isolated. We need to regain command and control or we're going to be cut off and slaughtered!'

'How?' Sven growled. 'The vox-units are being jammed.'

Silvertongue stared across the smoke wreathed starport and reached a decision. 'Head for the command bunker!' he declared. 'We can use the long-range vox system to rally as many troops as we can and form a rearguard.'

Sven eyed the distant bunker and nodded grimly. 'Let's go,' he growled. 'It's as good a place for a last stand as any.'

A SQUADRON OF Chaos raiders picked up the *Holmgang* on their scopes halfway to Charys, and swung about on an intercept course. Augur operators studied the unknown contacts, struggling to divine their identities as gun crews raced to their mounts and torpedo crews hauled at the loading chains of their rune-etched missiles. Commanders invoked the blasphemous names of their gods and ordered their ships to flank speed. Vast rewards had been offered to the first crew to find the hated Wolf ships and bring them to bay.

The Chaos ships fanned out in a broad arc across the *Holmgang's* path, casting a deadly net for the oncoming vessels. Converging at maximum speed, the two forces reached extreme weapons' range within moments. The augur operators muttered desperate incantations and brooded over the icons glimmering on their screens, but they were taken by surprise when the unidentified ships were obscured behind a cloud of flickering energy readings.

Upon command, the remaining Thunderhawks of *Holmgang's* battle group rammed their throttles forward and streaked from the sensor shadow of their parent ships. By the time the Chaos commanders realised what had happened the strike craft were already starting their attack runs.

Fifteen seconds later the Wolf ships passed through the expanding debris clouds of the Chaos raiders. Hours later the light from the violent explosions would reach the hunter-killer squadrons stalking through the asteroid fields, but by then it would already be too late.

The fate of Charys was sealed.

ANOTHER LOUD BLAST reverberated down the curving tunnel, stirring the air of the cavern and causing the flames to gutter and spark. The scent of smoke and burned flesh reached the Space Wolves, causing the Wulfen to lower their heads and growl deep in their throats. Sigurd moved among the former Blood Claws, murmuring prayers in a firm, quiet voice.

At a nod from Bulveye, the pack leaders raced from the cavern, teeth bared and weapons ready. The Wolf Lord passed the ale horn back to Haegr and took up his ebon axe. A strange, deadly calm settled like a cloak over the ancient warrior as the sounds of war echoed faintly in the valley beyond. When he turned to the Rune Priest his eyes shone like bale fires. 'Get them as close as you can,' Bulveye said, 'and stay with them until the last.'

'Until the battle's done, lord,' Torvald promised. 'In victory or in death. You have my oath upon it.'

Bulveye nodded and clasped the Rune Priest's arm in farewell. Then he turned to Ragnar. 'Your destiny awaits, little brother,' he said. 'There's no telling how many of the foe we've drawn from the city, but I don't need to cast any runes to know you've a grim battle ahead of you.' He held out his hand. 'Fight well, Ragnar Blackmane, and hold to your oaths. The honour of our brotherhood, nay, the survival of Fenris itself, rests in your hands.'

Ragnar gripped Bulveye's wrist. 'The spear will be ours again, lord,' he said fiercely, 'regardless of the cost.'

The Wolf Lord's eyes narrowed at Ragnar's grave oath. 'Even at the cost of all you hold dear?' he asked. 'Even unto your very soul?'

Bulveye's words chilled the young Space Wolf, but he answered without hesitation. 'Even so, lord.'

With a rattle and a wheeze of hydraulics, a servitor limped from the shadows, bearing a polished silver helmet fashioned in the shape of a snarling wolf's head. Bulveye took up the helm and studied its scarred face for a moment. 'Remember all that I told you,' he said to Ragnar. 'War within. War without.'

Then the Wolf Lord's face disappeared behind the snarling mask, and he was gone, striding swiftly from the cavern towards the sound of the guns.

'War unending,' Ragnar answered softly, and felt the Wulfen swell within his breast.

As soon as Bulveye was gone, the Rune Priest turned to the assembled Wolves. 'It is time,' he said, raising his axe. 'Gather round, brothers.'

Ragnar turned to Torin and Haegr. The older Wolfblade was already on his feet, weapons ready, while his burly companion stared disconsolately into the depths of his empty ale horn. Murmured verses echoed across the cavern as Sigurd summoned the Wulfen with the stern tones of the Benediction of Iron.

Inquisitor Volt touched Gabriella on the arm, and the Navigator's eyes blinked open. They spoke softly to one another, and then climbed slowly to their feet. Ragnar watched them approach, concern etched deeply upon his face. 'Are you well?' he asked as they approached.

Gabriella looked up at the young Space Wolf and summoned a resolute smile. 'Of course,' she said coolly. 'Don't concern yourself about me.'

The distant tone in the Navigator's voice struck Ragnar like a blow. A bewildered frown darkened the young Space Wolf's face, but before he could reply the old inquisitor spoke. 'I asked Lady Gabriella to try and contact Lady Commander Athelstane or Lord Stern-mark and warn them of Madox's plan, but with no success. Though Charys and the shadow world are extensions of one another, the turbulence in the aether is too great for her mind to penetrate.'

'I need a physical link to them that I can focus upon,' Gabriella said. 'That would make all the difference.'

The young Space Wolf thought it over, but finally shook his head. 'I can't think of anything here that would help,' he growled, irritated at the idea of failing Gabriella yet again. 'I'm sorry.'

Volt sighed. 'No matter,' he said, although there was a look of concern in the old inquisitor's eyes. 'We will have to trust that they will endure until we can set things right.'

Ragnar nodded gravely. With a last glance at Gabriella, he turned to the Rune Priest. 'We stand ready, Torvald,' he said. 'Tell us what we must do.'

The old Rune Priest surveyed the assembled warriors and drew a deep breath. Pale blue arcs of power crackled along the length of his axe, and Torvald's bearded face split in a fearsome grin. 'Hearken to my voice, brothers,' he said in a booming voice. 'Hearken well, and follow me.'

Then the priest threw back his head and began to chant, the words ringing like hammer blows in the echoing space. Arcs of psychic power leapt from axe to priest and back again, growing more intense with each passing moment. Ragnar felt unseen energies crawl across his skin. The Wulfen snarled and snapped at the charged atmosphere, their yellow eyes narrowed in fear.

Lightning radiated outward from the Rune Priest, the arcs merging into a blue-white haze that surrounded the warriors in a nimbus of near-blinding light. Ragnar heard Gabriella let out a startled cry, and then the cavern floor seemed to tilt, propelling the young Space Wolf into the building storm.

RAGNAR FELT A dry, desert wind on his face and heard the cries of his companions echoing through the haze. He felt the first stirrings of panic as he tried to comprehend what has happening. His mind struggled to keep a mental image of the Wolf Lord's cavern, but his steps didn't match what he remembered. The faster he walked, the more the ground beneath him seemed to tilt, until it felt as though he were running downhill. Through it all, Torvald's voice rolled like thunder. Ragnar focused on the Rune Priest's chant and kept running, hoping that the old warrior's imposing form would take shape out of the whirling maelstrom at any moment.

Then, just as it seemed that the storm would go on forever, the white haze parted like mist and Ragnar found himself reeling like a drunkard down a rubble-choked street. The open sky stretched above him, dark and empty, hemmed by the jagged bones of burned-out buildings. His boot struck a large chunk of broken masonry and he went down on one knee, cursing fiercely under his breath. Wisps of grey smoke curled from the surface of his armour.

More cursing and startled shouts rang out behind the young Space Wolf. Ragnar heard Torvald let out a warning hiss. 'Quiet!' the Rune Priest warned. 'Not a sound.'

The young Space Wolf leapt to his feet, weapons ready, his eyes scanning his surroundings. Ruins stretched away from him as far as he could see. The road ahead of him was cratered by shell holes, but there were no vehicles or bodies that he could see. Off in the distance, Ragnar could see a broad, fortress-like structure brooding over the kilometres of devastation.

A column of shifting, pulsing energy rose from the dark palace, apparently woven like a burning thread into the night. Even from such a great distance the sight of it filled Ragnar with dread.

He knew where they were. Torvald had brought them to the very edge of the shadow city.

'How?' he gasped, turning to the Rune Priest. 'What manner of sorcery is this?'

Torvald was wreathed in vapour, like a blade drawn from the quenching barrel. His grin turned fierce, and tiny arcs of lightning flickered through his iron grey beard. 'We've learned a few of the enemy's secrets on our long hunt,' he replied. 'A keen mind and a bold heart can accomplish much, even in this terrible place. I can cross leagues in but a few steps, so long as I can see the destination in my mind.' The Rune Priest winked conspiratorially. 'Soon we'll be able to walk between the worlds as well as our enemies can.'

Inquisitor Volt stepped from the shadows across the street from Torvald. 'Pride goes before the fall, priest,' the old man warned. 'What you speak of dances upon the edge of damnation.'

Torvald gave the inquisitor a flinty stare. 'We've spent the last ten thousand years here, Volt. We've forgotten more about damnation than you will ever know.'

Dark shapes glided swiftly around the Rune Priest. The Wulfen recovered swiftly from the shock of the sudden transit, and whatever else had become of their minds, their training still held true. Sniffing the air, the former Blood Claws slipped silently into the shadows along both sides of the rubble-strewn lane, followed closely by Sigurd. Haegr and Torin paced into view behind Volt, warily eyeing the lightning-shot sky. Gabriella walked between them, her pineal eye blazing like a brand.

'We're at the south-east edge of the city,' Torvald continued. He pointed further east. 'A few hundred metres that way is the city's main transit route, but there's not much cover to shield our approach.'

Ragnar nodded, breathing in the crypt-like air and trying to clear his thoughts. He could still feel the curse clawing at his insides. Focus on the mission, he thought. 'What are we likely to encounter from here?'

The Rune Priest shrugged. 'I cannot say. This is as far as any of us has ever come.' His yellow eyes surveyed the ruined city blocks. 'The place is much changed since I was last here, and there are no signs of patrols. Bulveye's plan appears to have worked.'

'Or the Imperial troops on Charys have been driven from the capital,' Volt said, looking to the east. A look of horror leached the colour from the inquisitor's face. 'Blessed Emperor,' he said, fumbling for his chrono. 'What is the hour? Does anyone know? My timepiece isn't working.'

Torvald let out a grunt. 'Time is fickle in this place, inquisitor.'

'But not on Charys,' Volt whispered. 'If the Imperial forces have been forced back to the starport and Sternmark has been affected by Madox's ritual…' He gave Ragnar a stricken look. 'Before we left I ordered the *Holmgang* to destroy the planet if they didn't receive a signal from the planetary commanders at a set time each day. If Sternmark and his warriors have fallen under the sway of the curse, the surviving defenders will have been thrown into disarray–'

'Morkai's teeth!' Ragnar snarled. 'Have you gone mad, inquisitor?'

'Perhaps I have,' Volt said shakily. He ran a trembling hand across his face. 'We must be swift,' he said, thinking quickly. 'If we can disrupt the ritual in time, and Sternmark regains his senses, perhaps he can contact the battle-barge and stop the bombardment.'

'And if he can't?' Gabriella asked. 'What will happen here if Charys is destroyed?'

Volt turned to the Navigator. 'I don't know,' he said. 'Look around you. The shadow realm changes to reflect the reality of the physical world. If Charys burns…'

'Oh, damnation,' Torvald snarled. 'Not only have you put Charys in danger, but Bulveye and his warriors as well. You risk more than you know, Volt!' The Rune Priest took a step towards the inquisitor, his hand tightening on the haft of his axe.

'That's enough!' Ragnar snapped, stopping both men in their tracks. 'What's done is done. Our only chance to set this right is to get to Madox and recover the spear, and the sands are running from the glass as we speak.'

Torvald glared at Volt for another moment, and then relented with a curt nod. 'You're right, little brother,' he said. The priest pointed his axe in the direction of the palace. 'Lead on,' he said, 'but be careful. I've shielded us from sorcerous detection, but there may still be patrols guarding the streets.'

The young Space Wolf nodded, considering his options. 'Very well,' he said. 'Sigurd, take charge of the Wulfen and cover our flanks. Torin, Haegr, you're on point with me. Lady Gabriella, Inquisitor Volt, stay close to Torvald.' He locked eyes with each of the Wolves in turn. 'No shooting unless absolutely necessary. We can't risk being discovered before we get to the palace.'

Each of his companions nodded their understanding. Ragnar felt a welcome calm settle over him at the prospect of battle. 'All right,' he said, 'let's go.'

Torin and Haegr joined Ragnar without a word, and the Wolfblade set off at a swift, stealthy pace through the ruins. He breathed deeply, tasting the air for the scent of his enemies, and his eyes roamed the wasted landscape ahead for telltale signs of movement. The young Space Wolf bared his teeth in the darkness, glad to be back on the hunt once more.

They moved through the rubble wherever possible, avoiding the easier but more exposed roadways and charting a direct course for the distant palace. Ragnar caught multiple scents covering the broken stones, and thought he glimpsed distant movement in the direction of the palace, but the lightning made it difficult to discern truth from illusion.

It was Torin who saw them first. A warning hiss sent Ragnar scrambling for cover behind a toppled section of wall. His eyes darted warily left and right, but there was nothing to see.

Then he heard it, a thin, whistling sound, like wind over broken stones, approaching slowly from the north. Ragnar pressed closer against the stone and looked back along his line of march, hoping that everyone else had gone into cover as well.

Twin beams of lurid red light swept across the ruins from overhead, sweeping back and forth across the rubble. The whistling turned into a faint wail, and a strange, bat-winged figure glided swiftly overhead. Ragnar caught a glimpse of glistening, leathery wings and corroded metal ribbing, a long tail made of steel barbs and a pale, misshapen head. The creature's fleshy mouth was distended around the rusted grille of a vox speaker, and the crimson beams shone from its augmetic eyes.

Still searching, the figure swooped off to the south, until the light from its eyes was lost in the distance. Ragnar waited a full five minutes before he rose slowly to his feet. 'What was that?' he mused softly.

'Some manner of daemon,' Torin muttered, still crouched low and scanning the dark sky. 'If we're spotted they'll draw every patrol in the city down on us.'

'Let them,' Haegr growled, gripping the haft of his thunder hammer. 'I haven't had a bite of food or a drop of ale in twenty-four hours. *Someone* is going to get a good thrashing.'

Ragnar tried to gauge the distance left between them and the palace. As near as he could reckon, they still had five kilometres to go. 'We'll have to take that chance,' he declared. 'It's in the hands of the Fates now.'

They signalled to the rest of the warband and resumed their pace, dividing their attention between the path ahead and the skies above. As they drew closer to the centre of the city they saw more signs of movement along the shadowy streets. Ragnar's keen sight picked out the shapes of men, traitor Guardsmen like the foes they'd fought on Charys, lurking in the rubble at every intersection along the main routes leading to the palace. More of the flying daemons circled and swooped above the broken ground in between, painting the rocks with their bloody gaze. More than once, Ragnar was forced to call a halt and try to find a way through the net of flying sentries. Fortunately, their movements were predictable enough to create gaps that a small party could slip through if they were careful.

The trek into the city seemed to last for hours. Ragnar's earlier calm had melted away, leaving his body tense and his nerves raw. Each passing moment was like a weight piling onto his shoulders. Every flash of pale lightning caused his heart to skip a beat as he imagined the *Holmgang* unleashing her cyclonic torpedoes and setting the agri-world afire.

They were within a kilometre of the palace when they came upon a cross-street that intercepted their line of march. By this point they were close enough for the pillar of coruscating fire, towering over the ritual site, to cast strange shadows across the ruins, sending shivers along Ragnar's skin. He could see a pair of flying daemons searching a bombed-out district further off to the north, but sensed no other movement ahead. Signalling for his companions to halt, he crouched low and crept closer to the street.

Ragnar slipped silently through a defile of broken stone, and settled onto his haunches near the burned-out shell of a small building. Moving only his eyes, he scanned along the length of the street, first to the left, and then right… and froze.

Just twenty metres away, crouched against a low, broken wall, lurked nearly a score of traitor Guardsmen. Ragnar saw at once that they were not recent converts, like the rebels on Charys. Their armour was very old, and scribed with layers of blasphemous runes, and their bodies bore signs of terrible mutations. They clutched strange-looking autoguns tipped with serrated bayonets, and searched the darkness with cold, calculating stares. For the moment, their attention was directed to the north, towards the writhing column of Chaos energy.

The hackles on the young Space Wolf's neck rose. Faintly, he sensed movement behind him. Ragnar turned his head and saw several of the Wulfen moving across the rubble field towards him, and then Torvald, Gabriella and Volt. He bit back a curse. The rest of the warband had missed his signal in the darkness.

Moving as quickly as he dared, Ragnar slid backwards until his position was hidden by the same low wall that hid the daemon pack. Thinking quickly, he waved to his companions to head for the wrecked building. To his relief, the Wulfen changed course and slipped into cover behind the building's broken walls. Torvald and the others quickly followed suit, and Ragnar motioned for the Wolfblade to join them.

They made their way cautiously across the broken terrain and through a gaping window frame into the ground floor of the building. Part of the second storey's floor was still intact, as well as two of the structure's four walls. The warband crouched in deep shadow. Ragnar could hear the panting breath of the Wulfen, and saw the eerie glow of Gabriella's pineal eye. They watched Ragnar intently as he crouched down and described quietly what lay in their path.

'We can try to work our way further down the street, cross over, and then work our way back towards the palace,' Ragnar said, 'or we can wait and see if the patrol moves on.'

'Can't we just kill them?' Sigurd replied. The Wulfen shifted on their haunches and growled, as though in agreement.

'Not quietly,' the young Space Wolf said. 'We're still more than half a kilometre from the objective–'

'Then we'll cut our way through them and charge towards the palace,' Sigurd shot back. 'As you said before, we're wasting time.' The priest rose to his feet, and the Wulfen moved with him.

'Don't be a fool!' Ragnar hissed, bolting to his feet and stepping into Sigurd's path. Rage seethed within him as his body responded instinctively to the Wolf Priest's challenge. The Wulfen picked up on the change and bared their fangs. One of them, possibly Harald, took a step towards Ragnar and let out a warning snarl.

The bestial sound echoed like the roar of a chainblade in the confines of the ruined building. Sigurd hissed a warning at the Wulfen, but Ragnar waved him to sudden silence. Everyone froze as something sharp scraped along the ferrocrete above them.

Red light washed over the Wolves. Ragnar looked up and found himself staring into a pair of glowing augmetic eyes.

TWENTY
The Last Battle

IT WAS NO simple thing to turn a living world to ash.

Cyclonic torpedoes operated on the principle of igniting a planet's atmosphere and creating a self-sustaining firestorm that spread across entire continents. Kindling such a fire was no easy task, however; the warheads had to be seeded in a complex pattern and their detonations synchronised in such a way as to ensure a proper chain reaction.

The calculations began while the *Holmgang* was still an hour away from Charys. Like pieces of a puzzle, data about the agri-world's magnetic field, rotational speed and atmospheric density were computed, and orbital patterns for the bombardment took shape. This translated to manoeuvring orders for the fleet as the flagship choreographed insertion patterns for her attendant cruisers. Huge warships shifted positions with funereal grace, taking their places for the dreadful dance to come.

Holmgang's master and her command officers watched the green orb of Charys fill the grand viewports along the command deck and listened as the ordnance officers determined landmass ratios and population densities, turning over the last pieces of the puzzle and fitting them carefully into place.

THE RED-EYED daemon reared back like a striking cobra, its leathery wings spreading like a black hood around its misshapen skull. A squeal of static issued from the battered vox speaker that passed for the creature's mouth, and then it began a high, skirling wail that grew louder and more manic with each passing moment. More pairs of crimson eyes blazed to life in the shadows of the building's second storey. By ill luck, the Wolves had sought refuge right underneath the lair of an entire pack of the flying daemons.

Ragnar snarled a curse and brought up his bolt pistol, but the daemons were already in flight, leaping from their roost onto the surprised warriors. They moved with preternatural speed, diving low and lashing at their victims with their barbed steel tails. One of the creatures flashed past Ragnar, striking sparks across his breastplate and left arm with its raking tail. It spread its wings and raced skyward, but the young Space Wolf spun on his heel and shot the daemon in the back of the head. The smoking corpse struck one of the ragged walls and crumpled to the earth.

Unholy wails and the thunderous beating of wings shook the musty air as the daemons pressed their attacks. Haegr let out a wild yell and swept his hammer through the air at the darting figures, blood streaming from a ragged wound along the side of his face. Torin ducked low as a daemon swooped overhead, and sliced away one of its wings with a neat stroke of his sword. Other daemons crashed to earth in a tangle of wings and fur as the Wulfen grappled with their swift moving attackers and ripped them apart. The feral Wolves were every bit as swift as their monstrous foes, and their armour was proof against the creatures' barbed tails.

The surviving daemons fled skyward, circling above the ruined building and spreading the alarm far and wide. Bolt pistols barked, and within moments the last of the flying daemons crumpled and fell to the ground, but the damage had already been done. Ragnar could hear the sounds of armoured boots scrabbling across broken stone and heard the answering cries of other winged daemons approaching from every direction. There was only one thing left for the Wolves to do: fight their way to the palace, or die in the attempt.

Ragnar raised his keening blade. 'Follow me, brothers!' he cried. 'Our course is set, and the foe awaits. Let none stand against us. For Russ and the Allfather!'

Sigurd raised his crozius arcanum and began the Benediction of Iron. Torvald threw back his head and howled at the sky, and the Wulfen joined in, singing a hunting song older and more elemental than mankind.

Lightning raged overhead as the Wolves charged from the concealing shadows of the ruined building and crashed head-on into the oncoming platoon of traitor Guardsmen. Wild shots tore through the air, blasting craters from the rubble or ricocheting off ceramite plate. An indigo beam from Gabriella's pistol burned a hole through one onrushing Guardsman and toppled him to the ground. Inquisitor Volt cried an oath to the Emperor and shot another Guardsman full in the chest. The sanctified bolt pistol shell punched through the traitor's desecrated armour as though it were made of tissue, and the blessings carved onto the round's surface consumed the man in a sheet of silver fire.

Ragnar leapt a boulder-sized chunk of masonry and shot an oncoming Guardsman point-blank. The traitor staggered, and he finished the man off with a sweep of his blade. Another traitor lunged at him from the left, slashing at him with dagger-like claws, but he spun beneath the blow and sliced off the soldier's mutated arm at the elbow. Man-made lightning crackled as Torvald laid a traitor low with his rune axe, and Haegr smashed another apart with a furious blow from his thunder hammer.

'Forward!' Ragnar yelled, orientating himself on the distant palace. 'Don't stop for anything.'

Another Guardsman reared up in front of the young Space Wolf and they both fired point-blank. The traitor fell backwards, his head blown apart, even as the autogun shell ricocheted from Ragnar's ancient armour. He vaulted the Guardsman's bloody corpse and slid down a slope of shattered rubble, all but tumbling onto the debris choked street beyond.

A storm of shells criss-crossed over Ragnar's head or dug furrows from the roadway as more enemy patrols fired from either end of the street. Ragnar ducked low and crossed the street at a run, firing aimed shots at the mob of Guardsmen to his right. Torin and Haegr added their fire moments later as they emerged onto the street and followed the young Space Wolf's lead. Torvald, Gabriella and Volt followed, surrounded by Sigurd and the Wulfen. The inquisitor's armour and robes shone with burning silver runes, and the wards of protection seemed to confound the enemy's aim long enough for the group to reach cover on the far side of the street.

By that point Ragnar was already charging ahead through the lightning shot darkness, stumbling, leaping and scrambling over piles of rubble and twisted metal while listening to the sounds of pursuit approaching from the east and west. Shrieks echoed overhead as more of the flying daemons joined the chase. One swept low, angling for Ragnar's back, but a shot from Torin's bolt pistol sent it tumbling to the ground. Shouts, curses and feral howls shook the night. Shots from the traitors' autoguns hissed through the air, but the broken terrain provided ample cover for the running warband. Ragnar couldn't afford a single backward glance. He could only trust that his companions were still behind him.

Ragnar cut the most direct course over the ruins that he could, navigating by the twisting column of Chaos energy rising from the palace roof. The traitors continued to pursue the racing warband, sometimes drawing close enough for a brief exchange of fire with the Wolves. Once Ragnar clearly heard a howl of pain, and he knew that one of the Wulfen had been hit. Steeling himself, the young Space Wolf pressed on.

After several long minutes, the broken walls and piles of debris abruptly ended at the edge of a vast, open square that stretched before the palace gates. The square was pocked with craters and scarred with blackened furrows that were the hallmarks of an orbital bombardment. Ragnar fetched up against the remnants of a shattered wall and cursed under his breath. He ought to have expected a parade ground or marshalling field in front of the palace. This one, near as he could tell, looked to be a kilometre across. Faint signs of movement at the far end revealed mobs of traitor Guardsmen rushing into the square from the west, drawn by the wailing daemons overhead.

Far across the plaza, the palace's tall gates stood open, but for how much longer, Ragnar wondered?

Torin and Haegr pulled up alongside Ragnar, their armoured forms coated in dust and splashes of ichor. Haegr was red-faced and breathing hard from the difficult run, but his expression was set in a determined scowl. Torin peered across the open square and shook his head. 'I don't like the look of that,' he declared. 'We'll be taking fire the whole way across.'

'Best get it over with, then,' Ragnar growled. He peered back over his shoulder, trying to ascertain where the rest of the warband was. He caught a glimpse of Sigurd and a few of the Wulfen, and then saw Torvald, Gabriella and Volt climbing over a pile of rubble just behind him. 'We'll stay close to the inquisitor and see how well those wards of his work. Let's go!'

Ragnar leapt from cover onto the edge of the square. Moments later Torin and Haegr followed, and then Sigurd, Torvald, Gabriella and Volt. The dark, swift forms of the Wulfen flowed like shadows out of the rubble to either side. They were close to the south-west corner of the square. Ragnar could see more movement farther north, where a side street emptied into the square, and saw more pursuing mobs approaching from the north and east.

He didn't see the traitors hidden in the rubble to the south until they rose from cover and opened fire.

A storm of shells tore through the surprised warband, ringing off the curved surfaces of ceramite plate, and buzzing through the air. Two shells flattened against Ragnar's armour; another clipped Haegr's right leg, nearly dropping the burly Wolfblade to his knees. One of the Wulfen dropped without a sound, shot through the head.

Gabriella spun, raking the ruins with bursts from her xenotech pistol. Then a shell struck her high in the chest, knocking the Navigator from her feet.

Ragnar roared in anger and opened fire on the ambushers, knocking one traitor backwards with a shell through his helmet. More enemy shells hissed past the young Space Wolf's head as he leapt for Gabriella. 'Head for the palace,' he cried. 'Go!'

Torvald took up the cry, leading Sigurd and the Wulfen towards the palace. Still firing, Ragnar knelt beside Gabriella. 'Are you hurt?' he asked.

'Fine... I'm fine,' the Navigator gasped. 'It flattened against my armour. Help me up.'

A shell ricocheted from Ragnar's left pauldron. Volt, Torin and Haegr stood their ground, trading shots with the ambushing Guardsmen. The young Space Wolf got his sword arm around Gabriella's shoulders and lifted her to her feet. 'Run!' he yelled, pushing her after Torvald. Holstering his pistol, Ragnar pulled a grenade from his belt, threw it towards the ambushers, and then loped along in Gabriella's wake.

Lee Lightner

Shells hissed through the air from three different directions as the Wolves raced across the square. Traitor Guardsmen were charging at the warband, forming an armoured barrier across the warriors' path. Torvald was hit again and again, skipping a single step when one of the shells found a weak spot in his armour, but the old warrior only redoubled his pace, his axe held high. The Rune Priest began a dreadful battle chant as he charged into the fire, a song of split helms and splintered shields, a merciless song of vengeance and red ruin.

If the traitors meant to bar the path to Madox, they would have to stand their ground before the Wolves of Fenris.

Torvald crashed into the enemy ranks like a battering ram, his axe reaping a terrible harvest among his foes. Armour plates split and smoking corpses were flung skyward with each upward sweep of the warrior-priest's blade. The traitors slashed and stabbed at him with chainswords or jagged talons, but none struck more than once.

The traitors reeled from the priest's terrible onslaught. Then the Wulfen struck. Having suffered a constant hail of shells since the battle began, the cursed warriors leapt at their foes with bloodthirsty howls and flashing, razor-edged claws. Sigurd charged alongside them, roaring out the Litany of Detestation and crushing skulls with his glowing crozius. The enemy line recoiled from the impact, its survivors pushed step by step back towards the waiting palace, and the mobs of Guardsmen along the flanks rushed forwards, trying to encircle the Wolves.

'Forward!' Ragnar shouted to his companions. 'Break through and keep going.' As he spoke, he snapped a pair of shots into the swirling melee and brought down another foe. Then he wove past the snarling Wulfen and crashed into the line alongside Torvald. His frost blade howled as the young Space Wolf hacked open a traitor's breastplate, and then severed another's claw arm.

An indigo beam flashed past Ragnar's shoulder and punched through two of the struggling foes. Then Volt appeared, brandishing a glowing silver falchion and shouting a prayer of detestation in a terrible voice. The traitors faltered before the furious inquisitor and his powerful wards. Many threw up their arms and staggered away, hissing curses at Volt and the Wolves.

Haegr rushed forward with a bear-like roar and smashed two Guardsmen aside with a sweep of his hammer. Ragnar saw the opening and shouted to Sigurd. 'Forward, priest!' He pointed to the palace gates, just a few hundred metres away. 'Keep moving!'

Sigurd blocked a traitor's sweeping blade, and then glanced quickly at Ragnar and nodded. The Wolf Priest shouted something at a trio of Wulfen close by, and the warriors surged forwards. In moments they had broken through the encirclement and were racing across the parade field, drawing fire from several of the traitors as they went. More of the Wulfen caught sight of their comrades and broke free as well, and within moments the warband was on the move again, firing at the mob of Guardsmen closing ranks in their wake.

Shells chased after Ragnar and his companions, but the shots were poorly aimed and flew wide of their mark. The war band was widely scattered in the wake of the melee, with Sigurd and a trio of Wulfen well ahead, followed by Torvald, Volt, Gabriella and the rest of Harald's pack. Ragnar, Torin and Haegr brought up the rear, firing shots at the pursuing traitors as they ran.

Ragnar saw that the palace gates were still open, and from what he could see there were no foes waiting on the pockmarked battlements. He turned his attention from the pursuing Guardsmen long enough to try and peer beyond the gateway into the courtyard beyond, but all he caught was a fleeting glimpse of flickering purple flame.

More traitor Guardsmen were racing onto the parade ground from the south and west, but they were too far away to reach the Wolves in time. Once past the gates it would be a short run into the palace, and the confined spaces would favour them rather than their foes.

The young Space Wolf turned to shout encouragement to Sigurd, and caught a flash of movement just beyond the palace gates. At first he thought it was a mob of traitors positioning themselves in front of the shifting flames, but then he realised that the flames were in motion, advancing implacably towards the gateway.

Ragnar's eyes widened in realisation. 'Sigurd!' he shouted, but his warning came a moment too late.

Sigurd half-turned, glancing over his shoulder at the young Space Wolf just as the Chaos Dreadnought lumbered through the gateway and opened fire, bathing the Wolf Priest and the trio of Wulfen in a blast of crackling plasma.

* * *

THE CRACKLE OF small-arms fire echoed through the darkness across the Charys starport, punctuated by confused shouts and the cries of dying men. Flames billowed skyward from warehouses or refuelling nodes hit by enemy fire, illuminating large sections of the landing field while leaving others plunged into abyssal shadow. Sven and his companions kept to the darkness as they raced back to the command bunker, their preternatural senses alert for signs of danger.

Strange, gibbering howls and blasphemous cries rose from all directions as packs of daemons stalked across the landing field after the fleeing Guardsmen. The regiments had all but ceased to exist. All that remained were isolated platoons fighting for their lives as they searched for some way to escape the slaughter unfolding around them.

Men screamed in the night, calling to the Emperor to deliver them. Sometimes, their plea was answered by a low, savage howl. The sound made Sven's blood run cold. He'd heard it often enough along the mountain slopes and ice fields of home as the Fenrisian wolves hunted their prey. After that there would be terrible, unnatural screams and savage cries as the daemons found themselves fighting a beast every bit as terrible as they were. Sven, Gunnar and Silvertongue shared uneasy looks at every wolf-like howl. Our battle-brothers have gone mad, the Grey Hunter thought dreadfully, feeling his skin crawl. His gaze turned to the north-east, where the company had laid Berek in state on a bier strung with melta charges. Sven pictured Thorin Shieldsplitter kneeling at Berek's feet, his hands trembling as he lifted the access panel to the first charge and awoke its detonation runes. *Not long now,* Sven thought bleakly.

As they ran the five kilometres to the centre of the landing field, Sven listened for the rising whine of engines, and scanned the dark skies for thruster flames. Nothing had taken off from the doomed starport as far as he could tell. He feared that when they reached the command bunker they would find a burning, cratered ruin, blown apart by a salvo of powerful Earthshaker artillery shells.

Instead, the three Wolves arrived to find the low, slope-sided bunkers largely unscathed. Three cargo haulers were parked outside the main entrance, their petrochem engines rumbling. The armoured doors to the bunker were open, but there was no one about.

They surveyed the scene for a moment from the deep shadows beyond the bunker floodlights. 'What do you make of this?' Sven asked, feeling his hackles rise.

Gunnar shook his head. 'No signs of a firefight. Maybe the Guardsmen lost their nerve and ran off?'

'Perhaps,' Silvertongue said, but the skald's voice sounded less than certain. 'Let's check out the back of those trucks.'

The warriors spread out and approached the cargo haulers at a crouching run, their bolters trained and ready. Sven reached the tailgate of the first truck and swung around, aiming into the bed. 'Logic engines, data-slates and a pair of generators,' he declared, lowering his weapon, 'but no soldiers.'

'Same here,' Silvertongue said from the back of the second truck. 'Gunnar? What have you got?'

'Crates and more crates,' the Long Fang said from the third cargo hauler. 'Looks like they were emptying out the bunker. Except...'

The skald looked back at the old Wolf. 'Except what?'

Gunnar nodded towards the bunker entrance, just a few metres away. 'I smell blood,' he replied, 'and it's fresh.'

Silvertongue looked over at Sven and indicated the bunker entrance. The Grey Hunter nodded and edged towards the open doorway, bolter at the ready.

When he was within three metres, he could smell the blood as well, along with the stink of scorched ferrocrete and overheated power cells. Sven crouched low and tried to peer into the tunnel beyond the threshold. Most of the lights in the passageway were out, but the Wolf's keen sight picked out a body slumped on the floor just beyond the doorway.

Another savage howl rose into the darkness off to the south. Sven took a deep breath and edged closer.

The body was clearly that of a Guardsman, collapsed against the right wall of the tunnel and sitting in a pool of blood. The soldier's left arm was flung out to the side. In the faint light Sven could see that it had been torn open from shoulder to elbow. More worrying, the soldier had been facing *into* the bunker when he'd been killed.

Moving carefully, Sven stepped around the body and entered the tunnel. The Guardsman's lasgun lay in his lap, covered in gore. A faintly blinking light on the weapon's power cell showed that it was completely empty. Scorch marks from wild lasgun fire marked the reinforced walls all the way down the narrow passageway.

Sven crouched low, aiming down the passageway. There was another faint scent in the tunnel, something savage and wild that set his nerves on edge. He was so intent on the strange smell that he didn't hear Gunnar and Silvertongue creep up to the bunker entrance behind him.

'What happened here?' the skald asked.

The Grey Hunter started, his finger tightening on the trigger of his boltgun. Heart racing, he half-turned to his battle-brothers. 'There's something in here,' he said quietly. 'I don't know what it is, but I can smell it.'

Gunnar looked down at the dead soldier. 'Looks like daemon's work,' he said grimly.

Silvertongue nodded thoughtfully. 'If so, they're between us and the vox-units,' he said. 'Sven, you've got point.'

The Grey Hunter nodded, checking his bolter. Six rounds left, he thought. If there's more than one of them in here, this is going to be a short fight.

Weapons ready, the Wolves made their way into the bunker. Outside, a chorus of hunting howls rose into the fire-lit sky.

THE CHAOS DREADNOUGHT's armoured hide bore the marks of ten thousand years of battle. Gruesome trophies from dozens of unholy campaigns hung from corroded spikes across its wide shoulders, and its scarred front hull was daubed with evil runes painted in the blood of the innocent. The war machine's sarcophagus was wrapped in black iron chains, and strange charms had been affixed to its metal surface.

Wreathed in a nimbus of multicoloured fire, the oculars of the Dreadnought's pitted helm were as black as the depths of the abyss. Ragnar looked into those depths and knew that no living thing lay within that adamantine shell. The warrior within had been turned to dust by the sorceries of the Rubric of Ahriman, thousands of years past. All that remained was a hateful spirit that longed for nothing but slaughter.

In the middle ground between Ragnar and the Dreadnought, an armoured figure staggered amid three blackened and melted corpses. Smoke rose from Sigurd's armour, and the ceramite plates shimmered with heat, but the power of the iron wolf amulet had saved the priest from a gruesome death. The blast had left the Wolf Priest stunned, and for a moment he seemed unable to comprehend the peril looming before him.

With a groan of ancient servo-motors the war machine took a ponderous step forward. An inhuman growl issued from the Dreadnought's vox-unit as it reached for Sigurd with a huge, saw toothed power claw.

'For Russ and the Allfather!' Ragnar cried, charging between Sigurd and the war machine, and leaping at the Dreadnought's head. Purple and gold flames licked at him like deadly whips as he drew near, leaving long scorch marks across his shoulders and chest. His frost blade struck sparks as it rang from the war machine's heavy armour, but with all his strength he could not penetrate the thick adamantine plates.

Howling in fury, the Dreadnought turned at the waist and swiped its claw at the offending Wolf. Ragnar leapt backwards, just out of reach, but was struck with a hail of shells as a twin bolter in the war machine's shoulder opened fire. Mass-reactive rounds smashed against the young Space Wolf's breastplate, driving him to his knees.

More of the Wolves rushed forwards. The Wulfen swept around the Dreadnought's flanks, risking the deadly flames to leap in and rake their claws against the war machine's armour. Enraged, the Dreadnought lashed out wildly against its antagonists, catching one of the Wulfen in its claw and cutting him in two.

Then came a booming laugh, and Haegr strode towards the towering war machine with a berserker grin on his broad face. 'Curse your false gods for your ill fortune, traitor,' he called, hefting his thunder hammer. 'Mighty Haegr has been looking to give someone a good thrashing, and he's chosen you!'

The Dreadnought let out another savage roar and pivoted again, bringing its plasma cannon to bear, but Haegr saw the move and rushed forward with surprising speed. His hammer crackled with power as he swung it in a brutal arc, smashing the cannon's projector to pieces. Sorcerous flames lashed at the burly Wolfblade, but Haegr kept moving, spinning on one heel and smashing his hammer into the war machine's right hip. There was an earth-shaking detonation that sent pieces of torn metal spinning through the air, and the Dreadnought's right leg bent at an awkward angle. The war machine was immobilised.

However, the Dreadnought was far from finished. Howling in rage, it swung at Haegr with its power claw, striking the Wolfblade a glancing blow that hurled him through the air. Haegr hit the ground five metres away, his thunder hammer spinning across the paving stones.

'Haegr!' Ragnar shouted. The big Wolfblade slowly rose to his hands and knees, shaking his head in a daze. A burst of bolter shells blazed across Haegr's flank as the Dreadnought opened fire again. Other shells tore into the paving stones and buzzed through the air around the rest of the Wolves. The traitor Guardsmen and their daemon packs were drawing near, pressing in on the warriors from three sides. Ragnar looked back and saw Torvald, Torin, Volt and Gabriella standing back to back, blazing away at the oncoming foes.

The young Space Wolf staggered to his feet, trying to think of some way to stop the daemon-possessed war machine. Suddenly, he caught sight of a swift figure charging the Dreadnought from the right. A Wulfen dashed beneath the daemon's swinging power claw and leapt onto the machine's left leg. Flames enveloped the warrior, burning away his blond fur as the former Blood Claw climbed nimbly onto the Dreadnought's back. The war machine bellowed in fury, groping clumsily with its power claw at the bold warrior on its back, but the Wulfen crouched between the Dreadnought's twin exhaust towers and tore at the engine's power couplings with his charred hands.

Burning like a torch, Harald turned and met Ragnar's eyes. White teeth shone in a wolfish grin, framed by a blackened face. Then the Wulfen threw back his broad shoulders and heaved. Ensorcelled metal tore with a chilling shriek, and the Dreadnought's power plant exploded in a dazzling white flash.

The concussion flattened everyone within ten metres. Molten shrapnel rained down on the Wolves. The Dreadnought's power claw spun end over end across the paving stones less than a metre from where Ragnar lay.

The war machine was gone from the waist up, standing in a shallow crater melted in the stone. Beyond, the palace gates lay undefended. The young Space Wolf leapt to his feet. Shells buzzed past him as the traitor Guardsmen resumed their fire. 'Let's go!' he shouted to his stunned companions. 'Follow me!'

Ragnar charged past Haegr and the Wulfen and ran beneath the tall gateway. Beyond lay a long, rectangular courtyard, empty of life, and cloaked in deep shadow. The entrance to the palace was at the far end.

With a heavy tread, Haegr, Sigurd and the four surviving Wulfen swept through the gate. Shots chipped stone from the arch and rang from the steel gates. The burly Wolfblade had lost most of his whiskers to the searing touch of the Dreadnought's sorcerous flames, but other than that he seemed unharmed. Within moments the rest of the warband joined them, Torvald and Torin firing their bolt pistols at the daemons in their wake.

The pillar of Chaos energy overhead shone upon the Wolves with a sickly, furtive glow as they ran along the length of the courtyard. Shots whipped past them as the traitor Guardsmen boiled through the gateway and gave chase, but they could not gain much ground on the fleet-footed warriors. Ragnar felt a sense of righteous rage swelling within his breast with every step. The moment of reckoning was at hand. Madox was finally going to pay for all that he'd done. Nothing could stop them now.

Ragnar charged up the steps to the palace and put his shoulder to the doors. The dark wood smashed inward, revealing a silent, empty nave. Towering statues of daemon princes in ornate armour leered down at the Wolves as they raced inside.

Cadmus Volt pointed to the doors at the far end of the nave. 'The governor's audience chamber lies beyond,' he said over the bark of bolt pistols and the buzz of ricocheting shells. 'That was where Berek was ambushed. It must be the locus of the enemy ritual.'

The young Space Wolf nodded. His heart was racing, and his blood was afire. 'Whatever else happens, Madox must fall,' he said. 'Nothing else matters. If we die here, so be it, but Madox and his ritual must die with us.'

'Well said,' Sigurd replied solemnly. The young priest's face was blistered from the plasma blast, and the brush with death had left a grim look in his eyes.

'Enough talking,' Torvald said, hefting his axe. 'Now, go.'

Ragnar frowned at the Rune Priest. 'What about you?'

'I'm staying here,' he said. 'Someone has to hold the door and keep our pursuers off your back long enough for you to deal with Madox.' The ancient warrior studied the doorway and nodded. 'From here, I can hold those fiends at bay almost indefinitely.'

'Almost?' Ragnar said.

The Rune Priest smiled. 'Go, little brother,' he said. 'Fight well, in Leman's name.'

The young Space Wolf nodded. 'And you,' he replied.

Shots struck the doorframe and whipped around the darkened nave. With a nod of farewell, Torvald turned to face the onslaught. Ragnar and his remaining companions looked to one another and left the Rune Priest to his fate.

They crossed the nave quickly, their skin prickling at the touch of unseen energies. Ragnar heard the Wulfen growl uneasily, and felt the curse within him respond. Beyond the audience chamber's double doors, they could hear a chorus of wild, unnatural chanting.

Behind them, at the far end of the nave, Ragnar heard the first blows being struck as Torvald faced the traitor horde alone. A grim and terrible wrath came upon the young Space Wolf, like a red tide rising up behind his eyes. With a howl, he raised his boot and burst the wooden doors asunder.

Unholy light washed over Ragnar and his companions, along with a chorus of tortured shrieks from the souls of the damned. Scraps of tattered skin fluttered in on an unseen wind from the tall pillars lining the great chamber, drawn towards a whirling pillar of sorcerous energy that rose like a cyclone above the temple's black altar.

Upon the desecrated stone burned the stolen geneseed of Madox's victims, their precious genetic material spun free in a fine, red mist that rose in twisting tendrils into the heart of the psychic whirlwind. Scores of cult sorcerers filled the great hall, standing atop the charred remains of their peers as they stretched their hands to the obsidian altar and fuelled the workings of Madox's great spell.

The foul sorcerer stood behind that same black altar, gripping the Spear of Russ in his left hand. Madox's right hand was outstretched, as though in greeting, beckoning the Wolves to their doom. His eyes burned with hate from the depths of his ornate helmet, and his baroque armour glowed with unholy power. Patterns of runes carved into the ancient armour pulsed and writhed, radiating energy like heat from a forge, and foul energies leapt in arcs of lightning from the tips of his horned helm.

Behind Madox, wreathed in the very energies of the warp itself, shone the glowing semblance of a single, terrifying eye. It glared at Ragnar with palpable malice and inhuman evil, piercing his armour and sinking invisible talons of despair into the young Space Marine's soul.

A lesser soul might have shattered before such an awful sight, but Ragnar Blackmane looked upon his old foe and felt only a savage, merciless joy. 'Madox of the Thousand Sons!' he roared. 'Your wyrd is upon you! By Russ and the Allfather, your death is at hand!'

The chanting faltered with those fierce words, and the sorcerers spun around, hissing invocations to the Ruinous Powers. Howls shook the vaulted chamber as Ragnar led his companions into battle.

Bolt pistols hammered, sending heavy shells smashing through the massed ranks of the enemy. Ragnar fired again and again into the press, scarcely marking where his rounds struck as he forced his way step by step towards his goal. Sorcerous energies flashed through the air, striking the armoured warriors, but the wards etched into Volt's Inquisitorial armour seemed to turn aside the worst of the enemy spells.

Haegr and Torin stood to either side of Ragnar, wreaking a terrible slaughter with hammer and blade. On the flanks, the Wulfen pulled cultists off their feet and tore them asunder with tooth and claw. Sigurd stood among the Wulfen on the left, bellowing out the Litanies of Hate and slaying the enemy with blows from his glowing crozius. Gabriella stood on the right, moving easily among the bestial Wulfen and slashing at the cultists with her curved power sword.

The cultists fell back in disarray before the relentless assault. Scores died every moment, reaped like wheat before the Wolves' iron fury. With every step, Ragnar drew closer to the black altar, but Madox made not a single move to stop him. The master sorcerer simply waited, his eyes gleaming and his hand outstretched.

Within moments they had advanced almost two-thirds of the way across the chamber. Ragnar felt a hint of unease through the red currents of bloodlust. By then, however, it was already too late.

Swift figures emerged from the deep shadows behind the parchment covered pillars: broad, powerful figures in blue and gold armour, wielding bolt pistols and chainswords of arcane design. Their armour was decorated with grisly trophies from countless battlefields, including the burned and broken helms of Space Marine champions, and the skulls of Imperial heroes. They moved with a speed and skill beyond that of even normal Chaos Marines. They were veteran warriors who had slaughtered tens of thousands of foes in their time, and were the chosen men of powerful lords such as Madox.

'Look to the flanks!' Ragnar bellowed, but the veteran Chaos Marines were already pressing forwards, smashing the cultists out of their way in their eagerness to spill loyalist blood. Still more of the warriors were circling behind the warband, cutting off their retreat.

The only way left was to go forward. Redoubling his efforts, Ragnar threw himself at the cultists in front of him, severing limbs and splitting torsos with fearsome sweeps of his blade. He was less than three metres from the steps leading to the altar, and only about a dozen cultists stood in his path.

Ragnar heard the shriek of a chainblade biting against armour, and then heard Torin grunt in pain. A Chaos Marine had darted in alongside the older Wolfblade and struck him hard across his left vambrace, leaving torn armour and a deep cut above his elbow. Then Haegr let out a yell as a pair of enemy warriors attacked him from the right. The Wolfblade crushed one of the Chaos Marines with a downward stroke from his hammer, but the other drove his chainsword into Haegr's midsection with unnatural strength, and inflicted a bloody wound.

Anger and desperation drove Ragnar on. Madox had to die. The future of the Chapter depended upon it. He slashed left and right with his blade, killing every cultist he could reach. Then, without warning, the remaining sorcerers turned and fled from the berserk Wolf, scrambling for their lives up the stone steps.

For a fleeting instant, Ragnar felt a surge of triumph, but then a pair of Chaos Marines charged at him from each side, their swords flashing.

Ragnar howled in fury as he parried a blurring cut to his head, and then dodged a stop-thrust aimed at his midsection. A sword flicked out and struck his leg, the chainblade scoring the armour, but failing to penetrate. Another sword struck at his shoulder, biting deep into his right pauldron. The young Space Wolf struck back, aiming a feint at one warrior's head, and then switching to a back-handed cut that he buried deep in another Chaos Marine's chest. The enemy warrior staggered, and then surged upright, slashing his sword deep into Ragnar's forearm. The chosen warrior's unnatural vigour drove the Chaos Marine onward despite the terrible wound.

The young Space Wolf pulled his weapon free just in time to parry another blow arcing in from his left side. Suddenly he found himself entirely on the defensive, ringed by a semicircle of flashing blades at the very foot of the altar steps. He snarled with wild rage, feeling the red tide pounding in his veins as he slashed and hacked at the deadly warriors.

A bolt pistol barked just past Ragnar's shoulder. Without warning, the Chaos Marine to the young Space Wolf's right screamed as his body was wreathed in silver flames. Inquisitor Volt darted past the burning form and set his foot upon the stone steps, his eyes blazing with murderous hate. Raising his pistol, he fired a shot at Madox. The blessed round rang from the sorcerer's ancient armour, but the inquisitor took another step and fired again. Each time he pulled the trigger, Volt cried out a name.

'Gunter Mault. Kyr Sirenus. Mattieu Van Dorn. Yrian Kar'Doma. Issedu Orban.' Each shot struck Madox square in the chest, a relentless, punishing barrage that caused him to stagger with each hit. Volt kept coming, his face twisted into a mask of rage. 'Edwen

Barone. Jedden bir Gul. The souls of my friends cry out for vengeance, you bastard. And now–'

A bolt pistol cracked from the shadows behind the altar, and Volt staggered as an armour piercing shell tore through his side. The old inquisitor reeled, blood pouring from the exit wound in his back, but he straightened and took another step. He raised his pistol, but another enemy shell tore through his left shoulder. The glowing falchion clanged onto the steps as it fell from Volt's nerveless hand.

Figures were gliding from the darkness to either side of Madox: fearsome sorcerers in ornate armour, bearing dreadblades and aiming bolt pistols at the struggling inquisitor. Their guns hammered, and Volt's body twitched as the heavy slugs riddled him from neck to hip. The old man swayed, for an instant, on his feet, his pistol still raised. With a final effort, he squeezed the trigger, gouging a crater from the front of the stone altar. Then his lifeless body crumpled, sliding in a trail of blood back down the stone steps.

Ragnar bellowed a savage curse, and cut a warrior's leg out from under him, dropping the veteran Chaos Marine to the ground. Cries of rage and pain echoed around him as his friends were beset from all sides. A blade bit into his hip. Ragnar growled like a wounded wolf and shot his attacker point-bank in the face. There was only one enemy warrior left, but the Thousand Son sorcerers were gliding like snakes down the bloodstained steps, their black blades poised to strike.

A wave of blinding pain speared through him as the last veteran warrior slipped past Ragnar's guard and drove his chainblade into the young Space Wolf's chest. He felt one of his hearts stop beating, and pure, animal rage took hold. Dropping his bolt pistol, he grabbed the warrior's sword wrist and hacked off the Chaos Space Marine's helm with a single swipe of his blade.

Ragnar pulled the foe's chainsword free and fell to his knees. He could feel his muscles writhing like snakes beneath his skin, and his mind was afire. The young Space Wolf looked up the steps, past the oncoming sorcerers, to the altar and the towering figure of Madox. The spear was right there, just out of reach.

A pure, wordless cry of anguish tore through Ragnar's throat, and he felt his body begin to change. His frost blade clattered to the floor as he tore madly at his gauntlets. By the time he pulled them free, the talons were already starting to grow from his fingertips.

Ragnar looked back at Torin and found the older Wolfblade on his knees as well, writhing painfully in the grip of the curse. The Wulfen continued to fight, snapping and slashing at any foe that came within reach. Sigurd was still standing, fighting two veteran Chaos Space Marines at the same time. What he lacked in skill he made up for with pure, animal ferocity. His eyes shone yellow-gold, and his curved fangs were bared.

Howls filled the air as the curse took hold. At the top of the blood-soaked steps, Madox threw back his head and laughed, savouring his triumph.

Then a furious bellow shook the rafters, like the roar of a wounded bear. A shadow passed over Ragnar, and the ground shook beneath the tread of heavy, armoured feet. Haegr reached the foot of the stairs at a dead run, charging right at the line of sorcerers with his hammer ready to strike.

Streaming blood from half a dozen wounds, the burly Wolfblade swung his thunder hammer in a fearsome arc, smashing two of the sorcerers from his path. 'That was for Russ!' Haegr bellowed. Another sorcerer lunged in from the right, stabbing his sword into the Wolfblade's thigh. Grunting, Haegr slew the Chaos Space Marine with a swift, overhand blow. 'That was for Torin!' he said, and continued up the steps.

Another sorcerer darted in from the left, thrusting his sword deep into Haegr's side. The huge Space Wolf staggered, and then brought down his hammer and crushed the sorcerer's skull. 'That was for Gabriella,' he said grimly.

Haegr took another step. Then he drew back his hammer and swung it with all his strength, smashing the obsidian altar to bits with a deafening thunderclap. Madox reeled backwards, spitting curses as the Wolfblade reached for him with one broad hand.

'And this, you black-hearted bastard, is for my brother Ragnar!' Haegr cried, raising his fearsome hammer.

The Wolfblade closed his hand around his foe's throat, but as he pulled Madox towards him, Ragnar saw a glimmer of black metal as the sorcerer drew the hellblade at his hip.

Haegr and Madox crashed together. For a moment, neither figure moved. Metal creaked as Haegr's hand tightened around the sorcerer's throat, but then he slumped, falling to one knee as Madox pulled his sword free from Haegr's chest.

The thunder hammer fell from the Wolfblade's grasp. Still gripping the sorcerer's neck, Haegr lunged forward with the last of his strength and seized Russ's spear. Madox shouted a curse, struggling to keep hold of the relic. Desperate, he drew back his hellblade and buried it in Haegr's shoulder, right at the base of the neck. Blood fountained from the wound, but the Wolfblade would not relent. With a final, wrenching heave, Haegr tore the spear from Madox's grasp and cast it down the steps behind him.

Madox shouted with rage as the Spear of Russ plunged amid the surviving Wolves. It arced past Ragnar's head and landed, point-first, right behind Gabriella. The Navigator, fighting alongside one of the Wulfen, turned away from the Chaos sorcerer in front of her and ran for the weapon. Her xenotech pistol fell from her hand as she grabbed the haft of the ancient relic and closed her eyes, as though deep in concentration. Her pineal eye flared like a newborn star.

Abruptly, Gabriella's eyes opened again. She looked at Ragnar, just a few metres away. The Navigator's mouth opened, but no sound escaped her lips. Then her gaze fell to the black blade jutting from her abdomen and she sank slowly to the floor.

TWENTY-ONE
The Spear of Russ

HIGH ABOVE THE war-torn world of Charys, the dance of death began.

At a signal from *Holmgang*, the seven strike cruisers of the Space Wolf fleet broke away from the flagship on divergent courses, setting up orbital insertions that would carry them over their designated bombardment zones. The fleet's eight surviving escorts quickly fell behind the onrushing cruisers. Standard procedure for the *Hunter* and *Falchion* escorts was to provide a cordon in high orbit to protect the capital ships while they were locked into their attack runs.

Aboard the battle-barge, orders were passed to the helm, and *Holmgang* came about, setting up her own bombardment run. Her track would carry her over the capital city and the planet's starport. It wasn't the ideal placement for the cyclonic torpedoes, but the ship's master wanted to give the lost warriors of Berek's company the heroes' pyre that they deserved.

Across the command deck, the chief ordnance officer tapped a rune above his control station. A timer whirred and ticked, counting down the minutes remaining until launch.

THE COMMAND BUNKER was as silent as a tomb.

Sven moved through total darkness, sliding forward a step at a time, and tasting the scents in the air. He could hear the faint sounds of Gunnar and Silvertongue following a few metres behind him, and feel the pulse drumming in his temples, but little else. The Grey Hunter navigated by memory, working his way through the narrow, maze-like tunnels towards the war room at the bunker's centre.

They'd found no more bodies since entering the site, but the scent of blood hung heavy in the stale air. Sven could smell patches of it beneath his feet, the scent turning sickly sweet as it cooled and congealed. He couldn't make sense of it at first, until he realised that the spots appeared at regular intervals down the passageway. They were bloody footprints, left by whatever killed the soldier at the bunker's entrance, and they led in the direction that the Wolves needed to go.

Typical, Sven thought grimly. Never see a daemon hiding out in a supply closet or stalking the lavatories. No, they always seem to find the one place where they can cause people the most trouble, like cats, only with thumbs.

Sven grinned in the darkness and continued on.

Faint light shone around a sharp corner just ahead. The Grey Hunter paused, consulting his memory. If he remembered rightly, the war room was just around the corner, and the signals room about ten metres beyond that. *Nearly there*, he thought.

Just short of the corner, Sven paused and took a deep breath. His eyes narrowed as he tasted the charnel reek of a slaughterhouse.

The Grey Hunter swung around the corner, bolter ready. A single light strip glowed from the ceiling right outside the door to the war room, revealing a scene of carnage.

Bodies and pieces of bodies littered the ferrocrete passageway in a tremendous pool of dark blood. Broken weapons, crushed helmets and torn pieces of carapace armour were scattered among the remains, and scorch marks on the walls revealed that the victims had put up a brief but doomed fight before they'd been overwhelmed.

'Blessed Russ,' Sven whispered, studying the slaughter. There were at least six bodies lying on the ferrocrete, one of which was stretched across the threshold leading into the war room.

Gunnar and Silvertongue slipped up quietly behind Sven and took in the awful scene. 'Looks like a bomb went off,' the Long Fang said softly.

'Just claws and teeth, like the soldier at the entrance,' the Grey Hunter said. 'Those two would have been the sentries posted outside the war room,' Sven said, indicating the savaged remains of two men splayed against the wall opposite the doorway. 'The rest are logistics troops, I think.'

Silvertongue nodded thoughtfully. 'If there were still sentries here, then Athelstane hadn't left the bunker yet.'

The Grey Hunter nodded. 'See the body across the threshold? He's face-down, legs pointing into the room. He was trying to escape the war room when he died. Whatever happened,' he said, nodding at the doorway, 'started in there.'

'I agree,' the skald replied, drawing a deep breath. 'We have to check it out,' he said. 'If there's even a chance the lady commander is still alive, we need to find her.'

'I was afraid you were going to say that,' Sven replied. Stepping carefully and keeping low, he picked his way through the charnel scene and cautiously entered the room.

As bad as it was in the passageway, the war room was worse.

Blood and bits of torn flesh were everywhere, splashed on the floors and sprayed across the walls. Heavy tables had been splintered or hurled across the room, and pieces of wrecked logic engines gleamed like polished coins amid the gore. More scorch marks could be found almost everywhere Sven looked, suggesting a wild, desperate fight. Whatever it was the Guardsmen tried to stop, it was clear that they hadn't stood a chance.

Sven worked his way further into the room, peering closely at the bodies he came across. There were at least a dozen, as near as he could reckon. Gunnar and Silvertongue entered the room in the Grey Hunter's wake. Though they were veterans of scores of brutal campaigns, the sight of the vicious slaughter left them stunned. The Long Fang paused, just inside the door, while the skald picked his way carefully through the piled wreckage.

The Grey Hunter reached the far end of the chamber. 'Large group of bodies here,' he said, kneeling among the savaged corpses. He lifted a scrap of dripping cloth and studied the blood-smeared medals pinned upon it. 'Looks like senior regimental officers,' he mused. 'I guess now we know why no one got the withdrawal order.' Sven tossed the cloth aside and studied the bodies carefully. Frowning, he reached down and shifted one of the victims aside to reveal another body underneath.

'Morkai's teeth,' Sven hissed. 'Here she is. What's left of her, at least.'

Silvertongue made no reply. Worried, the Grey Hunter looked back and saw that the skald was kneeling beside a toppled table. Sven frowned. 'What is it?' he asked.

The skald reached down, pushed the table aside, and picked up a long, blood-stained power sword. 'It's Redclaw,' Silvertongue said grimly, holding the ancient blade up to the light. 'Blessed Russ,' the skald said in a bleak voice. 'Sternmark, what have you done?'

Sven felt a chill run down his spine. It was the same sensation he'd felt as a child, walking through the pine forests close to home and knowing that there was something watching him from deep within the wood. He felt his mouth go dry as he caught the same, feral scent he'd smelled at the bunker entrance. Then he saw the hulking figure just outside the war room door.

Gunnar caught the look in Sven's eye and whirled, bringing up his bolter, but the move came half a second too late. With a deep, liquid growl, the beast that had once been Mikal Sternmark lunged through the doorway and smashed the weapon from Gunnar's hand. Then it struck the Long Fang across the face with bone-crushing force. Sven heard the crunch of Gunnar's skull from clear across the room, and the old Wolf flew backwards onto a pile of broken furniture.

'Mikal Sternmark!' Silvertongue shouted. 'Stay your hand, lest you be labelled kinslayer, and forever damned.' The skald took a step forward, Redclaw held at the ready. 'Submit yourself into the keeping of your brothers, and save your tormented soul.'

The terrible beast grew still, its dripping claws poised over Gunnar's unconscious form. Sternmark had been transformed into a creature born of nightmare. His once glorious armour was drenched in dark blood and scraps of torn flesh, and his clawed hands were matted with gore. Slowly, the wolf-like head turned to regard the angry skald. Yellow-gold eyes regarded Silvertongue coldly, and then drifted to the sword in the warrior's hand. Thin lips drew back, revealing bloodstained fangs, and the Wulfen let out a predatory snarl.

Silvertongue drew a deep breath. 'I'll hold him off,' he said calmly. 'When he attacks me, you slip past and make for the signals room. Do you understand?'

Sven looked from the skald to Sternmark and back again. 'There's got to be another way,' the Grey Hunter said, feeling a cold fist of dread settle in his stomach. 'Together we could subdue him, or perhaps–'

'Do as I say!' Silvertongue snapped, taking his eyes off Sternmark just for a moment to give Sven a commanding glare.

That was all the time Sternmark needed.

The Wulfen was a blur as he charged at the skald with a bloodthirsty roar. Silvertongue's head snapped around and on pure instinct he dodged left, slicing low at the beast's right leg. The ancient power sword glanced from Sternmark's Terminator armour, but the skald's swift movement carried him beyond the reach of the Wulfen's fearsome claws.

Silvertongue fell back before the Wulfen's fierce attack, drawing the creature deeper into the room. Sven saw the skald's plan and started to move, skirting wide of the desperate battle and heading for the door. Shame stung him. Despite the skald's command, the young Grey Hunter knew he was abandoning both of his battle-brothers to a terrible fate. Though the skald fought skilfully and with great courage, he was no match for Sternmark's prowess. Silvertongue was going to die.

Sven was well past the fight, and his path from the room was clear. Still, he hesitated, his hand tightening on the grip of his bolter. Six rounds left, he thought.

The skald feinted at the Wulfen's face, and then swung low, aiming at the beast's right knee. It was a swift, crippling blow, but the Wulfen was swifter still. The creature caught the skald's wrist and pulled Silvertongue off his feet, drawing him within reach of the beast's gaping jaws. Snarling, the Wulfen sank his teeth into the skald's throat, and then felt the cold edge of a boltgun barrel press against the side of his head.

'Let him go, brother,' Sven said quietly. 'At this range, I can't possibly miss.'

The Wulfen let the skald's unconscious form slide heavily to the floor. A fearsome growl rumbled deep in the creature's chest.

Sven let out a slow breath. 'All right, that's good,' he said. 'Now, my lord, I want you to–'

He never saw the blow. The beast's arm crashed into Sven, knocking the bolter from his hand, and then clawed fingers closed around the Grey Hunter's throat. Sven drew back his power fist, in desperation, but he knew that the blow would not land in time.

'Stay your hand, Mikal Sternmark,' a voice spoke quietly from the doorway. 'Remember yourself, and the oaths you swore to me.'

The Wulfen's fierce gaze swung from the Grey Hunter to the tall figure framed in the doorway. Sven saw the beast's eyes widen, and the hand slipped from his throat. An anguished whine escaped the creature's lips, and the beast fell to its knees amid the carnage it had caused.

Berek Thunderfist looked haggard and pale in the wan light. Decked in his resplendent armour, Sven thought at first that he was looking upon the Wolf Lord's ghost. 'My lord,' he gasped in wonder. 'When I saw you last, you stood at death's door!'

'So I did,' Berek said gravely. 'Madox wounded me sorely, and his magic trapped my soul in a realm of shadows from which I could not escape, until a lady came to me and showed me the way back to the land of the living.' A faint smile pulled at the corners of Berek's mouth. 'Our debt to House Bellisarius is deeper than ever. I only hope we live long enough to repay it.'

Sven frowned in consternation. 'Forgive me, lord, but I don't understand.'

'Nor do I Sven, not entirely,' Berek said, 'and there is no time to explain. Even now the *Holmgang* is in the sky above us, preparing to bombard the planet. We have to reach them and call off the attack.'

'The *Holmgang*? Here?' Sven exclaimed. At once, the Grey Hunter bolted for the door, his scalp prickling at the thought of the doom looming high above the agri-world, but then he saw Gunnar's unconscious form and stopped in his tracks. He turned back to the slumped form of the Wulfen. 'What shall we do about him, my lord?'

Berek gazed upon the tormented face of his champion. 'He will stay here and watch over his fallen brothers,' the Wolf Lord said, in a voice like iron. 'Mikal Sternmark has been bewitched, like many of our brothers, by the sorceries of Madox and the Thousand Sons. But he is no monster,' the Wolf Lord declared. 'He has ever been true to his oaths, and he will heed me now.'

Wulfen and Wolf Lord locked eyes across the blood spattered room, and a look of comprehension shone in the creature's yellow eyes. The beast bowed low, touching its snout to the floor, and Berek turned away.

Sven followed the Wolf Lord into the hall, heading for the signals room. 'This curse, how are we going to stop it?' he asked.

'It's already begun,' Berek replied gravely. 'Once we've halted the bombardment, I'm going to turn the fleet's guns on the rebel positions while you and I rally our surviving brothers. Then we're going back into the city to finish what we started.'

GABRIELLA SEEMED TO fall in slow motion, sliding off the sorcerer's hellblade and sinking with dreadful grace to the floor. Her hands still gripped the Spear of Russ tightly, even as her life's blood poured out onto the dark stones. The Chaos sorcerer loomed above her, gripping the relic and trying to pull it free, but the Navigator held the spear's haft in a death grip. The warrior spat a hateful curse and drew back his blade, aiming a blow at Gabriella's head.

Ragnar crashed into the sorcerer at a full run, driving his shoulder into the warrior's chest. The Chaos Space Marine flew backwards with a snarl, slashing wildly with his blade and slicing open the young Space Wolf's cheek. Ragnar's hand closed around the haft of the spear, and he looked down at the stricken Navigator. Their eyes met for a single instant, and he could see the pain etched there. With a faint sigh, her hands slipped from the spear haft and she settled onto her back in a spreading pool of crimson.

He could hear her heartbeat slowing. The breath in her lungs was shallow, like a fading breeze. Horror assailed him as he looked down at the lady he had once sworn to protect.

The Wulfen called to him, beyond the red tide. It promised a simpler existence: a life without oaths or duty, living only for the moment and the red joy of the hunt. For an instant, he longed for that forgetfulness, and the feeling of power it promised.

He dimly heard the sorcerer clamber to his feet. Then came the voice of Bulveye, echoing in his head. *War within, war without.*

The Wulfen called, and Ragnar answered. *Come to me.*

With a furious hiss, the sorcerer rushed at the young Space Wolf, but Ragnar let the fury of the Wulfen drive him. He was a blur of motion, whipping the spear around and knocking the Chaos Space Marine's thrust aside. Then he brought the spear head back into line with a tight, circling motion and thrust it into the sorcerer's neck. The point of the ancient weapon punched through the ceramite plate as though it were paper, bursting from the back of the foe's neck in a gout of vile fluids. Ragnar jerked the weapon free and let the warrior's lifeless form fall to the ground.

Suddenly, Ragnar was bathed in lurid, red light, and he felt unseen hands grapple for the spear. Tendrils of energy wrapped around the haft of the relic, trailing from the foul eye floating above the ritual space. The young Space Wolf spun, glaring up at the semblance of Magnus, the foul primarch of the Thousand Sons.

He could feel the dreaded primarch channelling his energies into the spear, fighting to maintain the ritual that was corrupting the Space Wolves. Every moment the spell continued, the taint sank deeper into their souls.

Ragnar tightened his hands around the relic. He knew that he could not hope to match wills with one such as Magnus, and he did not intend to, for while he could sense the primarch's fury and his implacable hate, he could also feel the pain from a wound that had not yet healed. The spear had wounded Magnus sorely, and he was still weak.

The young Space Wolf gazed defiantly at the blazing eye and hefted the spear in his hands. With a howl of fury he drew his arm back for a murderous throw.

At once the tendrils recoiled, and a disembodied voice roared with thwarted rage. Then there was a thunderclap, and Magnus the Red, Primarch of the Thousand Sons, was gone.

Ragnar felt the echoes of the primarch's retreat reverberate across the surface of the shadow realm.

The red tide began to recede in his mind, flowing back into the deep recesses from whence it had sprung. However, the young Space Wolf wasn't ready to let it go, and he seized it by force of will, stoking the rage once more. The ritual was finally broken, but Madox, its foul architect, still remained.

The sorcerer stood above Haegr's slumped form, still clutching his bloodstained dreadblade. His left hand clenched into a trembling fist. 'Ruined!' he hissed. 'The labour of a hundred years, undone by a pack of fools.' Madox lashed out with a boot and kicked Haegr over, knocking the Wolfblade onto his back. 'But you've doomed yourself as well, Ragnar Blackmane. This world has already begun to unravel. Soon, it will return to the warp, and the things that lurk there will feast upon your soul! I shall savour your agonies like wine,' the sorcerer said, and then lowered his glowing eyes to the Navigator. 'Her, I may choose to keep as a plaything. Her spirit could entertain me for a very long time, I think.'

A chorus of hungry snarls answered Madox as the Wulfen turned from the bodies of their foes and caught the sorcerer's scent. As one, the four beasts charged at the foul sorcerer, their bloody jaws agape.

'No!' Ragnar shouted as the Wulfen charged up the stairs. Too late, the sorcerer sprang his trap.

Madox's left hand opened, and he uttered a string of blasphemous syllables. There was a rushing, wailing sound, like a merciless wind, and then a torrent of unnatural energy poured from the sorcerer's palm. The foul stream engulfed the four Wulfen, shrivelling their massive forms to smoking husks in an instant.

Ragnar was charging up the stairs as the first of the lifeless bodies fell to pieces on the stone steps. He'd sensed that Madox had been trying to bait him, and now that the sorcerer had expended his terrible spell Ragnar was determined to strike before he could ready another.

The Spear of Russ gave the young Space Wolf the advantage of reach, which he used to full effect. Madox fell back from the furious assault, his blade moving in a dark blur as he parried a flurry of lightning-fast jabs and thrusts. Though at a slight disadvantage, Madox had ten thousand years of experience on his side, and he moved with the deadly grace of a viper.

Ragnar pushed Madox relentlessly, driving him steadily backwards. The sorcerer reached the top of the steps and continued to retreat, until the young Space Wolf found himself fighting on level ground. Almost immediately, the sorcerer counter-attacked, knocking the spear aside and darting in to plunge the tip of his blade into Ragnar's thigh. Ragnar felt no pain from the blow, only a spreading coldness that sank deep into the limb.

Madox fell back, a faint hiss of laughter escaping from the depths of his ornate helm. Ragnar knew that he was being lured into playing the sorcerer's game. He remembered the fight back at the Fang, when Torin had played upon his aggression and killed him with small, precise blows. Madox was going to do the very same thing, and there was little that Ragnar could do about it.

The young Space Wolf darted forward, aiming a series of thrusts at the sorcerer's head and chest. Madox fell back, parrying them with ease. Then he lunged in and stabbed his blade into Ragnar's left hip.

'You're getting slower,' the sorcerer said, 'just a bit, perhaps, but I can tell. It's the cold, yes? You can feel it, sinking into your bones a little at a time, and each time I hit you, the feeling will get worse, until finally you're stumbling like a wounded steer.' Madox chuckled. 'I can make this last a long time, Ragnar, a very long time.'

The young Space Wolf staggered. Then, with a furious bellow, he leapt forward, stabbing at the sorcerer's sword arm. Madox expertly gauged the blow and lunged past the expected second strike, stabbing his hellsword into Ragnar's midsection.

Ragnar felt the icy coldness of the sword spread through his torso, and smiled. Madox looked up, and saw the point of Russ's spear, poised to strike.

There hadn't been a second blow. Instead, Ragnar had paused, letting the sorcerer's blade strike home. He reached out with his left hand and grabbed the sorcerer's wrist, driving the hellblade deeper into his chest and trapping it there.

Ragnar bared his teeth in a cold, wolfish grin. 'This, on the other hand, won't take very long at all.'

Madox's scream was cut short as the young Space Wolf drove the Spear of Russ through the sorcerer's faceplate.

FOR MANY YEARS to come the officers aboard the *Holmgang* would speak with pride of the part they played in the salvation of Charys. It was only in private, after several stiff glasses of amasec, that they would confess their horror at how close they'd come to unleashing their torpedoes on their lord and his men.

Berek's urgent call stopped the countdown with three seconds to spare, leaving the ordnance officers scrambling to transmit the abort code and silence the weapons' hungry spirits. Cheers erupted across the command deck as the Wolf Lord's steely voice barked orders to his fleet. The fight on the agri-world was far from over, and the guns of the great battle-barge were needed to turn the tide.

Within minutes the bombardment cannons were brought into action, unleashing a rain of devastation upon the massed rebel forces outside the planetary capital. Caught by surprise, the traitor regiments were devastated by the onslaught, and the survivors were forced to retreat in confusion back to the ruined streets of the nearby city.

But an even greater reversal was occurring invisibly across the entire world. As Madox's ritual failed and the shadow realm began to pull away from Charys, the daemon packs that had overrun the starport were forced to dissipate, drawn back to the maelstrom from whence they came. The Thousand Sons, faced with the real danger of finding themselves trapped without support on a planet so close to Fenris, chose to retreat too. They faded from sight one last time, leaving the rebel commanders screaming in vain for deliverance. Abandoned, exhausted and under fire from orbit, the rebel offensive became a panicked rout.

Berek strode out into the darkness like a vengeful god, calling his warriors to his side. The survivors of his company fell to their knees at their lord's miraculous deliverance, and soon word spread through the battered Guard regiments that the Lord of Wolves had risen from his deathbed to drive the

Chaos spawn from Charys. Within hours, an armoured column of recaptured vehicles had been assembled and was making its way up the Angelus Causeway with Berek's Wolves in the lead.

Their objective was the governor's palace, and they slew every living thing that stood in their way.

RAGNAR DREW A deep breath and wrapped his hands around the hilt of the hellblade. He gritted his teeth and slowly, carefully, he pulled the vile weapon free.

The black blade clattered to the stones beside Madox's lifeless form. Ragnar peered at his blood-stained hands for a moment, noting absently that the claws were no longer there. Then he planted his boot on Madox's chest and pulled the Spear of Russ from the sorcerer's helm. There was no blood upon the adamantine spear tip, just a dark stain of dust.

Ragnar could still feel the cold spreading through his body as he turned and limped carefully down the blood-stained steps. The air felt strange. It was thin and very dry, like ozone, and he heard the ominous rumble of thunder somewhere far away. He remembered what Madox had said about the world returning to the warp.

The young Space Wolf made his way among the shrivelled bodies of the Wulfen and sank to one knee beside his fallen friend. Haegr's face was as pale as alabaster, and blood still ran freely from the terrible wound in his shoulder, staining the steps crimson beneath him. The Wolfblade's eyes fluttered, and he puffed out his singed whiskers with a short breath. 'You look awful,' he said breathlessly.

Ragnar tried to grin. 'So I'm told,' he said. He rested his hand on Haegr's breastplate, amazed that the burly Wolf hadn't already sunk into the Red Dream. 'Save your strength,' he said, looking down to where Sigurd knelt with Torin beside Gabriella's prone form. 'I'll get the Wolf Priest–'

'Are you... are you saying that the mighty Haegr is lacking in strength?' the Wolfblade smiled weakly. 'I should thrash you for that.'

The young Space Wolf felt a terrible ache in his chest that had nothing to do with his wounds. 'Get up and try, then. Torin will take bets, I'm sure.'

Haegr's grin faded. 'Some other time perhaps,' he said softly. 'Is Gabriella safe?'

Ragnar glanced again at the Navigator, and tried to sound dismissive. 'Torin's with her,' he said. 'She's resting, I think.'

'That's good,' the Wolfblade said, his voice growing faint. 'Tell her I'm sorry. I didn't want to leave her.'

'She knows, Haegr.' Ragnar said, his heart heavy with grief. 'She knows.'

The Wolfblade's eyes grew unfocused. He blinked once, and smiled. 'Don't take too long getting to the Halls of Russ,' he said, almost too faintly to hear, 'or I'll have drunk all the good ale before you get there.' He tried to laugh, but the breath escaped in a gentle sigh and the mighty warrior grew still.

Ragnar reached down and clasped his friend's broad hand in farewell. As he did, he saw the black gleam of Haegr's ale horn, lying on the steps beside him. Madox's hellblade had severed its carrying strap, but the vessel itself looked unharmed. The young Space Wolf picked it up and tied it to his belt as he stood and made his way down the steps.

A tremor shook the Chaos temple, shifting the stones beneath the young Space Wolf's feet. He slipped on something slick, and realised numbly that there was blood on his boots. But for the terrible ache in his heart, he could feel nothing from his waist to his neck. Using the spear as a walking stick, he made his way to Gabriella's side.

Sigurd was bent over the injured Navigator, pressing a bandage to the wound in her abdomen. Torin looked up as the young Space Wolf approached. His eyes were dark again, and his expression was bleak as he clutched the Navigator's hands in his own. 'She told me she tried to send a warning to Berek,' he said. 'Perhaps she saved Charys.'

Ragnar nodded dumbly. As terrible as Haegr's death had been, the sight of the wounded Navigator was more terrible still. He touched Sigurd on the arm. 'How is she?'

The young Wolf Priest shook his head. 'My unguents and salves are made for Space Wolves, not people,' he said, his voice full of regret. He caught sight of the wound in Ragnar's chest and his eyes widened. 'Your wound is still bleeding,' he said, his voice taut with concern. 'Sit down and let me see to it.'

'It's nothing,' the young Space Wolf replied. 'Save your energy for Lady Gabriella.'

Sigurd started to protest, but saw the look in Ragnar's eyes and thought better of it. He nodded his head in the direction of the steps. 'What of Haegr?'

Ragnar shook his head. Tears stung at the corners of his eyes, and he couldn't bring himself to speak.

Sigurd nodded gravely and rose to his feet. He had one last duty to perform for the burly Wolfblade. Though he had fallen in battle, his gene-seed would need to be returned to the Fang, for implantation in a new initiate. Drawing a short, curved dagger from his belt, the priest made his way to the fallen warrior.

Torin looked up at Ragnar. 'What now?' he asked. 'It sounds like the whole world is coming apart.'

'It is,' the young Space Wolf said bleakly, gazing down at Gabriella's face. Her eyes were closed, as though she were sleeping. The bandage over her chest was already stained red. Gently, he reached down and touched her cheek. 'Forgive me, my lady,' was all he could manage to say.

'Bulveye must know a way off the planet,' Torin said. 'They got here somehow, after all.'

'No doubt,' Ragnar agreed, 'but he's a day's march away. I don't think this place is going to hold together that long.'

'It won't,' a deep voice growled from the temple entrance, 'but we'll be gone long before then.'

Torvald moved with a limp as he entered the temple, and his left arm hung at an awkward angle. His armour was battered and his face bloodied, but the ancient warrior still lived. He looked at Torin and Ragnar and frowned. 'Don't act like you're looking at a ghost,' he snapped. 'It was just a horde of Guardsmen. I've fought worse in my time.'

The Rune Priest surveyed the bloodstained battlefield and then knelt by the fallen Navigator. 'This was well done, brothers,' he said solemnly. 'Leman would be proud.' Then he glanced down at Gabriella's prone form and laid a hand gently on her arm. 'Can you carry her? There's no time to waste. We have to get back to Bulveye's camp–'

Suddenly, the Navigator's eyes fluttered open. 'No,' Gabriella said weakly. 'There's another way.'

The Rune Priest's brow furrowed in concern. 'What is she talking about?'

'The co-location,' she said, 'the bridge between worlds. We can cross it.'

Torvald listened and shook his head sadly. 'No, lady. Would that I could, but crossing between the realms like that is still beyond my abilities–'

'Not for me,' she said. Gabriella pulled a hand from Torin and grabbed the Rune Priest's arm. 'Open the gate. I can guide us through.'

The Rune Priest considered this. 'What you're suggesting is fraught with risk,' he began.

'*Please*,' she said. 'Please.' Gabriella looked up at Torin and Ragnar. 'I don't want to die in this place.'

Ragnar looked into the Navigator's eyes, and nodded. 'Do it,' he told the Rune Priest.

Torvald's scowl deepened. 'Very well,' he said. 'Call the young priest. We need to be quick.'

Torin called for Sigurd, and then gently took Gabriella in his arms. Ragnar stood beside Torvald. 'We should go back to Bulveye's camp first,' he said. 'If Gabriella can guide us home, she can bring all of you with us. You can come home, after all these years.'

A strange look passed over Torvald. He looked at Ragnar, and smiled sadly. 'The thought tempts me brother,' he said, 'but our work is not finished yet. One day, when our oath has been fulfilled, we will return. You may count upon it.'

Sigurd rejoined them swiftly as pale lightning began to crackle from the Rune Priest's axe. The crackling energies reminded Ragnar of the first time he'd seen Torvald, outlined by the lightning above the shadow world. Suddenly, he glanced over at the Rune Priest.

'Torvald, when I first saw you at the agri-combine, you said you'd been looking for me, but Sigurd had no way of knowing I was on the *Fist of Russ*. How is that possible?'

The Rune Priest raised his head in the young Space Wolf's direction. His eyelids opened, revealing glowing orbs instead of eyes. '*It was foreseen*,' the Rune Priest said in an unearthly voice. '*Farewell, Ragnar Blackmane. We shall meet again*.'

Before Ragnar could reply the gate opened, and the world vanished in a haze of white light.

BRITTLE BONES SNAPPED beneath Berek Thunderfist's heels as he returned in triumph to the governor's audience chamber. Sven and several members of Gunnar's Long Fang pack followed close on the Wolf Lord's heels, and a pair of Guardsmen brought up the rear, glancing fearfully around the great chamber, and fingering the triggers of their hand flamers. Berek had brought them to finally put an end to the governor and his household, but by the time they had arrived the huge tapestry of flesh was a brown, shrivelled husk, already disintegrating in the faint breeze.

Small-arms fire crackled in the distance as Guard units began the arduous task of hunting down rebel holdouts. With the *Holmgang* in orbit, the Imperial forces were able to overcome the planetary vox jamming, and had already regained contact with several isolated packs across the planet. Charys had been won back from the brink of ruin, but at a terrible cost.

Berek surveyed the ruined chamber one last time. 'Let's go,' he told his men. 'There's nothing left to see here.'

But as the Wolf Lord turned away, Sven's eyes widened and he pointed back at the dais. 'You may want to take another look, my lord.'

The Wolf Lord glanced back. A white haze was taking shape where the governor's throne had once stood. It thickened, like mist, and he could see vague figures moving within it.

There was a clatter of bolts and a hum of power converters as the Long Fangs rushed forward, weapons at the ready. Berek held out his hand. 'Hold your fire,' he said. His nose caught a faint, familiar scent.

The figures grew more distinct, as though they were approaching from a great distance.

'Ragnar!' Sven shouted.

The young Space Wolf appeared first, the Spear of Russ held upright in his hand. Torin the Wayfarer followed, with the limp body of a Navigator in his arms. Bringing up the rear was a young Space Wolf Priest with eyes far older than his meagre years.

A vague, towering figure stood beyond the limping, battered Wolves. Berek studied the silhouette, and despite the gulf that lay between them, he knew that he was looking at one of his kin. The warrior raised a mighty axe in salute, and then vanished in the haze. In moments, the strange fog was gone.

Ragnar approached the astonished Wolf Lord, his face pale as alabaster. Blood dripped onto the stones with every step he took. He sank slowly to his knees before Berek, and with both hands he offered up Russ's spear.

'We have won back our honour, my lord,' the young Space Wolf said. 'The Spear of Russ is ours once more.'

EPILOGUE
War Within, War Without

RAGNAR STALKED DOWN the ruined passageways of the *Dominus Bellum*, feeling the ghosts of old friends loping silently in his wake.

It had taken four more months to pacify Charys, as bands of cultists and rebel Guardsmen fled the capital and took to the hills. The Chaos uprising across the subsector had virtually ended with Madox's death. When the ritual collapsed, the agents of the Thousand Sons abandoned their campaign and vanished back into the shadows. The Space Wolves and the battered Imperial Guard regiments across the region restored order swiftly and brutally, but rebuilding the damage wrought by the Chaos forces would take decades.

Victory had come at a terrible price for the Chapter. Many battle-brothers had been lost in the fighting, and many more had sunk into the Red Dream until they could recover from their injuries. Some warriors who survived the campaign bore scars on their souls that would never fully heal. Mikal Sternmark was given over to the Wolf Priests after the events on Charys, and spent many years in seclusion as he struggled with the things he'd done during the battle at the starport. He returned to serve with Berek Thunderfist during the Wolf Lord's last campaign, fighting with honour and dying beside his lord as a champion ought during the awful battle on Hadsrubal.

The Imperial authorities never learned the truth of Lady Commander Athelstane's fate. As far as anyone knew, she died as a hero of the Imperium, which wasn't very far from the truth. It was assumed that she'd been slain fighting the daemons that had penetrated the perimeter wards, and none of Berek's warriors contradicted the official account. The Chapter looked out for its own.

Ragnar and the Spear of Russ were placed aboard a strike cruiser and despatched to Fenris as soon as the warp was safe to travel. Much of the time he spent in the Red Dream while his body recovered from the terrible wounds he'd received, but back at the Fang he was questioned at length by Ranek and the Old Wolf himself. Ragnar spoke of the Thirteenth Company to Logan Grimnar alone. After he'd told his tale, the Old Wolf had the Spear of Russ brought up from the vaults, and made Ragnar swear upon the relic never to tell another soul of what he'd seen.

For many years afterwards Ragnar tried to learn what Grimnar knew of Bulveye and his secret mission, but the wily Old Wolf claimed that such things had been lost in the mists of time. Eventually, Ragnar had stopped asking, but he remembered the last words that Torvald had said to him. Sooner or later, he'd see the Rune Priest again, and then he'd have his answers.

Six months after Ragnar placed the spear in Berek's hands on Charys, the Thunderfist's company made a solemn pilgrimage to the ancient shrine on Garm. The world still lay in ruins in the wake of the great uprising, years past, but the Chapter had spared no expense to restore the resting place of the legendary Wolf Lord to its former glory. Ragnar walked behind Berek, carrying the spear that he and his companions had won in battle. With most of the great company bearing witness, he returned the relic to its rightful place and fulfilled the oath he'd sworn. Then Berek declared to his men that by winning back the Chapter's honour, Ragnar had redeemed his own as well. The Wolf Lord declared that, by Logan Grimnar's decree, Ragnar's time among the Wolfblade was at an end.

Hours later, Gabriella and Torin found him in the shrine, standing before Garm's ivory sarcophagus. The Navigator had never fully recovered from the terrible ordeal she had suffered at Charys. She seemed weak and frail as Torin led her into the shrine, and there was a thick streak of white in her long, black hair. They said farewell to one another beside the tomb. Torin and Ragnar spoke of Haegr, and laughed once again at the memory of the burly warrior with an ale bucket on his foot. Gabriella listened, and smiled, but her eyes were haunted and her expression distant. She told Ragnar that he would always be welcome in her house on Terra, and invited him to return one day, if the Fates permitted. By then she was growing tired, and so took her leave. Torin led her gently away, her hand resting upon his arm. The next day her ship departed on the long journey to Terra. Ragnar hadn't seen either of them since.

That night, Ragnar stood vigil before the silent tomb. He left Haegr's ale horn upon the sarcophagus when he left at dawn the next day. As far as he knew, it remained there still.

A HOWL ECHOED from the darkness. Ragnar stopped in his tracks, still so deep in his reverie that he thought he was back on Charys once more. Then he heard the vile screech of a xenos beast and he was back aboard a derelict Imperial battleship, hurtling towards Corta Hydalis, and the warrior he sought was somewhere up ahead.

The Wolf Lord crouched, peering down the long, debris-strewn passageway. The sounds of battle were unmistakeable, steel ringing against bone and claws hissing across ceramite. From the sound of it, Hogun was facing off against a horde of alien horrors.

Readying his bolt pistol, Ragnar raced towards the fight.

A hundred metres ahead the passageway opened into a small, debris filled room some thirty metres across. Shafts of weak light shone down into the space through access shafts overhead, providing just enough illumination for Ragnar to see by. There, in the centre of the room stood Hogun, surrounded by a pack of genestealers.

Two of the beasts lay dead at Hogun's feet, split open by the Wolf Guard's power axe. Blood streamed from a number of minor wounds along Hogun's chest, arms and back. Four more genestealers circled Hogun warily, waiting for their prey to weaken and make a fatal mistake.

The genestealers were so intent on their prey that they didn't realise Ragnar was stealing upon them until it was too late. The Wolf Lord raised his bolt pistol and fired two quick shots. One of the creatures let out a hideous screech and collapsed, ichor streaming from wounds in its side, but Ragnar was already on the move, charging another of the genestealers before the first body hit the ground.

'For Russ and the Allfather!' he roared, hacking at the genestealer with his frost blade. The blow was swift, but the genestealer was swifter, ducking beneath the blow and lunging forward. Talons pierced the Wolf Lord's armour, digging deep into his chest. Clashing jaws snapped at Ragnar's face. He bellowed a curse, shoved his pistol under the creature's chin and pulled the trigger. Ichor and bits of chitin splashed against the far wall as the body slumped to the floor.

A heavy weight crashed against Ragnar's back, driving him to his knees. Clawed hands reached around his suit's backpack, grabbing for his neck. The Wolf Lord spun, trying to dislodge the genestealer, but the alien monster clung like a swamp tick. Talons raked across Ragnar's cheeks. Any moment those same talons would find his neck, and then he was done for.

Ragnar hurled himself backwards, smashing the genestealer against one of the walls. He heard chitin crack, but the creature refused to let go.

There was another hissing screech across the chamber as the last of the monsters fell before Hogun's axe. Then the Wolf Guard loomed in front of Ragnar, his dripping axe ready to strike. His yellow-gold eyes shone in the faint light.

Ragnar felt the genestealer's razor-sharp claws dig into his neck. Trusting to the Fates, he turned his back to Hogun.

Hogun's power axe hissed through the air, and steel rang against chitin. The genestealer let out a shriek and fell heavily to the deck.

By the time Ragnar had turned around again, Hogun was racing down a passageway on the far side of the room. 'Wait!' he called after the Wolf Guard. 'Remember your oaths to me, Hogun, and *stand fast!*'

Years of training took over, stopping the fleeing warrior in his tracks. Hogun turned like a wolf at bay, his teeth bared and his shoulders heaving. 'No oaths bind me now, my lord,' he said in a ragged voice. 'I've slain my packmates in a fit of madness. I'm wolf bitten, and damned for all time.'

'Not true,' Ragnar said, edging slowly towards Hogun. 'Did you not just save me from certain death? What is that, if not fealty to one's lord?'

'All I wanted was to kill something,' Hogun snarled. 'If I had not run I would have tried to kill you next.'

'Is that what you think?' Ragnar said. 'Do you hold yourself in so little regard that you think you could raise your hand to your sworn lord?' He holstered his pistol and sheathed his sword. 'Very well,' the Wolf Lord said, taking another step forward. 'Strike me down, if you can.'

Hogun's eyes widened. 'What madness is this?' he said, taking a step back.

'*Stand your ground!*' Ragnar roared. He took another step closer. 'I said strike me, Hogun. Slay me with your axe if you can.'

The Wolf Guard snarled in fury. His hands tightened on the haft of his axe, but he made no move to attack. 'I cannot,' he said through clenched teeth. 'I cannot!'

'That's right,' the Wolf Lord said. 'The wolf does not rule you, Hogun. Fight it! Master the beast and make its strength your own! That is what we do. That is who we are.'

Hogun wavered, torn by shame and rage. 'Slay me then, lord,' he cried. 'I spilled the blood of my packmates. My life is forfeit.'

'So it is,' the Wolf Lord said. 'You have killed my liegemen, and so your life belongs to me, as tradition demands. Do you agree?'

The Wolf Guard straightened, accepting his fate. 'That is so, lord. Do as you will.'

'Then hear me: you are a part of my company until the Fates deem otherwise, and you will fight alongside me until there is no life left in you. You are wolf bitten, and you have lost your honour by spilling the blood of your packmates, so from this moment forward you will fight to win it back. Do you understand?'

Hogun stared at Ragnar. 'Is such a thing possible?'

'That, and more besides,' the Wolf Lord said. 'Follow me, and serve the Allfather, Hogun. That is all I ask. Will you do this?'

The Wolf Guard fell to his knees. 'I will, my lord,' he said. 'I will follow you into Morkai's jaws if I must.'

Ragnar clapped Hogun on the shoulder. 'Let's not get ahead of ourselves,' he said with a faint smile. 'Right now, we've got to get the company back together and fight our way to the ship's reactors. Now get on your feet.'

The Wolf Lord headed back the way he'd come with Hogun following close on his heels. As they emerged into the chamber where they'd fought the genestealers, they found the Wolf Priest waiting for them.

'Petur's found Einar's pack off Jotun Three and is leading them to us,' the priest said. 'The rest of the packs are assembled back at the junction and are awaiting orders. Jurgen has checked his data-slates and believes he's found an accessway nearby that should take us right to the reactor deck.'

Ragnar took in the news with a curt nod. 'Well done,' he said, and then indicated Hogun. 'I commend this warrior into your keeping, priest. Whatever else he may be, he is still a member of my warband, and he will fight alongside us as any other warrior.'

The Wolf Priest studied Hogun for a moment, and then reached up with one hand and disengaged the clasps on his wolf skull helm. Sigurd lifted the helmet away and smiled grimly at the Wolf Guard. They fell into step behind Ragnar as the Wolf Lord rushed back to the junction, his mind already working on the tactics he would need to defeat the genestealer threat.

Behind him, the jarl's son spoke to Hogun in quiet tones. 'Listen closely, Hogun, and mark me well. I've a story to tell you of the Wulfen, and of the heroes they can become.'

ABOUT THE AUTHOR

Lee Lightner is the penname for two authors who live in Baltimore, USA. Lifelong friends, they are both avid Space Wolf fans.

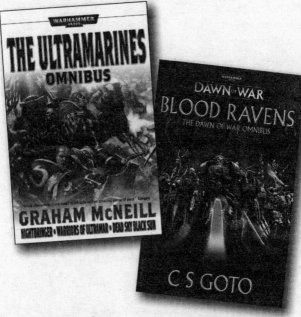